# NINE EXPENSIVE FUNERALS

HAYDEN SMITH

First Trade Paperback Edition published November 2020
First e-book Edition published November 2020

Cover by: Rocking Book Covers
Lighthouse logo by: VendeDesign
Author photo by: Kenny Hekhuis Photography

ISBN 978-1-7359983-0-5 (Trade paperback)

ISBN 978-1-7359983-1-2 (e-book)

Library of Congress Control Number: 2020922299

Published in the United States of America by: The McKinley Company

*This book is dedicated to my children, grandchildren, and great-grandchildren.*

*You are my joy, my raison d'être.*

# 1

When Tom walked into Doo Drop Inn's small room by the bar, Fred was there drinking a beer, playing a rat-a-tat rhythm with his ball point pen, and shaking his head. The restaurant was nearly empty. Just one other guy in the booth right behind Fred. "Hey, Fred, you're one ahead of me. This isn't like you," Tom said, as he slipped into the high-backed red leather booth across from Fred. "What's up, my friend?"

Fred was red-faced. His hands trembled as he took the final swig of his beer. He had scribbled a note on a bar napkin. He showed it to Tom and said, "Nine expensive funerals, Tom. That's what it will take."

"What is this about?"

Fred was quiet when their favorite waitress, Joan, brought Tom's beer, along with another for Fred. Fred Thomas is the mayor of Muskegon, Michigan, and Tom's good friend ever since Fred's son first sang in Tom's high school choir. They met at Doo Drop for lunch every other week or so to catch up and let Fred pick Tom's brain about the thorny issues he faces as mayor. Fred frequently told Tom that he was a good sounding board and laughed when he added, "for a high school choir director."

Fred continued, "Do you remember that I hired a consultant to see if he could find out why it is so hard to change the industrial base here? Well, he just called me with his report."

Tom arched his eyebrows and nodded, thinking back to the lunch conversation about Fred's frustration with the resistance he was getting. He was trying to bring in more tech companies and light industries and move Muskegon out of the smelly heavy manufacturing that was taking up the Muskegon Lake lakeshore.

"He told me there are nine powerful men who sit on each other's boards of directors. They control everything that happens here. The city commissioners seem to have no power. He found out nine men already have their agenda for the city. It's more of the same of what we have, a major lakefront industrial development, and they have big money invested. You know I've been pushing to diversify the industrial base for the city and move industry off the lakefront so we can reclaim it for the residents and tourists. But my plans evidently conflict with their agenda so mine will never happen. Not until that cabal is broken. And to quote him, 'there needs to be nine expensive funerals in this city before anything they don't want can happen. While they are alive, no progress, no change.'" Fred took another sip of beer.

"And there's more." Fred slammed his fist on the table. Tom jumped back in surprise. Fred was never violent or this angry. Fred went on, "He said that they want me gone as mayor, or better yet, out of town, maybe even dead."

"Calm down, it can't be that bad." Tom was shocked. This couldn't be true – this was Muskegon. Things like this didn't happen here.

"It is! They said that word, dead! But I...I just...I can't just give up."

Tom sipped his beer and gathered his thoughts. He stalled and studied his beer as if it were the first time he had seen it, even though he had the same thing every time he came into the Doo Drop.

"Who besides me knows about your plans? Does anyone in City Hall have your back? Is there anything I can do to help, Fred? Maybe I could spread the word in the neighborhoods, you know, get the people behind your ideas. Some pressure from the citizens could force a change."

Fred said, "I'm not surprised that you want to get involved and I appreciate it. I know how much you care about Muskegon, but it's not a good idea. I don't want it to affect your job at the high school nor would I want to see you, or your sweetheart Maria, put at risk. Remember they said, *dead!*"

"I think the death threats may be just an empty threat, a scare tactic. How about you meet with the boards, let them know you want their inputs, and smooth things over?"

They were quiet as Joan brought their perch lunches.

After she left Fred continued, "I thought about that, but I don't want to tip my hand that I know about them until I've had some time to think this through and get some proof of their existence."

Tom asked, "What about the unions? Do they have influence over these guys?"

"Right now, the union leadership is too busy trying to keep their jobs. Several highly placed officials in Michigan unions were recently voted out of office.

"No, it's this group of nine city fathers on these boards that I have to figure out. I may get together with the union leaders later but I'll try the group first. I have one member of the city commission open to my plans. I think I can get more of them behind me."

Fred finished his last bite of the perch and continued, "My friend, the consultant, says he doesn't have the names of the group of nine."

Tom jumped in, "Fred, who is this consultant? You've never told me his name. Is he a reliable source of this information?"

"He is reliable. I met him when I first ran for Mayor. And no one knows his name except me. I pay him out of my own funds so no one at City Hall knows we have a connection."

"I ask again, Fred, is he reliable?"

"He is. He is respected in the community. He was there during my interviews for the job of Mayor. We both agree that it is better if no one knows about our relationship. Most important, he has never let me down. Everything he has told me has been solid information.

"He is well known at City Hall and seems to be trusted by all of them. He picks up a lot as he talks with people there. But he said he has to tread carefully. They all clam up when he asks about the men who run the major companies in the city."

Fred slugged down the last of his beer. "I have to go. I'll ask Eleanor to call Maria and work out a time for a Christmas celebration dinner at our house. I'll be more settled down by then and we'll make it a pleasant evening. You and Maria can fill us in on what you are up to."

"Sounds good, Fred. We'll look forward to that."

"Let's get together in a couple of weeks to catch up. How about Saturday, the 15th?"

"Ok, Fred. See you then."

Neither of them noticed the reaction of the big man in the booth behind Fred, his back to them. But he had jerked his head around when he heard the words "nine expensive funerals," He called for his check and continued to listen while he waited for it. Later at the cashier's stand, he looked back to where the mayor and his friend sat. He fixed the friend's face to memory. He made a point to remember the name "Tom." He needed to talk with Antonelli before the next meeting of the group that hired him.

## 2

Nine men sat around the table in the private upstairs dining room of the members-only Century Club. They had just finished their bi-monthly dinner, without much conversation. Over the last month, several purchases or options-to-buy of the lakefront properties had been made through a shell company that protected their identities. The only member with any ties to the purchases was Antonelli — his name was on the bank account that held the funds the individuals had contributed to make the purchases. Several automotive-related industries had made tentative agreements with them to locate new divisions on the lakefront in Muskegon, the same kinds of manufacturing that already took up most of the lakeshore. The meeting continued after the servers brought coffee and after dinner drinks and left them behind closed doors.

George Anderson, the presumptive leader of the group, said, "You all seem quiet tonight. I sense some concerns or fears that I don't understand. We're doing ok. We've made good progress on the lakefront properties. Now is a time to keep our ears open for anything that might derail our plans. We stand to lose a lot of money, millions of dollars, if that happens."

George, who was well-respected in the business community, often calmed the waters. It was no surprise that a number of heads nodded in agreement. Then Wendell grabbed the floor. "Look, we don't know much about this mayor yet and that concerns me. He has only been here a little over a year. So far, no one seems to know much about his plans."

Tim Samuels shook his head and said, "I've heard some stories of some sentiment against industries on the waterfront. I have no idea where they came from. Maybe the mayor is testing the waters with ideas of his own."

Joe Antonelli decided to tell them about Harry. "I've found someone who can help with all of those questions. His name is Harry. He has already set up contacts in City Hall. He can keep us tuned in with City Hall. But we can also call on him for some muscle work in case we need it."

Tim asked, "Joe, are you sure of this man? Where did you find him?"

Joe didn't tell them the whole story. He met Harry when he came into Joe's restaurant one night to sell bootleg whiskey. What he shared was, "I checked Harry out with friends in Detroit and Chicago. Harry works alone and can be trusted to keep his mouth shut about us."

George squinted through the cigar smoke and growled, "How is it that you have friends in Chicago and Detroit who know people like Harry? You continue to surprise me, Joe. But tell me this. Can he be controlled? Will he take orders? And is he expensive?"

Joe flushed, not sure of George's thinking about Harry...and him. "He's not cheap but we don't want to stint here. I paid him a retainer from our slush fund. Trust me. He'll be a good investment. It's already paid off. I asked him to follow the mayor. Not a tight tail, but just enough to see where he goes and who he talks to. He called me this afternoon with a report. At lunch today he was in the Doo Drop Inn near the mayor and a man named Tom. The mayor told this Tom about a consultant he had hired. This consultant somehow has found out about us. He knows there's a group of nine who don't want changes made unless those changes agree with what the group believes is right for the city. He seems to know about us but has no names as yet."

George said, "Joe, that's good input. We need solid info about what the mayor thinks he knows. You'll keep a tight rein on him?"

"Yes, I will. You'll see, we'll know every move the mayor makes almost as soon as it happens."

Wendell broke in, "Maybe we need to be more careful not to be seen together. Does anyone have a concern about our annual Christmas party at the Occidental Hotel?"

Joe interrupted, "I don't have a concern about that. It seems to me that when your wives are with us, we are just a group of friends at a Christmas brunch. The ladies enjoy it as much as we do. It's not only a good time, it is a good tactic. People would be surprised if business and industry leaders didn't interact socially."

Tim added, "My main worry is that we can't afford to be found out as the group behind the changes. We've taken precautions with that shell corporation Joe set up. It hides our names. The corporation has bought up all the properties and our slush fund is in the corporation's name. But with the new inputs from this Harry, we might have more cause for concern. This consultant might be able to tie us to the corporation."

Joe said, "Don't be a fear monger, Tim. We don't need negative thoughts — we have to stay positive. We know we are on the right track and we can't lose sight of our goals."

Tim shook his head. "I'm not afraid, Joe. I'm just cautious. We all have a great deal of money tied up in these plans. We can't afford to let down our guard at this stage."

Several of the nine nodded agreement with Tim. Each of them had a lot at stake in this venture. When the group first formed and a plan of action evolved, all were excited about the potential. Yet, as time went on, their fears grew.

Joe added, "All the more reason for Harry. We will know what moves the mayor makes the same day he starts them."

George said, "Joe's right. We now have a way to know what City

Hall is up to. I still feel a lot of concern in the room. But look, there is a lot of business talent around this table. We put together a great business plan. Our attorney, Harold Evans, has kept things legal and we need to continue to trust that he has protected us. Let's stop the worry. This will work. Any final questions?"

Joe laughed and twirled his handle bar mustache. "You know I like to eat, what's on the menu for next Saturday? Anything special?" The mood lifted, they chuckled as they thought ahead to the brunch.

George added, "Alright, meeting's adjourned. I'll see you next Saturday at the Occidental for our annual Christmas brunch with our wives."

## 3

Harry called Joe at his restaurant at 1:30 Sunday afternoon. Joe said, "The group has accepted the fact that we need someone like you, and I've assured them that you are the man for the job. I'm the only one who knows your full name. They only know you as Harry. Let's keep it that way."

Harry quizzed Joe, "How long do you think the job will take?"

Joe hesitated, "I think it may be six months or more. It depends on a number of things like what you find out about the mayor, how fast our business interests come together, how many other factors may come up that we'll have to resolve."

Harry said, "That's going to be expensive if I keep living out of the Ramada motel. I might be better off finding a small house to rent. I can cook my own meals so expenses will be lower and I'll be more out of the public eye."

"I can get to the bank in the morning so I'll have the money we agreed on by this time tomorrow. Come to the restaurant between one and one-thirty and have lunch. The staff knows you sold us the bootleg whiskey so it will be natural that you come back here to get paid. I'll just join you at your table as though I'm making the payment for it. The money will be in an envelope. There will be enough in expense money to get you a house. You should pay ahead for six months. That way you won't have to sign a lease. Your day-to-day expenses as well as the first installment of your fee will be in there. You'll also have instructions on how we'll talk and make contact as time goes on. We don't want to be seen together any more often than we have to. I'll also have a note in there as to how we handle future payments."

Harry smirked, "You've got it all worked out, haven't you, Joe?"

Joe said, "Yes, I have. And just remember my neck is on the line for this. Your friends in Detroit and Chicago told me you were the man for the job. I will count on you to get it done. Don't let me down, Harry."

"I won't. You only have to let me know what needs to be done and I'll make it happen. You keep the money coming and everything will be hunky-dory. I'll see you tomorrow at the restaurant, one-thirty for lunch."

For a time after the call ended, Harry sat in his motel room thinking about what a great gig this was. It had the potential to set him up for the rest of his days. It would amount to over $200,000 over the next six months. He just had to make sure there were no loose ends, but he knew how to do that. And they didn't even know that he was double dipping with the union leaders. At the end of this job, he could just disappear and live someplace warm.

He needed to go out for dinner and celebrate a little. He would pick up a Sunday paper tomorrow. Sunday was a good day to find rental houses.

Harry walked into Tony's at six. The Ramada motel manager recommended it as the best place in town to get a good steak and made the reservation for him. It was close enough that Harry just walked over. The hostess showed him to a small booth in the bar area. Just perfect for a little private celebration. There were many tables filled in the dining room, but not so many in the bar. It looked like a typical Saturday night in most restaurants. The red leather booths were tall enough that Harry couldn't see the couple seated next to him nor hear a thing they were saying. The thick carpet and heavy drapes also muted the sounds of other diners and the soft easy swing jazz music muffled the usual restaurant noises. Harry felt invisible in this classy environment.

The waitress brought a little dish of a cheese dip and some crackers and asked, "What will you have to drink, sir?"

"I'd like bourbon on the rocks to start."

She brought the drink and took his order, a medium rare filet mignon with all the trimmings and a glass of the house cabernet sauvignon to go with dinner.

Harry sat sipping his bourbon and his thoughts went back to how to make sure there were no loose ends. Harry hadn't told Joe Antonelli everything. The last job Harry had in Chicago had turned out well — eventually. The job had gotten complicated and Harry had to go further than he usually did to clean it up. The family he worked for needed him to teach a competitor a lesson in the booze business. They had to learn that they weren't welcome in Chicago.

Harry had spent some time learning the guy's habits. He always came back to the warehouse by himself late on Tuesday nights to tally up the books from the week before. That night Harry parked two blocks away from the warehouse on W. Adams St for a quick getaway to Union Station. Dressed in black, Harry blended into the shadows and waited for the guy to show up. Just before 9:00 PM Harry put on a black ski mask. The guy didn't see him in the shadows by the door he always went in. Harry went in right behind him and knocked him out with a baseball bat. He woke up tied to a chair and all he could see was this big man dressed from head to toe in black. Harry told him he had to quit the booze business. To emphasize the order he broke both the guy's knees with two well placed baseball bat swings. Repeating the warning that he had to quit the business, Harry told him that if he didn't, next time it would be his wife and two kids who got hurt.

Harry had left him there, took off his mask, and walked back to his car. What he didn't realize at the time was that he had been seen by a man who was up and happened to be standing at his window. Since he had seen two people go in and only one came out, he must have gotten suspicious and called the police. Harry heard the sirens start just as he was getting into his car. Harry drove off, turned on S. Halsted quickly and was gone before the police were there. Safe, he thought.

As it happened there was a second police car coming from the direction Harry was headed. He pulled in to wait for the car to go by and could see that there was only one officer in the car. For whatever reason he did a U-turn and pulled up behind, lights flashing, sirens blaring. Harry had his gun ready when the cop came to the window. When he leaned in to shine the light in his eyes, Harry shot the cop in the forehead. Harry hated to kill a cop — they never stop looking for cop killers.

Harry slowly drove another block to W. Jackson and turned toward Union Station. He abandoned the car in the 7-11 parking lot a couple of blocks from Union Station. The car was stolen, and he had always worn gloves so there wouldn't be any clues there. He walked briskly to Union Station — he already had his ticket to Detroit and the train was leaving in 30 minutes. He mused as he sipped his drink, "I'm safe. They will never find me." The plan was to lie low for a while and start moving bootleg whiskey around the state of Michigan again. Joe knew none of this. Harry thought, *he might not have hired me.*

The waitress came with his order. The steak was done perfectly, and the wine was just the right complement to it. It was a great way to celebrate this new job. Tomorrow — find a furnished house and get back to tailing the mayor Monday or Tuesday.

The Sunday paper had three furnished houses for rent. Harry found all three on the city map. The first one he saw was too expensive as well as more house than he needed. He drove next to the house on Estes Street in what was called the Lakeside area. The owner was there waiting for some potential renters who were late. Harry walked up to the owner and asked if the place was still available. When he said it was unless the other couple showed up in the next five minutes. He showed the house and quizzed Harry about what he did. Harry said he was a consultant from the east side of the state working with a group here in town. Harry told him he liked the house and would take it right now. The other couple still hadn't shown up so the owner agreed to rent it to Harry. The owner wanted a lease with the first and last month's payments, but Harry said, "Look, I'll only be here for six months. How about I pay you in cash now for the whole six months and forget the lease? Just give me a receipt for six month's rent."

The owner thought for a minute and said, "You've got a deal."

Harry paid him and asked, "Where's the closest grocery store? I need to get some food in."

"Etterman's is just down on Lakeshore Drive. It's only about ten minutes or so from here. It's one of the best in town. They have a great meat department."

"Thanks. I'll get my things at the motel and move in this afternoon."

Harry went back to the Ramada, checked out, and came back to get settled in. Once done, he found Lakeshore Drive, drove to Etterman's, and did his shopping. Now it was time to get back to work and see what the mayor was up to.

# 4

---

T om heard the horn, twice. Doug was in his driveway, impatient as always. Tom hurried through the swirling snow and jumped into the passenger seat.

Doug said, "Hey buddy, our meeting is at 11:00. We need to go."

Tom replied, "I know, I know. We're ok for time."

"Where's Maria? I thought she might have come with you. I hoped I would have an ally today." But... *What he meant was he was hoping to see her this morning.*

"She had something to do early this morning. She'll meet us at the Occidental."

They headed downtown. Tom hadn't wanted Doug along. But Doug had insisted and here he was, a nuisance and argumentative as usual. Yes, he was Tom's best friend, but he was messing with tradition. He wanted to change the annual Christmas concert by adding a small orchestra. The Muskegon High School Acappella Choir sings on the balcony of the downtown Occidental Hotel lobby every Christmas. It was a fun thing to do when Tom was a boy in high school. The hotel and audience loved it the way it was and that was good enough for Tom. Why fix something that wasn't broken? Tom wanted to continue the tradition as it has always been.

Doug said, "Tom, I have new thoughts about our conversation yesterday at lunch. I want to help you bring your *Acapulco* singing into the sixties. Why not add a few instruments?"

Tom smiled, "Good ole Doug, always the funny man. The word is acappella. It is the Acappella Choir. That means we sing without accompaniment."

"I know what it means, smarty. By the way, I've wanted to talk to you about that. Acappella has a space between the A and the C. It is more properly spelled a Cappella."

Tom laughed, "How did you know that? That is the correct spelling, the Italian way. But words change, at least in America. Here, it has been one word, acapella, for a long time. And it still means we sing without accompaniment."

"Yet the kids love those new jazzy pieces with you on the piano. They've told me. Why not add a few strings, maybe a horn or two and some percussion? Use some of those ideas from your club work over in Grand Rapids."

"I don't like it, Doug. I thought you would have learned by now. People in this town don't like change. You know that. You have to follow the rules. If you don't, you are in trouble here."

Doug just shook his head. Tom thought Doug was going to drop it. But Doug wouldn't let it go.

"Why can't we give it a try with a small group? That's not much of a change."

"Doug, stop pushing. We're almost there. Drive on past Western Avenue, park further on down Third Street, and we'll walk back up to the hotel."

"There's a place right here. Why can't I park here?"

"Just do it, Doug!"

Tom always liked this walk back up toward the Occidental. There she was, in all her glory, a lovely old lady. The shadows from the early morning winter sun made her appear mysterious. But that took nothing away from her stateliness. Tom could see why she had the reputation as the most dominant building in the Muskegon downtown. First opened in Muskegon's lumber days in the 1870s, a number of additions had been made until by the 1920s she was an elegant Renaissance Revival eight story structure. The grey arches at the ground level with large windows gave way to red brick for the upper stories. Tom said, "Just look at that, Doug. Isn't she a grand old building?"

"Yeah, I guess. It's just another hotel."

"Where's the romance in your soul? This place has been the focal point of activities in Muskegon for a lot of years. The annual Lumbermen's ball, the Christmas formal dance and dinner party are both held here. I hear the city fathers do a lot of their business here."

"Yeah, yeah."

As they entered the lobby from Western Ave., one could see the balcony where the choir would sing. The balustrade on the mezzanine extended around the two sides and the back where the choir stood. Black columns with gilded crowns spaced around the lobby supported the mezzanine and provided a striking contrast to the cream walls and ceiling. Plush gold velvet sofas and easy chairs were scattered about the lobby on the Prussian blue patterned carpet. These were even now filled with guests who relaxed and talked with their friends. The period lamps close to the seating enhanced and softened the lighting from the great crystal chandelier and ceiling lights two stories up. A festive air filled the lobby with poinsettias all over and a thirty foot tall Christmas tree in the center. The overall effect was of understated elegance with a touch of at-home feeling.

Tom said, "See in the back and up where the balustrade crosses the back? That's where we'll be singing."

Doug pressed, "There is plenty of room up there for a small orchestra."

"Doug! Leave it alone! I'm tired of the pressure."

Doug and Tom were still at it when Maria walked up. Tom grabbed her and gave her a big hug.

Doug put his hands over his eyes. "Hey, you two, cool it. Not in front of the kids."

Maria asked, "What is the argument about? I could see something wasn't right as I walked over. "

Tom said, "I'll fill you in later."

Mrs. McKay, the events manager, came across the room. Tom took Maria's hand as they walked toward Mrs. McKay's office. Doug frowned. *He was disappointed that Tom hadn't changed his mind and annoyed that it was Tom who was holding Maria's hand. He had wanted to do that and more for a long time before Tom was around.*

As they passed by a meeting room, the door opened. A group of men and women in Christmas finery came out chattering away happily. Tom didn't know any of them so he just smiled and gave them a nod. Mrs. McKay said to one of them, "I hope everything was satisfactory, Mr. Antonelli."

Maria and Tom did double takes at the name "Antonelli." They both knew a troubled girl named "Sara Antonelli" at the high school. Tom wondered if they were related. The name Antonelli wasn't that common in Muskegon.

"It was great. You have a merry Christmas, Mrs. McKay."

When the couples had gone, Tom asked Mrs. McKay about the group and she said, "That's some of the town's businessmen. They just finished their Christmas brunch. The men and their wives come here every year for this special occasion."

Doug blurted, "What do you think about the addition of a small orchestral group, Mrs. McKay?"

"I think that would be marvelous! Something new. The townspeople will love it."

Maria exclaimed, "Tom, I didn't know you had instruments in mind. I think it is a terrific idea."

Tom glared at Doug.

Doug smiled. "See there. Seems as though you are outvoted."

Mrs. McKay asked, "Didn't you want to make the change, Tom? From what I have heard from my daughter, the kids all love what you are doing with the music. And there's plenty of room in the balcony."

So Tom just threw up his hands. "Ok! Ok! We'll do it. Truth to tell, the idea is growing on me. We have a little over two weeks till Saturday the 22nd. We'll be ready, Mrs. McKay."

Maria smiled at Tom as if he had just performed a miracle. Doug grinned, a big wide smile, and clapped his hands. "Bravo!"

# 5

___

F red and Tom got to Doo Drop Inn at about the same time. When they walked in, Joan greeted them, "Hi Fred, Tom, grab your favorite booth and I'll bring your brews."

Tom said, "Hey, Joan, the Christmas decorations are up! The room looks great. It's always so warm and cozy, but these decorations add to the room. They are perfect."

Joan blushed and teared up. "I did them myself yesterday. This is my room to work and I wanted it to be just right."

"You did a great job with it. Makes it feel so homey."

"Thanks, guys. I'll get your drinks."

When she brought them, Tom raised his glass, "Salud! Merry Christmas to us all." Joan held up an imaginary glass and said, "Cheers. Do you want your usual?"

Tom and Fred both nodded yes, and said, "Is there any other choice than the perch dinner?"

Tom turned to Fred, "Anything new? Like names of the nine men in the group?"

The side door opened, and a big man walked in. He took the booth behind them even though there were many empty tables in the dining room. Neither Tom nor Fred paid any attention to him except to note that he was a big man, probably 6' 5" and maybe 260 pounds. Joan came with their perch lunches, and turned to the man behind Tom. "Can I help you, sir?" She took his food order and brought him a bottle of Bud beer.

Fred answered, "No, nothing new. My consultant hasn't been able to find any names."

"I've talked this over with some friends who promise to do a little probing to see if they can find out who they are. For the most part, they can't believe anything this bad could happen in our town. Do you think a private detective could figure out who they are?"

"My consultant is on the lookout for a detective who specializes in people searches. If we can just get one name, we might be able to pull on the string and start to unravel who else is in this group. If we can just get them identified, we can at least start a conversation. Maybe we can find some common ground. But for now, just a lot of ifs."

"Sounds like a good plan, Fred. I'll keep talking to neighbors and colleagues and see what turns up. Will you be at the Occidental concert next Saturday?"

"Yes, we will. Eleanor and Emily will be there too. We wouldn't miss Freddy Jr's first concert there. I am so proud of him for this, he's worked hard."

Tom said, "Yes, he has. By the way, do you remember I told you about Doug's pressure on me to add some instruments?"

Joan brought the big man's check and he got up to leave. Fred said, "I think I'd like coffee. How about you, Tom? Hey, Joan, how about some coffee? It's cold out there."

The big man left to pay his bill. Fred looked at him as he walked by, but didn't recognize him so he turned back to Tom. "I do remember Doug's ideas. What happened?"

"Doug, Maria, and Mrs. McKay at the Occidental convinced me. They were right. We've been in rehearsal with a small orchestra for a week now and it's great! The kids love it."

"Freddy Jr. didn't say a word."

"I asked them not to. We wanted it to be a surprise for the audience. It's a first."

"Well, I won't say anything either. How is Maria?"

Their coffee came. "Maria is great. She'll be there next Saturday. We'll have an early lunch in the Occidental café. It will be a celebration for the start of the Christmas break. We're officially off for the holidays on Christmas Eve day."

"Tom, let's try and put all this business behind us for the holidays. We'll look at it again after the first of the year. I really appreciate you helping me think through this. You always see things from a different perspective and that helps me think more clearly."

They signaled Joan for their checks. When she came with them, they both handed her a Christmas money envelope. She wiped her eyes and gave them hugs when Tom sang, "Have yourself a merry little Christmas ..." Together, they said, "Merry Christmas, Joan."

TOM DIDN'T GO HOME RIGHT AWAY. He drove out Sherman through the Beach Street area to the Ovals beach on Lake Michigan. This was one of his "thinking spots."

He parked and left the car running so he could warm up fast after a walk down to the water's edge. The wind was brutal and there was a hint of snow or sleet in the air. But it was what Tom wanted, to be shocked out of the lunch torpor so he could think. He turned back toward the car and pushed through the sand against the wind. Unlocking his car, he got back into the warmth.

He took his gold colored meditation coin from his pocket. It was etched with the statement, "Be fair, be just, always. It is the most important thing in life after love." It was his version of Proverbs chapter two, verses nine and ten. He needed to find a way to help Fred. It was the right thing to do and Fred was a good friend. How could he help Fred figure out who this mystery group was? Time to ask some more questions and see what he could find out. But right now, it was time to go. He had a dinner date with Maria tonight.

## 6

Maria and Tom had an early lunch at the Occidental café on Saturday before the concert. It was a beautiful room, the brilliant white tablecloths contrasted with the rust and silver chairs. Each table was topped with a mini Christmas tree decorated with gold bows that matched the water silk covered walls. They finished their lunch and sipped more coffee while they waited for the choir.

"Do you remember our first date here? I was so nervous. I really liked you and I wanted the date to be perfect," Tom mused. "I was really happy when you agreed to more dates, a second, third..."

"Oh, Tom," Maria laughed. "You had me hooked when I discovered that you love music as much as I do. I can't think of a better turn of karma than you becoming the choir director at Muskegon High where I am the theater director. It's a match made in heaven. I'm only glad it didn't take you too long after you started teaching at the high school to ask me out."

Tom couldn't believe how lucky he was. He loved Maria. His parents loved Maria and Maria said her parents approved of him. He knew he was going to ask Maria a question soon and he hoped she would say yes. But he also knew he had to come clean about a serious issue before he could ask her that important question.

Maria raised her coffee in a toast, "To a terrific concert today. The orchestra addition worked well for the school show this past week."

Tom said, "All of you were right! I can't wait to hear the reaction of the townspeople this afternoon."

Keeping an eye on the lobby from where we were seated, they finished their coffee and talked about plans for the Christmas break. When they saw Doug and the students come in, Tom said, "We have to go. It's show time!" He quickly paid the bill and headed out to join the excited students. They could hardly control themselves. Many had never been inside the Occidental and they were overwhelmed by the beautiful lobby.

Doug and Tom got the students together in the upstairs ballroom, did a few warm-ups, and tried to settle the kids' nerves. By the time the choir was set up on the balcony and the orchestra was seated and ready to go, the lobby was jammed with over 100 people. The townspeople loved this concert – it was standing room only. The downbeat was promptly at the promised 2:00 p.m.

The concert was a hit! The townspeople loved the changes, the jazzy Christmas tunes, the addition of the orchestra, and of course, the traditional carol sing at the end. Doug and Tom held the students there on the balcony for an extra couple of minutes as they enjoyed the warmth of the applause. Tom told them, "Remember Tolstoy said, 'The purpose of art is to connect one person with another.' You, each of you, made the connection with the people down there. You touched them with your singing and playing. Now go downstairs and meet your admirers."

Doug's smile covered his whole face. To put it more accurately, he was beaming like a 'Cheshire' cat, as though he was the one who made it all possible. He said, "Why don't you get down there and join them? As you told the kids, go meet some people."

Tom spotted Fred and wanted to tell him how well Freddy, Jr. had done with his solo. Tom made his way across the room and saw several of the men who had been at the breakfast meeting a couple of weeks ago – the ones Mrs. McKay called the "city fathers." Fred met Tom halfway and introduced Tom to one of them.

"Tom," he said, "this is Joe Antonelli. Joe, Tom O'Banion. His daughter Sara sings in your choir, so he wanted to meet you."

Mr. Antonelli said, "Yeah, you're the guy my daughter thinks so much of. She has a crush on you."

Tom laughed and replied, "That sometimes happens to a choir director. Not to worry, Mr. Antonelli, it will pass. Here come Maria and Doug, my friends and colleagues from school. Maria is the theater director and Doug is the orchestra and band conductor."

Mr. Antonelli said, "Nice to meet you both. I have been to your musicals and band concerts." He added, "I appreciate that you keep up this tradition at the Occidental. It adds to the city's celebration of the season."

"We enjoy it," Tom answered. "For some of the students, it's the first time they have been exposed to a place like this grand old hotel."

A group of the choir members crowded around and said, "Mr. O, where will we have our hot fudge sundaes?" They had started a new tradition last year. When the concert was over, the choir was treated to one of the Occidental Candy Shop's famous hot fudge sundaes. Tom wouldn't let them have it before the concert – ice cream and hot fudge don't mix well with singing or playing an instrument. Tom wasn't sure if the kids liked the concert or the ice cream better, but it didn't really matter, they deserved a treat for working so hard.

Tom replied, "They'll be in the small banquet room over in the corner of the lobby. They are ready right now. Better hurry in so you don't miss out. We'll be right along."

"Nice to meet you, Mr. Antonelli." Tom thought it was interesting that Antonelli was in that group of men that he saw two weeks ago coming out of the conference room upstairs. Tom wondered what his role was in town to be included with the big muckity mucks. Tom continued, "See you at a future concert. You too, Fred, see you soon."

Doug, Tom, and Maria hurried into the small banquet room. The choir kids and orchestra musicians were just finishing their sundaes.

Tom turned to Doug and Maria, "Let's not have sundaes. I have something I want to run by you both."

"What's that?" they said in unison.

"It is about unseen forces driving people in this town and the townspeople don't have any idea. But patience, grasshoppers. Let's get the kids on the bus with their chaperons so they can get back to school and their rides home. We'll go to Drelles' Restaurant. It's just across the street and we can have a drink and relax over an early dinner. And since their expansion, it holds a big crowd. Makes for good privacy. Best of all, my treat."

It was snowing lightly as they walked over to Drelles. Tom broke out with a chorus of "It's beginning to look a lot like Christmas." Maria smiled as always and said, "Tom, what will people think?" Tom smiled back because she had confessed earlier she liked that he felt the freedom to just break into song any old time and that Tom followed his own drummer frequently. Doug frowned. He had once told Tom it wasn't in good taste, no matter that it was for Maria's benefit.

It was early, only 5:30 p.m. so the hostess led them to a somewhat private booth. Doug took a seat where he could see most of the room as well as both front and back doors. The waitress took the drinks and appetizers order and left with a promise to give them some time before they ordered dinner.

"Well what did you both think of the concert?" Tom prompted.

"Oh, no, you don't. What is this thing you wanted to run by us? It can't be just the performance which, by the way, was terrific. The audience ate it up." Maria scolded Tom.

Doug added, "The orchestra addition, a beautiful lagniappe, took it over the top. But come on, spill it. "

Tom told them about the conversation with Fred at Doo Drop. Mostly it was about how upset Fred was over the "nine expensive funerals" comment his consultant made. "Fred can't understand how nine men can hold the town back. Frankly, I can't either."

"Maybe it is that way in a lot of towns, not just ours," Maria said. "You know, unseen forces that drive things and the townspeople don't have any idea."

"Could be, but Fred has a real love for this town and wants to see it grow in a different direction. The funny thing is, that comment slipped my mind until last week when we came down to set up the concert."

"What happened that morning that brought it back? I don't remember anything unusual."

"Remember when we went to Mrs. McKay's office? A group of men and their wives — could have been nine or ten couples — came out of a meeting room. I asked Mrs. McKay who they were, and she said they were some of the town's business and industry leaders. You'll remember that Mrs. McKay spoke to one. Well, I met him tonight, Joe Antonelli. And you know what? I think he may be part of that group of nine."

While Tom was talking, Doug had been looking around, and now said, "Tom, keep your voice down. You don't know who is in here and how the sound might carry. I know you're upset but calm down."

Tom looked around and lowered his voice, "You're right, I'm upset. So is Fred."

He continued, "How is it you are always checking out any room you are in?"

Doug said, "It's just a habit of mine, I like to be aware of anything going on wherever I happen to be."

Maria jumped in, "I remember at the time I wondered if Joe Antonelli is related to Sara. I was curious about him so I checked Sara's school records. He's her father. And by the way, there is no Mrs. Antonelli. She died of cancer some four years ago when Sara was only twelve. I think he has done a good job with Sara through some difficult years for a girl. She'll be 16 in August and has done well in her classes. The only concern I have is that she seems more aggressive toward older men than most girls that age."

"Interesting info, sweetheart, but the relationship doesn't necessarily mean anything. It's just that the incident makes me think. Fred's consultant said there are nine men that hold the town back, and guess what, I'm wondering if that group at the Occidental just may be them. From what Mrs. McKay said, they meet there once a month. This one happens to be their Christmas celebration."

"Is there any way we can find out who they are?"

"I don't know how. The group is pretty secretive from what Fred's consultant told him. Do you suppose the consultant knows but didn't want to tell Fred?"

"I don't know but Fred seems to believe he's pretty reliable. There's something else that Fred was uptight about. This group of nine wants to get rid of him. Permanently. Not just fire him but do him physical harm."

Maria gasped, "No, that can't be. Not here in Muskegon. Maybe the consultant got some bad information."

"Maybe so. But I'm determined to help Fred get to the bottom of this. Keep your ears open and see what you can find out. And be careful. We don't know what these guys are up to."

The waitress interrupted the conversation to take their dinner orders. Though it was a Greek-American restaurant, Drelles still had good old American dishes. Maria ordered her standard – pork chops with apple sauce, mashed potatoes, and green beans. Tom went with his usual – meat loaf, mashed potatoes, and peas with a dinner roll. Doug decided to try their moussaka even though it had eggplant in it. Nothing fancy, simply good food.

During dinner they continued to kick around ideas about the group of nine. Tom tried to wind it up over coffee and dessert and said, "I have to do something. You should have seen Fred at our lunch. I've never seen him so upset. Fred is like the older brother I never had. He has always been there for me. I can't let him down now."

## 7

"Fred," his secretary Alice said, "they are waiting for you in the conference room. Mr. Milford and Mr. Saunders said they have a meeting at 11:00 this morning, so they need to catch you now."

Fred was dressed in his usual gabardine slacks, tweed sport coat with the leather patches on the elbows. His trademark bowtie, tied as usual this morning by his wife, was a red one. He didn't look forward to dealing with the city manager, Sam Milford, and Sam's assistant, Jerry Saunders. A company that manufactured electronic circuit boards wanted to start a new business in Muskegon. Fred had been working hard to get the firm to put their new plant in Muskegon and start the transformation of the lakeshore area. But there were those who didn't want it to happen. For some reason, it didn't fit their image of the city. Even Sam was reluctant, and Fred wasn't yet sure why. Fred believed that the town should shift away from heavy industry that was dependent on the automobile companies. He just hadn't sold the idea to enough people yet.

"Well, might as well get to it," Fred thought.

Fred stepped into the conference room. Sam and Jerry were deep in conversation but stopped when he came in.

"Good morning, gentlemen," Fred said, "Let's do it, shall we? I want to see Jones Electronics come to our town."

Sam said, "We have a problem. They don't want an electronics business in the city. They don't think it fits in."

"Who are they? The city's business leaders or the unions?"

"This time it is the group of city fathers opposed to change. They want to keep the status quo."

"Yes, I know who you mean, the group of nine," Fred said, watching Sam and Jerry carefully to catch their reactions to the "group of nine."

Sam replied, "What do you mean, group of nine? Where did that number come from?"

"I heard it somewhere," Fred said evasively. "What you are saying is they don't think it fits in with the way they think the city should go. Well, I think it will be good for the city's economy in the long term. We need it here and I'm getting a little weary of the push to do it their way. We'll probably hear from the union leaders, too. They don't like it that this circuit board company isn't unionized."

"Fred, you know what will happen if we buck them on this. There is an election coming up next year and I'd just as soon stick around for a while."

Fred stared him down, "We need to do the right thing for the city, Sam. It's time. They have run things too long. I talked to Joe Antonelli at the Christmas concert last week. I think he may be a member of the group, but he could be on our side on this."

"From what I heard about their last meeting, it sounded like all of them were in agreement, even Mr. Antonelli," Jerry chimed in.

"Where did you hear that? How do you know about their meetings? And what makes you think Antonelli is a member of the group?"

"In answer to your last question, I don't know that he is. I've just heard things. And as for the meetings, word gets around. Maybe the group of nine lets things leak out so it gets back to the people they think need to hear it," Jerry stammered.

"So maybe city hall should do that too, let things leak out. I sometimes think it is happening already, but the problem is, I haven't figured out who is doing the leaking." Fred got up and walked to the window that overlooked the lake. He turned back quickly and saw the uneasy look on Sam's face before he looked down at his notes. Fred added, "We need to find who's doing the leaking."

Fred thought back to the last time he proposed a change. It was another business, this time the new business was in direct competition with Larry Olsen's casting manufacturing business. Larry Olsen came to see him. The town didn't need two companies making castings. Fred pointed out to Olsen that there were two automotive spring manufacturers in town, and both were doing well. Olsen said that this was different, and he had the support of a group of the town's business people who wanted to keep the new competitor out. He also said Fred "better come around to their way or maybe there would not be a next time." Usually the hints were more subtle, but this was direct and threatening. Fred remembered that he hadn't reacted well and told Larry in no uncertain terms, that he and whoever was with him on this were holding back the development of the town with their attitudes toward new business. Larry was not happy hearing that and stormed out of Fred's office slamming the door behind him. In the end the new castings company had backed out – Fred never got the real story about why they did.

"We're moving ahead on this new business. You need to get on board, Sam," Fred said. "What do we have to do to get ready to sell it to the city council?"

Sam replied, "I'll have everything ready and on your desk Wednesday morning. Why don't you read it over and see what you think? I can put it on the agenda for the first city council meeting of the New Year and we can have it polished up by then. It will also give me some time to do some arm-twisting."

As their meeting broke up, Alice came in and said, "Fred, there is a Mr. Charles Jacobs waiting to see you. He represents the AFL-CIO and doesn't have an appointment but said this wouldn't take long. What should I tell him?"

Fred asked if there were any other appointments. Alice shook her head no so he told her, "Tell him that another meeting is scheduled, so he would only have a few minutes. Then send him in."

Fred continued saying to Sam and Jerry, "See what I mean. How did the union find out about this? Why is he here?"

Sam answered, "It may be nothing at all. I think you are being paranoid."

Fred shook his head and walked to his office. He wondered why Sam was being so difficult and why did he look so uneasy when Fred talked about leaks. Could Sam be the leak? Fred was looking forward to talking to Tom this weekend and getting his take on the situation. Tom had a good way of helping him clarify things. Fred buzzed Alice and told her to send Mr. Jacobs in.

"Good morning, Mr. Jacobs."

"Mr. Mayor, I'm here out of courtesy to you," Jacobs said. "You are trying to bring in a non-union electronics firm to the city. I'm here to let you know that we object to a non-union firm. While we can't stop you, nor would we try, I want you to know we will do everything in our power to discourage them. If you are successful, we will be working on bringing them into the fold right away."

"Mr. Jacobs, I appreciate the courtesy of your visit, but it is going to happen. I'm going to the city council just after the New Year for their final approval to move on it. I thank you for your time, but I have to get to another meeting. Oh, by the way, how did you know we are trying to bring in an electronics company? That is not common knowledge outside this office."

"Things get out, Mr. Mayor. No one can keep secrets in this town. You should know that by now."

Fred walked to the window, digesting this latest piece of information. So many questions. How did Jacobs know about the electronics company? "No one can keep secrets in this town," he had said. And yet somebody was good at keeping secrets — no one had any idea who the men in the group of nine were. He heard what Jacobs said but he wasn't buying it. Where's the leak? And...why are Sam and Jerry dragging their feet? Are they concerned about their jobs and/or are they the source of the leak? Fred thought he might have to plant something different with each of them to see if it got out. He'd know if one was involved.

SAM RUSHED BACK to his office, closed the door, and got right on the phone. He misdialed at first in his haste and had to recheck the number. His call was to Harry to let him know what happened. Harry was his contact with the unions. Harry wasn't in so he left a message with the answering service, "Sam here. Call me."

When Jerry got back to their offices, Sam was already on the phone; their secretary was off somewhere, so Jerry went back to Alice and said, "I have a quick errand to run. Our secretary isn't at her desk though, so would you tell Sam? And tell him, please, I'll be back in plenty of time for our 2:00 o'clock meeting."

Alice thought, *Here we go again. I'm going to follow him this time.* She buzzed Fred and asked if it was alright for her to run a quick errand over lunch. Fred said, "Sure, take your time. I'll be in but not here for anyone until you get back."

Jerry grabbed his coat and walked out into the brisk December day. He had to meet Harry. It was snowing lightly again. It was just a short walk from city hall to the Hostess Café, but he kept his head down against the snow. When Alice came out of the building, he was already half a block away down Clay Avenue. Alice was sure she hadn't been seen.

Jerry went in, looked around and found Harry Walker, a big tall muscular man. He looked like a former football player. Jerry didn't like the man, but he was the contact for the group of city fathers, so Jerry had to deal with him. And he didn't want the extra money to stop. He just needed to report what was happening inside city hall. He sat down and asked the waitress to bring him some coffee and a donut. When it arrived and she left, he told Harry that the news wasn't good.

Alice stood just inside the door and saw Jerry talking to a big man. The man noticed her standing by the bulletin board just inside the door, but he turned back quickly to Jerry and his conversation. Alice hesitated a moment, pretending to write down a number from the bulletin board. She exited quickly, turned left toward Western Ave, and had lunch at Walgreen's so she would have a good story if Jerry happened to ask her why she was at the Hostess Café. *Now she knew for sure that Jerry was up to something. He had been sneaking out a lot frequently. The question was should she tell Fred?*

In the meantime, Jerry was telling Harry that the mayor was determined to bring the new company in and was going to try and convince the city council. He finished his coffee and made the walk back feeling some uneasiness. He didn't trust Harry and to tell the truth, was a little afraid of him.

Harry asked for more coffee and sat thinking about what he heard. He would, he was sure, hear soon from Sam Milford. This was a sweet little deal he had going, being the muscle for both the unions and the city business fathers. Sam was a kind of bumbler about supplying information. Jerry was the real player. His information was better, and he was hungrier. With two different feeds from City Hall, Harry was sure no one would ever know that he was playing both sides and taking in a nice buck from each.

## 8

It was Wednesday, January 2nd, the first day of school for the new semester. The snow was the kind that made Michiganders say, "Snow fine, stay long time," whatever that meant. It was cold and blustery with the winds off Muskegon Lake. Even though the high school was some distance from the lake, you could still feel that wind. Tom parked his car, felt the blast of the wind and fine snow. He saw Maria get out of hers. They walked together into the north end of the building, went past the bookstore, the biology classrooms, and came to the little theater side entrance.

Maria stopped outside her office door and turned to Tom. "Dinner was great Saturday night. Tony's is so special. What made you pick it?"

"I just wanted a romantic evening with my favorite girl," Tom replied with a heated look.

"I better be your only girl after what you said to me," she said with a laugh.

"You know you are," Tom moved closer to her as he sang, "It's A Lovely Day Today."

Maria danced away, "Tom, you know we have to be careful here at school. We don't want any rumors to get started."

"Too late! The kids and the faculty likely know anyway." Tom like a magician pulled a single red rose out of his inside jacket pocket and handed it to her, 'pour toi, ma Cherie, tu es belle' Her perfect smile was radiant. She blew Tom a kiss, "I'll see you later at the teacher in-service...you just behave yourself in there Mr. O. People are watching."

Tom continued on, turned right at the corner, down past the school's main entrance, and on to the choir room, also his office. Maria was still on his mind, *I'm a lucky guy. She is beautiful and seems to care for me. A tall, 5' 9", willowy blonde, Maria was a terrific musical comedy singer and actress who had starred in several West Michigan amateur productions.* He had seen her as Anna in The King and I, she was wonderful. A fabulous dancer as well – she could do it all! Over a glass of wine after the cast party, Tom told her, "You could make it on Broadway."

She gazed into his eyes, "That's not for me, Tom. I'm happy as the drama teacher here."

Tom loved his job here, too. It was hard to believe he had been here a year and a half. He had been teaching at a high school in southern Michigan for four years when he ran into his former high school choral director, John, at a state directors' meeting. John had inspired Tom to become a choral conductor. John was excited about his new job as the state music education director. He let Tom know that his director's job at Muskegon High School was open. When John asked Tom if he was happy where he was, Tom told him he was but he would really love to get back to Muskegon. John encouraged Tom to apply and told him that he had a really good chance to come home to teach in Muskegon, and that he would put in a good word for him.

Tom took his advice and got lucky. He was the Choral Director at his alma mater, Muskegon High School. His students were great. His parents were here. And he was back in his hometown that he loved. Best of all, there was Maria. They started dating almost as soon as Tom started at MHS. And now though she didn't know it yet, she was the future Mrs. O'Banion.

Tom frowned as he thought about the serious conversation he had to have with Maria before they went much further. Tom was infertile from a childhood illness. He was somewhat apprehensive about talking to Maria after what happened in college. He had dated a girl most of his junior and senior years and thought she was the one. But when she found out he couldn't father children, she dropped Tom like a rock. He was crushed and didn't date much until he met Maria, almost five years later. Maria was so important to him – he was worried about her reaction. He thought she cared about him the same way he cared about her. He prayed she would react differently. Tom shook himself and thought, *I better think about this another time, I have work to do.*

An in-service day for the teachers meant there were no students in the building today. Teachers could get their classrooms set up and materials ready when the students showed up tomorrow. Doug, the orchestra band director, and Tom's best friend at school dropped in for a chat. Doug played the French horn in the local symphony. He was that good!

A funny guy, Doug always had a good story or a bad pun and could tell them well. He didn't disappoint as he regaled Tom with stories of his family Christmas. Tom guffawed at the vision of the new kitten racing up the Christmas tree chasing the blinking Christmas lights. Doug wears wildly colored shirts that his orchestra students love. He is, well, a little irreverent at times and sometimes a little corny but that made him all the more endearing. He is the epitome of W. Somerset Maugham's quote, "Impropriety is the soul of wit."

Tom asked him, "Doug, why don't you find yourself a lady friend. You're a funny guy, women like you. How about Nancy? Then we could double date, what do you say?"

"I like things just the way they are. No complications." Doug wondered, *Maybe I should tell Tom about my past. The military after two years of junior college, special ops training, even a stint as a mercenary in South America. Tom knew he had finished his B.A. and M.A. in music at Western Michigan University, but nothing about the military. No, not yet.*

He started to leave but turned back to launch his daily challenge, "What's the meaning of decimate?"

Tom gave him the dictionary definition "to destroy or demolish."

"Wrong, choir man, it means the tenth wife of a Middle East potentate." Tom groaned and Doug left with his usual cackle.

When he was gone, Tom sat at his desk in the back behind the pianos and looked over his class rosters to check the balance among students in the choirs. It was time to recruit again at the first assembly with the students next week. Always more women than men. Maybe Freddy, Jr., the mayor's son, could recruit some of his buddies.

Tom sat down at the piano and started to play. He was classically trained on the piano, thanks to his mom who insisted he start with the classics. But Tom was really into jazz. He would love to play in some of the clubs around town. Problem was, this was 1963, in West Michigan, and the administration would frown on it – outside employment in clubs wasn't allowed, even if it was on his own time. Last summer he sat in at some jazz spots in Grand Rapids and Detroit, just for a few gigs. He hoped they were far enough away from Muskegon that the administration wouldn't find out. Doug and Maria knew Tom did it but no one else at the school did. Doug would waggle his fake cigar and say, with his best Groucho imitation, "You have to watch out for those jazz musicians."

With no one else around, Tom lost himself with some jazz tunes, "Take Five" by Dave Brubeck, "Here's That Rainy Day" by Jimmy Van Heusen and Johnny Burke, and "Spring Can Really Hang You up The Most" by Tommy Wolf and Fran Landesman. He was still at it when Maria stuck her head in the door and said, "Tear yourself away from that piano, Mr. O, we have a meeting to get to."

All the teachers and staff convened in the little theater off the main auditorium and stage. Maria and Tom found seats with Doug and Nancy. Nancy is Maria's best friend and confidant. She teaches speech, radio production, and script writing as well as being Maria's assistant and technical director for plays and musicals. As the "fearsome foursome" of the creative arts at the high school, they spent a lot of time together. Finally after a two and half hour meeting with announcements and nothing really different as far as procedures and events, the teachers and staff scattered like students at the end of a school day. The Fearsome Foursome wrapped up their preparations and took off to US 31 B-B-Q for an early dinner.

# 9

The students poured in the next morning, full of stories about their Christmas break. Tom's first class started at 8:00 a.m. with one of the two math classes he had for this semester. The 8 o'clock was Advanced Algebra and the second math class was Trigonometry at 1:00 p.m. Some people thought it was strange that the choir director taught math, but math and music are closely related. In fact, Tom toyed with the idea of teaching math and doing music on the side, but he knew he needed more music in his life than a part-time gig.

Second period, 9:00 a.m. was Mixed Chorus. This group was the starting choir and most students sang here first then moved up to the more advanced choirs, sometimes Acappella II if they were good. Acappella I met third period at 10:00 and Acappella II, the top choir, at 11:00 a.m. It was a good schedule with last period Tom's planning period that gave him a chance to catch up on his grading and get ready for the next day.

As always Tom played the piano as the kids came in. Sometimes they would join in singing, sometimes they would just listen. Just before Acappella II, Tom shed his jacket so the kids could see his special Schroeder tee shirt — think the Peanuts comic strip. As they crowded around the piano, they could see the name Schroeder on the back. Tom switched to a Beethoven sonata. As more of them caught on, the kids started giggling and burst into laughter. Tom stood up and showed them the front with Schroeder at the piano and Lucy watching him with adoring eyes. By then everyone was in on it and the class was in an uproar.

When they settled down, the elite groups of singers went about getting acquainted, reacquainted, and sharing stories about their Christmas vacation. On the first day back from any vacation, Tom liked to have the class talk about new music the kids discovered over the break. The kids shouted out new and old tunes like "Up on the Roof" by the Drifters, "Loco-Motion" by Little Eva, "Twist and Shout' by The Isley Brothers, "Runaround Sue" by Del Shannon, and "Twistin' the Night Away" by Sam Cooke. Tom couldn't catch all the titles, but as always, he was impressed by how well tuned into the latest they were. They loved the new rock and roll.

"Ok! Ok! I have an assignment for you," Tom held up his hands in mock surrender.

"Oh, no," they moaned. "Not already. You wouldn't do that to us, Mr. O. Not on the first day back!"

"Over the weekend I want you to do a little research. Think about all the concerts you've heard or been in, talk to your friends and relatives, check out the Top 40, and make a list of what music you think might be fun to do for the spring concert this year. I already have some ideas, but I'd like to hear from you."

Sara Antonelli's hand shot up, "What kinds of songs do you want?" She was always trying to catch Tom's attention.

"We always have classical choral works in the first half of the concert. We need some classics, with a few surprises I have up my sleeve. In the second half, I'd like to shake it up a bit more and focus on Broadway and pop tunes and maybe a rock and roll number or two with some jazz mixed in. One of the classical pieces I've already picked has both a standard choral arrangement and a jazzy version by a new group, the Swingle Singers. Anyone ever hear of them?" They shook their heads no so Tom continued.

"Let me show you how it works. I'm going to play you a sample of each version so you can see what happens. We'll start with the classical version of Bach's "Ode to Joy" – listen to this. Nice, huh? We'll move right into the Swingle Singers version of the same. Pretty cool, don't you think? And just for a fun ending to the first half of the concert, we'll go right into the Swingle Singers' version of Beethoven's Fifth Symphony. We'll bill it in the program as "A Fifth of Beethoven with a little Bach on the Side." They all applauded and laughed aloud. It was good to see them excited about fun things ahead.

Tom continued, "Several new musicals have been released this year like "A Funny Thing Happened on the Way to the Forum" and "How to Succeed in Business without Really Trying." And some new musical movies like "State Fair" and "Gypsy." Plus, there are some new tunes with jazzy arrangements. Let's see what you can come up with. We'll put together a master list and I'll see what I can find in choral arrangements. Monday, we'll start work on two pieces, a classical piece and a Broadway song I arranged back in the summer. Everybody clear on the assignment?" They nodded and even looked a little intrigued.

Sara sidled up to Tom's side. "Broadway tunes will be fun, Mr. O. Do you know what Miss Vitale will do for the school musical this year?"

"She hasn't decided yet, Sara. Do you plan to try out for the show?"

"I'm not sure yet. My voice isn't very strong. And I would really like to do a lead."

"If you don't get a lead, you could be in the chorus. It's good experience and lots of fun."

Sara stepped a little closer, "I guess, but I'd really like a lead. Maybe you could give me some extra help?"

Tom backed away and put the desk between them, "Sara, I have to get back to my paperwork. You need to get to your next class." Sara looked irritated and flounced out of the classroom. Tom was uncomfortable with Sara sometimes. He thought she might have a little schoolgirl crush on him.

Tom finished straightening up his room and making sure everything was ready for the trig class after lunch. It looked like the choirs would be in good shape if he could recruit some more male voices and if they could shift their schedules around so they could join choir.

## 10

Maria's morning classes went well. In her free time before lunch she wandered into the little theater. This small, cozy theater was perfect for one-act dramas, smaller comedy, and drama productions as well as induction ceremonies for student organizations like the National Honor Society. It had a small proscenium stage and seated about 200 people. The décor was simple but elegant as she sat down in one of the soft red cushioned seats. She looked up at the stage and thought about the plays she would do this school year. The aroma of student, grease paint permeated the room. She loved it. It was her life.

Her thoughts drifted to Tom, as they did frequently throughout the day. Thinking about his surprise gift of the rose this morning made her smile again. There was always a twinkle in those blue Irish eyes as he did those special things. He often whispered little endearments in French, more romantic because of the language. He told her he did some short drama roles in this little theater and musical comedy roles in the big room when he went to school here. She could imagine him on stage with his fine tenor voice — she actually loved it when he serenaded her with her favorite Irish ballads. They shared a love for both the theater and good music. It was easy to see why they hit it off right away when he came last year.

As she walked to the main auditorium, she heard the music from his choir room. She slipped in the back door of his choir room to listen. She was behind him and gestured to the students not to let on she was there.

When the piece finished, she clapped softly, "Beautiful, Mr. O. I had to come in to hear it."

He turned at the sound of her voice with tears in his eyes that he wiped away, no self-consciousness. Tears often came when the music got to him. Seeing her there, all he could say was, "Well, hi there Miss Vitale, meet the makers of those beautiful sounds."

The students burst into applause.

She waved goodbye to the students, gave Tom a quick wave, and left the room.

Maria made her way to the big auditorium, still moved by the music. She sat down in the center about seven rows back and thought about what had just happened. She had seen the tears and heard the catch in his voice. She loved his intensity when he gets lost in his music. Sometimes he is so focused that he often doesn't even know anyone else has come into the room as just happened. Of course, she relates to that since she sometimes forgets to eat when she's staging a play. Even though he's pretty serious, he loves life and it shows in his dry wit and when he's playing jazz. She smiled dreamily as she thought about his slightly curly auburn hair and his blue eyes – he looked like an Irishman. He was not much taller than she was and slender – they fit well together when they danced. She had really strong feelings about Tom and she was fairly sure he felt the same way about her.

Back to her reason for being in here. All the musicals were performed here in the big auditorium. The stage was large enough for big musical casts and there was an orchestra pit.

The acoustics of the room were great. One could do shows here and no one in the audience would miss a word. She imagined as Tom did, that she could hear traces of the music of the shows done here. A little trace of Ado Annie's "Cain't Say No" from last year's production of Oklahoma and then a hint of "Shall We Dance" from Civic Theatre's production of "The King and I."

Assemblies were also held here as this room could accommodate the entire student body. She was so fortunate to get hired here. The facilities were great, the administration very supportive of the arts, and she was having a great time teaching and directing.

As she sat there absorbing the ambience, Tom came back to mind. She thought of the conversation she had with her mom. After her mom met him, she later said to Maria, "Watch out for that one, he can charm the socks off you. He's part Peter Pan and part Pied Piper."

Maria laughed and said, "Aw, Mom. He's ok. Tom is a good friend and that's important first, so we'll see. But I like him. And you're right, he is a charmer. I've told him that might get him in trouble someday with his girl choir members. But he just says that the only one he wants to charm is me."

Mom smiled and said, "Sounds to me as if it's more than like."

"I don't know. Maybe. There is much to like. Sometimes he is so serious, but his love of life and sense of humor comes out and he changes, his face just beams when he smiles."

Now as she thought of that conversation, Maria wondered, *I think I am in love with him but is it too fast?* The heart doesn't always know about the "right time" to fall in love, and maybe later would be better. Yet they had been an "item" for several months now, dating at least once a week. She found she could easily bring him out of his serious mood and have him laughing. He could do the same for her. But she knew there were things to learn about Tom yet.

She and Tom's mother talked about that at Christmas. His mom seemed to think that much of his serious nature and wisdom came during a long sickness and recovery in his teenage years. Confined to bed, and unable to go to school for several weeks, Tom read a lot in that time, classics such as the writings of Plato as well as good fiction. He had once told Maria that if he could find one idea in a book that helped him find his way, then whatever the book, the read was worthwhile. He developed his serious demeanor during that time, maybe because he confronted his mortality so early, as well as his strong sense of fairness and justice. His mom said that Tom never lost that habit of reading. She told Maria, "He also seemed to develop an extra sense, an ability to read situations and people. He has an uncanny knack for seeing the situation from different perspectives, so he finds his way more easily."

"That must be why he seems to know what I'm thinking," Maria said laughing. She frowned, "He's never told me about being sick."

"He'll tell you when he's ready. You should know as well that Tom had a sister who died young. She was three years younger than Tom and he adored her. We lost her when she was ten. Losing her was as hard on him as it was on us."

Maria hugged her and said, "I'm so sorry. It has to be hard to lose a child."

Tom's mother had teared up and said, "It hit us all pretty hard. When Tom was so ill later, we were afraid that we would lose him too. The doctor told us that it was a close call with Tom."

Maria thought she would ask Tom soon if he didn't bring it up. It was puzzling to her that he hadn't. They were so open with each other. Maria corralled her thoughts, checked her watch, and realized it was already lunchtime. She slipped out of the auditorium and walked across the hall to Tom's office.

She stuck her head in the back door and asked, "Are you going to lunch now? I have lunch duty this period, so I have to be there."

"That sounds great. Let's go."

Lunch duty wasn't really a chore. It was interesting to see which kids had paired up, who sat with whom. Today there was a table full of basketball players. They practiced for several days before the New Year started and were a team again after the layoff. Bob Fowler, the team's star forward and Sara's boyfriend, was at the table with several others.

At another table, there were members of his choirs chattering about their holidays and the music assignment Tom had given them. Maria said, "I hear you have your kids at work already."

"Yes, I asked them to make a list of new music they heard recently and oh, are they really up on the new songs! They are to think of some classical pieces, and some Broadway tunes we could consider for the spring concert. By the way, what show do you plan to do for your spring musical?"

"I haven't made a final decision yet. I would love to do the "Fantastiks" but I'm not sure it has been released yet for schools. If that doesn't work out, I will do "The King and I." I need to talk with you about your singers to see which ones have strong voices."

Just then, the bell rang for the first afternoon class. Maria and Tom stayed an extra minute, still talking about their morning classes. Sara Antonelli came up behind them and said, "Here are two of my favorite people. Miss Vitale, do you know what musical you are doing this spring. Mr. O has encouraged me to audition. I'd like a shot at a lead."

"Yes, I did, Sara. But remember what I said when you were nervous about the strength of your voice?" Maria watched Sara with interest.

Sara said coyly, "But if you were to coach me after school, maybe I could win a role."

"Sara, I can't do that for you and not for everyone else. That wouldn't really be fair, would it?"

She pouted, "I just thought you could help." Sara, long blond hair swinging from side to side, took off to catch up with her friends.

When Sara was out of earshot, Maria warned, "Tom, you might want to be careful around Sara. Did you see the way she looked at you? And she was definitely flirting with you."

"I know. I saw it. But it's just a schoolgirl crush. I don't sense that it is serious. But I'll take the warning and make sure I'm never alone with her."

Maria went to her planning period and Tom went to teach the trigonometry class. His planning period was the last period of the day. He waited for Maria to finish her Stagecraft class and walked her to her car. It was a good start to the semester.

## 11

Tom was lucky to find a small rental house in the beach area not far from Lake Michigan. It was just a one bedroom with a small kitchen, bathroom, and a good sized living room. The best part of the house was the fireplace. Tom loved sitting there enjoying the flicker of a log fire. He was looking forward to buying a house and he hoped he would be doing that with Maria but, for now, this worked.

After a lazy Saturday morning, Tom ran his errands and got home in plenty of time to catch the first showing of "The Music Man" which was playing at the Michigan Theater. Maria and Nancy were on a Girl Only Saturday, so he was footloose and fancy-free. The ladies were going to spend the day shopping and enjoying a Chinese dinner.

Tom knew Maria wanted to see "The Music Man," but she told him, "You go ahead. We can go together one night next week. You know how you like to see these at least twice."

Tom had seen the stage version, but he wanted to see how Robert Preston handled the role in the movie. And he could listen to the music all day long, especially the rhythmic "Rock Island" that set up the plot for the show.

Tom got to the theater early as usual so he could just sit, enjoy the sights, sounds, and smells of the theater, and watch people. He liked to sit front and center about 15 or so rows back so he could get the full effect of the glorious furnishings. The Michigan Theater was so beautiful and another one of the old buildings that Tom loved in Muskegon. Originally done in a Spanish Renaissance style, the décor had been carefully preserved to maintain its elegance. A floral design of red and gold leaves rimmed the walls just below the ceiling. In the front of the room above the stage was a heraldic style shield, also in red and gold-leaf with the mask symbol in its center suggesting the drama and music to come. The side walls featured marble facets and columns reminiscent of a Victorian décor. The curtain, drawn nearly to the top for the movie, was a rich burgundy and gold brocade accented with thick gold tassels that drew the curtain up in graceful loops. Tom as always stood and looked around the back of the house and up at the balcony. All the seats were in a matching deep red with embedded gold filigree. The seats, though narrow, were quite comfortable. Running down each side were Tiffany-style hanging lamps. The ceiling completed the luxurious picture with deep red and gold swirls that drew the room together and accentuated the pink translucent inverted dome in the center of the ceiling.

If one sat quietly and tuned out the buzz from the people coming in, one could imagine you could hear the music of past performances. Howard Keel singing "Old Man River" seemed as though it was still resounding, you could almost smell the river he was singing about. So many stage shows were also done here, and Tom liked to think he could hear the traces of all the musicals from years back.

He smiled and thought maybe he could even catch a glimpse of the ghost of the theater. He knew it was probably not true, but it was fun to think about. People probably wondered what he was smiling at.

Several of his music students came in. There were some groups of girls and a few couples, Sara and her boyfriend, Bob Fowler, among them. Sara and Bob saw Tom and walked over.

Sara asked, "What were you smiling about, Mr. O?"

"Hi to both of you. You caught me. Remembering the music of

past performances here often makes me smile. You should try it. Let your imagination go when you are here and try to go back to something you saw and heard. Just let it in."

"How do you do it?"

"Tell you what we'll do. In Monday's class we'll have a discussion on this show, and we'll talk about letting them run through your mind. Spread the word. There are a number of other choir members here. It will make for a good start to Monday's class."

Bob said, "I think that's great, Mr. O. We'll see you Monday. Come on, Sara, let's find our seats."

They went on further back from where Tom sat. Tom remembered what Maria said about Sara at lunch the other day and he felt a premonition of trouble. The movie started and Tom put it out of his mind. The show was terrific. Robert Preston was masterful as Professor Harold Hill. Shirley Jones was surprisingly good, too. Her portrayal of Marian the librarian was superb and what a voice, even though she had too much vibrato for his taste. The music was wonderful. He couldn't get it out of his head, danced across the street to his car, and went home singing "76 Trombones."

## 12

T he monthly shopping trip was on! Nancy and Maria would hit the major department stores and ladies' fashion shops in downtown Muskegon. Next, as they often did, they would have dinner at Chan's. They had their route all mapped out, Hardy Herpolsheimer's department store, Hughes Ladies Shop, Grossman's and Federals Department stores.

On a Saturday afternoon, downtown Muskegon was busy, so Nancy parked in the lot behind 'Herps' as Hardy Herpolsheimer's was called by the locals. They started their shopping afternoon there. By the time they reached Grossman's, they had bought some new clothes for work and, of course, shoes for Maria. Maria loved her shoes! They stopped for afternoon tea and "cookies" upstairs in Grossman's coffee shop.

When they left, they went back to Federals. There was a blouse that Nancy saw, and she wanted to go back and get it. While they were there, Maria spotted a tie that she was sure Tom would like. She bought it and had it gift wrapped. Nancy asked, "Is this for a birthday gift?"

"No, Tom's birthday isn't until September. This is one of those 'just because' gifts. He's always doing something like that so now I do too. The other day at school he gave me a single rose. I've learned to keep a tall bud vase just for times like that. He doesn't buy me clothes. I think he's not comfortable with that."

"Are things getting more serious with you two?"

"I want to talk with you about that at dinner."

They continued on back down Western Avenue and took a left turn at Second Street. Maria always checked out what was new at Buel's Shoes. But nothing caught her fancy, so they went on down Clay past the Hostess Café to the parking lot behind Herps. They dumped their packages in the trunk.

Maria asked, "Are you about ready to go to dinner? It's getting along toward 5:00 p.m. and with all this walking, I'm starting to get hungry."

"You're always hungry and even get a little cranky when you don't eat right away."

"I know. That's what Tom says too. He keeps me well fed."

"I don't know where you pack it all in. You are always thin."

Maria smiled, "I'm just lucky, I guess."

"Let's drive down to the House of Chan. This early we should be able to find a parking spot somewhere in that block. We won't have far to go in the dark when we get out from dinner."

They found a parking place in front of the Rescue Mission and climbed the stairs next door up to Chan's. They both enjoyed Chinese food, and this was the best in town. They were seated quickly and ordered tea while they looked over the menu.

"What are you up for?"

Maria answered, "I always get Mongolian beef. I love it. But maybe I'll try something new tonight. How about you?"

"Let's get the combination, three choices of Mongolian beef, sweet and sour chicken, and moo shu pork. We can share!"

The waiter came, took the order. Each added egg drop soup to start along with an egg roll.

Nancy asked, "You were going to tell me something about you and Tom. Have things changed? By the way, where is Tom tonight?"

"He's at the Michigan Theatre seeing the movie production of "The Music Man,"

"Have you seen it yet?"

"No, I haven't, but Tom promised to take me later this week."

"Well then, what's up? Has he asked you to marry him?"

Maria laughed, "No, not yet. Sometimes I think he is close to asking, but he hesitates. I know I love him, and he loves me, but something seems to be holding him back."

"Do you have any idea what that might be? I think you two are a great match."

"I don't know what might be holding him back. His mom and I talked at Christmas time and she told me about a childhood illness that kept him out of school for a while. It was a long recovery she said."

"Do you know what it was?"

"No, but I've decided that if he doesn't open up soon, I'll ask him. Since his mom brought it up, I think I can ask him now. His Mom didn't say what it was. We just talked about how it affected him. It gave him a lot of time to read and think and dream, she said."

Maria went on, "There's the matter of his converting to Catholicism. I think he'll be open to that. He doesn't go to church now, but I sense that he is spiritual. So many things to learn about each other yet and questions to get settled. Maybe I'm just thinking too much. One of these days he'll surprise me and ask. I'm ready, I think."

"Do you want me to talk to Doug? He and Tom are close friends."

"No, let's just wait. But that brings up something else. I know it is coming and when it does, I would like you to be my maid of honor."

Nancy teared up, "I was hoping you would ask me. Yes, I would love to."

"We'll have so much to do when the time comes. I want a big wedding with three or four bridesmaids. But enough for now, I'm getting ahead of myself."

"It's ok to dream about it. It is what all we girls want, isn't it?"

"Yes, it is. I can see us now. Both teaching as we are doing, raising a family. I want two or three children. I'm an only child so I want more than one."

"Any doubts? You'll say yes?"

"I will. I love him and like him. He feels deeply about the things that are important to him. He can be quite intense sometimes. He is so much into his music that at times he doesn't even know I've come into the room. He feels that same way about other issues too. Some of them concern me a little but they'll work out. That's a conversation for another time."

They finished their dinner while chatting about other things. Maria told Nancy about her choice of "The King and I" musical she would do this year. She asked Nancy if she would take the assistant director's job again.

Nancy said, "Count me in! That is exciting. I saw you when you were Anna a while back. With that behind you, you should be able to bring the students up to a great level."

"Good! Thank you, Nancy."

When the waiter brought their checks, he left them each a fortune cookie. Maria's was "A good change is coming into your life soon."

She said "See, my fortune says it's coming soon."

## 13

F red asked his secretary Alice to arrange a meeting with the city manager for the next morning. She asked, "Alright, Fred, do you want me to tell Sam what it is about?"

"No, just tell him I have an agenda change to discuss."

When Fred met with the city commission back on that Thursday in early January, they hadn't bought his arguments about the new business. They wanted more time to think about it, and revisit it later in the month. Fred's long term plans were to let the electronic business be the starting point for an industrial park away from the lakefront. The lakefront needed to be developed to attract the tourist trade as well as other lake uses for the locals. The commission wasn't in on this part yet. Fred didn't think they would be swayed.

Fred went home that day disturbed by the turn of events. The city commission wanted to think, but he knew that it was the right path. The community needed this new type of business and needed it away from the lakefront. He thought the commission would come around, but the real question was how to get past the movers in the town, the business group. They were the nine men who didn't want things to change from their ideas of what the town should be.

Fred sat down for dinner with his wife, Eleanor, and their two children, Fred Jr. who was a rambunctious 15 year old and Emily, their 12 year old sweetheart. Fred Jr was full of stories about the spring concert. He didn't spill all the beans, but he hinted they were in for some surprises. Eleanor watched Fred and wondered why he was so quiet. Emily begged to play a game of Monopoly, "just a short one," which was pretty hard to do in a game of Monopoly. After a couple of hours, they finally called the game and sent the kids off to bed.

Fred turned to Eleanor, "I have something to talk with you about."

"Is this serious?" she said. "Shall I get us something to drink?"

"Yes, it's serious. A glass of wine would be nice."

Fred followed her into the kitchen. He thought about staying in the kitchen, but the dishwasher was still running and was a little noisy. It was a new dishwasher, just installed last week, and it was Eleanor's pride and joy. Fred was happy with it, too, because it gave them more time to just be with each other.

It was hard to believe they had been married almost 20 years. They got married just after college, but they were as much in love today as they were in the early days. It was a different love, mature and satisfying. They trusted each other and could talk over anything that came along.

Fred and Eleanor settled down on the sofa with their wine, looked deeply into each other's eyes, toasted each other, and sealed the toast with a kiss. Eleanor looked at Fred expectantly. She questioned, "What's up, Fred? You've been preoccupied all night. Emily never beats you in Monopoly."

"Remember when I told you about the city commission meeting and how the city commissioners were dragging their feet?" He started. "I've been hearing rumors that they are not on board at all. I don't really understand why, but I need to keep moving on my lakeshore vision. I'm just afraid of the consequences. I want to see it happen. It's the right thing, but I'm concerned that the decision might have a serious impact on our future. I need the benefit of your wisdom."

"Fred, you know I'll support you all the way. Your vision is right for Muskegon. What are you going to do?" she asked.

"After these four years here, I think of this place as my town, our town. I want it to grow. I think the right thing to do is to go ahead and ask this business to come to Muskegon. You remember my long term plans to build the industrial base out south of town and open the lakefront for area and tourist attractions? I'm convinced that the town's future lies in finding the best balance of the two. We have a beautiful lakefront with almost no 'lakefront' development on it."

"You're preaching to the choir, darlin'." She leaned back into Fred's side. "What do you think might happen?"

"I suspect my mayor's job might be in jeopardy. The city commissioners aren't going to go up against this cabal of business leaders. From what the consultant told me, this is a pretty powerful group of men. They sit on interlocking boards and have for a long time made the decisions about what direction this town should take. They don't want any change that doesn't fit with their plans. And on top of that, the union is strong here. Between the cabal and the unions, they might make sure I don't get re-elected next year so they can put in someone they can control. That means we'll have to start over again somewhere."

"You're sure you can't convince them to change their minds?"

Fred shook his head and said, "No, it won't work. Remember what happened last time when Larry Olsen came to see me? There was a direct threat that if I didn't go along that time, there might not be another chance. The thing is, I never felt quite right about what happened. I just can't go along this time. Someone has to stand up to them."

"Are you sure it has to be you?"

Fred slammed his fist on the coffee table so hard the wine sloshed out of their glasses. He grabbed the wine glasses and said, "I'm sorry, darling. I'm sure it has to be me or it won't happen. If I don't, the town will likely languish as it has since the mid-50s. The problem is that between the mayor's salary and my small law practice on the side, we finally have some good times. The kids like it here. You seem to be

happy here. And I've grown to love this town. It has so much potential to grow in some different directions."

"It does, Fred. But if we have to start over someplace else, that's
what will have to be. I can always go back to work if we need me to.
You know I haven't worked since the kids were little and it would be
kind of exciting to get back into nursing now that they're older. It
wouldn't be easy on Freddy and Emily, but they are young, and they'll
adjust. Fred, do what you have to do."

The next morning, Fred went to work determined to bring the
situation to a head. He wanted to call the new company's owner but
thought he should talk to the council before he did. Fred had asked
his secretary to give the city manager a note that he wanted to see
him. Sam popped into Fred's office and said, "I didn't think we were
meeting this morning, what's up?"

Fred told Sam that he had decided to go ahead with the electronics company. Sam's reaction was what Fred thought it would be
— he was visibly shaken. And Fred added, "Sam, this also fits in with
my longer term plans."

"What plans, Fred?" Sam asked.

"Not yet. When the time is right, you'll be the first to know."

Sam said, "But you can't push this, Fred. They'll crucify you.
They'll ruin you in this town. You won't be re-elected, might even be
recalled."

"I know all that and it's a chance I'm ready to take. As I said back
in December, it is time to stand up to this group and the unions and
take our town forward. This afternoon at the city commission meeting, I'll be asking for their approval and Sam, I hope that you'll
back me."

"Fred, I can't do that. I like my job here and I will be gone too if
you do this and I support you."

"Well then, the city commission and I will have to go it without
you, Sam. Alice already has it on the agenda. I'll see you at the
meeting."

Sam hurried back to his office and as he rushed past, Jerry called out to him asking what the rush was. Sam said, "Get in here, Jerry. We have a problem."

"What's going on, Sam?"

"Fred is going against the group and will be asking the city council this afternoon to approve the new electronics business. I've told him I can't go along with this, but he thinks he can get it passed."

Jerry exclaimed, "Doesn't he remember what will happen if he does that?"

"I'm sure he does but I don't think he realizes what it might mean to members of the city commission. Some of them may be hurt in this too. But he just might make it happen. We don't have enough time before the meeting to talk to each of them. I have a luncheon meeting to attend. Let's talk about it again around 2 o'clock."

Jerry went back to his office and made a phone call to Harry, "We need to meet and quickly. There's an emergency that needs to be dealt with."

Jerry grabbed his coat, told Sam's secretary that he would be back in time for his 2 pm meeting with Sam and headed for Drelles' restaurant. He arrived before Harry and ordered a drink to steady his nerves. Harry came in and said, "This better be good. What can be so important?"

They ordered lunch and before it came, Jerry recounted the events of the morning. Harry asked, "Couldn't Sam talk him out of it?"

When Jerry told him no, Harry said, "I need to get back to my people with this. Just tell the waiter I had to leave." Jerry fretted that this whole thing could turn ugly. He hoped he wasn't going to be collateral damage.

## 14

The atmosphere in the back room of Joe Antonelli's restaurant was tense. Eight of the members were there. Joe was talking with Harry and would be in soon. Joe left Harry cooling his heels in the bar in case they needed him soon for a new assignment and then rejoined the group. He relayed what Harry had told him. One, the mayor was going to push for a decision on the new electronics firm at the city commission meeting. Two, his contact said that Fred hinted at some long term plans that he wasn't quite ready to reveal yet. Finally, it was about the meetings between the mayor and the as yet unidentified man named Tom at the Doo Drop Inn. They seemed to meet pretty regularly. Harry didn't know everything they talked about, but he reminded Joe about "the nine expensive funerals" comment.

"We can't allow this," said George Anderson, their leader. "It isn't only that this new business doesn't fit with our plans. It will open the door to others who want to move here and that will mean competition for the land we need. And what is this long term plan that we haven't heard about? We're close to a lock on the lakefront properties and the agreements with the new firms are almost ready. We just can't have this now. Fred has become the problem we were afraid of. He's idealistic and strong-minded. You remember what he said to Larry a year ago. But we know what's best for our town.

"He needs to be stopped. Let's have Harry lean hard on him, you know, rough him up a little so he takes the warning. Our mayor needs the fear that something might happen to him if he doesn't cooperate."

"I know a lot of the members of the city commission. I'll go to each of them individually and tell them what's at stake. If we cast some doubts there and Harry can make Fred toe the line, we can stop it," Joe declared.

Wendell asked, "Does anyone know the owner of this electronics company? I think we should work it from that end as well."

George mused, "I think I can find out. Maybe we can get something on him and use it to keep him out."

Tim fretted, "I hate to resort to these tactics, but I don't see any other choice." Tim was the owner of the largest section of lakefront on Muskegon Lake and had much to gain if their master plan went through and much to lose if it didn't.

Joe continued, "I'll get Harry started on what we want done. We should also have him check out who this fellow named Tom is. We need to know in case he starts to make trouble."

MEANWHILE, Charles Jacobs met with his union's executive board and told them of the new developments in the mayor's office.

His vice-president asked, "Should we do something about this, like have one of our boys lean on him."

Charles said, "Let's wait. My contact, Harry, tells me that the businesspeople will likely take some action."

# 15

Fred got off the phone and buzzed Alice. She bustled in and Fred said, "Remind me of what I have for the rest of the day?"

"Not much today. You've got a budget meeting this afternoon that should be over about 5:00. You have a few phone calls before then – concerned citizens. Tomorrow you have a lunch meeting with Mr. Jones about the new electronics business and the city council meeting is at 3:00 p.m. And, oh yes, Chief Johnson called and asked for some time with you. I made an appointment for tomorrow at 9:00 a.m. and said he could have a half hour at most. He said that would be fine, nothing serious. He just wants to run some things by you."

"All right, thanks Alice. Would you get Eleanor for me? I need to double check on where we're meeting for dinner."

When his phone rang, Fred picked it up on the first ring and said, "Hi sweetie."

Eleanor said, "Fred Thomas, someday you're going to get in trouble doing that. It might be someone else on the line."

"That could be fun depending on who's on the phone," Fred said laughing. "The meeting won't be over until 5:00 so I'm going from here right to Doo Drop. We have a reservation for 5:30 so we'll have plenty of time before Freddy's concert. I love you, see you soon."

"I love you, too, Fred."

When Fred came out to his car at 5:15 p.m., he was annoyed to see there was a car parked behind his. Fred walked over to see if he could get out around it. Just at that moment, hidden in the shadows, a big man got out of the car and started moving toward Fred. Fred asked, "What's going on, my friend? Would you mind moving your car? I need to get to my son's concert."

Fred realized the guy was wearing a black ski mask. he started to head back to the building. The big man stepped in front of him, "I'm not a friend, but this is a friendly warning." Grabbing Fred's arm, he yanked it behind Fred's back and slammed him face down on the hood of his car.

"Now you listen, Mr. Mayor and listen close. There are people in this town who don't want the business you're trying to bring here. They don't want the change. You are a problem we don't want. Got it! Just drop it or the next time I come to see you, it won't be at all friendly."

With that warning he pushed Fred's face again down hard on the hood, got in a good punch to the kidneys, and Fred slid down into the snow beside the car. The big guy walked casually back to his car and drove away.

Fred stayed down in the snow for a few minutes, catching his breath, and assessing his injuries. He had a slight nosebleed and was able to stop it with his handkerchief. He sat up, felt a little woozy, and thought he would just rest a bit more. He struggled to his feet and cleaned the snow off his clothes.

Fred got in his car, checked out his damage in the visor mirror and sat there for a few minutes while he thought about what just happened. He was shocked and dismayed at this turn of events. He hadn't expected that the group would resort to physical threats. *Who was it? Was it the nine city fathers behind this or the unions? With that mask he was wearing, I had no idea who the man was. Now what do I do?* I don't want anyone else to get hurt, but I need to talk to Tom about this. He's really good at deducing what's happening by looking at the facts.

Fred didn't want Eleanor to get worried so he hurried to the restaurant. Fortunately, he was only 5 minutes late, and the family was engrossed in their appetizers and garlic toast and chattering about the concert, so they didn't notice his slightly disheveled appearance right away. Eleanor looked at him with a puzzled look, but he shook her off and she understood they would talk about it later.

Fred kidded Freddy Jr. about the garlic toast. "You'll be in among a lot of other students. You'll have to have a mint or two before you start singing." He blushed and Fred wondered if there was a girl Jr liked in the choir.

They tucked into their dinners. Eleanor knew what Fred liked so she had already ordered two perch dinners – the best in the state of Michigan. The kids still liked their hamburgers and fries. Of course, they also had a large order of the famous Doo Drop onion rings. Dinner was great as always, and service was quick. They left in plenty of time to get Freddy, Jr. to the high school for the 7:00 p.m. concert.

When Fred and Eleanor were settled in the center section in the auditorium about six rows back and Emily was off talking with a friend, Eleanor turned to Fred and asked, "Ok, what's going on? You were pretty quiet at dinner tonight."

Fred shook his head, "Not here. Not now. Just things at the office. I'll tell you all about it later tonight."

Eleanor was about to push for more, but Tom walked up. He often walked through the early crowd in the auditorium visiting with parents while his accompanist and assistant director put the choir through their warm-ups.

Eleanor said, "Hi Tom. Freddy is excited about this concert and can't wait to audition for the Acappella I Choir this spring."

Tom replied, "He does well. He has a great voice and I think he'll make it. I may even move him up to Acappella II before the final concert. I need some more tenors up there." Turning to Fred, he said, "Well Mr. Mayor how's everything down at city hall?"

"About the same, Tom. It's going to be great just to relax and enjoy the music. We need to have lunch again to get caught up and talk about that matter we discussed earlier."

"We'll do that, I'll call you. Good to see you both here. I have to move along and talk to some other folks."

As Tom walked away, Eleanor looked at Fred and caught the unfamiliar worried frown on his face. She said, "Something's up, Fred. I can see it in your face. We will talk tonight."

The concert was terrific. It was a preview of the big spring concert, so the audience just got a taste of what Tom had planned. Mr. O seemed to have a gift of bringing out the best in the kids. Their sense of the right dynamics was great under his direction. And the blend was so good. His love of all kinds of music was contagious. They loved him too because he was defying the old traditions and including some jazzy tunes and tonight there was even one song with a rock beat, following the new trend that was just started.

Later that night Fred told Eleanor what happened. She fretted, "How is your arm?"

Fred admitted, "It's a little sore but I don't think it's serious. I just didn't think they would resort to violence. That's what is most upsetting. I told Tom that I thought they were a dangerous group. I'm not sure I believed it then, but I do now."

"Is this going to change your mind?"

"No, but I think I better take some precautions. I won't go out that back door to the parking area without someone else along. Jim, the chief, is coming in tomorrow morning and my guess is that he'll want to have a squad car there when I leave."

Fred soothed Eleanor and told her not to worry, that he would talk to the police chief tomorrow, and he was sure that would be the end of it. Eleanor wasn't so sure.

# 16

The group was having breakfast in the Century Club's private dining room. Later over coffee, some lit up cigars and amid the heavy smoke, the conversation turned to Harry's confrontation with the mayor.

Joe said, "He got a little more physical than I thought he would. Harry left the mayor lying in the snow with a bloody nose and a twisted arm. He got the message all right. Now we'll have to see how he reacts to it. Harry said he was in Doo Drop last night with his family putting on a good show. I don't think he was hurt too badly."

George said, "I got to my friend who knows this Jones from the electronics outfit. So far, he seems clean. I asked several people to call him and press the issue that there are influential people who don't want him and his business in this town. I called in a favor from some banker friends and put some pressure on him from that direction. From the reports back, he was indignant at first but began to waver as the number of calls increased. We should know in a day or two whether this will work or not."

## 17

When Chief Johnson came in for his appointment at 9:00, Fred had coffee brought in and they settled in for a chat. "Fred, I just need a few minutes with you to keep you in the loop on some changes I have made in the department. I want to make things run smoother, but it will take a few months to see what happens. By the way, where's your tweed sport coat?"

Fred laughed, "Well, I have a meeting shortly with the president of an electronics company, so I wore my three-piece-suit. Anyway, what's on your mind?"

Fred listened to him for the next 15 minutes, asked questions along the way and said, "Jim, I think these are good changes. Will you keep me posted on how they work out?"

Jim replied, "I will. Thanks for the coffee and the time. I'll let you get back to your schedule."

Fred hesitated, "Jim, have some more coffee. There's something I need your advice on. I was attacked last night as I left the office."

"What?" Jim asked with alarm. Fred filled him in on what happened and that he wasn't seriously injured. Fred also told him about the threat of future violence unless he changed his mind.

"Did you recognize the man?"

"No, it happened so fast. And he had on a black ski mask. But he is a big man, I'm sure I've never seen him before."

"Can you describe him for me?"

"Not really. The only thing I remember is that he was big, could have been a football player. He's taller than I am, probably over 6 feet and well built. Big guy! As for the car, it was gray. I think maybe a Buick."

Jim asked, "Will you change your mind?"

"No, I won't. We need to diversify our industry. I think the future economic growth of our city will be severely impacted if we don't. No, I won't change my mind, not on your life ... or mine."

"I'm going to arrange for a car to be in the parking area when you leave. You'll have to give us a heads up for a time to be here."

"Do you really think that's necessary?"

"We don't want to take a chance. Let's just keep an eye on you for a little while until this gets resolved."

"Alright then, I'll call when I'm ready to leave."

Alice buzzed Fred and said, "Mr. Jones of Jones Industries is on the phone."

Fred said, "Excuse me, Jim. I have to take this. Jones is the owner of the electronics company we're talking about."

The chief left. Fred buzzed Alice and said, "Put Mr. Jones through." Fred stood up to walk to the window as he talked. He often paced while talking on the phone. It helped him think through what was being said and how to respond.

"Mr. Jones, how are you? I'm looking forward to our lunch and the meeting this afternoon."

"That's why I'm calling, Fred. We have to postpone things."

"Is there a problem?"

Mr. Jones replied, "Yes, we had an emergency board meeting this morning and decided to put off the expansion."

"Is it the terms we discussed? I thought you were happy with those."

"I am," he said, "but the board was adamant. We need to move more slowly. We'll get back to you sometime in late spring or early summer. I'm sorry, Fred, goodbye."

Fred hung up and sat down hard. *What happened?* Fred wondered. This was supposed to be a done deal. *What will I tell the commission?* This didn't make sense. As Fred brooded on it, *he wondered if there was a connection between the attack last night and the shift in plans by the Jones Company. But what could it be? Was it one of the groups? Did they have that much power? So many questions and no answers.*

Fred called the chief and said, "Jim, I've had some disappointing news. The electronics company deal is off for now. I'll talk to you about the details later. I'm leaving in a few minutes to go take a ride out to the Ovals to think a little. This probably means you don't have to worry about the squad car here."

Jim said, "Let me have someone there for a while just in case. Your man from yesterday may not have gotten the word yet and I'm not ready to take a chance. The officer will be there in five minutes. Is there anyone else who might be threatened, maybe a commissioner or the city manager?"

"No, the commissioners haven't been involved directly yet and Sam, the city manager has some reservations about the project. I don't think anyone would come after any of them. I wonder if they might come after my family."

"Does Eleanor know about all this?"

"Yes, she does, and it concerns me that I see the fear in her eyes. We talked about what it might mean if they push me out of office. But we never thought it might come to this."

"We'll have a cruiser that is on patrol go by more often, just in case. Anyone else?"

"You should be aware that my friend Tom O'Banion is on board too. He doesn't know about the attack yet. He is talking to people, trying to build up grass-roots support. I asked him not to get involved, but Tom is a good friend and isn't afraid to push things he believes in. He has a good mind for this and might well be able to make a difference. Problem is he might say something to the wrong person. And my guess is when he hears of the attack on me that will make him even more determined to help."

"I'll keep that in mind." The Chief hung up.

Fred told Alice he would be back by one o'clock and headed for the Ovals, followed by a squad car. The Ovals, a big beach area near the channel from Muskegon Lake to Lake Michigan was his favorite spot to go and think. It was pretty cold this time of the year but he would go for a walk to clear his head and have lunch at the café in the old bathhouse building.

By the time Fred got back, he was a little more settled but still had no answers. Fred called each of the commissioners and told them about the change. They were surprised to hear of it too and most wondered why and what would they do next. Fred told them he would be back to them early next week and they would talk then.

## 18

The following Monday January 21, Fred was up earlier than usual. The night before was one of those nights when the problems of the past week woke him up several times. Finally, at 6:00 a.m. he decided that he would just stay up. Fred made some coffee and sat listening to a local radio station for the latest news. It was a bitter cold morning, near zero according to the radio. He kept the volume low so as not to wake Eleanor and almost missed the bulletin about a fire in downtown Muskegon. Fred called the police, and was immediately connected to the chief.

"Jim, I just heard about the fire. What can you tell me?"

"Good morning, Fred, Fire Chief Amundsen tells me it started in Drelles and there are about 70 firemen on the job by now, including some from Muskegon Heights and North Muskegon. Captain Bob Tanner said that it was almost out of control by the time they battered in the back door. Their job was not made easier by the cold and wind that freezes the water so quickly. It is looking like Drelles will be a total loss."

"How about the adjacent businesses?"

"The firemen seem to have it contained. Some of the immediately adjacent businesses have smoke damage. The only one the smoke missed was Scholl's shoe shop. And some apartments on the south side of Western were evacuated because of heavy smoke. Oh, and a little smoke got into the east end of the mezzanine of the Occidental. The manager, Mr. Baker said there is nothing to worry about there."

"I need to be down there. I think I'll set up a temporary head-quarter in the Occidental. Would you let people know I'll be there?"

Jim asked, "Do you think it's wise, Fred? You know, in view of the assault out back of your office?"

"That doesn't matter right now. It is important that I be where people can see me and talk to me if they want. I'll park up on Clay by the Chronicle and walk the block to the hotel."

"Let me send a car for you. It will be there in 15 minutes or less."

"All right, Jim. That should give me enough time to get dressed and ready. Once I'm in the Occidental, there will be safety in numbers. I'd better get ready, talk to you later."

Fred jotted a note to Eleanor and was waiting at the front door when the squad car pulled up in his driveway.

When the policeman dropped Fred off, he went in the Third St. side door directly into the lobby of the hotel. He went right to the registration desk and asked for the manager, Mr. Baker. When he came out, Baker asked, "How can we help, Mr. Mayor?"

"Can you find me a space where I could set up a temporary office-like area in the lobby, kind of a command center, with a phone I could use? I want to take a walk over to talk to one of the fire chiefs, but I won't be there long. They don't need me in the way."

"I'll have it ready for you when you get back."

Fred thanked him and walked out the front door. He stood first just watching the activity and trying to locate the chief or one of the captains of the fire department. Fred spoke briefly to Leo Drelles, one of the four brothers who ran the restaurant. "I would guess you are insured against this kind of loss."

Leo answered, "Mr. Mayor, we are, but this is years of our lives. We'll have to start over."

"I understand that. Let me know if there is anything I can do to help."

"Thanks, Mr. Mayor, I appreciate that."

Fire Chief Amundsen came rushing out of the building, grabbed a ladder and with the help of two other men, took it into the building. A few minutes later, they came out with a fourth man who apparently was injured. After making sure the injured fireman was being checked out by the EMTs, the chief spotted Fred across the street and walked across through the trucks and hoses. "Mr. Mayor, I'm glad you are here. We just about have the fire contained. The Drelles restaurant is going to be a total loss, but we've managed to keep it from spreading. There's only just minor damage to the other businesses."

"Is the man you just brought out going to be all right?"

"He will be. He has a groin injury from a fall down into the basement, but yes, he will be fine. I'll tell him you were asking about him."

"I have an office area set up in the Occidental. Please let me know if there is anything else you need. Any other resources you might want brought in."

With that Fred walked back into the hotel and was immediately besieged by reporters from the Chronicle and the Grand Rapids Press as well as the Grand Rapids TV station. Fred caught them up on what the chief told him and said, "Chief Amundsen will quite likely have a press conference for you in a few hours."

Joe Antonelli walked over from his restaurant and was standing on the edge of the group of reporters. "What is the story, Fred? Are the firemen truly able to get it under control?"

"That's what the chief told me. You heard me tell the reporters. Barring any unforeseen factors, we can save the other businesses."

"It's good of you to be here, Fred. The people will feel better knowing you're here."

"Well, Joe, it's the right thing to do."

"How long do you plan to be here?"

"As long as it takes, Joe. What else would you expect? If you'll excuse me, I need to call my secretary and let her know where I am."

As Joe walked away, Fred was shown a temporary office area and called his secretary. He told Alice he would be here for a while and asked her if anything else was going on that he needed to deal with.

"Eleanor called. I told her that I heard you were on the scene and that you would call her. I've cancelled two meetings that can wait and told them we would be in touch later. I have some phone calls you might need to make." She gave him the numbers and asked if there was anything she could do.

"Yes, please get all the information you can about the firefighters, their names, any injuries. In short, find all the details you can about the fire and the job they are doing. Some of it you won't be able to get until it's over. But I want to be able to have a commendation ceremony within two or three weeks. Do what you can, and Alice, put your thinking cap on about the details. We'll put it together after I talk with the Chief. Thanks, Alice."

Fred called Eleanor to catch her up on what was happening. She answered, "Fred, where are you? Are you all right? I saw your note when I got up. The television reporters said Drelles is destroyed."

"Slow down, sweetheart. I'm ok. I'm in an office area in the Occidental. I'll probably be here till sometime in the afternoon. As soon as I know it is under control, I'll head back to the office. Jim sent an officer to pick me up. He let me off right at the side door of the hotel. I'll give you a call when I get back to the office and we'll figure out what to do about getting home. I love you, sweetie, I have to go. The chief is here to talk."

WHEN JOE GOT BACK to his restaurant, he called the leader of the group of nine. "George, this fire is going to cause us another problem. Fred is at a command center in the Occidental. His presence is only going to serve to enhance his reputation as mayor."

"We'll deal with it later. Why don't you just stick around as long as you can, see what you can learn. I'll call all the others, and some may show up down there. I can't come. We should be careful not to be seen together in public."

# 19

Maria and Tom had lunch duty when she announced she made her decision about the spring musical. She was going to do 'The King and I." "Many of the students have only seen the movie, and it is great. But on stage is a more compelling experience."

"Don't I remember that you played the part of Anna in Muskegon's Civic Opera production?" Tom gazed at her adoringly.

"Yes, it was a fun role. We have the talent here to do a great show and they'll love the experience. It will be a good way for them to learn about another culture. And you know how much the power this play has to draw a good audience."

"How are auditions coming?"

"Great. I want to start rehearsals this week or at the latest the week after. First, I have a couple of roles to fill. We should be ready by late April. Doug has started the pit band on the music. Nancy has agreed again to be my assistant director, supervise makeup, and help with costumes. We had lunch last week and she got all excited and said, 'Count me in!'"

"She's such a good friend for you."

"Yes, she is. I think Nancy and Doug would make a good pair and she is interested in him, but he just shies away. What do you think?"

"I don't think he wants a relationship. He doesn't seem to be interested. He never talks about it. I don't know much about Doug's past – he plays everything pretty close to the vest. Maybe he had a bad break-up some time ago. He did once tell me that he likes things just the way they are. No complications."

Maria shook her head, "Well anyway, you and I should talk about your singers and who could play Anna, the King, Tuptim, and Lun Tha. We need to encourage them to audition. And, of course, we need a strong contralto for Lady Thiang, the King's chief wife. Can I count on you to prep the chorus and coach the leads vocally?"

"Count me in too. You don't even have to ask. I'll set up some after school rehearsals for the chorus and the soloists. And just so you know, I remember what you said about Sara and it worries me. She keeps stopping by after class to talk, but I move out into the hall with her as though I have somewhere else to be."

"I'm glad you're doing that. She could be trouble."

"How about the technical stuff? Do you have the people you need?"

"I do. The group who did the tech work for last year's musical are back as seniors. They know their business. I've also contacted the elementary schools. We need a big group of children."

Tom raised a brow and asked, "Do you see any problem with the community about this musical?"

Maria frowned, "I think not. But you never know. There is a reference to Buddhism in the story and some may not like the *Uncle Tom's Cabin* ballet."

As they talked, they watched the kids in the cafeteria. Spring was in the air and young blood was running hot. Maria said, "Maybe we better finish this conversation over dinner tonight. We're being watched."

"You're right. But they're always watching. They're likely wondering what's up."

SARA and her girlfriends were at their usual table close by the football players. Sara and Joanie were whispering to each other and watching Tom and Maria.

"What do you think, Joanie, are they doing it?"

"I don't think so. They seem to be close, but I heard that they were just friends."

"Whatever, that just may be what they want us to believe. I just think he is sexy. And have you seen the way he looks at me in choir," Sara purred.

Joanie said, "He doesn't look at you any more than the rest of us."

"I think he wants me, and I know I want him. If I get a chance, I'm going to give it to him."

Joanie gasped, "What about Bob? How could you do that to him?"

"I don't want to marry Mr. O, I just want him. Bob and I will eventually marry after college."

Just then Bob walked up and said to Sara, "Hey, sweetheart, how about a movie tonight?"

Sara gave Bob a sultry look, "No, let's just stay in at my house, have some popcorn, and watch TV. Route 66 is on and my Dad is going to be out playing cards with friends until after 11. We'll have the house to ourselves."

Bob got to Sara's house about 8:30 p.m. Sara told him her Dad would leave just before 8 p.m. She turned the TV on and sat on the sofa. Bob walked over to the gun case, "Hey, this is quite a gun, telescope sight and all."

"Don't touch that. That's Dad's pride and joy. Last fall he taught me how to shoot it and took me hunting. I got my first deer. And anyway the cabinet is locked. Come on over and we'll find a good show to watch."

But it soon became clear that Bob wasn't the least bit interested in TV. She snuggled up to him as soon as they settled on the couch. "See isn't this cozy?"

Bob wanted more. He started kissing her and touching her where he shouldn't.

She said, "Stop it, Bob. I don't want this."

Bob said, "I remember how you looked at me in the cafeteria. Didn't you mean it?" He continued touching her until she finally gave in. She couldn't believe how rough and awkward he was.

Bob smiled, "Should we have used a rubber?"

"Well, it's too late now. You better hope I don't get pregnant."

Later after they were dressed Sara told Bob he better go now.

"Can't I stay longer? I won't be able to see you tomorrow. I wish I could, but my parents invited relatives for the weekend. That usually means I have to stay pretty close to home. I'll call if I can get away."

Sara stamped her foot, "Just go, Bob. I'll see you at school next week."

After he left, she sat crying softly, thinking, *Mr. O wouldn't do what Bob did. He's a real man.*

## 20

---

Two weeks after the fire Fred almost had his speech for the commendation ceremony finished when Alice buzzed him and said the fire chief was there.

Fred met him at the door, "Good morning, John. Thank you for coming in. Would you like some coffee?"

"Yes, that would be good. Nothing in it." Alice brought the coffee in, and they settled in to plan the ceremony.

John said, "Fred, I appreciate what you are trying to do with this award, but it isn't necessary. We were just doing our job."

"I know, but it's the right thing to do. Your men did a great job of containing it in the worst of conditions, it was really cold, and water was freezing everywhere. And except for some smoke in nearby buildings, there is no other damage. We were lucky that no one was seriously hurt. How are Sam Jones and Jim Stewart?"

"They're both fine. As good as new."

"Any more word on where and how it started?"

"No, nothing new. We may never know. The clean-up company has been particularly good about alerting us to what they are finding. But nothing is obvious."

"John, is this Friday afternoon all right for the ceremony?"

"Everyone can be here, of course unless there is another fire. It's to be held in the big meeting room where the city council meets?"

"That's right. At 4:00 pm. Here's what is planned. The Chronicle will be there for some pictures. If you think of anything else, please let me know."

"Ok, Fred. And thank you. See you on Friday."

ON FRIDAY, Fred walked into the big meeting room promptly at 3:55 pm. Alice did a great job of arranging all the details. He walked up to the podium at the center of the curved tables.

"Good afternoon, ladies and gentlemen. Thank you all for coming. I believe this is as full as this room has ever been. Let me start off by introducing everyone up here. To my right, Fire Chief John Amundsen, fire Captain Bob Tanner, and to his right, are two firefighters who were injured in the fire, Sam Jones and Jim Stewart. To my left is City Manager Sam Milford along with, to his left, three members of the Drelles restaurant owners, Leo, Gus, and Tony. They have all agreed to be here with just one condition. They don't want to make a speech. Well, except for Leo – he has promised to say just a few words." Fred smiled at Leo.

"In addition, most of the members of the city commission are in the front row. You'll have the opportunity to speak with all of them as well as the people up here after the ceremony. There will be coffee, punch, and cookies from Rykes. I know you all love their butter cookies as much as I do.

"We so often take our firefighters and policemen for granted. They put their lives on the line all the time. It seemed to me that we need to recognize their service. So here we are."

Fred spotted Joe Antonelli in the crowd. He stood near the back and talked with another man. The second man looked somehow familiar, but Fred couldn't put a name to the face.

Fred continued, "I have here a plaque that will soon hang in the main fire station. It says, 'From a grateful city, to the men of

Muskegon's Fire Department, we honor you for your extraordinary service to the community. We recognize your courage as you do your job, going above and beyond in this particular case. You saved the surrounding businesses, contained the fire to Drelles Restaurant. We thank you.'" As he handed the plaque to the chief, the Chronicle photographer took pictures.

Chief Amundsen said, "Thank you, Mr. Mayor. We appreciate the recognition and the honor it conveys."

Fred nodded to Leo Drelles who stepped up and said, "Thank you to you, Chief Andersen, and your men, especially Sam Jones and Jim Stewart. We'll start over. We've already talked about a new building in the same spot. But we are just so happy that everyone is safe and that Sam and Jim are healing well. The family appreciates your efforts and your service."

Fred said, "Thank you, Leo and Chief Amundsen. I promised to make this short. What I would like to see happen now is that you all enjoy the goodies. Just be sure to shake the hands of these men and thank them face to face."

Fred rushed down from the dais and headed to the back of the room. He wanted to get a better look at the man with Joe. By the time he worked his way through the crowd, the two of them were gone. "Funny," he thought, "they didn't stay to mingle."

JOE AND WENDELL left quickly and walked to their car. As they drove away from City Hall, Wendell said, "We need to get something done. He is a popular Mayor and did himself a lot of good in there today."

Joe acknowledged this and said, "I'll get back to George with this. We'll have to factor it into what we do. We may have to change our strategy and move more strongly on the mayor."

## 21

After the City Hall presentation, Tom and Maria went to the Doo Drop Inn for dinner. They were seated in the bar lounge area near the little stage that featured local musicians. They often enjoyed their dinner in that area since both liked the lounge acts.

Their conversation turned to the auditions. "Who do you think is strong enough to do the King?"

"Well, Gil has a strong baritone voice. He could handle 'A Puzzlement' and he's good enough on his feet to do 'Shall We Dance?' He has a regal look about him as well."

"What do you think about Sara for one of the leads?"

Tom shrugged. "She's just not strong enough for a lead. Maybe she would be happy with a special role in the 'Uncle Tom's Cabin' scene. I know just the person for Anna. She did the part of Annie Adoo last year in "Oklahoma" and her voice has gotten much stronger."

Maria agreed. "I've spoken to her; I think she'll do it. She will make a great Anna."

They continued discussing the cast. Tom told Maria there was a good group of talented girls for the King's wives. Maria said her auditions at the elementary schools went well and her children were ready to go.

They ordered coffee and sat listening to the guitar playing vocalist as she sang "Can't Take My Eyes Off of You." Tom looked deeply into Maria's eyes and sang softly to her, "can't take my eyes off of you..." He whispered, "Je t'aime, Maria."

Lost in the music and the moment, they sat like that for a while. Tom noticed that Maria was quiet, "What are you thinking about?"

Maria took both of Tom's hands in hers, "Tom, you know I care very deeply for you. But before we go further, there's something we need to discuss. Your mom told me about your childhood illness."

"You're right. It's time. I've wanted to tell you, but I've been afraid. You'll understand, I hope, when I tell you the whole story. So here goes. I was 16 years old and in my junior year of high school when I developed a pretty severe case of the mumps. There was no vaccine for it in those days and the only treatment was complete bed rest and the proper treatment to reduce swelling. I was diagnosed with the mumps in January and I couldn't get back to school for the rest of that year."

Tom continued while searching Maria's face, "My mother was a high school teacher and worked with me so I could keep up with my studies. Even so, I lost a semester, so I graduated a semester later than expected. I was almost 19 and I didn't start college until January, but I made up the credits by taking summer school classes and graduated from college on time.

"Anyway, during that semester I was sick. I satisfied my natural curiosity and spent a lot of my bed time reading so that I was able to keep up with the next class behind me and stay with them the following year. My habit of reading paid off since.

"I started reading mysteries including Sherlock Holmes stories. I dreamed of becoming a detective like Holmes, I liked the way Holmes thought. I was able to keep up with my piano lessons by taking it easy practicing. You know how much I love music and it kept me sane."

Tom hesitated and took a deep breath. "The big problem arose later when the family doctor did a thorough physical follow-up and discovered that the mumps had turned into mumps orchitis, a rare but very serious form of mumps. I wasn't concerned about that at the time. But now I am because of you.

"I've wanted to talk to you about it," he said. "But I've been uneasy. Maria, you are so important to me. I don't want to lose you."

"Tom, you won't lose me," she took his hand and said, "Don't you remember the other night at Tony's? I love you and I want to be with you."

Tom shook his head. "But you've always said you loved children and wanted a big family."

"That's true, but you said you wanted that too."

"I do, but the problem is, Maria, my illness left me sterile. I can't father children."

Maria went silent. Tom thought, *Oh, no. She's gone quiet on me. Not again.* But she said, "Tom, there are a lot of children out there who need homes. We could adopt. My mom is always talking about her volunteer work at Catholic Services where there are girls who have babies and don't want to keep them." Maria blushed and asked, "Does that mean impotent, too?"

"No darlin'. That part is ok!"

She blushed deeper and said, "Thank goodness!"

"Just think about it, Maria." Tom took her home, kissed her good-night, and drove to his house. Tom promised to call her tomorrow.

Tom knew he wouldn't sleep right away so he parked in his driveway and walked to the beach. The ovals at Lake Michigan were about a half mile from his house and he needed to think and clear his head. He remembered what happened at college when his girlfriend found out he was sterile. He wasn't sure of Maria's reaction to the news about his infertility. He was afraid he'd lose Maria.

Maria called her mom as soon as she got inside her apartment. She said, "Mom, I know it's late, but can I come over and talk to you?"

Her mom said, "Of course, come on over. I'll put some tea on. Is everything alright? You're home early from dinner with Tom."

"I'll be there soon, Mom. Everything is fine. I just need your advice."

When she walked in, her mom gave her a big hug. She said, "Do you want your dad in on the conversation?"

Maria said, "Yes, please. You'll see, I need both of you."

They sat at the kitchen table with their tea and some fresh baked cookies. Her dad said, "Well, sweetie, what's up?"

Maria told them about Tom's childhood illness and its effect on Tom's ability to father children. She ended with, "I told Tom tonight that we could always adopt, but the truth is I'm unsure. I always wanted children of my own, you both know that."

Her mom said, "Do you love him?"

"Yes, I do, and I know he loves me. In fact, I have been expecting him to ask me to marry him. We've been dating for over a year now and I couldn't understand why he hadn't before. Now I know."

Dad said, "You have a choice to make, don't you?"

Maria said, "It affects you two as well. I'm an only child and I know you want grandchildren."

Mom hugged her again and said, "You know we'll love them just as much if you adopt them. You will too. When you and Tom are ready, Catholic Social Services and Father Flannery will help. By the way, do you want to talk to him too?"

"No, you two are all I need right now."

"Do you want to sleep on it and then decide?" Dad asked as he too hugged her.

"No, I want to go to Tom right now and tell him so he doesn't lose sleep over it."

## 22

Maria went home, got her toothbrush and everything she needed for school tomorrow. When she got to Tom's house, she saw his car was there, but the house was all dark. She knew where he would be. He was over at the Ovals thinking. That was his favorite place when he was troubled. She drove to the Ovals and there he was on one of the swings.

She walked up behind him, waved a red rose in front of him, "Hey there mister, would you like some company?"

"Guess who I was thinking about? I'm glad you came," Tom said as he took her into his arms and kissed her.

Maria sat on the other swing and told him again that it didn't matter about children. Tom asked, "You are sure?"

"I'm sure, Tom."

Pulling their swings together, she kissed him again more deeply and said, "We better go to your house, I'm not sure I can wait till we get to mine. There's something I've been wanting for a long, long time."

Laughing with her, Tom said, "Me too, let's go."

Maria and Tom jumped into her car and made the quick trip to his house. She grabbed her bag from the car and went in. Tom asked,

"Shall I light a fire? It's ready. I built it before I left for the beach. And would you like a glass of wine?"

"That would be great, Tom. Let's make this a special time."

They sat watching the fire and sipping their wine. They talked about the loss of Tom's sister, his illness, and what they had done for him and to him. Losing her at such a young age forced Tom to think about his own mortality and realize that he needed to live his life fully. It also made him aware of how important family is to him. Without his mom and dad's support, he wouldn't have survived her death and his illness. And he was sure that he was important to their support, too. They sat quietly gazing at the fire.

"So much for you to deal with, Tom. I'm sorry you and your parents had to go through that. And I know it's why you're so strong now. You make me feel protected," Maria sighed. She set down her wine, put her hands on Tom's face, and pulled him in for a deep kiss. After a few minutes, Maria took Tom's hand and led him down the hall, "Tom, is this ok? Is this the way to your bedroom? We can take it slow, Tom."

"This is definitely ok, Maria. I love you so much."

In the bedroom she started unbuttoning her blouse. Tom said, "Let me, Maria."

Later they lay close, sharing the moment, talking, holding each other, and finally slept.

The next morning, they drove separately to school, met in the parking lot as usual, and walked to their offices. As Tom slipped into Maria's office with her, Tom said, "I love you, Maria."

No one noticed the special glow that shown on their faces except Doug. He, as usual stopped in the choir room to talk after home room. He prodded, "What's up with you, Tom?"

Tom replied, "We don't have time to talk about it now. But Maria knows I can't father children and it's ok! I'll catch you up later."

Doug just grinned as if he knew it would be all along. He was happy that issue was settled for his friend. He asked, "Did you ask her to marry you?"

"Not yet. I have something special I want to get planned to do that. It will happen next weekend. And, by the way, I want you for my best man. What do you say?"

With a big smile, Doug said, "You know I will!"

Doug left for his classroom, anger simmering but not showing. Doug had learned to keep a "wooden" face. He was sure Tom didn't know about his feelings for Maria and of course, she didn't either. But there it was and Doug had no idea, especially now, how to change it.

## 23

M aria asked, "Tom, where are we going? I mean, it's a beautiful spring day and I'm enjoying it. I haven't made this drive in ages."

Tom laughed, "We're just driving to see where the roads take us. My parents used to do that with us. They would let one of us kids pick the next turn and which direction to go. We saw some interesting scenery that way."

They drove north on Scenic Drive past the burned out Blockhouse area. The Blockhouse was an old log fort built for protection from the natives during the mid-1800s. There was evidence of some clean-up and new construction. When they reached the dead end with the golf course on the right, Tom said, "Let's go left and see where this leads."

After a block or so, Tom turned right toward White Lake. Maria said, "I'm getting hungry. Where and when are we going to eat?"

"How about right here and right now?"

Maria said, "The Lakeside Inn. I've heard of this place. Looks nice."

"It is, it opened officially as a resort and restaurant about 1915. The ambiance is still retro to that time. You'll see. They open every spring as soon as it warms up. We'll be out on the deck."

Tom left Maria off at the front entrance and went to park the car. The flower gardens, buttercups, lavender, and roses were in full bloom alongside the entryway. For Maria the delicate aroma of the roses created a heady atmosphere while she waited for Tom. Tom walked up, took her arm, and said, "Tonight is going to be special, Maria. I'll get you fed, and we'll talk. We can celebrate the coming success of your musical."

Maria spotted the gift shop off to the right as they came in the lobby. Tom gave a questioning look at the hostess, who in return gave him an 'all set' nod. So Tom put his hand on Maria's back and quickly followed the hostess into the cocktail area for diners. Maria exclaimed, "Mr. O, you did that deliberately, rushed me by the shop. You know how much I love gift shops."

Tom laughed, "There will be plenty of time later."

The hostess escorted them to their table out on the deck. A white tablecloth, white cloth napkins, a candle, and flowers on the table painted an elegant picture. "Oh, Tom, this is so lovely. What made you pick this? And, why haven't we been here before?"

Tom said, with a grin, "I saved it for tonight. The views of the lakes and the sunset are gorgeous from here."

Maria had more questions but their waitress, Annie, brought water with lemon slices along with a cheese and cracker basket. She asked what they wanted to drink besides water. Tom turned to Maria and said, "Why don't we have some champagne for a change? And we'll have a shrimp cocktail to share."

"What are you up to, Tom?"

"I'll tell you. Wait until we get our champagne. Look at that view. Let's take a quick walk down by the water."

"But Tom," she said, "this cheese is great, and the champagne is on the way."

"It will be alright, you'll see. Come on, you'll love the view."

Tom grabbed Maria's hand and they walked hand in hand across the lawn to the narrow beach and enjoyed the view of beautiful

White Lake and the channel. Further on they could see Lake Michigan in the distance. The late afternoon sun shining on Maria's face gave her such radiance that Tom's breath caught. He was so enchanted he almost forgot what he was up to. Tom smiled at her and said, "Maria, look back at the Inn. It's such a lovely old place, a delightful setting, don't you think?"

As Maria started to turn, she said, "Tom, that's one of the things I love about you. You're so sentimental about older places like this." When she looked back, there was the entire wait staff on the deck. They held up a banner that read, "Maria, will you marry me?" She whirled around to Tom, now down on one knee, and said, "I will, Tom. I will." Tom jumped up, took her in his arms, and twirled her around on the beach.

"Tom, put me down. What will people think?"

Just then, applause broke out from the direction of the restaurant. The other deck diners were on their feet with big smiles. On their table, Maria now saw a bottle of champagne and a small wedding cake with a candle and a little white box on it.

"Let's go, Maria." As they ran back to their table, the applause continued. The champagne was poured. Tom opened the white box and showed Maria the ring.

Her eyes shone as he slipped the ring on her finger. More applause rippled around the deck including a group at a large round table on the other side of the patio.

When the staff left, Tom picked up his glass of champagne, "To us, Maria." They touched glasses and sipped as they looked deeply into each other's eyes.

Annie checked in with them. "I'll put your cake away for later. May I take your orders?"

Tom thanked Annie and asked her to let them enjoy their champagne and shrimp cocktail for a while before they ordered dinner.

Maria smiled at Tom, took his hand and said, "This has been planned for a while, hasn't it? This is a wonderful surprise. We have to tell our parents!"

Tom grinned and said, "Do you suppose I should ask your dad for your hand?"

They both laughed. "I think they'll be happy for us."

Tom answered, "Why not tell them right now?"

"I'm hungry. Can't we eat first?"

"Maria, look over at the other side of the patio."

She looked and saw her parents and Tom's parents at a round table for six across the patio. They stood champagne glasses in hand and toasted the bride and groom to be. Maria and Tom rushed over. Hugs were exchanged. Annie brought their appetizers and their champagne to their new table.

After their orders were placed and the wine ordered, Maria turned to Tom, a twinkle in her eye, and asked, "Tom, what would you have done if I said no?"

Tom winked at her parents and said in his 'ok' Irish brogue, "Well now lass, I had it on the highest authority that ye would say yes!"

Her mother asked if they knew the time and place for the wedding.

Maria said, "No, but I've always wanted a Christmas wedding. Does that give you enough time to get it planned?"

Maria's mom said, "I think we can make that happen."

The conversation continued about the wedding plans as their parents got better acquainted. Annie brought the cake back along with ice cream and coffee for all.

Maria and Tom stole a look and a nod. Tom said, "We're going to slip away. The check is all taken care of. The four of you can just sit and enjoy. We'll see you later this weekend."

As they walked out, there was another round of applause and congratulations from the other diners.

## 24

W hen Fred first came to Muskegon, he and Eleanor drove all over the town just to get acquainted with the various neighborhoods. Since he was the mayor, they felt they should live in the city of Muskegon. They considered near the downtown but gravitated toward the lake, areas like Lakeside, Pinchtown, or Bluffton. They bought a great house on Lakeshore Drive near Pinchtown and they loved it. It had an enclosed porch on the back of the house with a great view of Muskegon Lake. Their two children were in the Muskegon school system, Fred, Jr. now in high school and Emily soon to be.

Fred made the drive from Ottawa Street along the Muskegon Lake shore to Lakeshore Drive, past the smelly paper mill, and on to the Ovals many times over. As he did, he began to dream of building industrial parks on the edge of town away from the lake. He wanted to bring in new industry and eventually move some of the lakeshore industries out to the parks. The lakeshore could be restored to lake oriented activities for residents and tourists and build a tourist industry to take advantage of its beauty. He wanted to bring more balance to the economy – keep the heavy industrial jobs but move them off the lakeshore and bring in more light industry and some of the new tech industries that were beginning to develop in California. Fred also wanted to restore and rebuild a lot of the older buildings around town like the Hackley House and the Hume House as well as the train station and even the Blockhouse.

Fred believed in that dream. He had only shared it with two people, Eleanor and Tom O'Banion — Eleanor, because she was his wife and she supported him completely and Tom, because he loved Muskegon as much as Fred had grown to love it. He and Tom both liked to go to the Ovals and walk the beach to relax and think. They shared lunches often and after swearing Tom to secrecy, Fred told him of his thoughts for the future of the city. Tom was interested from two vantage points. He grew up in Muskegon and loved his hometown. He also loved old buildings and was concerned with preserving them. He made a number of suggestions about remodeling and preserving the old Occidental Hotel, and the Hackley Public Library where he spent many happy hours among the books.

Tonight Fred and Eleanor were looking forward to Tom and Maria in their home for dinner. When Tom told Fred about the engagement, Fred said, "Congratulations! Let us celebrate with you, come to dinner and we'll make it a special occasion." The four of them were out on the enclosed porch with cocktails and appetizers. It was enjoyable watching the sailboats already out even this early in the spring.

Maria asked, "Where are Freddy, Jr. and Emily?"

Eleanor responded, "They are both on sleepovers, Freddy at one of his friends and Emily at Grandma and Grandpa's house getting spoiled."

She continued, "Maria, I hear your engagement was quite a surprise. You didn't have any idea about it?"

"No, I didn't even pick up on it at the Lakeside Inn. I was just hungry and wanted to get to dinner."

"Are you that hungry tonight?"

Maria laughed, taking another bacon-wrapped date, "Well, Tom says I'm nearly always hungry, but I'm enjoying these appetizers for now. I'm good."

After the laughter died down, Fred said, "Tell us about it."

Both started talking at once. They laughed and Tom deferred to Maria.

"We think a December wedding. Mom and Dad feel they can get it ready by then. We're just about finished with the program for the church's Pre-Marriage class that Father Flannery set up for us. And Tom has completed everything he needed to do to complete his conversion to Catholicism. Everything is on schedule."

She added, "Our honeymoon isn't set yet. We'll decide soon. We've talked about Ireland next summer. You know Tom is Irish. He was there once right after graduation from college. His Irish worry stone, a piece of Connemara marble, came from there. He calls it his good luck stone. He's told me a lot about Ireland and wants to take me to see it. But then, Tom has always wanted to go to Paris as well and I like that choice too. Tom studied French in high school and college. I took some French in college. There is so much to see and do there plus it's supposed to be the most romantic city in the world. We'll see where we end up."

Eleanor said, "Both sound like great places to honeymoon."

She continued, "I'd better check on dinner. It should be about done. The sauce should be ready, so I just have to do the pasta."

Maria asked, "Can I help?"

"I'd appreciate that. We'll be ready in about ten minutes, guys."

The dinner was great. Spaghetti, garlic toast from Cole's bakery, salad, and a smooth Chianti. After coffee and apple pie, Fred and Tom took their refilled wine glasses to the deck and left Maria and Eleanor in the living room talking wedding plans.

Tom asked Fred if there was anything new at City Hall.

Fred said, "Jerry said something the other day that puzzled me. He said he heard something about the group all being on the same page or something. He added that even Antonelli agreed. It sounded like he thought Joe Antonelli was a member of the group?"

"Maria and I saw Antonelli coming out of a room at the Occidental with a group of men and their wives. Mrs. McKay said it was a group who met there occasionally. I wonder if that could be your group of nine."

Frustrated, Fred said emphatically, "Who knows? Tom, remember I told you at lunch that I didn't want you to get involved because I didn't want you to get hurt. Well, it has come to that now."

He told Tom how the man assaulted him in the City Hall parking lot.

"Were you badly injured?"

"No, just some pulled muscles in my arm and a bloody nose. The chief has a man with me now."

"Do you think they'll try again?"

"I don't know. That's why the police escort. Eleanor and I talked about it and we're here to stay. This is our town now and we want to be here and help make it what it could be."

Tom noticed Fred going quiet so he asked him, "Where are you, my friend?"

"I was just remembering that about a year ago, I tried to bring in a new castings business. Larry Olsen, the owner of a casting business in town, came to see me at the office and after a fierce argument, left angry, slamming the door behind him. I wonder if he might be part of the group of nine. I don't want them to force us to leave."

Eleanor and Maria came out on the deck just then and Maria said, "What group of nine? And what's this about staying? Here? Why would you want to leave?"

Tom looked at Fred, "Can I tell Maria what is going on?"

They spent the next hour or so, talked about how the city was run, and how Fred wanted to change it. Tom noticed that Maria was quiet. He took her aside and asked her what was wrong. She said, "I didn't know about all this. I wonder how many people are as much in the dark as I am. It scares me."

"I'm sure it does, sweetheart. But Fred has the police in on it. And they are with him wherever he goes."

As Maria and Tom were about to leave, Tom told Fred again, "If you need me to do something, just let me know. I'll help. Let's have lunch again soon and figure out what I might do."

Neither of them noticed the gray car parked across the street or the man smoking in it.

## 25

It was a Wednesday near the end of May, only a week or so left in the school year. Tom was in his office thinking about what a good semester this had been. All his choirs performed well. Their last responsibility was to sing "The Lord Bless You and Keep You" at the Baccalaureate next week.

There was a knock on the door and the principal's secretary, Darlene, came in. She said, "John would like to see you."

Tom said casually, "I'm supposed to be with Maria and Doug in the cafeteria. Can it wait?"

"No, he insisted that it be right now."

He walked with her to the main office. Darlene knocked and said, "Mr. Mann, Tom is here."

"Hello, John, what's up that couldn't wait?"

"You better sit down. We have a problem."

"What kind of problem?"

John said, "Just let me lay it out for you. You have a student in choir, Sara Antonelli. She and her father just left my office about an hour ago."

"Yes, Sara is my student but what does this have to do with me."

"She is pregnant, and she says the child is yours."

Tom jumped up and said, "That's not true, John. Why would she say that?"

"Please sit down, Tom. It is worse than that, Mr. Antonelli has hired an attorney. They've been to the district attorney and have filed for a paternity judgement against you. He and the police should be here any minute now. I've been asked to keep you here until they come."

"This can't be. She has been cozying up to me all semester. Maria noticed and warned me to be careful of her."

"Has it ever gone any further?"

"John, I can't believe you would even ask that. Of course not!"

"It will be out in the community soon. I have to ask you to leave school immediately, within the hour."

"That's not fair, John. I'm innocent. I've never touched her that way and besides..."

"I know. Of course, it's not fair. But it is what I have to do. I spoke to the superintendent right after Mr. Antonelli left. He agrees with me, actually suggested it. Your pay will be continued until you are cleared. You better get yourself a good attorney. When the police get here, clean out your things and don't plan to come back until next year."

"My students will be upset that I'm not here. What will you tell them?"

"We'll handle it. We'll tell them you had a family emergency."

Darlene knocked and when John answered, a policeman and a man who introduced himself as Harvey Swensen, the district attorney, came in. Swensen said to Tom, "Mr. O'Banion, you are to appear in court Friday afternoon at 2:00 p.m. for arraignment on the charge of sex with an underage minor. That is statutory rape. We are also seeking a judgement of paternity. You have a day and a half to get an attorney or for us to appoint one for you from the public defender pool. What is your preference?"

"I have an attorney who handles my civil affairs. He'll take care of it."

"Because Mr. Mann has vouched for you as someone who keeps

his word, I accept that, and we'll see you Friday afternoon. Should you not, a warrant will be issued for your arrest. Do you understand?"

"Yes. I'll be there. John, I was supposed to meet Maria and Doug in the cafeteria. Can I go let them know?"

"No, I can't let you do that. Just go right to your office, get your things, and leave the building with the officer."

"Would you please let them know only that something has come up and I'll be in touch with both of them tonight?"

"I'll have someone notify Maria and Doug. Please keep me posted about what happens."

The district attorney went back to city hall. The police officer and Tom went to the choir room. The officer waited while Tom cleaned out his desk, taking those things he normally took home each summer. He didn't take any music because surely this would be cleaned up before fall.

MARIA AND DOUG were both on lunch duty. They were waiting for Tom to join them. Maria was basking in the glow of the success of the play. The community feedback was great. But the students were talking about the engagement. There had been an announcement during home room that morning. They noticed the ring right away and the buzz was still going.

Maria said, "I'm so ready for our trip. I wish we had planned it for earlier. It's in late July and early August."

She and Tom were going to celebrate their engagement with a sunset cruise on the Milwaukee Clipper.

"Say, Doug, why don't I invite Nancy and the two of you could go too? We would have a great time, the four of us."

Doug turned away. "Thanks for the invite, but no. You two need the getaway — it will be good for you both. This last term has been busy, exciting, 'engaging'."

Maria groaned, "Doug! I wonder where Tom is. He's never this late for lunch."

She was interrupted by the appearance of Mr. Mann's secretary, Darlene. "Tom wanted me to find you and let you know that something came up and he had to leave school. He said he would call you either later this afternoon or evening."

"What is it? Tom and I were supposed to have dinner tonight."

"I don't know. I wasn't in on the conversation in the office, oops, I shouldn't have said that. But don't worry. He'll call you"

"Who's office, Darlene?"

"I can't say anymore. Tom will let you know."

When Darlene was gone, Maria said, "Can you cover for me, Doug? I'll look in Tom's office to see if he has gone yet or if he left me a note."

"I'll cover for you. Lunch period is almost over and I'll be right behind you."

Maria went to Tom's office. It was locked...strange. She had a spare key in her office, she hurried to get it. When she returned, Doug was just coming from the cafeteria. Maria went right to Tom's desk. She thought Tom might have left her a note, but nothing. And his desk has been cleaned out.

"This isn't like Tom, something's very wrong, maybe something with his family."

"He'll find us tonight, Maria. We have to get to our afternoon classes."

"Call me if he contacts you."

"I will. But, Maria, he'll call you first. Please let me know."

## 26

Tom was led out of school with a box of his office possessions. The officer walked him all the way to his car. He was so thankful the parking lot was behind the gym so there were no windows for students or staff to see him escorted by the police to his car. Tom said to the officer, "I resent this. It's not necessary. I've got my stuff. I won't go back in. You can go now."

The officer replied, "Mr. O'Banion, it's just procedure. Don't get upset over it."

Tom replied heatedly, "I'm sorry but this whole business is just not right. I haven't done anything wrong."

The officer said, "Mr. O'Banion, you shouldn't say any more to me. I will be asked what you said as we walked out."

"Great. You're right, Officer."

Tom put his stuff in the back seat and climbed into the driver's seat. He looked back at the school and prayed that this would all blow over and people would know the whole thing was a mistake. He drove away slowly. The officer waited at the school until Tom was out of sight.

Tom thought, *Don't be upset. How can I not be upset? This isn't even possible! And the only person I've been with is Maria. Oh no, what will Maria think?* He was in a state of shock. He couldn't understand what was in Sara's mind that she would do something like this. She knew nothing had happened with him. Why would she have told her dad this lie? And why would he have believed it? She must have worked hard to convince him.

Tom headed for home. He needed to get to his phone and call his attorney, Paul Becker. He rushed into the house and immediately called Paul.

"Paul, I have a serious problem." Tom filled him in on Sara's accusation and the police at school.

Paul, who knew Tom was sterile, asked, "Didn't you tell them that you couldn't father children?"

"No, I started to, but it wouldn't affect the rape charge, so I stopped. Statutory rape is serious. That is a criminal case, sex with a girl under 16. I got the impression from the district attorney that he felt he had an open and shut case and would prosecute no matter what I said."

"Just as well. You remembered what I told you about clients talking too much. I guess neither of us thought you would need the advice but here we are. We should talk before the arraignment. I'm due in court at 1:00 p.m. and there for the rest of the afternoon. Come in tomorrow morning at 8:00 a.m. and we'll talk strategy. Who else knows you are sterile?"

"Just my parents, Maria, her parents, and Doug."

"Tell them not to say anything to anyone about this, not the press or the district attorney's office, not a single person. I don't want anyone at the Prosecutor's office to know about your sterility for now. The press likely won't be on this yet nor will the prosecutor contact them until after the arraignment, if even then."

Tom replied, "I'll tell them all. Should I bring anyone with me tomorrow?"

"No, let's just you and I meet first, then we'll see."

*Maria will be angry about this. But would anger be the only reaction? She knows I can't father children, and will she believe me about the rest? She will, I know she will.*

Tom knew how upset his parents would be as well. He needed to tell them together so they could hear it at the same time.

Tom called his dad at his office. "Dad, I wonder if you could do me a favor."

"Of course, son, what is it?"

"You and Mom often eat out on Wednesday nights. Could I persuade you to get some takeout and eat at home tonight? I need to come and see you. Something has come up and I want to talk to you both about it. I'll come by after I see Maria this evening, maybe about 8:00 p.m. or so?"

"What's going on, Tom?"

"Dad, I'd rather not say on the phone. If you eat out, don't go to Antonelli's. Just trust me. I'll tell you everything tonight."

"Alright, your mom and I will work something out and we'll be ready for you. Love you, Son."

"Love you, too, Dad."

After Tom hung up, he checked the time – 2:30 already and school is out at 3:15. He wanted to be at Maria's house when she got home. She was sure to be frantic to find out what is happening after Tom missed her at lunch.

Tom was parked in front of her house when she drove up. He put his keys and worry stone in his pocket and went to meet her at the back door. Maria rushed over to Tom. After a quick hug and a shake of his head, Tom let her know that he didn't want to talk in the driveway. They went into her apartment and sat down at the kitchen table.

"Alright Tom, what's happening?"

"I've been suspended from my teaching position. Sara Antonelli is pregnant. She convinced her parents that I'm the father. Mr. Antonelli went straight to the district attorney who is a friend of his. The charges are sex with an underage girl or statutory rape, and paternity. I was escorted out of school by a policeman."

Maria gasped, "Why would she do such a thing? Did you tell them that you can't father children?"

"I started to, but with the district attorney there, I thought better of it. When I called Paul, he agreed it was better not to have told them until he and I talked. We'll meet tomorrow morning at 8:00 a. m."

"Maybe it would have been better if you had. It would have cleared you of the charges right away."

"The paternity judgement, yes. But there's the charge of sex with an underage girl. It's her word against mine. I remember that you warned me about her. I was so careful when she was around. Nothing ever happened with us. But will they believe me?"

"I do, Tom. And that's what counts. You'll convince them."

"I'm so relieved to hear that, Maria. I hoped that you would believe me because the only woman I've been with is you.

"I'll find out tomorrow morning what we will likely do, what our strategy will be. The arraignment is on Friday. The trial probably won't be for a while if there is one."

"Do you want me to go with you tomorrow to see Paul?"

"No, Paul said it would be better with just the two of us. Maybe later if it is needed. I should call Doug. He's probably in a stew wondering what is going on."

"Why don't you ask him to come over? I'll fix some sandwiches and we'll have a light supper."

"It'll have to be early. I told my dad I would be over about eight to tell them what's up."

Tom, Maria, and Doug talked through dinner. None of them could figure out the why of this. After Doug left, Tom and Maria cleaned up. Tom said, "Let's meet at my house Friday evening and we'll go somewhere and have dinner. I'll tell you all about the arraignment then. I told my parents that I would come and talk to them around 8:00 p.m. Could you go tell your parents and ask them not to talk to anyone about this, especially about the fact that I can't father children?"

Maria hugged him, "I'll tell them and Tom, darling, it will work out. I'll see you at your house tomorrow evening so you can tell me what Paul says, and Friday night we'll go out for dinner. Maybe all this will be resolved."

## 27

Tom's parents were on the front porch when he drove up. He got a hug from his mother and a handshake from his dad. His mother asked, "Would you like something to eat?"

"No, Maria, Doug, and I had a light dinner at her apartment. Maria went over to see her parents and Doug went home."

His dad said, "Why don't we go inside, and we'll have something to drink and you can tell us all about whatever is going on."

After they were settled in, Tom told them what happened at school. How he was accused of raping one on his students and got her pregnant, and asked to leave the school, and how embarrassing it was to be walked out of school escorted by a policeman. "I wasn't sure if any of my students saw that. I hope not. They wouldn't even let me go to the cafeteria so I could tell Maria and Doug."

Tom's dad steamed, "That seems like pretty shabby treatment. I have some friends on the school board. Do you want me to talk to them?"

"No, Dad, it won't do any good. They probably don't even know anything about it yet. The principal and the superintendent discussed the situation and made the decision to put me on suspension. The superintendent didn't need board approval to suspend me until this gets settled. At least they didn't stop my pay."

"Have you talked to an attorney yet?"

"Yes, I talked to Paul and we're going to be meeting tomorrow morning early to get him on board. He said that I did well not to say a lot. Paul taught me that if ever got in trouble to never volunteer information and don't even talk without him there. Oh, and by the way, he told me to ask you not to say anything about the fact that I am sterile. Maria is doing the same with her parents. That's why I didn't want to take a chance that you might have bumped into someone who knows what happened. I hope you don't mind."

"No, we don't, son. Does he think that it might be useful in your defense?"

"It might, but we don't want to let it out until we develop a strategy. I need to talk to Paul and work out a strategy together. I'll come and talk with you again after the arraignment. That's at 1:00 p.m. on Friday."

"Son, do you have enough money to take care of his fees. This is likely to be an expensive trial if it comes to that."

"Dad, I'm ok, thanks. The two of you taught me to save my money and I have. I'd better leave. I have to be at Paul's office at 8:00 a.m. It's going to be ok, Mom. Don't cry. Please don't cry and don't worry. It'll be ok."

"I know, Tom. It's just that it's so unfair. You'll keep us posted?"

"I will. You know what I love about you two?"

"What's that, dear?"

"You didn't even ask me anything that would hint that you thought I might have done something wrong."

"Of course not, we know you."

"Maria knows me too. She is quite upset and can't figure out any more than I can what Sara is thinking. I'll talk to you after the arraignment on Friday. I love you both."

Tom drove straight home, called Maria.

"Hi sweetheart, how did it go with your parents?"

"They were shocked by it but know that you are innocent. They wanted to know how they could help."

"So did my parents. Dad asked me if I needed any help with the money. But I told him they had taught me well about saving. I'm ok."

"Sleep well, darling. I'll see you tomorrow after school at your house."

## 28

P aul said, "Good morning, Tom. Would you like some coffee before we begin?"

"That would be good."

Paul called his secretary and asked for two coffees. After she left, he asked Tom to go over just what happened the previous day, "Don't leave anything out. I need to know all they said. I won't ask questions this time. I can read the charges later."

Tom told him how he was called to the principal's office. "When I got there, the principal told me that I would be suspended till it was settled. I was told that a police officer and the district attorney were on their way. When they came in, they read me the charges — paternity and statutory rape. They told me that there would be an arraignment at 2:00 p.m. Friday." Tom went on, "I wasn't given any choice at school. I am suspended until the charges are cleared by order of the superintendent of schools. I cleaned out my personal things and you know the rest. My parents and Maria's won't talk to anyone, nor will Doug. I'll catch them up after the hearing."

Paul said, "Here's how tomorrow afternoon will proceed. The charges will be read in court. The judge will have read them earlier. He will ask the prosecution if the charges can be backed up with evidence. They will have Sara's statement and judges typically take the side of the girl in these things and don't doubt her word at this stage. You will be charged formally and asked how you will plead."

"I want to plead innocent because that is what I am."

"You are only allowed to plead not guilty or guilty."

"But, I'm innocent of both the charges."

"That's what you say, but the law doesn't allow that as a plea. You'll have to plead not guilty."

"That's not right, Paul."

"But it is the law. I'll meet you at the courthouse at 1:45 p.m."

Tom left, found a phone booth, called Fred, and said he was in the downtown area, and asked if it was convenient to drop by for a few minutes. Fred told him to come on over. They settled down at the table in Fred's office and Tom said, "I have a problem." He continued and told Fred about what had happened at school earlier. "I just met with Paul, my attorney and the arraignment hearing is tomorrow afternoon. It seems the Mr. Antonelli got things rolling with the district attorney before they came. Out of the blue, I'm off the job till this is over. I still have a year on my contract. We have to get this cleared up so I can go back to work next fall."

"You should be able to get a speedy trial. It appears they want it that way, too. Do you want me to talk to the DA?"

"No, thank you. Paul is on top of it."

"Tom, why didn't you tell them about your infertility?"

"That's what everyone has asked me. But as I told them all, with the district attorney there, I thought I shouldn't mention it. And at that time, I hadn't talked to Paul yet."

"I think that was wise and I'm sure Paul agreed."

"I have a strategy and I want to run it by you." Tom outlined what he wanted to do at the trial to prove he was innocent and not just 'not guilty.'

Fred said, "That might work but it will be tricky. It will depend how much leeway the judge will give you. Do you know who the judge is yet?"

"No, I'll find out tomorrow. Paul probably knows but I forgot to ask him."

"It doesn't matter. It is what it is. Paul is a good defense attorney, you'll be alright. What does Maria think of all this?"

"She's pretty upset but has every confidence I'll be ok."

"Does she know about your strategy in court?"

"No, not yet. I'll tell her tonight."

"It's a pretty bold idea. It just might work. Tell Paul if he wants to talk about it with me, I'm here."

"Thanks, Fred. I feel better but I'm still pretty nervous about this. I'd better get along. I have to go home and plan what I'll wear. Paul told me to dress a little more formally for the hearing. He wants me to set a good impression with the judge. I'll let you know what happens. Can we have lunch Saturday and talk about this some more?"

"I'm sure we can. If I get home and Eleanor has something planned, I'll let you know. By the way, may I tell Eleanor about this?"

"That's fine, but just her. I'll see you Saturday."

TOM AND PAUL sat at the defendant's table. Paul greeted district attorney Swensen. Tom just nodded to him and shook his head at Sara. Joe Antonelli was behind the prosecution table, Joe glared at Tom.

Judge McVie came in, sat down, and said, "Are you ready for the prosecution, Mr. Swensen." On a positive answer he asked the same question of Paul. Both of them waived the reading of the charges. Tom just sat still and since he didn't know what to expect, he just waited for the next shoe to drop.

Judge McVie went on, "I've read the district attorney's indictment. Mr. O'Banion, do you understand the charges?"

"Yes, your honor." Paul had coached him about proper etiquette in the courtroom.

"How do you plead, Mr. O'Banion?"

"Well, your honor, I know I am innocent of both charges. That is what I want to be found. I just want my teaching job back. Not just 'Not Guilty,' but innocent."

"Mr. O'Banion, that is not the way the law works. You will be found either 'Not Guilty' or 'Guilty.' You may believe yourself to be innocent, but the law can't say that you are. Didn't Mr. Becker explain that to you?"

Tom answered, "Yes, he did, your honor. But..."

"Well, let me repeat the instructions to you. You may not plead innocent, only guilty, or not guilty. What is your plea?"

Tom shook his head, "Not guilty, your honor."

"I am convinced that Mr. O'Banion will be here for the trial, I have decided that he is to be released on his own recognizance. I take notice of Mr. Becker's motion for a speedy trial to get this behind both the plaintiff and the defendant. My calendar is full through July. I am therefore setting a trial date for Monday, August 5th. Are there any other motions to be filed?"

There were no other motions. The judge declared the arraignment hearing ended. Paul and Tom sat in the courtroom for a while after everyone else left. Paul told Tom that he should be prepared for this to hit the papers soon. The prosecutor might be able to keep it capped because of Sara's age but there are always leaks.

## 29

The group finished their breakfast in the meeting room at the Century Club. After the staff brought fresh pots of coffee, George Anderson opened with, "Joe told me of a situation with his daughter Sara. Joe has been raising her on his own since he lost wife to cancer four years ago. Yesterday, a man named Tom O'Banion was arraigned for statutory rape of Sara and paternity. She's pregnant. Mr. O' Banion was released with no bond. He is a teacher at Muskegon High School. He has been suspended from his job with pay. I don't think he should have been suspended, but there is nothing we can influence at this point. Joe is with Sara and her grandmother this morning. They are quite distraught over this."

There were expressions of sympathy from all the other seven members for Joe and Sara. But they all wondered why they were told all this in an open meeting.

George continued, "Of course, we are all concerned for Joe and his family. I'm sure justice will be done. But there is another aspect to this. When Wendell and I were at the firemen's commendation ceremony, we saw this O'Banion man there. He looked pretty tight with the mayor. And our contact in City Hall has confirmed that this Tom is often with the mayor at City Hall. Now, I wonder if this is the same

Tom that Harry has told us about. As you all know, we do have a contact through Harry in the police department and he will keep us posted of any new developments."

Wendell asked, "What do you propose we do about O'Banion?"

Tim wondered, "Is there some way we could get a picture of him that we could show to Harry?"

Wendell said, "I think I might be able to get a picture of him from the district attorney or his office."

George jumped in, "I don't think you should do that, Wendell. It might cause some suspicion. Does anyone have a contact at the high school? Or better yet, there is likely to be a picture of him in last year's *Said and Done*, the high school yearbook. Everyone should keep their eyes and ears open. I'll ask Joe to get with Harry and have him go back to Doo Drop and ask around about this Tom who lunches with the Mayor. He may even catch them there again. In the meantime, his trial will be in a month or two. We'll make sure Harry gets in the courtroom. He can make the identification then."

He went on, "Anything else we need to deal with?"

Tim said, "Is there any sign that the Mayor will change his mind?"

"There's been no news for a while. We'll meet in a couple of weeks unless something happens."

## 30

Maria was late. They usually had dinner out on Friday nights. On Wednesday, she told him she wanted to pick him up this time. Tom needed to tell her what happened at the arraignment, Tom was waiting and was getting worried that she was late. *Maybe she changed her mind about believing me*, he thought. Today's arraignment had upset him more than he expected.

Tom was waiting for Maria on the porch swing. When she pulled in, he jumped up and rushed to Maria. When she got out of the car, she reached into the back seat and brought out a picnic basket. She said, "I thought we could talk better here than at a restaurant. I made lasagna last night and just put together a salad. There's a bottle of Chianti and a loaf of French bread in here. If you will open the wine, we'll have a glass and talk while the lasagna warms up. What do you think? If you don't stop rubbing that worry stone, you're going to wear a hole in it."

Tom took the picnic basket, set it on the porch, gave her a hug and a kiss, and said, "I'm so glad you're here. You always know what's best. I love you."

"I love you, too. Let's get this lasagna in the oven and talk."

Tom went over what happened with Fred yesterday and in court today. When he got to the part about his asserting his innocence vs. pleading not guilty, Maria asked, "Do you still think you made the right decision about not telling everyone about your infertility?"

"I do. And I think I have a way to prove my innocence in both charges. As my plan becomes clearer, I'll want to run it by you before I go to Paul with it."

"Let me check the lasagna. It must be ready by now."

"I'll refill our wine glasses and slice the bread. This Chianti is quite good."

"It is one that Doug recommended. He really knows his wines – almost like he was a sommelier in another life. Maybe he was – he never talks about his past. By the way, when will you tell him what happened?"

"I'll get together with him over the weekend."

Dinner was great because Maria's lasagna is the best. Tom thought, *I'll have to be careful after we get married, I might put on weight.* They took their wine out to the porch. They had an hour yet before they would see their respective parents.

"We'll get through this, Tom. There is no way they can find you guilty."

"I know. I remembered what you told me that day when the semester started. I was careful to never be alone with Sara after that. I can't imagine why she would do this."

"She was annoyed when I offered her a role in the *Uncle Tom's Cabin* scene. She said that she wanted something more substantial. But she took the role and did a good job on it. I wouldn't think that would be it, but you never know."

"I suppose Bob is likely to be the father."

"That would be my guess too. I feel quite sure that Sara is not promiscuous."

"We shouldn't say anything about that. Just let whatever comes out after the trial on August fifth."

"There will be a formal trial? Why is that?"

Tom said, "I guess there has to be a jury. Friday was just the arraignment before the judge. The judge looked over the prosecution's case and decided there is enough evidence to hold me for trial. Paul also told me that both the prosecutor and the judge will usually take the girl's side in these cases. So yes, there will be a trial."

"That's not fair."

"I know it isn't, but that's the way it is. It's time to go, sweetheart. I need to go talk to my parents."

"I'll call you when I get home, Tom. I should be there by 9:30 or so."

TOM'S PARENTS were on their front porch when he drove up.

His mother Mary grabbed him in a big hug.

His dad John said, "Hello, son. Would you like something to drink while we talk?"

"No, thank you. Maria and I just finished dinner, Maria's terrific lasagna, salad, bread, and of course, a great Chianti."

"You'll have to get us over there for dinner sometime so we can have some of that lasagna you claim is so good. Well, tell us what's up."

They went in, settled in chairs in the living room. Tom went through the events in court today and ended with, "Today was just an arraignment. They read the charges against me and I had to make a plea, guilty or not guilty. I pled not guilty. There could have been bail set, but apparently it isn't usual in these cases. The judge said my reputation and standing in the community before this happened is good."

Mom was indignant. "Of course, you're not guilty!"

"You're right, Mom. You both know I can't father children. Her accusation is not valid. Why she did it I don't know. But it is her word against mine about the rape at this point. Paul told me that in these cases, they usually believe the word of the girl."

"Why didn't you tell them that you are sterile?"

"Everyone asks that question. At first, in the principal's office it was because the prosecuting attorney was there. And both Fred and Paul have told me that if you are ever in trouble, don't volunteer information to your opponent. Law school basic advice for clients. And, oh yes, Paul said to remind you that the prosecutor may send someone around with questions before the trial. So again, mum's the word about my sterility."

Tom added, "Actually Paul and I decided that because of my wish to be found innocent, we shouldn't tell them. And of course, as Paul said, I have to be tested again to make sure it is still true when we go to trial."

"But there might not have to be a trial if you told them."

"No, Dad. There is the other serious charge of sex with a minor. That makes it statutory rape. My sterility wouldn't prove that there was no sex. I have a strategy in mind, but I'm still working on it. I had some time after meeting with Paul so I went and talked to Fred about it. He was a defense attorney, you know, before he became mayor. When I outlined the bare bones of the strategy, he said it was bold, but it could work. He has every confidence in Paul and offered to consult with Paul if needed."

"Fred is a good friend, Son. I have a lot of respect for what he wants to do for our town."

Mom asked, "What does Maria think about all of this?"

"She knows none of it is true but is quite upset. I don't know if I ever told you about it or not. She warned me early January that she thought Sara had a crush on me. She said I should be careful around her. And I was. I always made sure there were others around except for one time. That was when she was crying, upset that she didn't get the role she wanted in the school musical. That may come up at the trial which is, by the way, August 5th."

Tom added, "I'd better get back home. Maria wants to talk on the phone some more about it. She's with her folks to tell them what happened right now and will call when she gets home."

～

MARIA FOUND her parents in the kitchen finishing up dishes. They all sat down at the kitchen table with coffees.

"How was dinner tonight with Tom?"

"It was good as far as the dinner goes. I was so full of questions that it wasn't a normal conversation. This thing has me so upset."

"We know, Sweetheart. Tell us what happened in court today."

Maria caught them up on the events of the day. She said, "I don't understand a whole lot of what happened. The judge said no bail so Tom is free to work on his defense."

She continued, "The trial is going to be early August, the 5<sup>th</sup>, I think. I hope this doesn't affect Tom's status at school and our wedding plans."

"He isn't likely to lose his job, is he?"

"No, he shouldn't. He'll be found not guilty and it will all go away. Do you think we ought to go slow on the wedding?"

"No, I don't. You and I can keep on with our plans. We still have five months, so we'll be all right."

Maria said, "I almost forgot. Tom said to remind you that we should definitely not tell anyone about Tom's sterility, we shouldn't say anything about it. They think it might cause a problem with his defense. We have to keep it quiet, even if the prosecution comes around with questions.

"I need to get home. I told Tom I would call him. We'll talk more later."

Her mom said, "In a way, it's too bad you are not already married. You could be a great comfort to each other if you were."

Maria was surprised at what her mother said. She didn't say anything, just hugged them both and went off to home.

## 31

Maria didn't go home. She drove to Tom's house. Tom and Doug sat on the front porch with beers. "Hey, guys, you got some more of that beer handy?"

Tom jumped up to give Maria a hug and kiss. Doug came back with her beer.

"How did your parents take it?"

"They took it well. They know you are innocent. Mom said something that surprised me. She said it is too bad we weren't already married. We could be a comfort to each other. What do you think about that?"

"I think she is right, we could be."

Doug jumped in, "What you should do is move in together."

Tom and Maria both said, "We can't do that! It wouldn't be the right thing to do."

Maria added, "I don't think that's what Mom meant. But maybe we could move the wedding date up. Even that would raise some talk. People would think we had to get married. Let's just give it some time. I'll find the right time to talk to her and Dad about it."

Doug said, "Tom told me about what happened in court today."

"It will be alright, Maria. I'm innocent and the court will find that in a few weeks."

"But in the meantime, do we just drop everything and wait?"

"No, darling. We just keep on with our lives and we do what we would have done anyway. School is finished, so we can just enjoy our summer. I want to look for a summer gig over in Grand Rapids. I've played the jazz clubs over there. I think they will find a spot for me, maybe Friday and Saturday nights. I could sit in with them and you two could come and have a listen."

Doug looked thoughtful, "That sounds great, but what are you going to do long term?"

"I'll get my job back. I want to be back in school with my choirs next fall."

"But suppose that doesn't happen?"

"It will," he said with more confidence than he felt. "Hey, Dave Brubeck is in concert with the Si Zentner Famous Band for the Seaway Festival in a couple of weeks. The city did well to get him — this is only the second year for the Festival. Getting Dave Brubeck is quite a feat. He's the feature attraction this year. He has always been the best of the jazz pianists as far as I'm concerned. It will be a great concert."

Doug said, "I like his music too. Do you have the tickets?"

"Sure do. I bought them early so we would get good seats close up. How about you, Doug? Can you go?"

"I didn't get my ticket yet. I don't know if there are any left."

"Just so happens I have another one with your name on it."

"I might have known. By the way, the University of Michigan Symphony is playing at the Sunrise Service on Sunday morning. How about that? It's free. I'll get tickets for that. I can afford it." He grinned.

"Yeah, but that's early in the morning."

"Right, that's when the sunrise happens."

Maria jumped in. "There are events on through the July 4th fireworks plus an art exhibit in Hackley Park. I'm sure we can find lots to keep us busy."

Tom added, "And a couple of weeks later, the last week of July, Maria and I will be on our Clipper sunset cruise. So enough is happening that we won't worry about the trial. We'll have a good summer. Paul and I have to work on my defense so that will keep me busy as well."

Doug said, "Well, I have to get along home. Thanks for the beer. I'll see you two."

"Goodnight, Doug. See you."

## 32

F red asked Alice to type up a memo to Sam and the members of the city commission. He was calling for a special meeting to discuss a new idea he had to sweeten the pot for Jones Industries.

He asked Alice to send out the memo immediately. She was to follow up with phone calls to everyone for next Thursday.

When Sam got the memo, he immediately went to Fred's office and asked, "What's up Fred? I thought you said they decided to put off the decision until next spring."

Fred replied, "Sam, I think something or someone else is trying to sabotage our efforts. It may be another town — it may be someone in town here."

Fred didn't notice Sam's reaction to his last comment about "someone in town" but just continued, "I'm just not sure but I'm afraid if we don't take some action now, we may lose the deal. We need this industry."

"Fred, don't you remember our conversation last week about the possible repercussions? Do you really want to do this?"

"I think I can convince the commission to move to make the deal sweeter. It's getting into July and I don't want to wait any longer. I will take it to Mr. Jones and their board. I have to try."

They talked until Fred, frustrated, said, "Enough Sam, I don't understand your foot-dragging on this. You know what we have to do. We need this diversification. We need these new jobs to grow. If I can convince the commissioners, they'll ask you to move on this."

When Sam returned to his office, Jerry asked him what was that all about. Sam showed him the memo and relayed the details of his conversation with Fred.

Jerry said, "Sam, what are you going to do?"

"If he gets the commissioners behind him, I won't have a choice. I'll have to go along. Who knows, maybe he's right and it's what we should do? I'll see you after lunch, Jerry."

Jerry left for lunch and made a phone call to Harry. Harry in turn called Joe Antonelli to let him know of the new developments.

Fred asked his secretary to come in and said, "Alice, I have a few things to get done, some letters to dictate. I have some phone calls to make. I'm leaving early, taking a late lunch, and heading to Marsh Field. Freddy Jr. has his last pony league ball game this evening that I want to see."

Alice said, "Fred, I think there is something going on with Sam and Jerry that is not necessarily city business."

"What do you mean?"

"Well, they are always in private huddles and they get quiet as soon as you or a commissioner comes close. I first saw it awhile back and I've caught them at it several times over the last few months."

"Alright, Alice. Thanks. I'll keep an eye on them from now on. Let me know if you see anything else suspicious, but don't confront them. I don't want to tip our hands that we suspect something is going on."

Alice said, "Do you want me to call the chief and let him know?"

"No, all that trouble seems to have blown over. I don't need a police escort anymore. Get your pad and we'll do the letters. You can type them up tomorrow morning."

∾

Joe called all the members of the group and invited them to lunch at his restaurant to discuss the changes and decide on a course of action. When it was laid out to the members, the reaction was to get Fred stopped. Now!

Tim said, "How do we do that? We can't get him ousted in time to prevent this, but we need to set an example. There are some members of the commission who might take up the cause."

Joe hesitated. "There needs to be an accident...he has to disappear...tonight."

"Now hold on a minute," said Tim. He went on, "I didn't sign on to this to condone killing anyone."

"If we don't take care of it, we may lose all the money we have tied up in the development. It has to be done."

"Remember, we agreed a long time ago that important decisions had to be unanimous. Remember this, Tim, when this plan goes through, you stand to make a great deal of money. We can't back down now. Are you with us or not?"

Tim relented and the unanimous vote was made. Joe said, "I'll let Harry know to take care of it."

He called Harry and told him what the decision was and said, "It needs to be done before the day is over. We don't care how you do it. He needs to be gone. Do you need some help? I'm a crack shot with a deer rifle."

"No, I don't want anyone else involved." Harry said, "He's not a big man. I can handle him. I've watched him for a while. He's back to leaving by the back entrance to city hall. He still parks in his parking spot — the first one outside the door. The police don't come anymore so he must have called them off. I'll just tell him that you and a few others want to see him and that I'll take him to you and bring him back. He won't suspect a thing until we get in the car and by that time, I'll have him out."

Joe said, "I don't need to know what you do with him. Just make sure he doesn't get away, make it permanent."

Harry said, "It will be. He will never be found. Let me call my contact and make sure the mayor is in." He called Jerry Saunders's office and said, "Jerry, I need you to find out when the mayor is leaving. Call me when you have the info."

Jerry strolled over to Fred's office and said to Alice, Fred's secretary, "How much longer will Fred be here? Sam wanted to see him for a few minutes if he could."

Alice replied, "It will have to wait until morning. When Fred finishes some last minute work, he'll be leaving for a late lunch and to Marsh Field for his son's ball game."

To cover himself, Jerry asked and was given a 9:00 a.m. appointment for Sam the next morning. He went back to his office, called Harry and filled him in.

WHEN FRED CAME OUT, there was a car with its engine running behind his car. He could see someone sitting in the driver's seat, but the visor was down so he couldn't see who it was. Fred thumped on the trunk, "Hey, would you mind moving your car?"

Harry got out and opened his passenger door and said, "Get in. There are some people who need to talk with you a few minutes including Joe Antonelli. They won't take long. We'll get you some lunch and take you to your son's game."

"No...hey, how did you know I was going to my son's game? Get your car out of my way. I'm not going anywhere with you. They can make an appointment if they want to talk to me."

Harry brought the gun out from behind his back and said, "You don't have a choice. Get in the back seat and I'll take you to them. We want you to understand that you can't cross us and get away with it. When the word spreads about you, no one else will try anything."

As Fred bent over to get in the back seat, Harry hit him hard on the back of his head with his gun and pushed him into the back seat. Fred was out cold. Harry took a tarp out of the trunk and covered the mayor with it. He looked around and up at the windows of City Hall. No one. He didn't see the man off to one side of a third floor window.

Harry drove off along the Causeway and out Ruddiman Drive

toward the old deserted cabin in the woods off Scenic Drive. Though it was only a quarter of a mile or so from the old Blockhouse, the cabin couldn't be seen from the highway or the Blockhouse. He stumbled on it a couple of weeks ago when he walked down away from the Blockhouse to take a leak. He saw a reflection off a window and climbed down the dune to explore it. There was a one-room cabin, an outhouse, and a shed sitting on a little peninsula near the middle of Lost Lake. He was surprised to find an overgrown two-track road leading back to Scenic Drive south of the Blockhouse. Harry figured if he cleaned out some of the brush on the two-track, he could drive a good part of the way to the cabin.

The Blockhouse had been burned down last September by a gang of local youth. They were finally rebuilding it but the crew would be done for the day soon, they always were. Harry wanted to be sure the workers wouldn't be a problem in case they were working late. When he got to the Blockhouse area, he drove right past the old two track, on up past both the south and north parking areas. He drove slowly as if he was interested in the rebuilding but it was really so he could see where they were working. He had already checked it out and knew they couldn't see the cabin unless they walked behind the newly rising structure and down into the woods.

He went on past and parked in the Duck Lake channel area, waited a few minutes, and started back down to take another look at the workers. As he did, he decided that he would be ok going up the two track since they were focusing on the front of the building today. Harry drove on by the north, then the south parking lots. After going around the next curve, the Blockhouse and the workers were out of sight. He slowed up, found his two-track, pulled away the brush that he had stashed there earlier, drove in and then stopped to put the brush pile back to hide the entrance.

As he drove deeper into the woods, he knew he couldn't get all the way in by the cabin so he stopped a few hundred feet away. He had only cleared the two-track partway. He hadn't known for sure that he would need the cabin, but he wanted to be prepared. At least his car was hidden from the road. He took a shovel and another canvas tarp out of the trunk of the car. As he came around to the back passenger door, he heard a groan. He pulled Fred out of the car, gun clubbed him again to make sure he stayed out and laid him on the tarp.

He needed to double check on the crew. He crept up the dune through the scrub pines and dune grass until he could just make out the back of blockhouse. No one working back there and he could see the guys packing up their tools so they would be gone soon. He turned and could tell that his car was hidden from them, too.

He went back down the hill, dragged the tarp with the mayor's body behind the cabin into a shed. He put a silencer on his gun and shot the mayor twice, once in the forehead and then the chest. There was a lot of blood. He rolled the body up in the tarp, tied the whole thing with rope, and weighted it with some pieces of cement block. He could have buried it out in the woods, but he had a better plan. He was going to drop it off the back of the Clipper – it would be a more permanent hiding place at the bottom of Lake Michigan. The Milwaukee Clipper owners were thinking about offering three hour sunset trips, so they had a promotional fee that was quite reasonable. He would go out tomorrow before sunset and drop the body when it got dark and no one would be the wiser.

He locked the shed and went back to his car. He needed to get more dry ice to make sure the body didn't stink by tomorrow night. He threw the shovel in the trunk and drove back down Scenic Drive into North Muskegon to Aron's restaurant. He ate dinner and listened to the music for a while. There was a country band there tonight and he made sure his presence was noticed by asking some of the ladies to dance. If he were there long enough, they wouldn't remember the time when he came and when he left.

## 33

Eleanor couldn't understand where Fred was. It wasn't like him to miss Fred, Jr.'s last game. It was already the 5<sup>th</sup> inning and now it was anxious Emily who asked, "Where's Daddy?"

"I don't know, honey. Something must have come up late in the day and he couldn't call us. I'm sure he'll be home when we get there."

Freddy Jr. was on deck so they got back to the game. He got a hit, a single to right field. They were both on their feet cheering. The Muskegon Jr. Varsity won over Grand Haven. Freddy had two hits.

Eleanor said, "Tell you what. We'll get a big Scrib's pizza and take it home. Daddy will be there and we'll celebrate your win."

"Yay," from two hungry mouths.

But when they got home, no Daddy. Eleanor said, "Sit down and eat some dinner. I'll get you some milk."

"Aren't you going to eat, Mom?"

"I will, just not right now, I have some phone calls to make."

She called Alice at home, who told her that Fred left for a late lunch and was going right to the game after lunch. Another piece of the puzzle, if he left early, where was he? Eleanor was trying hard not to panic. She called Chief Johnson. "Hello, Chief Johnson? This is Eleanor Thomas."

The Chief said, "Hello, Eleanor. What's going on?"

"Fred hasn't come home and didn't show up for Freddy's game. Alice said he left to have some lunch and go to the game. He didn't make the game, he's not home, and now I don't know where he is."

Jim said, "Let me check and I'll get back to you. Do you have anyone you can call to come and stay with you?"

"No, I don't need anyone right now. Just call me when you know something, please."

THE DISPATCHER on duty called the chief's secretary and told her there was a man on the phone who saw someone hit the mayor on the head, stuff him in a car, and drive off. She waited until the chief got off the phone with Eleanor and told him. Jim was strapping on his gun. She said, "Jim, you need to hear this before you leave."

He said, "What is it? I need to check something out for Eleanor. Fred's missing."

She said, "I know. We just had a call from someone at City Hall who said they saw the mayor being taken."

"Is he still on the phone?"

"I don't know. I'll ask the dispatcher."

The dispatcher said the man hung up on her after he gave her his name. He is Darrell Simmons, one of the second shift custodians. "He sounded pretty upset but said he would still be there when a policeman comes."

Jim said to his secretary, "Get me an officer with a squad car, quickly please. I need to get over there right now."

They drove to the back of city hall to see if Fred's car was there. It was, so where was Fred? Jim and his officer approached on each side of the car and walked up to it with hands on their guns. A check of the car told them nothing. And there were no other cars other than city vehicles. They checked them anyway. He wondered why Fred hadn't called for an officer to meet him outside City Hall. The Chief left the officer with the car and said, "I'll have a wrecker brought to tow the car to the police impound lot and send another squad car to pick you up. Don't let anyone near Fred's car. Let me have the keys to your cruiser. I'm going up to talk to the man who saw this and then on out to see Eleanor."

He went inside and found Alice, Fred's secretary. He asked her to find Darrell Simmons for him. When they brought a distraught Darrell to Fred's office, the Chief questioned him briefly about what happened. When asked about the car, Darrell could only say it was gray and he thought it might be a Buick. He quizzed Darrell, "Why did you wait so long to call this in?"

"I was afraid."

"Well, you did the right thing. Thanks for your courage and thank you for your call. I would like you to go over to police headquarters right away before you head home and let them take a statement."

"Do you think I'll be in any danger because I reported it?"

"No, Darrell. You didn't tell anyone else, did you? I'll tell Alice to keep things quiet about what you saw. You slip out of Fred's private door, stop at the station, and ask for a man named Mark Bergstrom, tell him what you saw, and head home. Don't come in Monday unless Alice calls you."

"All right, Chief. Thank you."

Jim showed him out the private door and called Alice into Fred's office. He said to her, "Keep things quiet about Darrell and what he saw. I told him not to come in Monday unless you call him. I'll let you know if I think it is safe for him. Until I get to the bottom of this, I don't want anyone to know he saw the whole thing. Oh, can you get me the station?"

Alice went to her desk, called the police station, and transferred the call to Jim. He got his lead detective, Mark, on the line, and told him what was going on, and said, "A man named Darrell Simmons will come in to give you a statement about what he saw. I'm going over to see Fred's wife, Eleanor, and I'll want to talk to you about this when I get back. And Mark, put out a BOLO for a gray Buick. It may not do much good. Too much time has gone by, but we have to try."

He hung up and came out of Fred's office only to find the city manager in a conversation with Alice. Sam asked him why he was there and why there was a police car out back.

Jim told him, "I had a call from Eleanor that Fred missed Freddy Jr's game. I'm just here checking it out. I have no idea where Fred is so I'm going to see her and let her know. I came with the officer in the squad car and he is staying until we can have Fred's car towed. You know all I know for now. I'll be over again in the morning to talk to all of you. Who knows, Fred may turn up before then."

"Thanks Chief, I won't say anything until we hear more."

"What are you doing here so late?"

"I was having dinner downtown and saw the police car and came in to check it out."

After Sam walked away, Alice said, "You didn't tell him about what Darrell said."

"No, I don't want anyone but you and Darrell to know about the man who took Fred. At least for now. Go on home, now, Alice. I'll let you know if I learn anything or if I need your help. Thanks for being here."

Jim left and drove straight to Fred's house. The instant he knocked, Eleanor opened the door.

"Come in, Jim. What did you find?"

They walked into the living room where Eleanor's parents were waiting. He said, "I'm glad you folks are here. Let's sit down and I'll tell you what I know."

He told her what he found, saying, "I don't like to think the worst without further investigation, but it doesn't look good. We have a witness who saw a man push Fred into a gray Buick and drove away with him. We have officers looking for the car but we're not likely to find it. I need to talk to a lot of people at City Hall. I can't do that till in the morning."

"It doesn't look good, does it?"

"Let's not jump too fast. I'll keep you posted. Try and get some sleep. I'll be in touch tomorrow."

## 34

The sun would soon drop into Lake Michigan and the boat would turn around and begin the trip back home. After the sun was down, there would be a light dinner and some time to dance in the ballroom. Tom and Maria got to the bow early to watch the sunset.

Sunsets over Lake Michigan in late July are some of the most beautiful in the world. This one was spectacular! The high clouds were tinged yellow. Down closer to the lake, it was a deep red with a rainbow of shades in between. No green flash this time, but they did happen. Maria and Tom watched it from the bow of the Milwaukee Clipper as they steamed westward out into Lake Michigan. This three hour cruise out into the Lake was the first trip of its kind for the Clipper. Tom and Maria had been lucky to get on it.

Tom loved The Clipper almost as much as he loved all the historical buildings in Muskegon. She was first commissioned in 1905 as the Juniata and started her life as a cruise ship traveling throughout the Great Lakes. Taken out of service in the late 1930s because of the fire danger from all the wood in its superstructure, it was completely rebuilt in 1940 in the Manitowoc, Wisconsin, shipyard. Its new construction was all steel. Very modern and completely fireproof, the new ship had air conditioned staterooms, a movie theater, and a ball room complete with live entertainment. In 1941, it was renamed the S. S. Milwaukee Clipper. Though it made trips to Chicago from both Milwaukee and Muskegon on weekdays, its primary run was back and forth across the lake between Milwaukee and Muskegon on weekends. The Clipper carried an average 112,000 passengers a year, many with their cars. Most often, the cruise across the big lake and back was a pleasurable time just to get away and enjoy.

Tom was so ready to get away this weekend. Preparing for his trial took up much of his summer. The arraignment was a while ago and the trial was a week from Monday morning. Tom could have stopped it back at the arraignment and been found not guilty, but he needed to show that he was truly innocent. Tom thought, *there's a difference at least to me – I wanted people to know that I would never do something like this.* Tom's attorney told him that innocent was not one of the choices legally, but he didn't really care about the law – he just wanted justice. Maria was supportive of his efforts, she knew he was innocent. She had warned Tom that he should be careful of Sara and he was, but . . .

Tom shook his head and cleared the dark thoughts out. He glanced around at the other sunset watchers. He recognized some of them by sight from seeing them around Muskegon at the Farmer's Market or the Michigan Theater, but he couldn't say he knew their names. Of course, the Milwaukee Clipper could carry nine hundred passengers, almost a little village. Today with the special deal, she had a full complement of people from all over from Grand Haven to Manistee.

A big burly man muscled his way through the crowd and claimed a spot near them. He took a big camera out of his shoulder bag that looked expensive and got set to take pictures. Tom thought he looked vaguely familiar, but he couldn't place him.

The guy turned and said, "These sunsets are gorgeous, aren't they?"

Startled to be caught watching the guy, Tom replied, "We never tire of them."

"Me, either," he said. "I take pictures all the time. Each one is different. I have quite a collection now, most of them taken from here or sometimes the fantail. Well, I think that's all the pictures for tonight. Enjoy the rest of your evening."

Maria said, "He was pushy getting a spot in front. I'm not sure I like him..." Tom was surprised since Maria was not one to be critical of people. Tom knew to heed her intuitions. She was most often right.

"What do you mean, you don't like him?"

"I just have the feeling there is more going on in his head than he shows. He hides it well, but...there is something there."

It dawned on Tom why he looked familiar. He told Maria, "I know him. Not his name, but he was the man who was in Doo Drop twice when Fred and I had lunch there. I wonder why he is on this trip on the Clipper. He doesn't strike me as a tourist, although he was taking a lot of photos."

Tom and Maria stayed at the bow rail, taking in the waves that were, it seemed, following them. They let the wind blow through their hair. Tom turned for another look at the big man and saw Bob and Sara go down the stairs to the car deck. *That's odd,* he thought, *the ballroom is upstairs.*

As the big man, Harry, walked away, he thought more about the couple he just spoke with. The guy looked at him as though he recognized him. Then it came to him. *This was the man with the mayor at the restaurant – they had lunch together frequently. The woman must be his wife or girlfriend at least. Neither one looked like they knew who he was so Harry wasn't too worried. The conversation was short and served to build his cover. And if the guy figured it out, Harry would just have to tie up another loose end.*

Harry made his way along the main deck and went down the stairs to the car deck. There weren't many cars on this trip but the light was fading. It still took him a little time to locate his car. Once he found it, he looked around at the other cars, saw only empty ones. He moved quickly to his own and opened the trunk. He untied the cement blocks and thought, *that was a mistake to have tied them on before getting here.* But he would need them to weight the body. He didn't want it to surface too soon, if ever. He carried one block in each hand to the ramp door on the stern end of the deck. Returning to the car, he bent to get Fred's body and heard a noise behind him. He put the trunk down quietly and listened. It sounded like whispers. Again, he listened, nothing. He opened the trunk again.

"Hearing things. It must be the waves," he whispered to himself. He took the tarp-wrapped body out of the trunk and hoisted it over his shoulder. With his other hand he closed the trunk with a bang, louder than he wanted. He quickly dropped down. After some time, he stood up, readjusted his load, and started aft.

BOB AND SARA were in the back seat of a car that they had found unlocked. They wanted some time alone to get away from all the people. They would have used her dad's car, but he had just dropped her off. He had some business to tend to. They met up with Bob and he said he would bring her home. Now they heard the trunk slam and rose up in the back seat.

"What was that, Bob?" Sara whispered.

"I don't know," he answered, "but look, there's a man on the way to the back of the ship."

"What is that he has over his shoulder? It looks like a body. This is scary. Let's get out of here before he comes back."

"Wait, he may turn around any minute."

"I'm not waiting," she said. She opened the door and started toward the stairs. Bob had no choice but to follow, so he slammed the door and ran after her.

As they started up the stairs toward the main deck, they looked back. The man had dropped the body on the trunk, grabbed his camera and snapped a flash picture. He dumped the body back into the trunk and took off up the stairs after them.

Bob and Sara scurried up the stairs. As they emerged from the car deck, a couple at the rail turned and saw them.

"Oh no," said Sara, "it's Mr. O. and Miss Vitale. I don't want to talk to them. Hurry, let's go the other way. They're probably going to the ballroom on the upper deck."


TOM AND MARIA were surprised to see Bob and Sara, and it looked like they didn't want to talk to them any more than Tom and Maria wanted to talk to them. Just then, the stairwell door opened again and out came the big man with the camera.

He said, "Did you just see two kids run up these stairs?"

Without thinking, Tom said, "They just ran..." Tom stopped and wondered why the guy was after Bob and Sara. And continued, "...I don't remember which way, we were talking."

Maria said, "Want to dance, mister, let's head up to the ballroom, how about a dance?" Off they went, hand in hand.

Tom wondered what was going on. This was just a little odd that this guy seemed to be chasing Bob and Sara. He remembered what Maria said about the man. Tom didn't have any idea it was the start of a nightmarish time.

# 35

When the Clipper docked just after 9 p.m. Maria and Tom held back. They didn't want their evening to end. The dancing had been wonderful. The sunset was breathtaking. Tom was finally relaxed a little.

It was dusky now but they could still see a lot as they stood by the rail, not far from the gangplank, watching the others leave the ship. Tom said, "Look there's that big man with the camera. He was the one who came from below deck after Sara and Bob. I saw him get off in the first wave, but he hasn't left yet. He's seems to be watching for someone."

Maria exclaimed, "Maybe he's still wants Sara and Bob. Don't you wonder why?"

"I see Sara and Bob, just at the end of the pier. Look, the big guy has seen them."

Bob grabbed Sara's hand and took off for the parking lot. When they did, the big guy followed them. When Harry got to the parking lot, he saw them get into an old Chevy, probably 1953 or 1954. He made a note of the license plate number. Right now, he needed to get his car off the Clipper and figure out what to do with the damn body.

Had it not been for those kids, he would have been done with it. Now it was a problem.

He told the gate agent that he had seen some friends off to their cars and needed to get to his car now. There was no problem re-entering the car port, but the gate agent said, "Hurry it up. We need to close up the ship." After the delay chasing down the kids, it was late. Harry needed to get the body back out to the cabin by the Block-house and figure out what to do with it. He guessed he could just bury it out there, cover up his track, and hope the Michigan winds would erase his tracks.

Being careful to drive under the speed limit, Harry got to the cabin when it was quite dark. There wasn't a full moon, but it was enough for him to make his way around the cabin. The body was still wrapped in the tarp and tied with rope, but all the dry ice had dissolved so he could smell the decay. *Where would he bury the body?* Behind the shed was the best spot. The digging was not difficult since the ground was mostly dune sand and a little dune grass. When the hole was deep enough, he untied the ropes and rolled the body into the grave. When he filled it in and smoothed it over, he put the shovel and tarp in the shed. There was enough other junk in there that it shouldn't stand out. He walked back to the car, carefully turned around without turning on his lights, and crept quietly down the two-track until he reached the road. Still with his lights out, he spread the brush to cover the entrance to the two-track.

Harry drove to Aron's restaurant about 10:30 p.m., had a burger and brew, and listened to music until almost midnight. He made sure that he talked to wait staff and told them how much he enjoyed the Clipper excursion.

He would call everyone tomorrow morning and let the group know the job was done.

TOM AND MARIA watched as Bob and Sara drove away in his old car. As they turned onto Lakeshore Drive, Tom and Maria saw Chief

Johnson drive up in a squad car. They disembarked and the Chief came their way and waved them to stop. They stood just off the gangplank.

"Hi Chief, what brings you here? And how did you know we would be here?"

"I just left Eleanor, Fred's wife, and she told me that you two were on your way back from a sunset excursion today."

Tom asked, "Why were you with Eleanor?"

Jim said, "I know you and Fred are friends. I have some bad news for you. Fred has gone missing and I'm afraid there may be foul play. Eleanor called me when Fred didn't show up for his son's ball game or at home. She's distraught. Her parents are with her."

Jim filled them in on what he told Eleanor last night. He continued with, "I talked to all the city hall workers today. The only thing we have to go on is that a custodial employee saw Fred forced into the back seat of a gray car by a big burly man. We have been on the lookout for a gray car, but it is like looking for a needle in a haystack with only that to go on."

Maria jumped in, "That's strange. There was a big man, definitely burly, on the boat. He just followed Bob and Sara to the parking lot."

"Who is Bob?"

Tom told him, "He is Sara's boyfriend. She is the girl accusing me of rape and paternity. And Bob is her boyfriend. You may have heard, my trial is Monday morning."

"Yes, I have heard. But what does that have to do with this big fella?"

Tom told him about him chasing the kids up the stairs on the boat. "I'm concerned that they may have seen something down there. He watched for them to get off the boat and he followed them."

The Chief asked, "Do you know him or, if not, can you at least describe him?"

"He was 6'2 or 6'3, weight well over 200 pounds. He has a round face, dark hair and, as Maria said, looked like a football player. Probably a lineman. I know this doesn't help much."

"We'll find him. It might take a while. I'll talk to Bob and Sara, warn them that they should be careful. Maybe they'll tell me about what happened down on the car deck. I'd like the two of you to come in as soon as you can after the trial to make statements. In the meantime, you two watch your back...and let me know if anything else happens."

They were so intent on their conversation, none of them noticed a gray car that left the Clipper's car deck.

Tom and Maria walked to his car in the parking lot. They drove off along Lakeshore Drive toward Tom's house.

Maria asked, "Do you think this has anything to do with what we talked about at dinner the other night?"

"I suspect it has. Fred and I met a while back and he said then that we needed to dig deeper to find out who the group of nine were. But he was determined to move his ideas forward. Even though he was threatened and told to hold to the line. He refused to do it. Whoever is behind this may have stepped up the pressure."

"The chief told us to watch our back, Tom. Are we in danger too?"

Tom pulled the car over and put his arm around Maria. "Don't worry; there is no reason for anyone to think either of us is involved. You remember that Fred said for me not to get involved right now. I haven't made any moves yet, but just talked to some people."

"Let's get to my house and call Eleanor. I would bet she needs someone right now."

Maria talked to Eleanor and found that her parents were still with her. She asked Eleanor how she was doing and told her that she and Tom were praying for her and Fred's safe return. Maria made a date for them to see her the next afternoon.

# 36

The prosecuting attorney, Harvey Swensen, and his staff were already in place. The courtroom was filled with people. The trial had created a lot of interest in the city and people wanted to see and hear all the details. When Tom and his attorney, Paul Becker, came in, there was a stir in the courtroom. The buzz increased as they walked to the defense table. From the comments he could hear, Tom thought that most of them were directed at him with some animosity. He wasn't surprised. The word spread fast through the community when the principal, Mr. Mann, suspended him back in May. He heard that there was a lot of outrage directed at what they believed Tom did. He saw Mr. Mann toward the rear of the courtroom.

"All rise, the Honorable Judge McVie."

Judge McVie brought the courtroom to order, called the jury in, and said to Tom, "Mr. O' Banion, you are charged with criminal sexual conduct with one of your students, Miss Sara Antonelli. She is now four months pregnant. Mr. Swensen seeks a paternity judgement. We are therefore here for a trial on the charges. Since then, Miss Antonelli, who was under 16 years old at the time, has said that force was involved and since you are more than five years older than she is, the prosecution has also filed a charge of statutory rape. How do you plead?"

Mr. Paul Becker, Tom's attorney, rose and said, "Not guilty on all charges, your Honor."

"I need to hear that from Mr. O'Banion."

Tom stood and said, "Not guilty on all charges, your honor."

The judge turned to the prosecutor and said, "You may proceed, Mr. Swensen."

The prosecutor called his first witness, Mrs. Morton. She refused to look at Tom as she walked to the witness stand. Tom wondered what she could possibly have to say about this. When she was sworn in, Swenson asked her, "Mrs. Morton, would you tell us how you are employed?"

"I am a counselor at Muskegon High School."

"Mrs. Morton, have you ever noticed any inappropriate behavior between Miss Antonelli and Mr. O'Banion?"

Mr. Becker jumped up. "Objection, your Honor. Leading the witness. Calls for an opinion from her."

"My apologies, your Honor. Mrs. Morton, can you tell us what you observed on April 14th of this year?"

"I walk by the choir room on my way out of the building. The door was open and I saw Tom hugging Sara. I wondered what was going on. She seemed to be in tears and pretty unhappy about something."

"What happened next?"

"Well, Tom saw me at the door and stepped back away from Sara, as if he was guilty of something."

Mr. Becker said, "Objection, your Honor that is again an opinion, with no basis in facts."

"Objection sustained." Judge McVie instructed the jury, "Please disregard the witness's last statement." To the prosecutor, "Proceed, Mr. Swensen."

"What did Sara do at this time?"

"She ran out of the choir room and down the hall like she wanted to get away from something."

"Objection, your Honor. Mrs. Morton continues to draw conclusions."

"Objection sustained. Mrs. Morton, just state the facts as you saw them and don't offer any opinions."

The prosecutor said, "No further questions, your Honor."

Judge McVie said, "Cross-examination, Mr. Becker?"

"Mrs. Morton, what kind of hug did you see?"

She said, "I don't understand, it was a hug. It just didn't look right."

Mr. Becker asked, "What do you mean, didn't look right? Did their bodies touch and where were his hands?"

"I don't think their bodies touched except at the shoulders and he looked like he was patting her back. But it didn't look right. Male teachers shouldn't be hugging their girl students."

"Mrs. Morton, isn't it just possible he was consoling her over something that had happened in her life?"

"Well, it is possible, but I don't think so. It just didn't look right."

The prosecutor said, "Your honor, redirect?"

Getting the nod from the judge, Mr. Swenson asked, "Mrs. Morton, have you seen them together since?"

"Yes, I passed by the choir room one day just before school was out. The door was open, and I could see them both and heard them argue. Sara was again crying and Mr. O' Banion tried to calm her down. I just kept on, but this was the second time she was crying with him in the picture. It just seemed like something is not right."

Mr. Becker objected again on the grounds of drawing a conclusion.

"I withdraw the question. No further questions, your Honor."

The prosecution now presented several other witnesses who professed to have seen Tom hugging and being hugged by female members of his choirs.

On cross-examination of the last one, a male teacher, Mr. Becker asked, "Do you suppose that all this hugging is just the natural enthusiasm of choir members because they just like Mr. O' Banion?"

Mr. Swensen objected saying, "Mr. Becker is testifying, your Honor."

The judge admonished Mr. Becker saying, "Move on. Do you have more questions?"

"No, your Honor. But I now make a motion to dismiss. What we have heard so far is a string of observations of behavior that, while perhaps not wise of Mr. O' Banion, does not constitute sex with a minor, statutory rape, and paternity."

Judge McVie frowned, "You may be right about these observations, Mr. Becker, but your motion is denied, you are premature. Miss Antonelli has yet to testify. Call your next witness, Mr. Swensen."

"I call Miss Sara Antonelli."

Sara was sworn in. She wouldn't look at Tom.

Mr. Swensen said, "Sara, I know this may be difficult for you. If you feel you have to take a break at any time, just let me know. Can you tell us what happened on the afternoon of April 14$^{th}$?"

Sara immediately teared up. Mr. Swensen offered her a clean handkerchief. "Take your time, Sara."

She sniffled. "I was upset during choir practice. I only got a small part in 'The King and I' and I just couldn't seem to get past it. My friends in the soprano section urged me to talk to Mr. O."

"You call him Mr. O. Why is that?"

"That's what all the kids call him. I went to see him after classes that afternoon. He's always been so nice, that's why I was so surprised and hurt by what he did."

"Why don't you tell us what happened?"

"I told Mr. O how I felt about the play and the role I had. I was in the chorus and one small scene, but it just isn't the same as a lead role. He was trying to console me, and he put his arms around me. I was still crying. I put my head on his shoulder and he pulled me closer."

"Go on, Sara."

"Well, there is a small couch back behind the piano and his desk. He sat me down on the couch and walked over and locked both the doors. I didn't understand that."

"Had he ever done that before, Sara?"

"No, and I got scared because he came and sat down beside me on the couch. He put his arm around me and pulled me close, saying he knew how to make me feel better."

A gasp went up from the courtroom and everyone glared at Tom, including the jury members.

"Please continue when you're ready, Sara."

"Well," Sara whispered, "he started touching my breasts and reached under my skirt. The next thing I knew he was on top of me and in me. I was crying and telling him to stop, but he wouldn't. When it was all over, he told me to get dressed, walked me to the door, unlocked it, gave me another hug, patted me on the back, and said, 'You'll feel better now. I'll try and get you an understudy role in the next play.' Just about then I saw Mrs. Morton and he let me go. I just ran off down the hall."

Mr. Swensen asked Sara, "Did he use a condom, you know, a rubber?"

She said, "No, he didn't."

Mr. Swensen said, "Your witness, Mr. Becker."

Tom leaned over to Paul and said, "That's quite a story. It's full of lies. Let me ask her a few questions."

Paul said, "Not yet. Let me set the tone first. I'm still not happy with what you want to do. The judge won't let you do it unless you fire me."

"Alright, Paul. But if you don't check with me, I will stand up and do just that."

Paul asked a lot of questions but aside from triggering the tears again, he couldn't get anything accomplished. He couldn't shake her story.

Tom stood up and said, "Your Honor, I would like to continue the questioning of this witness."

The prosecutor jumped to his feet and objected loudly.

The judge ignored him and said, "I can't let you do that, Mr. O' Banion. You have a competent attorney."

Tom said, "Your Honor, Michigan law says I am permitted to take over if I fire my attorney. I wish to do so now."

He turned and said, "Paul, you're fired."

Judge McVie said, "Mr. O' Banion, this is quite irregular. You are within your rights. But be advised I'll be holding you on a tight rein. Don't upset the witness."

Tom turned to Sara and said, "Sara, we've always been on good terms, haven't we?"

She teared up, not knowing what to expect, but said, "Yes, we have. That's why I was so surprised."

"How are you feeling these days?"

"I'm feeling ok considering. The morning sickness and all that is gone."

Tom said, "Sara, are you sure the child you are carrying is mine?"

The courtroom erupted in shouting at Tom. The prosecutor was on his feet saying to the judge, "Your Honor, Miss Antonelli is not on trial here. The suggestion Mr. O' Banion makes is outrageous."

The judge said, "I agree, Mr. Swensen. Mr. O' Banion, you may not continue on this line of questioning. Do you understand?"

"Yes, your Honor. May I go on?"

To Sara he said, "Sara, would it change your mind if you knew that I am not able to father children?"

Again, the courtroom erupted, and the prosecution objected. The judge said to Tom, "Mr. O' Banion, one more question of that nature and I'll hold you in contempt."

Tom said, "Your Honor, I have a document I'd like to introduce into evidence."

The judge said, "You can't do that. Only your attorney can and you fired him."

Tom said, "Paul, would you become my attorney again now?"

Tom sat down and Paul took over.

Paul asked the same question, "Sara, would it change your mind about who is the father if you knew that Mr. O'Banion is sterile?"

Sara broke down in tears. The judge said, "We will recess until 2:00 pm."

## 37

When court reconvened in the afternoon, Mr. Becker immediately asked the judge if he could bring in another witness before finishing up with Sara. The judge allowed it so he said, "Please call Dr. David Smith."

He took a few minutes establishing Dr. Smith's credentials. He determined that Dr. Smith was the family doctor for the O'Banions since before Tom was born.

"Dr. Smith, please tell us about Tom's childhood."

Mr. Swensen objected, "Relevance."

Mr. Becker said, "It will be shown, your Honor."

"Very well, proceed."

Dr. Smith told how he delivered Tom and gave him all his child-hood shots except for mumps. He went on to say, "Unfortunately for Tom there was no vaccine for the mumps. One wasn't developed until the late forties and even then, it only had short term effectiveness. To this day, there is still not an effective vaccine. When Tom was sixteen years old, he had a quite severe case of mumps. Tom developed 'mumps orchitis,' It is very rare, but it does happen. It put him in the hospital, and we thought for a while we would lose him. But he turned the corner and after a long recovery time, over six months at home, no school and limited activity, he seemed to gain full recovery."

"Please continue, Dr. Smith."

"When he was seventeen, I did a series of tests on Tom to see if there were any long term consequences of the 'mumps orchitis.' Sadly, there were. As a result of all this, Tom is sterile. I just did another test prior to this trial. Tom remains sterile. He will never be able to father children. Mr. Becker is aware of the results of that test."

The courtroom buzzed. They knew what this meant for Sara's testimony.

Paul Becker said, "No further questions. Here is the document Dr. Smith spoke of. It has the results of his recent tests. May we enter into evidence?"

After it was entered and the prosecution was given a copy, he went on, "Your Honor, I would like to recall Miss Sara Antonelli to the stand."

When she was seated, the judge reminded her she was still under oath.

Mr. Becker asked the judge if the court recorder could read back the portion of Dr. Smith's testimony about Tom's "mumps orchitis" and its consequences.

Mr. Becker asked her, "Sara, having heard the testimony of Dr. Smith, would you like to change your story?"

Sara started crying and said, "Mr. O, I never meant to hurt you." Turning to the judge, she said, "He never did anything to me. The baby is someone else's. Mr. O never touched me in that way. I'm sorry, Mr. O."

One more time the courtroom erupted. After the judge calmed the courtroom, he said, "Miss Antonelli, you will be charged with perjury. Do you know what that is? You should be ashamed for what you have done to Mr. O'Banion. I will see to it that a public apology asking for his forgiveness is added to whatever sentence comes your way when you are tried for perjury."

"I know. I lied. I'm sorry your honor."

To Tom, the judge said, "Mr. O' Banion, you have the apologies of this court. You have been unjustly accused. The verdict will be 'Not Guilty 'on all charges. But you have proven yourself innocent, without question. I only hope and pray that you will be able to be reinstated in your job and be able to return to a normal life."

He turned and said for the record, "Case dismissed."

The reporters rushed for the exits to file their surprise stories.

Maria met Tom halfway down the aisle, gave him a tearful hug and kiss. They walked hand in hand together out of the court and onto Terrace Street. Doug found them outside and said to Tom, "Well, it worked. You proved what we all knew. You are innocent. Everything should go back to normal and you'll be reinstated."

Tom said, "I hope so, Doug. I hated to do that to Sara, but it was my only chance to restore some sense to my life."

Mr. Antonelli came up to him and said, "I won't forget how you treated my daughter in there. Your turn will come." He walked away with Sara while Tom and Maria stood open-mouthed.

"Can you believe that? Tom, what do you think he means? Was it a threat?"

"I don't think it was a threat. He likely meant that 'What goes around comes around.' I just believed that it was the only way to clear my name. The whole experience will probably haunt me for a long time."

"What's next, Tom?" Maria went on to say, "Do you think Mr. Mann will reinstate you?"

"I don't know. I plan to meet with him tomorrow morning. Right now, we need to go and see how Eleanor is. We told her we would see her after the trial. She needs our help with all this."

ELEANOR PACED BACK and forth in her living room. Maria went to her with a hug, noticed the eyes reddened from tears. Her hair was unkempt, not styled in Eleanor's usual way. She apologized, saying, "I just can't get it out of my head that Fred has disappeared. I keep imagining all the things that could be wrong.'

Maria hugged her, "Oh Eleanor, just try to think and hope for the best. The police will find him."

Eleanor snuffled again, "I know they are doing all they can. But it has been four days now."

Tom said, "Eleanor, are your parents coming back?"

"Yes, they went home to get a few more clothes and will be back tomorrow afternoon."

Tom continued, "Please tell us what the chief told you. We learned a little from him when we got off the Clipper."

She caught them up on the chief's latest report. "They have your description of the suspect, as well as the city custodian's, and that of Bob and Sara. The department's sketch artist has put together a composite that has already been edited by all except you two. Jim said he would be contacting you to get your input. His officers already have copies and there is a search for him as a material witness."

"Has he given you any idea of what they are thinking?"

"No, Tom, nothing. He just says for me to be patient and let them do their job."

She teared up again. "It doesn't look good."

Maria put her arm around Eleanor. She couldn't imagine what Eleanor was feeling. She knew she would be devastated if anything happened to Tom. After a while, the tears stopped. Eleanor said, "I don't know what to say to the children. They are so frightened."

Tom said, "I meet with Mr. Mann tomorrow morning about my job. After that, the chief wants Maria and me to come downtown to help with the sketch. We'll check in with you after we do that. If you need anything, please let us know."

Before they left, Maria gave Eleanor her home phone number and said, "If you need me before your parents get back, please call."

## 38

Tom's appointment with Mr. Mann was at 9:00 am. He arrived a little early and was treated to an embarrassed smile this time from everyone in the outer office.

When the door to his office was closed, Mr. Mann said, "Thanks for coming in, Tom."

Tom waited after a slight nod, not sure just how to react.

Mr. Mann continued, "Tom, you probably think that since the trial results, you will be able to come back to work here."

"Only seems right," Tom said.

"But, you see, Tom," he went on, "we can't have this scandal hanging over the high school and particularly the music department where there is more contact with the students."

Tom exclaimed, "There was no scandal. That was proven in court. I am totally innocent. You were there. Sara admitted that it never happened and that the baby wasn't mine. You must have seen the story of my innocence in last night's Chronicle."

"I know that, Tom. I was in court when Sara testified. But there will always be a perception in the minds of the parents and the community that we have to deal with. You know how it is. Perception is what counts and it will negatively affect the school and the music department."

"What are you saying?"

"Tom, we can't take the chance. I've posted your job and contacted all the music schools. What I mean is that you will not be allowed back as choral director and teacher."

"That's not fair. It's not the right thing to do," Tom said, his temper rising.

"It may not be fair, but it is what will happen. We could probably find an administrative position for you somewhere, but no contact with students. The Board agrees with me. But no matter what you decide, they have decided you will get the balance of your contract pay. They will either continue your checks or just send you one check for the rest of this year and next."

Tom stood and said, "No! I will not accept a desk job, Mr. Mann. My life has been ruined and changed forever by a young girl's lies and the 'perception' as you call it, of some of the faculty, staff, and parents. I wouldn't have believed people in this town would be like that. But if you and the Board are an example, I guess they are like that. No! Mr. Mann, I will leave the school system. What will I do? I'm sure you don't care as long as you can shove your problem under the rug. But, you know, the unfairness of what you are doing will not go unnoticed. People will remember and you will hear of it later."

Mr. Mann stood up and said, "Is that a threat, Tom?"

"No, I don't threaten people. I'll just leave now. Send someone with me if you feel you must while I get the rest of my things."

"Please don't leave this way. It is what we felt we needed to do."

"This is how I feel. Goodbye, Mr. Mann. This is not right, it is not fair."

TOM'S ANGER cooled as he drove to Maria's house. He now regretted the remark about the townspeople. He wondered if he had any recourse but didn't know where he could find out. When he told

Maria, she burst into tears. "That's not fair, Tom. What are you going to do?"

"I don't know. We'll have to figure things out later."

"I'll talk to Mr. Mann and the board. This isn't right. And it's my battle too. I don't want to be there if you aren't."

"Maria, darlin'. I don't think that's a good idea. They might decide to let you go, too."

"Don't tell me what to do, Tom O'Banion. I'm won't sit by and watch them keep you away from the work you love."

"All right, but for now we better get along. We're due to see the chief."

They were ushered right into the chief's office. He said, "What happened at your meeting with the principal, Tom?"

Tom told him. The chief was shocked. "That's a surprise. I don't understand his rationale."

Tom said, "Neither do I. He said some mumbo jumbo about perceptions in the community. If it is true, I'm disappointed with the people of the town. But enough of that, any news about Fred?"

"The only leads we have are this man that the two of you saw on the Clipper and the man the custodian saw at City Hall. But we don't know yet if it's the same man. And there are more questions. The big man the custodian saw take Fred. Does he still have him or has something worse happened? Why would he just hold him? Tom, I'm afraid it doesn't look good. We're processing Fred's car for fingerprints. The custodian said the man didn't go near Fred's car but he might have been the same man who attacked Fred a few weeks ago and could have left prints then. It's a long shot but if we find a print, we can check through our fingerprint card file."

He added, "And I think that Bob and Sara aren't truthful."

"What do you mean by not truthful?"

"I think they saw something down on the car deck of the Clipper, but they are too frightened to say what. They tried to get away from the man, but no, they saw something."

Maria said, "Tom, you remember how they looked when they

came up from the car deck. They were practically running toward the upper deck stairs."

"I do remember, but they aren't about to confide in us after what happened in court."

"And I can't get much when their parents are here. The kids are being told not to say anything. They are all coming in again this afternoon after the final sketch is done. I'll get the artist in here. The two of you give him your input, and we'll show it to the custodian and to Bob and Sara. We'll see what they say. Maybe I can get them to realize that they may become victims."

"By the way, Chief, what about City Hall? Is there an interim mayor?"

"I don't know. We have a police presence there and will maintain it until we know what this is all about."

Tom said, "I'd like to go over there after we give our input on the sketch."

"Why?"

"Maybe they'll tell us something that they wouldn't tell the police. Everyone over there knows Fred and I were good friends so they might open up."

The chief said, "Don't do that, Tom. It might put you both into the line of fire."

"Chief, I think I am there already. Just let us try. Maria and I will come right back to take a look at the final sketch and see what Bob and Sara say."

The chief reluctantly agreed, "Ok, Tom. Tell you what I will do. I could tell you to leave it alone, but I respect your instincts. I would like to know what you find. It might help if you knew what our witnesses have said to our investigators. I'll get you copies of their interview reports. Just keep them to yourselves."

When he returned with a copy of the reports, he added, "Be careful out there. And keep me informed of any things you learn."

## 39

Tom and Maria walked over to City Hall. Alice was at her desk but looked like a lost soul. She burst into tears when they walked up. "I can't make any sense out of this. Who would do this to Fred?"

As Maria tried to comfort her, Tom probed, "Who have the police talked to? I want to talk to the same people. I'll start with the custodian that saw the man who took Fred."

"No one is supposed to know he saw anything. The chief thought it might put him in danger."

"Is he here?"

"He is. The Chief called me early Monday and said it would be alright for him to come in. So he's been working all week. I'll take you to him. Thank you for coming. You give me something to do."

She called the custodian's manager and asked where Darrell Simmons was working right now, telling him why he was needed. She led Tom and Maria to the third floor and introduced them.

Tom said to him, "The chief of police has asked me to come and talk to you. I am working with the department in a special capacity. The chief wants me to hear your story. We appreciate your help.

"I know you have been through this already, but can you take me to where you were at the window and take me through everything you saw?"

Darrell took them all to the window that overlooked the parking area out back. He pointed to the mayor's reserved spot, and said, "That's where Fred always parked."

Tom said, "Darrell, close your eyes and try to go back to the day it happened. Tell me everything that comes to your mind."

Darrell closed his eyes. "I was on my break, having a smoke. What got my attention was this gray Buick that pulled up right behind Fred's car. This big man got out and went around and sat in the driver's seat. I heard that the mayor was hurt a while ago." Joe opened his eyes, "Do you think it might be the same man?"

"Maybe, we just don't know yet. Go on. Keep your eyes closed, you'll remember better."

"Well, the next thing you know, this big guy opened his door and stopped Fred as he came out the back door. The guy said something to him. I remember Fred looked a little scared, but he balked and said something back. The man pulled a gun and pointed it at Fred. When I saw the gun, I backed up so I could just see but would be hidden if he looked up that way. The man opened the back door, motioned with the gun. As Fred bent over to get into the back seat, the man hit him on the head with the gun and pushed Fred the rest of the way in. The man closed the door, looked around but not up here. I just remembered something else. He opened the trunk, took out an old-looking tarp, and put it over Fred."

"He still had his gun out but didn't use it."

"That's right. But he kept it in his right hand as he got into the car. He must have laid it on the front seat so it would be handy if Fred woke up. It looked like it was a pretty hard blow."

"Could you see if there was any blood?"

"No, but I wouldn't be surprised."

"Anything else? Like, did you get the license number or were there stickers on the car?"

"I don't remember any stickers, but license plate numbers are a hobby of mine. I don't know how much it will help but the letters were for Muskegon County and the first two numbers after that were one and nine."

"That's great, Darrell. I'll tell the chief. You take care now."

They walked back down to the first floor and Fred's office. As they approached, Tom was surprised to see Joe Antonelli walking toward them and talking with the City Manager, Sam Milford. He told Maria to wait with Alice for a minute saying that he wanted to say hello to the City Manager.

He walked over to them. When Joe saw him, his face darkened. "I don't want to talk to you, Tom O'Banion. Not after what you did in court."

Tom replied, "Don't you mean, not after what your daughter did to me? I've lost my job. I won't be able to teach here anymore. And that's even though we now both know none of the charges had any truth to them."

Antonelli made a move toward Tom, but Sam Milford got between them. "Now, gentlemen, let's calm down."

"All right, Sam, I will, I want to talk to you about what happened to Fred. I'll come back at a better time. I am a little surprised to see you here, Mr. Antonelli."

"You just stay away from my daughter."

Tom walked away shaking his head in disbelief. He and Maria said goodbye to Alice and left to head back to police headquarters.

## 40

The Kelly family was on their way back home from a camping trip at Silver Lake. They came down Scenic Drive from Whitehall and had one more stop to make. Their children, 15 year old Tommy and 12 year old Alicia, weren't too excited about the stop this time. They toured the old blockhouse two years before and they were ready to get home. But their dad was a big history buff about the area and that interest included the Blockhouse.

Tommy's dad from early childhood always believed that the Blockhouse was a fort built to protect the settlers from the natives in the area. It must have been built back in the mid-1800s. But as his children grew, he began to look into the history. He found the story about the natives to be just that, a story. As it turned out, the former Michigan state parks director P.J. Hoffmaster and the state parks superintendent, Nicholas Trierweiler, first came up with the idea of building a fort on the site in 1931. It was to be a replica of Ft. Dearborn in the Detroit area. The Blockhouse was built by Franklin D. Roosevelt's Civilian Conservation Corps (CCC) and the Civil Works Administration (CWA). It was completed some three years or so later and opened to the public in 1934. Built on the area's highest dune in the state park, it stood 250 feet above the Lake Michigan level. It became one of the major tourist attractions for the area.

It was a shame the Blockhouse had been burned down by a local gang of boys last year. They were sentenced to some jail time, probation, and community service—part of that community service was they had to spend their summer as laborers to help rebuild it. Mr. Kelly wanted to see how the restoration was coming. He was happy to see the basic structure of the old fort was done, and they had started the caulking.

Tommy's dad found the foreman of the work group and told him he was a history buff interested in the Blockhouse. He asked, "When do you expect it will be done?"

"Well, as you can see, the basic structure is almost done. We have a lot of work to be done on the inside yet. We'll get that finished before the summer is over. Next spring the park service will come in and clean things up. It should open to the public likely next May."

Tommy got bored with the whole thing and asked his mom if he could walk around back. He went a little way down the path behind the blockhouse. He saw a flash of sunlight that looked like a reflection from a mirror or something. It could be a window, maybe something down there. He decided to check it out and started down the hill behind the work site.

Tommy's dad said, "Thanks for the info. I'll gather up my family and we'll be off until next spring." He walked around to the back to find Tommy and saw him climbing down the dune.

"Tommy, let's go. We're ready to head home. Come on back up and we'll go to Scrib's on the way home." Scrib's pizza was special to Tommy so he came back up the hill. He figured he would come out with one of his buddies later and check out what might be down in the woods. Jeff had a car and he would be up for it.

"What were you doing down there, Tommy?"

"I just looked around. I wanted to know what was down that hill. It looks like there might be hiking trails through there. It might be fun to get down there sometime."

"We've got another three weeks before school starts. Do you want to go for a hike too, Alicia?"

"No, Daddy, I don't want to go on a hike. I'd rather go to the beach. There aren't that many swimming days left."

Mom said, "I'll tell you what, Alicia. How about you and I spend an afternoon at the beach and let the guys have their hike. This is Wednesday, the 7th. How about a week from Saturday, that'll be the 17th? What do you guys think?"

"That sounds great."

Tommy thought that this worked out well. He and Jeff could get up there this Saturday, the tenth, and check things out firsthand.

They stopped at the Scrib's on Laketon Avenue. They decided to have their pizza there and then head home to relax. It had been a great vacation.

## 41

Maria and Tom got back to City Hall and found the Chief still with Bob and his parents. Bob said the sketch looked a lot like the man on the boat but couldn't be positive.

When Bob saw Tom, he said, "I'm sorry for what you were put through. Sara had to know I'm the father. I still don't understand why she accused you."

"Thanks, it's over now. What about you and Sara? Do you know what you will do?"

"We haven't made any decision yet, still haven't figured out what is the right thing to do. All of our college plans will have to change. We both want to be teachers. And I have a scholarship to State to play football."

"You'll figure it out, Bob. Are your parents with you on this?"

"They are. Mr. Antonelli is still pretty upset but he'll be alright."

"Tommy, did you recognize the man on the boat from the sketch?"

"It sort of looks like him, but I can't be sure."

"Maria and I are on our way to see the sketch. Since we talked to someone who looked like the suspect for a while on the Clipper, the

Chief thinks we might be able to help with his identification. You take care of yourself, Bob. If you want to talk about it, let me know."

The chief's secretary came over. "He's ready for you and Maria now."

When they walked into the chief's office, there was another man there. The chief said, "This is Jeff, our sketch artist. I thought since the two of you are the last to make final comments I would have him here to make the changes right away."

Both of them said that the sketch was a fairly good likeness. But Maria said, "I think his nose is a little broader, looks almost bulbous and his hairline is a bit more receded."

Jeff made the changes and showed it to them again. Maria said, "That's him!"

Tom said, "You're right, Maria. It's a good likeness. Now what's next?"

"All of my officers will soon have a copy. They'll be on the alert all over the city. I'll have a man over at City Hall to show it to Darrell, the custodian."

"Oh, I almost forgot. When I talked to Darrell, he remembered a part of the license plate. You know, Chief, if he says it is the same man as we saw and that Bob and Sara saw, that means..."

The officer knocked on the chief's door, was admitted, and said, "Sir, the custodian says he's sure that is the man. He signed a statement to that effect. And he said he now remembers part of the license plate. I better get that info to the patrol cars."

The Chief told him about the changes and said, "You'll have to show him the new one."

"Ok, Chief, I'll get right back over there."

"Alright, Tom, we now know that the two men, Fred's attacker and your man, are one and the same. But all it means is that he took Fred. What he did on the car deck of the Clipper, we don't know but it looks suspicious. Bob and Sara haven't said a word yet. I may have to get the prosecutor to talk to them about that, and how they could be charged with obstruction of justice. I have also told them they might be in danger. Maybe they'll believe it when they are told that he is Fred's kidnapper."

"Do you still think he is being held somewhere?"

"There is no way to know. But the more time passes, the more likely it is that something has happened to Fred. I'll keep you posted on what we find."

"Could I have a copy of that sketch?"

"Why, Tom? Who could you show it to that we can't?"

"You never know, but I have to do something! If this man was following Fred before he abducted him, maybe someone like a waitress where we had lunch saw the man as well."

The Chief gave him a copy. "Just be careful and let me know if anything comes up."

## 42

Harry was on his second cup of coffee in his small Lakeside house. He wanted to dope out what he should do. He figured that his time was limited here. But he was concerned that some of the people from the Clipper might be a problem. He knew the couple on the Clipper could recognize him and might eventually put things together. Maybe the two kids could recognize him, too. The pictures he took in the car storage area might help him figure out who they were. The film was at the Lakeside Pharmacy to be developed. What to do first? He could take a little time to think it through, dig up some information about all of them. In the meantime, he should call Joe to set up a meeting.

He called Joe at the restaurant after the lunch hour. Joe said, "We don't really need to meet right now. All we want to know is if you took care of things."

"I did. That's what you will pay me for. He won't be a problem again. And by the way you told me there would be a bonus when the job was done."

"I'll talk to the group this weekend. Can you lay low until then?"

Harry said, "No rush. I have a few things to clear up. It might take a couple of weeks. I'll call you after Labor Day to get the money."

"Do you know where you'll move to?"

"Yeah, somewhere warm before winter sets in."

"Well, we don't want to know where you are. We'll set up a way to contact you if we need you again."

Harry hung up. He figured he better stay put until things calmed down. The police must have started their investigation of the missing mayor, but they wouldn't have much of a clue yet. He thought he might have two or three weeks before they connected him with it. Time enough to get a lead on everyone, all the possible witnesses. He could in time decide on what to do with them. He could just pull another Chicago and kill them all. No one from Chicago had any idea who had been behind the multiple murders. He didn't want to leave loose ends here either.

He should call Jerry at City Hall. Jerry was afraid and would be hungrier than Sam, more likely to cooperate.

The operator connected him with Jerry. "Jerry, this is Harry."

"Yeah, Harry. Look, things are in kind of a jumble here. The mayor is missing. No one knows where he is or what has happened. I really can't talk now."

"Really, that's too bad. Jerry, remember what we said. The money keeps coming as long as you help us out. I have a license number and car make. I need to know who it belongs to. It's someone I need to track down. My clients want me to get this name. I'm sure you have a contact in the police department. You get this done for me and we won't call on you for a while."

"Ok, Harry, by the end of the day."

Harry said, "Call me" and hung up. He fixed himself a roast beef sandwich for lunch, grabbed a beer, and began to map out a plan. After lunch, he started a chronology of the boat trip. He put down everything he could remember that happened on the ship. *What was it about the conversation with the couple on the Clipper?* There was that moment just as he left that the man looked familiar. He realized the man was with the mayor at Doo Drop, his name was Tom. And he was at the mayor's house that night for dinner. The woman on the boat was also with him at the dinner. Find one and he would have the other. Tom and Fred had talked about who might be in the group of nine.

The boy and girl had probably been making out like rabbits in the car so they must be a couple too. Looked like about 15 or 16 years old. They probably went to Muskegon Sr. High. His pictures of the boy would help as would Jerry's information about the license plate of the boy's car. Jerry might also be able to help with the man on the boat. Maybe the man went there to see his friend the mayor at City Hall. Jerry might have seen them together and knows who he is.

Jerry finally called about 4:30 p.m. "All right, Harry, I've got the name that goes with that license plate. It's Henry Fowler. His address is out on Henry Street. They're in the phone book, address and all. I checked."

"Good, thanks. I have another question for you. Have you ever seen a man at City Hall who seems to be a good friend of the mayor? Probably shows up often. He would be just under 6 foot. He has jet black hair, an attractive man. I think his first name is Tom. And he has a lady friend who is tall and blonde."

"I saw him once. He came once in early June and again in July. I don't remember that he came in any other time than summer. I'll tell you who might know. I overheard Fred when he told Alice that they were going over to the U.S. 31 barbeque for lunch. Maybe someone over there might know him."

"Thanks, you did alright. I'll have a bonus for you in the usual spot after Labor Day; just keep an eye on it. I need to know who that man is." Harry hung up and went back to work. He made a list of what he had to get done over the next few days. He wanted to minimize his time out during the day. There was less chance of being seen at night. First job would be to get to the boy. If he had to get rough to get the girl's name, he would. He would put the fear of God in both of them.

He thought, *Wait a minute*. When he came up from the car deck, he was startled to see the couple from earlier at the rail. The man had been evasive when Harry asked about kids who ran by. Maybe they knew each other. He might be able to get both their names from the boy.

Tomorrow he would start. From the information Jerry gave him, he could find the boy tomorrow and pump him for info.

## 43

"Maria, do you have a preference for lunch?" Tom asked Maria. "We need to check out both Doo Drop and the U.S. 31 Barbecue. Those places were favorites for Fred and me on our lunch get-togethers. Maybe the waitresses will remember the man in the sketch."

"Well, it is Friday, and we need to eat fish. Let's go to Doo Drop."

They were soon settled into a booth in the bar area where Fred and Tom usually sat. When the waitress came, Tom greeted her with "Joan, this is Maria, my fiancée."

Joan said, "Nice to meet you, Maria. Where's Fred today?"

"You may not have heard. Fred has gone missing."

"Oh, no! Well, I did hear a couple of men who talked about the mayor but I didn't make the connection. Do the police have any idea about what happened yet?"

"Not yet, they don't. That's partly why we're here. But first can you get us a couple of beers?"

Maria said, "Make mine Miller's." Joan knew Tom's favorite.

She was soon back with them and asked, "Are you ready to order?"

They put in their orders—no choice really, perch for both of them plus a small order of onion rings. After Joan delivered an order to another customer, Tom motioned her over to their booth. Tom showed her the sketch. "Does this look like anyone you have ever seen in here?"

Joan said, "I wait on a lot of people, but I think I've seen him. He often sits in this area." She studied the picture once more. "You know, I think he was in here the last two or three times when you and Fred were here. Yes, that's right. He sat in the booth right behind the two of you and left just before you did."

"You're sure?"

"I am. I thought at the time that what he did was strange. There were plenty of empty booths, but he chose the one right behind you and Fred. He ordered another beer and wanted his check but didn't leave right away after I got it for him. He jumped up and headed out without drinking it. He usually lingers over his beer."

"Do you remember anything that stood out about him?"

"No, not really. Just that he was a big man. Tall and heavy."

"Thanks, Joan. The chief will probably send someone to talk to you."

She went off to get their food and brought it right back. Tom and Maria finished their lunch and took off for the downtown area. Tom asked Maria if she could use a cup of coffee and some dessert, maybe a piece of pie at U.S. 31 Barbecue. It was close to police headquarters and they might get lucky again.

Their dessert was great, but they got no further information. No one could remember the man. George, the owner of US 31 BBQ, asked Tom if there was any news of the mayor. Tom told him no, still missing. They headed back to the police station to let the chief know what they had found out. But the chief wasn't in. His secretary told them that the chief was with the Mayor's wife about the sketch. Tom left the word about what Joan at Doo Drop told him.

~

THEY HEADED BACK to Maria's. They had a lot to talk about regarding their future. Things had happened pretty fast in the last few days. They got into Tom's car and talked for a bit.

Maria said, "Let's go for a walk on the beach before you take me home. I need to walk off some of this food. I'm still full from lunch."

"Sounds good. Where do you want to go, Grand Haven beach or the Ovals?"

"The Ovals. We'll walk out to the lighthouse and along the beach to the Coast Guard Station. After our walk we can go to the concession stand and see Jimmy Coscarelli, the Popcorn man."

"Ha! I thought you were full. "

She laughed, "You know me, and I might be ready for a little something after our walk. Maybe some popcorn or a paddle pop."

They left the police station and drove down Western Avenue past Shaw Walker and up onto Lakeshore Drive. This was the long way around, but Tom liked to go this way now and then. There were some grand old homes all along the drive as they went around Muskegon Lake toward the ovals. They went through the Beachwood-Bluffton area where Buster Keaton used to hang out in the summer. They went back toward the channel and Tom followed the road around to the beach area and the concession stands. He parked and they took off hand in hand along the long jetty out to the lighthouse. There was a light chop on Lake Michigan today but not enough to splash up on them.

When they came back to the beach, Tom spread out the blanket he brought along. They shed their shoes and socks and walked through the shallows in the breakwater between the lighthouse jetty and the Coast Guard Station. It got to be late afternoon by the time they were at the Popcorn Stand. They got some coffee and went back to the blanket to talk.

"Tom, have you thought about what you will do? Things have been pretty hectic."

"I have called all the local schools, and no one has an opening. I have some savings laid by, so I'll be alright for a while. And the board paid me for next year, actually for the balance of my contract. In the meantime, I'm quite sure I can get in to play piano at some of the jazz clubs in Grand Rapids."

Maria said, "I have to stay where I am. I'm not happy about it. It isn't the same without you there. But nothing has opened up for me either."

"We'll have to keep looking for a place where there is something for both of us."

"That's going to be harder."

Tom took her into his arms and held her. "We'll find a way. I just need to know what is going on, why Fred is missing."

"Do you think you should? It really scares me. The man might remember us from the Clipper and connect the dots."

"It will be alright. I'll be careful. But I can't let it go. We can always back off if problems start coming up. I just can't stop yet. Fred was my friend. I have to find out who and why someone did this. I have to do my part."

"I know that about you and it's a part of why I love you, but I'm still scared." She kissed him.

"Nothing will happen. I know you are scared but I'll be careful."

Tom dropped her off and stopped at a phone booth to call Doug. He wanted to bounce some things off his friend, get another perspective on the latest.

## 44

Tom called Doug and asked him if they could get together to talk. Doug said, "Come on over. You need to catch me up."

Tom stopped at the grocery store and picked up fixings for a snack, roast beef, bread, tomatoes, and a six-pack of cold beer. He found Doug on his porch.

Doug said to Tom, "How about it? What's up?"

"I'm sorry I haven't been over to talk to you sooner. So much has happened since we got back from our trip on the Clipper. Fred is missing. I fear that worse news is coming."

"Don't jump to conclusions, Tom. Maybe he'll turn up. Is there a ransom demand?"

"No! I don't believe that will happen." Tom choked and started to tear up.

When he could control himself, Tom went on, "Jim, the chief of police, feels that something worse has happened. He doesn't say what, but I think Fred may be dead already."

Waiting for a minute to allow Tom to settle down, Doug asked, "Do they have clues about the man who took him?"

"Not yet. We have a composite sketch of what they are currently calling a 'person of interest.' Here's a copy of it. Have you ever seen him before?"

"No, never. Does he look like this to you? You saw him on the boat, you know."

"Yes I did. But it wasn't long enough to be sure now. Why do you ask?"

"Can I have that copy of the sketch?"

Tom was puzzled. "Why do you want one?"

"I want to do some looking for the man who may be coming after my friend, er, friends. Are you and Maria in danger? I'd like to get my hands on that guy. I'd take care of him."

"Doug, he's a big man. You could get hurt. You don't want to go after him with that attitude. What's gotten into you?"

"Alright but you two are my friends. I'll cool it but it wouldn't hurt to get another set of eyes looking."

"It's a long shot. He won't be easy to find. This composite came about by inputs from five witnesses, a custodian at City Hall, Bob and Sara from school, and the two of us. Maria and I got a good look at him when we talked to him on the Clipper. He was new to both of us except that I think I saw him at Doo Drop."

"How is Maria with all this?"

"She's pretty upset. She is frightened that I might do something to draw attention to us." Tom wondered, *why is Doug so concerned about Maria?*

Tom jumped up, agitated, and started pacing the porch. He said, "Doug, I have to do something. I've never been one to sit still when a friend is in danger. As I said a while back, I have to be involved. I just don't know where to turn. I think I better get on home and give Maria a call. She knows me well, knows what I might do, and is afraid for us."

"Keep me posted. If I think of anything or I catch sight of him, I'll let you know."

## 45

S aturday morning, Jeff stopped in front of Tommy's house and hit the horn. Tommy's mother said, "Jeff is here to pick you up. Go tell him to lay off that horn, then come back here and tell me what you two are up to."

Tommy hurried out and told Jeff to hang on. "Mom is just being Mom. She wants to know what we're doing. I'll be right back."

"Mom, we are just out for a ride. We'll end up at the beach, you know, out at the Ovals. Can I have some money for lunch?"

"Alright, here you are. Do you have your swimsuit and a towel?"

"Yes, Mom and thanks. I'll be home for supper."

Jeff was careful not to squeal the tires as he drove away from Tommy's Lakeside house. They drove up Laketon, Seaway Drive, and stopped downtown at US 31 Barbecue to get barbeque sandwiches and fries. They wanted to eat on the way so they would have more time to search the woods by the Blockhouse.

After they finished their lunch, Tommy said, "I can show you from the back of the Blockhouse grounds where I saw the sunlight reflections."

"We can walk down from the Blockhouse parking lot. It's Saturday and no workers around so we'll have the place to ourselves.

If we leave the car there, we can get out more easily. I'd hate to get stuck back in the woods somewhere."

They parked and went around to the back of the construction area. Tommy pointed off to the southeast. "It was right down there somewhere. Let's go, it won't be a hard hike."

It was pretty hot, being mid-August, so they were soon working up a good sweat even going downhill. The trees and underbrush were thick and they made slow progress. The dune was steep and Tommy slipped and hit against a tall birch tree. He hurt his side and it knocked the wind out of him.

Jeff went on ahead and called to Tommy.

"Tommy, look here. There's a two track road down here."

"Yeah, I wonder where it goes. If we follow it to the right, we ought to come out on Scenic Drive. Let's go the other way."

They made faster progress now on the two-track. They soon entered a small clearing and could see a cabin on the far side with a shed out behind it.

"Now who would have put a cabin and a shed back here? I wouldn't have thought you could build anything in this area. And look at the marshy lake surrounding it."

"It looks like it was built a long time ago. Do you think anyone lives there now? Let's go see."

"Jeff, I don't think we should. Let's just go back now."

"Don't be such a wimp. We'll just go take a look. There can't be anyone around. C'mon."

They walked through the brush to the front of the cabin. The wood siding was worn and gray. It looked like it might only be one big room, maybe two. The door was locked or stuck. Jeff peered in the window to the left of the door. There was an empty beer can on a table. "Tommy, someone has been here. Look at that, a shiny new beer can."

"Well, I told you I saw something."

"Let's go around back and see if there's another way in. I want to check it out."

The first thing they saw as they rounded the corner was the shed and on the other side, further down was an outhouse. Both the shed and the outhouse were in worse shape than the cabin. Both looked like they might fall down any minute. There was no other door in the back of the cabin so it seemed there was no way they could get in. They headed for the shed. Maybe they would be able to get in there.

The door was almost off the hinges, so Jeff just pushed his way in. Tommy hung back but eventually stuck his head in the door. Jeff was looking at an old tarp lying in one corner.

"This thing looks nasty – look at all the dark stains on it."

"I don't like this."

"Just hang on. I want to look around some more."

They went back out. Jeff started to walk around the yard. He eventually got to the back of the shed. Jeff called out, "Look here, this ground is freshly dug up. I wonder what's in there."

"I think we better go back and call the police."

"No, no police. At least not until we have some time to think this through. Come on, Tommy, we'll go back and spend some time on the beach. That's what we were supposed to be doing."

They climbed back up the hill and drove back to the Ovals. It was still pretty warm at the beach. Coscarelli's thermometer read 85°. The sun wasn't quite so intense by this time of the afternoon. They didn't feel like swimming after what happened at the Blockhouse, so they got popsicles and walked out the pier toward the lighthouse.

"What should we do, Jeff?"

"Just put it behind us, Tommy. We didn't do anything wrong yet and we might get in trouble with the police if we go to them."

"I wonder if it is a body and...whose body might it be?"

They sat on the edge of the jetty and watched the waves come in. They were strong enough that they splashed up on the rocks that lined the lake side. The other side where there was a little cove was always much calmer.

"Jeff, I still think we should go to the police. They may be on the lookout for somebody that we don't know about."

"May be true, but I won't go. We better get home. It's almost five. Isn't dinner time at your house always at six?"

Jeff let Tommy off and watched him go into his house. He was afraid that Tommy would go to the police.

DINNER TONIGHT WAS one of Tommy's favorites, spaghetti, garlic bread, and iced tea. It didn't take long though for his mom to notice that something wrong. "Tommy, what's wrong? You haven't eaten a thing, honey. Don't you feel well?"

"No, Mom. I'm ok. I just don't feel like it."

"That's not like you. This is your favorite. Something's has to be wrong."

"May I be excused?"

"Alright, honey. We'll talk later."

Tommy went upstairs to his room and sprawled across his bed. His side hurt. He needed to go to the police, but he didn't want to go by himself. He shouldn't have talked Jeff into taking him up there and his parents would be mad that he didn't tell them the truth about what he did today. He didn't want to tell them. But he had to. He just couldn't let it alone.

He went back downstairs. His dad and mom were still at the table with their coffee and apple pie. He sat down and said, "I have to tell you something."

His dad said, "What? You have a girl friend or what?"

"No, Dad, this is serious."

"Sorry, Son. Tell us what it is?"

"Do you remember that we stopped at the Blockhouse to see how far along the work was? And that I went around the back and a little way into the woods. Well, I saw something flash down the hill in back of the Blockhouse."

"What do you mean, something flash?"

"It was like a reflection off a mirror. It just flashed and went away."

"What happened next?"

"Jeff and I went up there today to see what we could find."

His mom said, "Tommy, you lied to me. You said you were going to the beach."

"I'm sorry, Mom. We did go to the beach. But we also went up there. We hiked down to the spot where I thought I saw it."

He told them all that happened, how he hurt his side. When his mom heard that, she wanted to see where he hurt. There was a big bruise. She said, "We'll have to get that looked at. Why don't you finish your story and we'll call the doctor?"

Tommy continued and when he came to the part about the stains and the freshly dug area behind the shed, both his parents reacted.

His dad said, "Tommy, you have to talk to the police."

"That's what I thought too but Jeff said we should just forget it and not get involved."

His parents looked at each other, and nodded, "We'll call them right now. This might be important." They got the police department on the line, telling them what happened. The police said that an officer would be right out to talk.

Detective Sergeant Mark Bergstrom was there in a half hour, listened to the story, and said, "You were right to bring it to us. I didn't know there was a cabin down there and a road to it. My guess is not many do except maybe the park service people. It may be outside their boundary. I'll talk to them tomorrow early and we'll check it out. It may be nothing but an animal buried back there, but it's fresh. That's troubling. Don't say anything to other people yet. We'll let you know if anything comes of it."

Tommy felt better after the detective left. "Mom, I think I can eat now. I'm hungry."

Later after a closer look at his side, she said, "I think this is only a bad bruise. I'll put some liniment on it, and we'll see how it is in the morning. Tommy, you did right to tell us. Sleep well."

# 46

When he got back to the office, Mark called the Chief. "Jim, sorry for calling you on a Saturday night but this could be important.'

He filled the chief in on the details and said, "The boy told me they found a road about a quarter mile south of the Blockhouse. They said it looked like it went back to the cabin."

"I want to go with you. Let's make it just you and me. I'll meet you at the office at nine tomorrow morning. We'll take a couple of shovels and see what's there."

Next morning going north on Scenic Drive, they missed the two-track road into the woods. After turning around in the parking area, they crept back slowly down the hill and found the road entrance. It was pretty well camouflaged, but they caught a change in the gravel. They turned left, stopped to clear the debris and branches, and started down the two-track. They made it about 200 yards in and decided not to take the car further. They grabbed their shovels and after a short walk down the road, they saw the cabin ahead. Mark breathed a sigh of relief. *You never know when a youngster would make up a story.*

"The boy said the freshly dug area is in the back of the shed and the tarp with the stains is inside the shed." They found the shed behind the dilapidated cabin. The shed was in even worse shape than the cabin. The door was hanging by one hinge. They pushed open the door and could see where the dust on the floor had been disturbed. In the back corner was a heavy dark green tarp, wadded up and thrown in the darkest spot of the room. Mark and Jim picked it up and carried it out into the sun.

"Those dark spots certainly could be blood, but we won't know for sure until we get it to the lab," Jim told Mark. "The boys were right to be suspicious."

Mark responded, "We better go check out the area behind the shed. They said it looked like someone had been digging back there. Tommy Kelly described it about six or seven feet by 3 feet. They didn't tear it up. They got scared and hightailed it out of there. They were afraid someone might still come around with that fresh beer can in the shed."

Behind the shed, it looked as though someone had dug in the soft ground behind the shed. The dune grass was on its side so they could see that it had been disturbed. It looked like whoever had dug the hole had tried to cover it up by sweeping pine boughs over the ground.

"Let's check it out, Mark. Grab one of the shovels. Be careful. We don't want to damage whatever might be in there. It could be someone burying trash."

They set to work carefully shoveling out the sand and dirt mix. A short while later, Jim said, "Look here, it looks like another tarp. Careful now. Let's use our hands to brush away the next layer."

As they cleared the remaining dirt, Jim looked more and more distressed. *Please don't let this be what I'm afraid it is.* "Mark, this doesn't look good. You take that end and I'll take the other. Let's lift this out."

They untied the ropes around the tarp, unfolded it carefully, and their worst fears were confirmed. It was the mayor. The inner layer of the tarp was soaked in blood from the shot to the head and the chest. There was so much blood. Fred must have bled out pretty fast. The smell was awful. The mayor must have been dead for a few days.

The chief covered the mayor's body with the tarp and shook his head. "Fred wanted to take the protection off. I should have insisted that he keep it.

"I'm going back to town. Mark, you stay here, secure the scene and see if there's any more evidence that we've missed. We'll need to get the beer can and the other tarp and get them to the lab," Jim said grimly.

"We need to find whoever did this quickly. The town will be in an uproar when the word gets out. I'll take the car, get back to the office, call in for some help for you, and get the coroner on the way. They should all be here in an hour or so. It's a long time, I know, but I don't want to take a chance that some newshound might have a police scanner. I'll stop at the first pay phone I see and call the office. That may speed it up. I want to keep it quiet till I get to talk to some people."

Mark nodded. "I know the drill. Don't put up the crime scene yellow tape out by the road yet. Try to hide the entrance to the road. When the others get here, they can set the crime scene boundaries."

"Mark, I don't have to but I will tell you to be careful. Whoever did this is dangerous, obviously armed and not at all concerned about using his gun. It's not likely he will show up before I can get some others here. But if he does, just fade back into the woods, don't try to be a hero."

Jim turned to go back to the car. *How am I going to tell Eleanor?*

## 47

Tom and Doug were at Tom's house, on the front porch. Tom was bouncing some ideas off Doug like how to go about finding out who the unknown man was. Tom said, "I have to do something to help the police track him down."

"What do you think you can do that the police can't?"

Tom shared what the waitress at Doo Drop told him, namely that this guy was sitting in the booth behind Tom and Fred at Doo Drop while they were having lunch – at least twice! Tom continued, "We also know that a custodian at City Hall saw him as he knocked Fred on the head with his gun and pushed him into a gray car. The police have been looking for that gray car, a Buick, with a big man in it."

Doug eyed Tom. "Again, what can you do that the police can't. Where do you fit in?"

"I'm trying to figure out a motive. I can't believe this is just a random abduction. If I find out why, we can maybe figure out who did it. I'm going to go to City Hall and talk to some people there. Maybe someone has an objection to what Fred wanted to do for the town."

Doug was quiet. "You know you might just put a target on your back, don't you? Do you think you can protect yourself?"

"Both Maria and the chief, too, think that it's possible and they both have warned me to be careful. But Fred was not just the mayor, he was my friend. I can't leave it alone."

He went on, "By the way, Maria is coming by after church. Doug, why don't you stick around? We'll have some sandwiches for lunch. Maybe a beer and talk some more about what I can do." Doug, lost in thought, just nodded.

*And if you are taken out by the killer, the door opens again for me.*

The phone rang. Tom jumped up, went inside, and grabbed it.

"Tom, this is Jim, er, Chief Johnson. I have some bad news. We found Fred's body. He was murdered."

Tom couldn't speak, choking up.

"Tom, are you still there?"

"I'm here."

"I need your help. Maria's too. I'm going over to tell Eleanor and I think it would help if the two of you were there."

"Maria is on her way here, so we can meet you there in about a half hour; say about 6:00 p.m. Will that be alright?"

"I'll be there."

They talked for a few more minutes. Tom wiped some tears away and returned to the porch just as Maria drove up. She came up the steps, took one look at Tom's face and said, "What's wrong? Doug, have you two been in a fight about something?"

"It's not that. He just got a call from the Chief. They've found Fred's body. He was shot."

Maria stepped up to Tom, open arms, hugging him for a long time. She knew how much Fred meant to him.

Both Maria and Doug jumped in with questions. Tom said, "Hold on! I don't have any details. The Chief wants us to meet him at Eleanor's."

Doug asked, "Me, too?"

"Let's all go. The kids may need some help."

## 48

The chief had just arrived as they drove up to Fred and Eleanor's house. He walked over to them. "I didn't call Eleanor, so I think I better go in first. When I say, 'Eleanor, I have some bad news', come on in. No, maybe that's not right. Let's just all go in."

Eleanor was in the living room, saw the chief, and ran right to the front door. "Jim, do you have something. Come on in. Oh...Maria, oh...what are all the rest of you doing here?"

The Chief, Jim, said, "Please sit down, Eleanor."

Eleanor sat and burst into tears. "Just tell me, what have you found out?"

"We've found Fred. He has been murdered."

"Oh, noooo..." Eleanor slumped and would have fallen, but Tom and Maria caught her. Tom and Maria were there on each side. Eleanor held onto Maria and burst into tears. Her sobs finally subsided. Tom and Maria walked Eleanor over to the dining room table and the others gathered around. Maria got her a glass of water.

When he could see she was settling down a little, Jim added, "There are some other things we need to talk about."

"All right, Jim. What else should I know? Fred's gone. Why didn't I

insist he keep the protection? Oh God, I have to tell the children."
She teared up again.

"Not just yet. Where are they?"

"Emily is upstairs in her room and Fred, Jr. is out with a friend."

Just then, Emily came down the stairs. "Mom, what are all these
people doing here? Are you crying?"

"I'm ok, Emily, sweetie, just some more questions the Chief has
for me. I'll tell you all about it later."

"Can I have a snack?"

"Sure, you can. Get a glass of milk and some of your favorite
Dutch Mill cookies from the cookie jar. Put some peanut butter on
them. I'll come up and we'll have a little talk later."

"Ok, Mother." She went back upstairs with her snack.

They watched her go back upstairs and close her bedroom door.
Eleanor turned to Jim. "So what else do I need to know?"

Jim told her where and how they found him. "We don't have any
idea who did this or why yet. We have a suspect. Have you seen this
police sketch? Do you know anyone who looks like this?"

Eleanor studied the sketch. "No, I've never seen anyone who looks
like this. I don't know him. How do you know about him and why is
he a suspect?"

Jim told her about all the people who saw the man or had contact
with him in some way. Fred described him after the early encounter
and told me he didn't know the man. There was the custodian at City
Hall who saw the abduction, Tom and Maria who spoke with him on
the Clipper, Bob and Sara saw him on the Clipper and so had Joan at
the Doo Drop where Fred and Tom would often have lunch. "The
waitress Joan saw someone who looked like this sketch in the booth
behind them."

Maria came back in with coffees. Eleanor teared up again and
Tom asked her if she wanted something stronger in her coffee.

Eleanor said, "No, I need my wits about me. Jim, that sounds like
your man. Will you be able to find him?"

"We will in time. The cabin is near state property so that's no help
except that the state police may get involved. They will be a big help.

We have no idea where he is. I'm thinking he is holed up somewhere here in town. If he is, he has to come out sometime and we are on the alert."

Jim continued, "We'll find him, Eleanor, and we'll get some answers. One more thing. We need to keep Fred's body for a little while yet. But you'll need to start thinking about funeral arrangements. I'll let you know when we can release his body to you."

At this, Eleanor broke down again, sobbing on Maria's shoulder.

When she was back in control, Jim added, "I need to get going. There's a lot to do. Can the rest of you stick around for a while?"

Tom walked out with Jim. "Tomorrow is Labor Day. I'll go to City Hall Tuesday morning and talk to some people. I'd like to stop in afterward and compare notes."

"I guess I won't be able to talk you out of that. I haven't figured how to make you official yet and I'll probably catch it from the city commission for letting you do this. I'll just say use that sensitivity of yours and those clue-sniffing skills you have. Watch for signs but be careful. I'll get hold of the Muskegon Chronicle. There will likely be a small story in tomorrow's holiday issue and the full story in Tuesday's edition."

By the time Tom got back in, Emily was told. Maria was with Emily as Eleanor finished a call to her parents. They were on their way. Fred's parents were notified and were driving over from the east side of the state.

Tom offered to go and get Fred Jr. But Eleanor told him it would be better to let him come home when he was supposed to. She said, "My parents will be here any time and can help."

Eleanor said, "We'll be alright until they get here. Thank you, Maria."

Tom, Maria, and Doug left and decided to grab a bite at Tony's restaurant. They were having a hard time enjoying their drinks and appetizers, but knew they had to eat. Tom said, "I spoke to the Chief before he left. I'm going to City Hall Tuesday morning and talk to him."

Maria said, "Oh, Tom, please don't get any more involved. No one knows just who is a part of this. If you start pushing Fred's ideas or looking for his killer, you might be next."

"That won't happen. I'll be careful about who I talk to. I just want to find out what is going on at City Hall that would be enough to make a motive for killing Fred."

"Doug and I will be at school. Our prep for the fall semester starts day after tomorrow. We'll be in session Thursday.

"What are you doing for Labor Day, Doug? Tom and I are just going to grill steaks at his place. Would you like to come over?"

"Nope, I'm taking a little trip to Lansing to see mom and dad. My sister and her husband are coming with their brood, so we'll have a fun day. Thanks for the invite though."

Their dinner came. Everything seemed tasteless as they were all grieving. They drove back to Tom's and Doug went on home.

# 49

Harry spent an uneasy Labor Day in his house on Estes Street as he planned what he would do. He was concerned about being out in the town. But then, there were only five people, besides Joe, who knew what he looked like — Fred, who was dead, the couple on the back of the boat, and the boy and girl from below deck. Nobody knew the Mayor was dead or that he was connected to the Mayor so he decided it would be ok to get out a little. They would likely all be busy with the holiday, cookouts, and all. He needed some groceries and should pick up his pictures from the boat. He decided he could take a chance, go down into the Lakeside business district, and pick up groceries and the pictures. There would be a lot of touristy types in the area for the holiday so he thought he would be safe.

He stuck his gun in his back under his shirt and left the house about 3:00 p.m. He drove down Bourdon St. to Lakeshore Drive, went left past the 'Our' theatre and the drugstore on the corner. Next block on, he took a left and pulled into the parking lot at the back of Etterman's Food Market. He walked back to the drugstore to pick up his pictures and a Muskegon Chronicle. When he saw the headline about the Mayor's body being found, he thought, *Uh Oh,* but just said to the clerk, "This is terrible."

She answered, "Yes, it is. What's the matter with our town?"

He stood outside to take a quick look at the pictures. But it was hot, in the mid-80s. He saw that the Lakeshore Tavern two doors to his right was open. *Why not,* he thought. That would be a great cool place to spend an hour or so and have a beer. It would be too dark to read the article about the Mayor or study the pictures. That would have to wait till he got back to the house. He sat in the back of the bar near the back entrance but faced front. He could watch who came and went. He had a couple of beers and the bar made a great hamburger. He paid his bill, put the pictures in his pocket, and went out into the heat. He turned left and started down to Etterman's.

Three doors away, the 'Our' theatre doors opened, and the matinee crowd poured out. Tom and Maria were in the back of the crowd, having sat about ten rows from the front. Tom said, "After the air conditioning in the theatre, this is like walking into a steam bath."

"Let's get back to the house. We can sit out on the back porch where it's cooler and enjoy something cold while the coals are getting ready."

"That sounds great. Now where did I park the car?"

"Tom, did you forget again? We're up the hill. If we hang a left just before Etterman's we'll find it about a block up on Moon."

Tom just grinned. "I know. I didn't forget."

"So which way are we parked, smarty?"

"We're headed down the hill. See I did know. Gotcha..."

"Tom, look up ahead. Look at that big man walking toward Etterman's. Does he look familiar to you?"

"We can't see his face. Let's get closer. Hurry."

"Tom, be careful. Look, he turned in to Etterman's. It sure looks like him."

"Let's turn left at the corner by the drug store and check Etterman's parking lot. Look, there it is. It's the grey Buick."

He turned to her. "Maria, there's a phone booth in the drugstore. Call the police and tell them we think he is in Etterman's. Tell them about the grey car. Here are my car keys. Get the car and park downhill on the street across from Etterman's parking lot. Stay low in the passenger seat. He'll come out the back door and I don't want him to see you. When I come out, I'll try to check out his car. Then I'll come to our car and when we see which way he goes, we'll follow him."

"What will you do now?"

"I'm going into Etterman's and see if I can get a better look, make sure it's him."

"Tom, I'm scared. Don't let him see you. He might be the killer."

"I know, but I'll be careful. He won't see me. Just get the police on the way."

Tom walked to the front entrance of the market, took a deep breath, and went in. He grabbed a bag of charcoal from the stack near the entrance. This was where he shopped all the time, so he heard, "Tom, how have you been. How were those steaks you got the other day?"

"Hello, Phil. Don't know yet. Maria and I took in a matinee at the 'Our' and I need to get this charcoal. The steaks are for supper tonight."

"Where is that sweetheart of yours?"

"She's in the car. If you'll check me out, I'll head out through the back, it will be quicker."

As Tom walked through the store toward the back, he looked for the big man. He didn't spot him until he turned the corner to the meat section. The big man was at the meat counter and turned in answer to the butcher's "Can I help you, sir?" It was him all right. Tom backed away into the aisle, went on to the back door and left. Tom saw Maria pull up and park across the street. Tom again saw the gray car, the only gray one in the lot, and walked over to check it out.

He stopped at the back of the car and wrote the license plate number on the charcoal bag. He walked up to the front of the car to see if he could find out anything else that might identify him.

Maria called out, "Tom, get over here. He'll catch you."

"Maria, start the car and get down. I'll be there in a minute."

Harry walked out the back door and casually looked around. He had seen the man who had watched him inside. Now that man was over near his car. Harry set his groceries down by the door and circled around to come up behind him.

Tom was peering into the driver's side window of the gray car when he heard a warning cry from Maria. Someone pushed his head into the top edge of the car. Nose bleeding, Tom slipped sideways, and hit the big guy in the groin with the bag of charcoal. When he doubled over, Tom took off on a run to the car. He jumped in the driver's seat and said, "Hang on, Maria."

Next thing they knew, a bullet hit the side view mirror, splintering it. Tom took off, squealing the tires. They didn't hear any more shots, but they kept moving as fast as it was safe with all the traffic.

Tom turned onto Lakeshore Drive, drove up to the next cross street, did a couple of right turns, and parked so he could watch Etterman's parking lot from up the hill.

Tom asked Maria, "Are the police on the way?"

"They said they would have a car here in about ten minutes. There! Now I can hear the sirens. But what do we do if the man comes after...Oh...there he is coming out of the lot. He's turning downhill toward Lake Shore Drive."

"Good. He must have heard the sirens too. We'll see which way he turns on Lakeshore and we'll follow him but keep our distance."

HARRY WALKED BACK to get his groceries. The man at the car was that Tom guy. He was sure of it. He got into his car and took a left out of the parking lot. When he got to Lakeshore Drive, he turned right.

Maria and Tom waited a couple of minutes and then followed. As they turned right, they heard the sirens getting louder. The man must have too, since he made a quick right onto Bourdon St. and disappeared.

"There. The police are just rounding the curve. I'll pull over close to Bourdon and wait for them."

As the police approached, Maria and Tom got out of the car and hailed them down.

Tom told the officers that the man just turned up Bourdon about a minute ago. "This is Maria. She's the one who called you. I went into Ettermans and saw him. It's the man from the boat."

"The Chief is on the way as well. Why don't you wait here for the Chief and we'll try to find our suspect? We have other cars coming down McCracken as well as waiting up on Glenside and Sherman."

Harry heard the sirens go silent. He was up on Fair St. by then. He turned left, went a half block, and turned right onto Estes. His house was halfway down the block, so he was in his attached garage and had closed the door before the police were anywhere near. He went through the breezeway, bringing his groceries, paper, and the pictures into the house. He didn't turn on any lights. He would have to hunker down until the police left the area.

When the Chief saw Tom and Maria, he pulled over. "You two did well. I'm glad you called us."

Tom said, "He took a shot at the car, smashed the mirror."

"That was close. We'll have to keep a closer eye on you two. It's a good thing you stopped at Bourdon. Let us handle it from here. If we can't catch him in the car, it will be because he lives in this area. It will be a matter of a house-to-house search. Unfortunately, without a warrant, we can't do that."

"Can't you get the warrant?"

"I'll get to a judge tomorrow. In the meantime, you two get back home and try to enjoy the rest of your holiday. I'll let you know what happens."

The Chief kept cars at the exit points from the neighborhood and sent two other cars plus his own cruising the neighborhood until they covered every street two or three times. Nothing was found. No sign of the gray car in a driveway, nothing.

Harry finally put his groceries away and sat down in his kitchen to look at the pictures. The pictures gave him a fairly good idea of what the kids looked like. Put it together with the information Jerry gave him about the car's owner, he felt he could find them all. After what happened today, he figured he also had to do something about Tom and his lady friend.

He turned to his paper. There it was, front page large headline, "Mayor's body found." Under the headline, "Body was buried near an abandoned cabin behind the Blockhouse." The article told the story about how two young boys discovered the burial site. The police were contacted, the body exhumed, and identified as that of Fred Thomas, Muskegon's mayor. Harry read the rest of the article that ended with the words, "The police have no suspects at the present time. An investigation is under way."

Harry no longer believed that they had no suspects. It seemed from the police presence here in Lakeside that somehow they were on to him. He was quite sure the man watching him in Etterman's or the woman with him was responsible for the police being here. He would need to get Jerry involved again. He would call him tomorrow and call Joe Antonelli as well. He was going to need some help from both of them to find all the witnesses. He needed a different car so he could move about more freely. He had to find a different place to live soon, just something temporary.

## 50

T he next morning Tom and Maria met for breakfast at the Cherokee. Maria was to start the fall term at school and Tom was going to City Hall to ask some questions. They finished their breakfast and were lingering over coffee. Maria said, "Tom, there's something we should talk about."

"And what is that, sweetheart?"

"I think we should move in together."

"I'm all for that. What will our parents say?"

"If they object, we could move our marriage up. We completed the church's pre-marriage sessions. There's no reason why we couldn't get married next week if we wanted to. And with only one of us working, we could save a lot of money with just one place."

"It sounds like you have this all figured out."

"It just makes good sense. We'll talk it through at dinner tonight, your place. I'll bring dinner. We'll figure out how and when to tell the folks. Right now, I need to get to school."

Tom walked Maria to her car, kissed her, and watched her drive off toward school.

When he got to City Hall, he started with the city manager, Sam Milford.

"Thanks for seeing me on such short notice, Sam. I just have a few questions. The chief has authorized me to do this. We're hoping that we might find some reason for why this has happened. Can you share with me if there is anything here at City Hall that might bear on Fred's murder?"

Tom noticed a change in Sam's demeanor. He appeared more wary of what was next.

Sam asked, "Why do you think it has to be something here?"

"We're looking at everything, that's all. What was Fred working on?"

"I don't believe there is anything that could trigger a murder. Let me call in my assistant, Jerry. He may have some thoughts." Sam asked his secretary to send Jerry in.

"Jerry, Tom O'Banion. Tom, Jerry Saunders. Tom is here with the Chief of Police's blessing. He has some questions — the first is if there is anything at City Hall that would cause someone to want to kill Fred." As Sam talked and the other two were shaking hands, Sam shook his head slightly at Jerry.

Jerry said, "I don't know of anything. What do you have in mind?"

Tom said, "Anything that might be a threat to someone in the community."

"Nothing." They said it almost in unison.

Tom looked at them in surprise. "You seem awfully certain."

"Well, when you've been around as long as we have, you'd know that it was pretty much business as usual around here."

"There wasn't some controversy about some new developments on the lakeshore?"

"Nothing out of the ordinary," Sam said decisively. Jerry looked a little uncomfortable, wouldn't meet Tom's eyes.

"Thank you both for your time. I'm going to move on to some other people. If you think of anything, please let the Chief know."

Tom walked away thinking, *I caught Sam's head shake. They know something, but neither will open up. I think I'll go see Alice and ask what she knows. She might have some idea.*

Alice said, "Hello, Tom. It's so good to see you. Are you alright? I know you and Fred were close."

"Yes, we were. And I can't let it drop so the Chief has agreed to let me talk to people. I just want to ask questions and see what comes up. Maybe it'll make some sense then."

"What do you want to ask me?"

"Do you know of anything Fred was working on for the city that would stir things up like this?

"No, Tom. Most things that he had on his plate were quite routine."

"Think hard. Is there anything that might have an impact on the town?"

Alice said, "I wonder if it could be the electronics company. I typed up a contract between the city and some company. I don't remember the name, but I could find a copy. I don't think it was ever signed."

"Would you get it, please?"

Alice quickly found the file and gave it to Tom. Tom scanned the documents. "It looks like the company planned to locate here. Fred told me about this a little while ago. Do you have a phone number for this Mr. Jones? I need to talk with him."

Alice got him the phone number. Tom added, "This is good, Alice. I'll call him."

"The last word was that the company changed their mind. Fred never said why that was, but the Chief knew about the change."

"Ok, Alice. You just lay low. By the way, who is interim mayor?"

"The city commission is meeting this afternoon to appoint someone. It will probably be the vice-mayor. If you call me back, I'll let you know."

"I'll be in touch. In the meantime, you take care. Be careful who you talk to."

Tom headed for the main doors. He was focused on his mission and so didn't notice that Sam and Jerry watched him as he walked out.

Sam said, "He isn't going to stop looking."

"I know, but we don't have anything to worry about. Our disagreement with Fred isn't known to anyone else here."

"You're right. Just the same, we better keep quiet at the city commission meeting this afternoon. The meeting is at two. I'm having lunch out today. I'll see you later."

Jerry went back to his office and called Harry. "That guy you were asking about was just here. He was asking all kinds of questions about things that might have caused someone to kill Fred. His name is Tom O'Banion."

"Do you know what he does and where he lives?"

"No, but I can find out. Let me talk to Fred's secretary. I bet she'll know."

Jerry hung up and walked over to Fred's office.

"Morning, Alice."

"Oh, hi, Jerry."

"You were pretty close to Fred. How are you holding up?"

"It has not been easy. I just wonder how Eleanor is."

"Alice, do you know much about Tom O'Banion? He's been asking a lot of questions."

"I've known Tom for a long time. He and Fred were good friends."

"Do you know what he does?"

"Yes, he is, or was, I should say, a teacher at Muskegon Sr. High."

"What do you mean, *was*?"

"He just went through a trial. He was found not guilty but still lost his job because of it. Fred was pretty upset about that. He knew Tom well and knew he couldn't have done what he was accused of. It was quite a relief when the charges against Tom were dismissed. Fred planned to work on the Board of Education to try and get him reinstated."

"What is he doing now?"

"He is working with the police to help find Fred's killer. He's trying to figure out the motive behind it. He lost a good friend. And, oh yes, he is going to be married later this year to the drama teacher and play director."

"This thing has impacted a lot of people. It's not good. Well, I'm going back to my office. I brought a lunch today so I'm going to work through the lunch hour. See you later, Alice. You take care now."

When Jerry got back to his office, he looked for Tom O'Banion in the phone book. There he was, out in the beach area. He took down the address and phone number. He called Harry and relayed all the information. He hoped that he wasn't getting Tom into trouble.

---

## 51

Harry called Joe Antonelli. "Joe, there are some new developments that may cause problems for all of us."

"What developments?"

"The man from the boat is asking some pointed questions about why Fred was killed. If he keeps pushing, he may make the connections. He has lost his job and seems to be going after this full time. He told my contact at City Hall that he was there with the blessings of the Chief of police and is trying to figure out what might be the motive for the Mayor's death."

"Do you know who he is? You're right. He could be a troublemaker."

"I think I should check him out. He's a loose end that might unravel the whole thing. I've warned him but I don't think he'll stop."

"I don't know, Harry. It's a stretch about making the connection. I don't see how he could do it."

"I don't know about that. He had a hand in the Lakeside dustup that almost caused me to get caught this weekend. Somehow, they now know what kind of car I drive, what I look like. Even now there's been a picture in the paper. I warned him, banged his head on my car, and even got a shot off at their car."

"I saw the picture. It's just a police sketch."

"You're right, but the sketch is pretty good. I'm sure much of the input to that sketch came from O' Banion and that woman of his. I ran into both of them on the Clipper. Also ran into a boy and girl on the boat that might have seen me enough to add to the sketch. There are just a bunch of loose ends that need clearing up."

"Maybe you should just get out of town now."

"I don't think that will work. I need to get rid of some people who could finger me...and maybe connect the dots to you and your eight buddies."

"Is that a threat, Harry?"

"No, no threat, at least not yet. You should tell the boys that I'm not going down alone on this. I just need some help to put this to rest. I also need that bonus so that when I do take care of things, I can split and be alright financially. I'll need a different car as well."

"You'll hear from us. I'll get with the group this afternoon. Just sit tight."

Joe called the group together. They met in their usual spot at the Century Club. The club manager said, "This isn't your regular day or time, Mr. Antonelli. Would you like some snacks and drinks?" Joe told her that would be great, and he would call down with the order after everyone was there.

When everyone got there, Joe called in their drink and snacks orders. He was told that the snacks would be up in about 15 minutes. Joe told them all that there were some new developments. He put someone on watch at the door to watch for the room service waiter. While they waited, he told them all that Harry said and told them, "Just talk about other things until the drinks come and we'll figure out what to do."

When the drinks came, Joe met the room service waiter at the door, gave him a big tip and said, "Just leave the cart at the door. I'll take it from here."

After everyone got their drinks, Tim said, "Alright, Joe. How about some more details on this situation that is so urgent that we had to have a special meeting?"

"It turns out the police are hot after Harry now. They don't know his name, but they have a police sketch that is pretty accurate. He was spotted by a man who saw him on the Clipper, the same man who has asked a lot of questions of people at City Hall about possible motives for the Mayor's death. His name is Tom O' Banion. You'll know him from this summer's farce of a trial. Harry says he knows too much and apparently has some influence with the police. In Harry's judgement, he needs to be dealt with. I wouldn't mind seeing him taken down a peg or two after what he did to my daughter on the stand."

"How does Harry propose to 'take care of him'?"

"Harry says he wants to scare him off with threats first. If that doesn't work, there may have to be more drastic measures."

Tim piped up, "It seems that Harry has gotten himself in some hot water. He seems to have lost control of the situation. We should just dump him."

Joe answered, "Yes, we should, but we are being threatened. Harry told me to pass on to all of you that he was not going down alone on this. He needs, he says, more money. He has to have another car since the police know his now, and he needs expenses until we pay him the bonus we promised him."

"That sounds like blackmail to me."

"I know that. But I don't think we have a choice. If our connection to him is exposed, we might be through in this town or even prosecuted for crimes that have been committed in our name. We need to expedite this."

Their leader, George, said, "Maybe we should get someone else to take him out."

Tim appeared panicky, "I don't think we should make that decision lightly. We don't want to dig the hole deeper."

Joe said, "You're right. But if he continues to get hemmed in, he may get desperate and panic. That could hurt us. And yes, I brought

Harry in to do the job you wanted done. Don't forget that – we all wanted the mayor neutralized. I didn't think Harry would kill him."

Everyone had an idea, but no one wanted to make the commitment.

George said, "Let's get him his bonus money and find him a different car. Get it licensed so we'll have a way to trace him. Take his $50,000 bonus out of the slush fund for the project plus another $10,000 for the car. That should be enough to shut him up for now. If he doesn't get out of town with that, we'll start looking for someone to take him out."

Since George was their leader and one with a lot to lose, they tended to listen to him. Everyone was uneasy about it, but they knew it had to be done.

Wendell suggested, "I think we should also try to figure out a way to point a finger toward the unions. They have a stake in this too and I'd be willing to bet they have been putting on some pressure as well."

"Good idea. How can we do that?"

"I don't know but if we can find a way, it will confuse the investigators."

George said, "Alright. We'll meet again on Saturday morning. Everybody comes with some ideas about how to turn this on to the unions."

Joe said, "I'll call Harry and tell him about the money and the car"

"Ok, Joe, remember, but only your name associated with the car in any way."

WHEN JOE GOT BACK to the office in his restaurant, he called Harry and told him of their decision.

"Just sit tight, Harry. I'll get you a car in a couple of days and have the bonus money for you. All you'll have to do is sign the papers and mail them off. No one but me knows your full name, so by the time anyone can make the connection, you'll be long gone.

Once you get it, you'll have to get things done fast and get out of town."

"How about the $50 g's?"

"It will be in a case in the trunk. We don't want to hear from you anymore. Call me Friday morning at nine and we'll get it done."

## 52

Tom got back to his house a little after noon. He ate a ham sandwich and a beer for lunch and thought about what Maria said this morning. He told her it was a good idea but now he wondered. If they moved in together before they were married, they would be frowned on around in this town. It would be better if they moved the wedding up a bit. He would talk to her about it tonight.

He pulled out the paper with the phone number on it. The area code suggested the company was in the southeast corner of the state. When he called, the lady said, "Jones Electronics."

Tom said, "My name is Tom O'Banion. I need to speak to Mr. Jones please. It is urgent."

"What is this in reference to? What do you mean, urgent? Does he know you?"

"No, but I am a friend of Mayor Fred Thomas of Muskegon. Or, I was, I should say. Fred was murdered and Mr. Jones might be able to help us with the investigation. He and the Mayor had negotiated a new plant in the Muskegon area."

"Are you with the police?

"No but I'm involved in the investigation. You can call Chief Jim Johnson if you need to verify. Please, I need to get some answers."

She transferred Tom to Mr. Jones' secretary where he repeated his story. She said, "Hold on, I'll see if he's available." She buzzed Mr. Jones and asked if he wanted to talk to Tom. He said, "It's ok. Put him through."

Mr. Jones picked up and said, "Mr. O'Banion. How can I help you?"

"It's Tom, please. I'm sorry I have to tell you that Fred Thomas, Muskegon's Mayor, has been murdered. We have a line on who did it but we don't know what the motive was, and if he was working alone or had bosses, and if so, who they are."

"I'm sorry to hear about Fred. But I don't see how I can help you. Our business together has been put on hold. Fred was down here last fall. We had some good discussions and came to a tentative agreement."

"I know. Fred was excited about your commitment to Muskegon. What changed, Mr. Jones?"

"I'm not sure I should share that with you, Tom. I don't know you."

"Please call the chief, he will vouch for me." Tom gave him phone number to the Chief's direct line.

"Hold on, Tom. Miss Smith, would you call this number for me?"

The Chief verified that Tom was on the case as a consultant with the department. Mr. Jones came back to Tom. "Tom, the Chief said we could talk. So here it is. Fred and I did have an agreement. We were supposed to have lunch and go to the City Commission meeting later in the afternoon. What changed? Two days before I was to go, I had a phone call from one of our board members. He was contacted by someone who said he was an attorney in Muskegon, a Mr. Andersen. Andersen told him that we should think twice about coming to Muskegon and that neither the unions nor the city fathers wanted us up there. He finished with, "You tell your Mr. Jones that his company would not be welcome here."

"Do you have a first name for Mr. Andersen?"

"No, I asked him. He was told that his first name wasn't important, just the message. I convened a board meeting. Come to think of it, we never did figure out how he got the name and number of the board member he called. We also don't know whether he is an attorney or not. We should have checked that out. Anyway, the board suggested that we stop the process until we can get more information. We are still extremely interested in building a new plant in Muskegon. But we want to get these issues resolved first. I called Fred and told him there was a delay. Fred asked if we could meet in Lansing after Labor Day to talk. I agreed to meet him. I wanted to tell Fred face to face what happened. I thought I owed him that much. Now we are back to square one. Do they know who is going to take Fred's place?"

"No, Mr. Jones. Not yet. I've talked to some of the people at City Hall. It's pretty unsettled and will take a while to get back to business. In the meantime, I need to get to the Chief with this information. We need to get a handle on this quickly."

"This sounds pretty important to you."

"Fred was my friend, almost like the older brother I never had. I won't let it go."

"I'm sorry about your friend. Keep me posted please."

Tom hung up and called the Chief. After he heard the gist of the phone call to Mr. Jones, Jim said, "I have a task force set up to move the investigation forward. I've been in touch with the State Police and they will send an investigator to be a part of the team, as well as a forensic person."

"Will I still be able to be a part of the investigation?"

"I'd like you to stay on. You have a skill that uncovers little bits of information and you put together theories about them. I think that skill could be useful as we get started. We have our first meeting at 9:30 a.m. tomorrow. Can you be here?"

"Thank you, Jim. I'll be there."

After he hung up, Tom thought about the past few days, what he learned, what was fact, and what was just conjecture. He decided to make a pseudo Ben Franklin analysis, not a positive or negative, but two lists. One was a list of known facts followed by questions and conclusions, what were the questions, what meaning did the facts have. The second list was the conjectures. If those were true, then what questions and conclusions are suggested. It might not be in final form, but it might lead him to the right conclusions.

The first list looked like:

- Fred was killed by person unknown, two gunshots, one to the head, and one in the heart.
- They had a suspect in the big man they had seen, twice now, on the boat and in Lakeside. But was he alone in this? If not, who did he work for? More likely the latter was the case since he wasn't known around town. If so, then the question became "why?"
- But it's one thing to find the man who pulled the trigger. It is more important to find the man or men who paid for the bullets. So again, who was he working for?
- The only thing they had on the suspect was a police sketch, pretty accurate. And that he drove a gray Buick and that he likely lived in Lakeside.
- After Maria and Tom found him at Etterman's, the police lost him in the warren of side streets of Lakeside. He was in hiding there now somewhere. Police were on the alert for the gray car.
- One possibility that might provide a motive was Jones Electronics. Mr. Jones was warned off by a supposed attorney, a Mr. Andersen, in Muskegon.
- The agreement between the city and Mr. Jones was real. Tom saw it, heard Fred talk about it, and Mr. Jones verified continued interest as soon as they could get some questions answered. Who is this "Mr. Andersen" who squashed the deal? Was he connected to the murder?
- Fred had been told by the consultant that there was a "group of nine" people in Muskegon who called the shots about business in Muskegon. He didn't know their identities.

Not many facts to go on.

The second list of conjectures included the following:

- Fred didn't know the identities of the "group of nine" but he had strong suspicions.
- The two possible groups were city businessmen who were planning something big in the city and didn't want anything in that didn't fit into their plans or the union leaders in the area who liked to keep things under their control.
- The businessmen seemed more likely, but how do we find out who they are?
- Their suspect was working for a local person or group. The big guy wasn't local, so it was likely that someone local hired him.
- The city manager and his assistant knew more than they were letting on. Tom saw this when he talked to the both of them.
- They could be connected to either of the two groups.

Tom was still at it when Maria drove in. After a hug and kiss, Maria told Tom, "I called Mom to tell her we wanted to talk to them. She said to come on over for dinner. Is that ok with you?"

"Of course, it is. That will be great. We can talk over dinner. When do we need to be there?"

"She said it would be ready about six. We need to talk before we go. I'd like a beer. How about you?"

Tom headed for his kitchen and brought back two cold brews. They sat on his front porch swing. "I've been thinking. We should move the wedding date up. What do you think?"

"I agree, Tom. We just have to do the final session of our Pre-Marriage counseling with Father Flannery. There is no reason we can't move it up."

"We should get going then. We'll need to get home fairly early. I have to be at the police station by 9:30 tomorrow morning."

On the way over, Tom told Maria about the new task force Jim had formed. And that Jim asked the State Police to send an investigator to help and that Jim wanted him to stay in to help with the analysis and to continue to interview people.

Maria reacted, "Tom, I wish you wouldn't get more involved. I'm so afraid you are going to get hurt somehow. Please don't do this."

"I know you're frightened. It will be ok. I can help but stay out of the line of fire."

"But we've already been shot at when we found him at Etterman's."

"I remember, but I have to do this." He told Maria about the phone interview with Mr. Jones of the electronics company how they were told to stay clear of Muskegon.

They arrived at her parents' home on time. It was out in the area across the float bridge on the south side of town. The Vitale family moved here from Grand Rapids a year or so after Maria got the job at Muskegon High School.

When they entered the house, the smells of meat loaf, scalloped potatoes, and green beans greeted them. Hardly a typical Italian dinner, but it was a favorite of the Vitale family. The Vitale crew, Poppa, Momma, Maria, and Tom finished dinner while they chatted about the investigation, at least as much as Tom could tell them. They adjourned to the living room to have coffee and a scoop of Spumoni splashed with Amaretto for dessert.

Maria's dad asked, "Well, what is it you want to share with us?"

"Right to the point, Dad? Here it is. We want to move the wedding up to quite soon. It makes good sense financially for us to be together now till Tom's job situation is resolved."

Her mom giggled and said, "It worked."

"What worked?"

"Do you remember what I said to you a week ago, that it would be so much easier for you both to deal with if you were already married?"

"I do remember but I don't think I showed how surprised I was that you said it. Do you think it can be done?"

"Sure, it can. Father Flannery is all ready for you to come and finish up. We'll finalize the arrangements and it will happen as quickly as you want it to."

Maria was excited. "This weekend or maybe the next?"

They all laughed. "Yes, I think next weekend would work."

"Can we just make it a private ceremony at the Parish house?"

"I'll ask Father Flannery tomorrow. Tom, what more can you tell us about how the investigation is going?"

Tom repeated all that he had told Maria and added only that the police couldn't find the man yet. He took a copy of the sketch out of his pocket. Neither of the Vitales recognized him.

Tom and Maria said their goodbyes and left. Tom said, "I'll take you home. I'll call my parents when I get home and let them know about these changes. We'll get together with them over the weekend."

## 53

The next morning Maria and Tom had an early breakfast at his place since there was so much planning to do and not a lot of time to get it done. They decided they would live in Tom's house when they moved in together. Maria's place was a furnished apartment and not nearly big enough for two.

"I like this, Tom, the two of us at our kitchen table while we talk over a last cup of coffee before we leave for work. The only thing that's not right about it is that we won't both be there."

"We'll get that worked out in time, ma Cherie. Another week and we'll be married. Doesn't that sound great? And later, maybe over Christmas we'll take a little honeymoon trip somewhere. Let's each write down our number one and number two choices for where we want to honeymoon. We'll compare notes and make a decision."

"That will be fun. I have some places in mind already. We'd better get going now."

"I can drop you off if you want. The task force meeting doesn't start till 9:30. I'll just get there a little early and have a chat with the Chief."

"I think I'd rather drive. You may get involved and not be able to pick me up after school. I should be home by 4:00 p.m. or so. I'll wait here for you. I love you. Be careful, Tom, please."

"I love you. I'll be fine. See you after school."

A kiss goodbye and Tom watched her drive off. Just as he finished cleaning up the breakfast dishes, his phone rang. "Tom O'Banion?"

"Yes, this is he?"

"This is your first warning. Back off from the Mayor's murder investigation and other business that doesn't concern you. You keep it up and you'll end up like him. You get the message?"

"Who is this? I hear you. You won't get away with this. The police almost got you the other day down in Lakeside."

"They weren't even close. You just remember what I said." He hung the phone up quietly, which was more ominous than if he had slammed it.

Tom sat for a few minutes and thought about what the man said. He should get down to police headquarters and fill Jim in on this call and the notes he made yesterday. He gathered them up and drove off.

Tom got to police headquarters about 8:30 a.m. He asked Jim's secretary if he could see Jim for a few minutes before the meeting started.

Jim looked up with surprise. "You're really early for our meeting."

"I got a phone call this morning just before I left. I'm pretty sure it was the killer. He told me that if I kept working on the Mayor's murder and his agenda, I would end up like the Mayor. If he knows my phone number, he probably knows where I live. Jim, Maria is moving in with me. We've changed the wedding date to next Saturday. What do I do?"

"Let me think about this for a minute. Does Maria have a place of her own?"

"She does, but it's too small for us in the long haul. We're doing this because we need to watch expenses until I find a job. And we just want to be married."

"Is there any reason to think the killer might know who Maria is?"

"I don't know. I don't see how. He saw us together on the Clipper. He must have gotten my name and number from someone at City

Hall, but there is no way he could get hers. But that's the only place I have spent a lot of time talking about this. You don't suppose that there is someone in City Hall who leaks information?"

"That's a possibility. I've thought about that. I wouldn't be surprised that some information about Fred's activities has gotten out. There would have to be someone at City Hall who is involved or maybe on the take from some group outside. Who knows? Could be Fred's group of nine? I wonder if Fred had any suspicions about all this."

"He did say something to me when we met back in December. He said he hired a consultant to find out what makes it so hard to bring about progress in this town. Let me see if I can remember right. The consultant told him there are interlocking boards of all the major industries here. Nothing could be changed until that cabal was broken. And then, an exact quote: 'There needs to be nine expensive funerals in this town before you can get anything done.' I asked him if the unions were involved. Fred told me he thought they would come around even though they oppose it now."

"Ok, Tom. You'll have to tell this again in the meeting this morning. I would suggest you and Maria move into her place until we catch this guy."

"Ok, I need to call Maria at school and make sure she goes to her place after school."

"My secretary, Gerri, will get you a temp desk with a phone you can use."

Tom made his phone call to the school office and said he would wait for Maria. It was important that they talk now. They didn't want to get Maria out of class. Tom asked to speak to Darlene, the principal's secretary. "Darlene, it is critical that I talk now to Maria. It's possible she is in danger."

"What do you mean, in danger?"

"I don't have time to explain. The Chief of Police is right here. Do you want me to put him on the line?"

"No, I'll get her right away."

Maria was on the phone in two minutes. "Tom, what's going on?"

"Listen carefully, sweetheart. After you left today, I had a phone call from the killer. He threatened me with Fred's fate if I didn't stop doing what I'm doing. When I got to police headquarters, I talked with Jim about it. He thinks we would be better off to move into your place and he will have a car outside until the man is caught. Would you do this for me, please? When you leave school today, go straight to your parents' house. When I get free from what's going on here, I'll come there, and we'll go together to your apartment."

"Ok, Tom. But are you even sure that we'll be safe at my place?"

"After our meeting, Jim and I will talk some more. I'll pick you up and we'll figure it out. I love you."

"I love you. You be careful."

"Always." Tom hung up, got some more coffee, and went to the conference room. He needed to sit and think about things. He wanted to contribute to this investigation and find out who did this to Fred. He was in the room about fifteen minutes when another man came in.

"Good morning, I'm David Smithson. I'm with the State Police. Call me Dave."

They sized each other up and shook hands. "I'm Tom, Tom O'Banion. I was Fred's friend. I've been doing what I can to help and the Chief allowed that I might be a part of the team."

"He told me about you. Do you know...?"

Jim, the chief and his lead detective, Mark Bergstrom walked in. There were more introductions, and coffee and donuts for all. Jim asked David, "Did you bring your investigator?"

"He drove up separately and started working at the morgue at 8:00 a.m. He'll have his analysis done before noon and the lab will get started this afternoon when he gets back. If he should find anything in his exam, he will call here to let us know."

"Good work. There are only four of us but not much else is going on so I can spend most of my time on this case. I know your schedule, Mark. Any reason you can think of that might take your focus away?"

"Nothing. I've been working full time on it since we found Fred's body. There are some new findings I want to talk about."

"Soon, Mark. Tom, will you be able to spend all your time with us?"

"I will. You probably have heard, the school board said I could no longer teach. They offered me an admin position, but I said no, I want to teach. They paid me for the balance of my contract. I am free to work for a while. Eventually I have to start looking for another teaching job."

"We need to start with a new development. Tom got a phone call this morning from our killer. He told Tom that if he didn't stop hunting Fred's killer, that the same thing would happen to him."

"That's not good, Tom. But there is a positive side to it."

"What do you mean, Mark?"

"At least we know he is still in town. And he seems to have another agenda. Is there anyone else he might go after?"

"Yes, Tom's fiancée, Maria. She is not doing anything active on the case, but he has seen her with Tom. And there are the two kids, Bob and Sara. They saw something on the boat. Let's get this done, get everyone up-to-date so we can see where to go next. Tom, you start with what you learned from Mr. Jones first and whatever else you want to add."

Tom started off with a quick summary of his phone call to Mr. Jones. "He was shocked to hear about Fred. Says that he was to meet Fred for lunch a while back and go with him to the City Commission meeting. They were going to sell the idea to the commissioners. But a couple of days before he was to come to Muskegon, one of his board members got a phone call from someone saying he was an attorney named Andersen, but wouldn't give his first name. Mr. Jones said he was told in no uncertain terms that he should stay away from Muskegon. There were people in the town who didn't want a new company of his type there. After a consultation with his board, they put things on hold until they got more data. They're still interested but don't even know where to start now."

Tom checked his notes and went on. "I finished two lists of facts and theories late last night, but now they seem a little mixed together.

Anyway, here are copies for you all. Fred was killed by a man who we suspect is the same person seen on the Clipper, he drives a gray car, and lives somewhere in the Lakeside area. It just doesn't make sense to me that he was alone in this, but there doesn't seem to be any reason for him on his own to kill Fred. I think he was working for someone or some group in the community. And then there's what Fred told me at lunch back in December. He hired a consultant to help him get at the problems. The consultant told him that until there were nine expensive funerals nothing would happen in Muskegon. So maybe that group of nine was paying this man. Or maybe the unions have a motive in this. The Jones Electric company is non-union, but Fred told me he could probably get their agreement. And this next is just a guess. When I talked to the city manager and his assistant, they dodged a lot of my questions. It feels as though they are hiding something.

"Mark, catch us up on what you have."

Mark consulted his notes. "We found Fred's body in a shallow grave behind a shed down the hill from the Blockhouse and near Lost Lake. He was shot in the forehead and in the left side of the chest. There was a lot of blood in the tarp we found inside the shed as well as on the floor of the shed. That would seem to indicate that he was shot inside the shed. Fred's body was wrapped in another tarp that was taped tight around him. For some reason, there were two ropes tied tightly around the wrapping. There was evidence of fraying on the rope where it was hanging free. The rest of the rope looked brand new. I'm not sure yet what that means."

Mark stopped. He couldn't seem to find what he wanted to talk about next.

Finally, he went on, "We have blood matches for Fred, the tarp, and the floor. It's as though Fred was shot on the tarp and later wrapped in the second tarp. At first, we didn't spot it, but when we got the ropes into the lab, we found fragments of concrete embedded where the rope was frayed. But we didn't find any concrete anywhere else. I also found marks along the two-track that looked as though someone dragged the tarp with the body in it. It's confusing though since it looks like it was done more than once, like two or even three times.

"Let me add one more thing. After the news came out that Fred was killed, we went back out to the site. You'll remember that the Blockhouse is being reconstructed. When we went back out to transport the body, we waited until the construction crew went home for the day. That way, no one would know anything happened out there until we had a chance to process the area. We didn't even put police tape out by the road but did cordon off the area around the cabin and shed. After the word about the mayor came out, I went back out to the site and asked the workers if they could remember hearing any shots being fired in the woods behind the Blockhouse. None remembered anything but one said that with all the hammering going on, they just wouldn't have noticed."

Tom said, "Can I say something?"

"Of course, no formalities here. Just jump in."

"I have a thought about the multiple tracks. Just theories but hear me out. Let's suppose that the day he knocked Fred unconscious out back of City Hall, he took him out there and dragged him back to the shed. Once he got Fred inside, he shot him and left him till he could make other arrangements. This pretty much fits your facts. This next step is pure conjecture but stay with me, it could fit. Suppose he wanted to dump the body off the back of the Milwaukee Clipper so it would never be found."

They all chuckled. "That's pretty far-fetched. What made you think of that?"

"Well first, the concrete pieces, the frayed ropes. I'd say he had concrete blocks tied to the ropes to make sure the body sinks and the concrete blocks frayed the rope. He needed to take them off again when he put the body back into the trunk. We may find them still on the Clipper. You remember what happened on our trip on the Clipper. Maria and I were talking on the main deck when Bob and Sara came running out of the car storage area looking scared. They took one look at us and ran off toward the back of the boat. A minute or so later this large man, which by the way, we have identified as our main suspect, came up from the same area and asked us about the two kids. We looked at each other and finally said that they went the opposite direction than we saw them go."

"I remember those details, but where do we go from here?"

"It's just a supposition mind you, but here's what could have happened. Bob and Sara were downstairs making out in her parents' car. They saw him take Fred's body out of the trunk and turn toward the back of the Clipper. When they argued over leaving, he heard them, put the body back in the trunk, and took off after them. He may already have put the cement blocks back at the drop off ramp and had to leave them there to chase the kids. And remember, Maria and I saw him take off following Bob to the parking area. He could have driven back out to the shed and buried him behind it. It would fit."

"Yeah, it could, though it is a stretch. We'll see. I better get that subpoena to serve on Bob and Sara so they will have to tell us about that incident." I'll get it this afternoon and see if we can get them in here tomorrow sometime. It's Saturday and they'll be out of school. And Mark, can you check the Clipper when it gets in today from its run?"

"I'll do it. And while I'm on the Clipper, I'll talk to the crew. One of them may be able to identify the sketch as someone who was on the Clipper recently."

Dave spoke up. "Even though some of that is conjecture, it is some pretty solid reasoning, Tom. Maybe we should offer you a State police job."

"Hey, wait a minute here. We get first dibs on his services here in his hometown."

Jim's secretary knocked and came in. She said, "Mr. Smithson, there is a phone call for you. It's your forensic investigator."

Dave left to take the call. While he was gone, Tom asked Jim, "Somehow the Chronicle found out my connection to Fred and that I am working on Fred's ideas and also that I am working with the police. I've put them off, but they keep coming back. What should I do?"

"Keep putting them off until I'm ready to make the announcement about the task force. When we do that, I'll make an announcement about your role on it. You can then, if you want, tell them about your efforts to continue talking up Fred's ideas. How does that sound?"

"Thanks, Jim. That will help."

Just then Dave returned saying, "Some interesting information. The Mayor had two deep contusions in his head, consistent with blows with a blunt instrument. I think this means that the blow with his gun your witness said happened in back of City Hall didn't knock him out long enough. He had to be hit again till the killer could get him back to the shed. By itself it doesn't necessarily mean anything. It's just the picture coming together."

"And one more thing. Your medical examiner said that from the condition of the body, the Mayor has been dead for some time. It is reasonable to assume he was shot on the day he was taken, now some four plus weeks ago. My forensic man is on the way back to Lansing. He'll have his full report ready late this afternoon with all the details."

When the Chief asked, Tom said, "When I spoke to Mr. Jones, he expressed his sympathy about Fred and said they are still interested in building a plant in Muskegon. That they are still interested may be the thing that stirred all this up. I'd also like to add something else to the mix. We all know how important it is to find the man who we now think is Fred's killer. But it is equally, maybe even more, important to find the people who bought the bullets. If the group responsible isn't found out, they will just find someone else to do their dirty work. They need to be stopped now."

Jim said, "You're right, Tom. We need to factor that into our approach. If we can catch this man alive, he may be willing to swap out some information for leniency in his sentence."

Tom was now finished, so the Chief said, "Alright everyone. We all have things to do. Mark, you cover the Clipper. Dave, I'll have all the files gathered up for you to review. Tom, you take the evening to think about everything. I'll have the warrants for the home searches and the subpoena for Bob and Sara's appearance this afternoon and serve them. We'll all meet back here at 10:00 a.m. tomorrow for the interview with Bob and Sara. I'll conduct it with a court stenographer to keep the record. I'd like all of you to sit in or maybe watch from outside the room but able to hear and observe. I'll decide that when I see how Bob, Sara, and their parents react to the subpoena. In case something breaks, Dave, do you know where you are staying yet?"

"I'll be out at the Holiday Inn on Seaway Drive just as you come into town."

"Good, well, let's get on with it. Tom, we need to talk a little more."

The two of them went to Jim's office. "Tom, I will try to get you a consulting fee. But it may be hard to get approved. However good I think you are, the board may not see it that way. I know I can cover your expenses. And, by the way, I am serious about the job offer. You'd have to get some training, but that should be no problem."

"That's good about the expenses. That will help. I would do it no matter what. As to the job, I thank you for the offer, but I really would like to get back to teaching and conducting."

"Just keep it in mind. What did Maria think about the move into her place temporarily?"

"She is ok with it. Her concern is about the intensity that has developed. She is concerned about me, very frightened."

"Here's what I think you should do. There is no real reason for you to be here in the morning. Leave your car in your drive or garage. Take her car, stay at her place tonight, and leave early in the morning. Go up north somewhere, Ludington, Manistee, or even Traverse City. Stay away until late Monday. When you come back to town, stop by police headquarters. We'll have a squad car follow you to your house. He will make sure you aren't followed when you leave your house. You can get over to Maria's. Start off next week with Maria going off to school and you can check in with me Tuesday morning."

"That sounds great. I'll head out now and tell Maria about the new plan."

## 54

Harry called Joe Antonelli at his restaurant. "Hello Joe, are things all set?"

"They are. The car is parked in the visitor's lot at Hackley Hospital. It's in the hospital parking lot near the corner of Larch and Peck and is backed in. It's a 1962 Chevy Impala 4 door sedan, dark blue, new tires, a little over a year old. It has a V-8 engine. Looks like a family sedan and it performs well. It should be reliable. The keys are on the top of the driver's side rear wheel. The money is in a briefcase in the trunk. The papers are on the floor of the passenger side front seat. I've marked the ones you have to sign and mail into the state. The envelope is already addressed. Did you get all that?

"Yes, I did. That will work. It will take me about an hour to get there. Thanks, Joe."

"How soon will you leave town?"

"I still have some loose ends to clear up. There's the..."

"Harry, why can't you just go now and not worry about anything?"

"I can't leave with all these people who are able to identify me or tie me to you and the group. I could never feel safe. I did what you all wanted me to. The Mayor is no longer a problem to your group.

There is no direct evidence to tie me to the Mayor. It's only a few witnesses who can testify to pieces of what has happened. If I lean on them hard enough, maybe I can leave and not be afraid of a nation-wide manhunt."

"Or maybe not, Harry. You might even make it worse. Will you do them real harm?"

"Maybe, we'll see. I know all the names now except one of the kids, the girl. I don't think the two kids will take more than a good scare. The one that worries me is that Tom O'Banion that we talked about before."

"I told you he was trouble. How will you shut him up? I hear he has asked a lot of questions at City Hall and that he works with the police."

"I'll be careful, Joe. I don't want any more trouble. I'll just do what I have to and go far away. You shouldn't need me again. I don't see how there can be any link between me and the group. You should now be clear. And once I'm gone, you won't ever see me again. You held up your end of the bargain. Thanks, Joe."

Harry hung up and thought about how he would get to the car. He could walk through Glenside and catch the Sherman bus downtown and transfer to the Peck Street. No, that wasn't good. If he started out right now through McGraft Park, he could get to Hackley Street and walk east to Peck Street. There's a 7-11 on the way where he could stop for a cup of coffee and a sandwich to go. He would eat it while he walked the last two miles to Hackley Hospital. He dressed conservatively, for him, and set out across the park. He forgot how hilly it was as you come up around the curve to where Hackley straightened out to go straight east. He was a little out of breath when he got to the convenience store. He stopped, got a sandwich and coffee and walked on.

No one paid any attention so far to a man who walked along as though on a Sunday stroll. By the time Harry reached Peck Street, he had finished the sandwich and coffee. From here it was only about five blocks to the hospital parking lot. It took him about 20 minutes. He found the car easily enough, got the keys off the tire, and opened the trunk. It was clean except for a briefcase. Harry opened it. Good old Joe. It was full of $100 bills. He closed the briefcase, shut the trunk, and walked around to the driver door. As he unlocked it, he looked around and saw no one except people as they walked to and from their cars. He didn't notice Joe with his binoculars in his white Buick LeSabre across the parking lot watching him.

He started the car, an automatic. That was good. He drove out onto Peck Street, and after a few blocks, took a left turn on Southern. He watched the rear view mirror constantly as always for someone following him. He saw no one but took the precaution of immediately taking a left turn onto Sanford Street. He drove on Sanford down past the Sealed Power plant where he turned right onto Delano Street and followed it till it dead ended at Sixth Street. Another couple of turns he was back on Hackley and home. He left the car in the driveway, took the money out of the trunk, went in the house, and finally breathed a sigh of relief.

Harry hadn't told Joe the whole truth. This was Friday. He would start on his plan tomorrow. He thought he better get over to O'Banion's place and see what he was up to. He wanted to be done with his business by Wednesday or Thursday at the latest. Then he would be gone.

# 55

Tom drove home and packed up some clothes. He didn't need to take much to stay at Maria's. He just loaded up a couple of suitcases. He picked up the phone and called his dad, "Hi Dad."

"Hello Son, what's new?"

"A lot of changes that we need to tell you and mom about. Our wedding date will be next Saturday, a private affair at the Vitale home or the Parish. We think we'll be safer together and we don't want to move in together till we are married. Can we meet with you somewhere for dinner and tell you all about it?"

"Let me make some reservations at Tony's."

"That sounds great. I need to talk to Maria. She's going to her parents after school and I'll pick her up there. How about I call you from there to confirm?"

"I'll tell your mother in the meantime. Talk to you later. Love you, Son."

"Love you too, Dad."

Tom had a sandwich for lunch with some iced tea. He thought about the turn of events. He knew he must be close on the killer and a solution to Fred's murder. Now he and Maria were in danger. He knew how frightened she was. But he was determined to find out what happened to Fred. They would be safe when he solved it and the killer was put away.

He drove to her parents but didn't notice the dark blue car that followed as he left his house. When he parked in front of the Vitales' house, the blue car drove on by and parked unnoticed, a block away on the other side of the street. Maria met him on the front porch with a hug and a kiss. "Guess what, darling. Father Flannery will marry us right here tomorrow morning out in the garden."

"What? That soon? I just told my dad it as going to be next Saturday! That's wonderful, sweetheart. We will take off right after the ceremony and go on a honeymoon up north. That was the chief's recommendation. It will work out."

"Will you be safe alone tonight?"

"We're supposed to meet my folks tonight for dinner and tell them what's up. When we leave the dinner, I'll bring you back here. My suitcases are in my car, so I don't have to go back home. I'll stay with my folks tonight and we'll all meet here tomorrow morning."

"Let's go in and talk to my parents until it's time to leave for dinner."

They went in to a surprise. Maria's parents sat at the coffee table in the living room with hors d'oeuvres and champagne in an ice bucket. Mr. Vitale said, "Can I pour you some champagne, Son? I know you're not married yet, but I couldn't wait till tomorrow to call you that."

"Thank you both for the welcome you show me. Champagne sounds great."

They all sat around the coffee table noshing on the hors d'oeuvres and sipping champagne. Tom told them of the chief's plan for their safety. He said, "When we get back from our weekend honeymoon, we are to go to the police station and a squad car will follow us to Maria's place. There will be someone on duty 24/7 by shifts."

"How about Monday when Maria has to go back to school to teach?"

"He will have a police presence with us both until this is settled.

Hey, you know who we haven't told yet, except for my parents? Doug, my best man, and Nancy, your maid of honor. May I use your telephone to call my parents and Doug?

"Hello Mom, is Dad there? There is another change. Can you both get on the phone extensions?"

"Yes, Son, we're both here. What's up?"

"When Maria told her parents about the chief's plan to send us out of town for the weekend, they got together with Father Flannery and moved the wedding up to tomorrow morning! It will be 10:00 a.m. at the Vitale's home. I'm sorry this is so fast. Maria and I wanted to tell you together over a quiet dinner."

"That's all right. We'll just make tonight a rehearsal dinner. Our reservations are at seven p.m. I'll call Tony's and ask them to move us from the booth to that little private room they have. I'm sure they'll take care of us. How many will there be?"

"Let's see. With Doug, Nancy, and Father Flannery, there will be nine. Thanks, Mom and Dad. We'll see you there."

Tom turned to the Vitales. "Dad and Mom want to make this a rehearsal dinner. We are all supposed to meet at Tony's."

Tom called Doug and told him about the dinner. He then made another call to the Chief, "Jim, there has been a change. Maria and I will be married tomorrow morning at 10:00 a.m. Could you have a squad car come by around 11:00 a.m. and make sure we're not followed on our way out of town?"

"I'll do that, Tom. And congratulations. They put things together in a hurry, didn't they?"

"Yes, they did. And we'll follow your advice. I've made reservations. We'll be in Traverse City for our honeymoon. We'll stay at the Park Place Saturday and Sunday nights. We should get back to Muskegon Monday afternoon as planned and come to the station."

"That will work, Tom. An officer from the station will follow you home and the rest will go as we planned. Be safe in the holiday traffic. See you Monday afternoon."

Mr. Vitale called Father Flannery and invited him to the rehearsal dinner and asked him about some other things. He left early. He told them he would meet the rest of us at Tony's. He drove downtown to Woolworth's as they would be open until 5:30 p.m. He just made it and with the help of the clerks, rounded up a white bell, wide white crepe ribbons, and some other necessaries. From there he drove to the church and he and Father Flannery loaded some folding chairs into the family station wagon. Father Flannery said, "This will be a great surprise for Maria tomorrow morning. It will be lovely out in your garden."

Maria called Nancy. Doug already knew. And by 7:00 p.m. everyone was ushered into the private room at Tony's. There were the Vitales, the O'Banions, Doug, Nancy, and Father Flannery seated at a round table so all could see and talk with everyone. Tom's dad had ordered the champagne so there were two bottles already chilling. After the waiter poured for them, Tom's dad raised his glass and said, "To tomorrow's bride and groom, may this be the beginning of a beautiful life together."

There was a chorus of "Here, here."

Tom's dad asked, "Tom, how about telling us how it happened that this got arranged so quickly?"

Tom said, "I think I'll let Maria and her mom tell it. This champagne is going to my head. I'm going to dig into this bar cheese and crackers."

Maria said, "Well, it all started when Mom said to me a couple of weeks ago, 'It's too bad you two aren't already married.' I was startled by that, but it got me to thinking. When I told Tom about it, he was all for it. We figured it was going to be next Saturday. When we got over to Mom and Dad's tonight, we had a surprise. The arrangements had all been made for the morning."

Maria's mother smiled. "I just planted the seed in her mind...and it worked!"

They all laughed at her cleverness. Their waiter came and took their orders. The families spent a great evening together, talking about how resourceful Maria's mom was, and how fortunate that Father Flannery was available on such short notice. Interesting how well things worked out.

Doug seemed thoughtful. *It seems that I have lost this round.*

Tom thought, *He is just happy the way things worked for Maria and me.*

The evening was a big success! It would be a lovely wedding the next day.

## 56

T he next morning Maria and her parents were up early. It looked like a perfect day for a wedding. Maria's dad said, "Close your eyes and come with me."

When she opened them, "Oh, Dad, this is just wonderful. I love you." Maria's dad had made the garden look like a chapel, complete with white wedding bells attached to white streamers, ribbons tied on the back of the folding chairs, and even a white arbor decorated with artificial white carnations and lilies, interspersed with little pink roses and greenery.

"Dad, when did you do all this? You must have worked all night. I love it! Thank you."

"I love you, Sweetie. Your mother and I are so happy for you."

"I know, Dad. I never thought our wedding would happen this quickly. But you made it perfect. Thank you. I love you."

Just then her mother came out. "Maria, you better get upstairs and get into that white dress we found yesterday. Nancy just came and the two of you can help each other pretty up. The rest of them will be here soon."

~

HARRY WAITED down the block from Tom's place. He got there at first light and thought he missed Tom. Maybe he stayed somewhere else and if so, Harry didn't know where. The only thing to do was see if he could pick up the trail at what had to be his girlfriend's parents' house. He saw all of them over there last night, so it was worth a try. When he passed the house, there were several cars parked there. He went on down to the corner to his watch spot. As he did, a number of other cars pulled up. Harry smiled a "Gotcha" as he watched Tom get out of his car. Tom looked quite dressed up for a Saturday – he wore what looked like a navy blue suit.

TOM, his parents, Doug, and Father Flannery arrived at about the same time. They were shown through the house, into the garden. Tom exclaimed, "Mr. Vitale, this is great. It looks wonderful. Thank you."

"Only the best for my Maria and you."

Father Flannery and Doug walked out into the garden. "They are ready to start. Tom, you, Doug, and I should get to the right side of the arbor."

Tom's parents came and sat on the left side of the circle of chairs. Maria's dad went back to the patio, took her mother by the arm, and walked her down to the right side of the circle of chairs. He turned on a record player with music that started Nancy down to the right side of the arbor. Maria stood at the back door with her bouquet of white carnations mixed with little pink roses. Her dad started a recording of Mendelsohn's "Wedding March", offered Maria his arm and walked her down the aisle. After he kissed her and put her hand in Tom's, he went to sit down beside her mother. When he sat, he reached down and unplugged the extension cord that led to the record player. Maria handed her bouquet to Nancy and faced Tom with both hands joined. Father Flannery married them.

When they were introduced as Mr. and Mrs. O'Banion, everyone gathered around them. Hugs and kisses were exchanged. Father Flannery took pictures of the bride and groom, and another with Doug and Nancy, one with the bride and groom and each set of parents. The last picture was one of the whole wedding party. He promised he would have them developed and in an album for them by the time that got back from their honeymoon.

They all went inside and sat down to a lunch provided by some of the ladies of the parish. There was champagne. Doug lifted his glass in a toast and said, "I would start with Shakespeare's words that you used in your vows, 'My heart is ever at your service.' But remember that you were Maria and Tom first, now Mr. and Mrs., but still Tom and Maria. Walk side by side together and as Antoine de Saint-Exupery said, 'Love does not consist in gazing at each other, but in looking outward together in the same direction.' You two are my best friends, I love you both. To you!"

The champagne glasses were filled again. Tom's dad rose. "The four of us agreed and I get to be the one to do a toast from all the parents. Maria, your mother told me what you said when you talked about Tom some time ago, that you and Tom have become best friends and the love will come. It did, we can see it and that brings us great joy. And so, a quote, 'It is written, when children find true love, parents find true joy.' Here's to your joy and ours from this day forward."

Maria and Tom looked at each other with tears of joy in their eyes. Tom rose for a toast to all of them. "Here's to those who love and honor us by being here. We cherish you all."

Their lunch ended with the cutting of a small wedding cake.

Tom looked at his watch. "Our escort will be here in ten minutes. We need to get Maria's suitcases loaded and be ready to head out. We'll call you both from the Park Place and let you know we got away safely."

HARRY SAT up when he saw Tom come out of the house and put two suitcases in the trunk of his car. He wondered, *what is going on? Looks*

*like a trip.* He saw Tom and his lady friend, in a white dress, no less, come out of the house followed by a priest, another young couple, and what looked like two sets of parents. *Hey, they got married. They must be headed for a honeymoon. I can get them both at the same time.* He started up his car and waited while they all hugged and kissed. *Now, ain't that nice.* He watched as they got in the car. He saw a police cruiser with two cops in it come around the other corner. It went into a driveway, turned around, and pulled up behind Tom's car. *Damn! Now I can't follow. The cop is sure to spot me even though I'm in a different car. I have no idea what direction they might go. I'll have to figure out a way to follow.*

## 57

A fter Tom's car and the police cruiser pulled away, Harry thought for a minute. *They're probably off on a honeymoon. Probably up north. I've heard that that's where people around here go since the country is so great up that way. Maybe if I wait up on U.S. 31 northbound, I could get lucky and pick up Tom's car when they go by. It's worth a try.*

Harry hurried away from Norton Shores on Henry Street. He turned right on Seminole Road and took it out Seaway Drive onto U.S. 31 north. He had to get far enough north to pick them up no matter which way they went through town. He stopped at a turnoff just north of Apple Avenue. It was on a stretch of the wild riverbed for the Muskegon River that was full of wildlife. He could stay here for a while with his binoculars and camera. If a policeman stopped to check him out, he could say he was a wildlife buff. He stood on the passenger side of his car and half faced the riverbed but with his eye out for Tom's car. When he caught sight of Tom's car, he would look through the glasses to make sure it was Tom in the car. They would never spot him alongside the road. They would be too much into themselves.

About 15 minutes went by and he spotted the car as it approached from the south. He swung around as though interested in the wildlife but watched them. As he looked, he saw that the driver was the man "Tom." The police escort was gone. As soon as they were past him, he came round the car and drove off behind them. He caught up with them and settled a safe distance behind. He had a full tank of gas so he figured he could get to wherever they were headed. Some three hours later, they neared Traverse City. As they got into traffic on the south side of Traverse City, he needed to tighten up his pursuit. He saw them turn right about half a block ahead of him. When he got there, he made a mental note that it was Front Street. They turned back south on Pine St. and took a left onto State St. with Harry two or sometimes three cars behind. He saw them pull into the entryway of a hotel called "Park Place." Harry thought, *Ok, I've got them. Now I need to find a place to park where I can watch the parking ramp exit and the front door. It's four thirty so I doubt that they will come out tonight, but you never know, so I'd better stay here.* Harry found his parking spot and settled down for the wait.

Tom and Maria got checked in and went up to the honeymoon suite on the fourth floor of the tower. They had a great view of downtown Traverse City and Traverse Bay further out. They stood at the window, admired the view, Tom with his arm around Maria, she with her head on his shoulder. Tom sighed and said, "Can you believe we're married? It happened so fast, but I'm so glad we did it. Are you hungry? Do you want to go out for dinner?"

She laughed. "When am I not hungry? Let's just clean up a little and have a nice leisurely dinner in the main restaurant. I've never been to Traverse City so tomorrow we can explore the downtown area and maybe find a beach somewhere later in the afternoon. What do you say?"

"Sounds good to me. While you get ready, I'll call down to see if we need reservations."

He made the reservation for 6:30 p.m. They promised Tom a special table since they were on their honeymoon. Tom ordered a bottle of champagne to be chilled and ready when they got there. He called in to Maria in the shower, "We're all set, darlin', 6:30 p.m."

She replied from the bedroom, "That means, Mr. O, that we have two hours. Whatever will we do? Why don't you come in here and let's talk about it?"

Tom walked into the bedroom and found the room dimmed. Maria was in the bed without a stitch on. "Hello there, big guy."

Tom caught his breath and said, "Hey there, sweetheart, hang on and I'll join you."

Later, they showered together and just made it for their dinner reservation time. The waiter opened the champagne, poured two glasses, and left them. He said he would check on them in a little bit to take their orders. Tom and Maria picked up their glasses and Tom whispered, "Here's to us, Maria. Mr. and Mrs. Tom O'Banion!" They did the traditional sharing by wrapping their arms together, gazing deeply in each other's eyes, as they took their first sips. They reminisced about how beautiful the day was, how much they appreciated Maria's father's decorations, while they enjoyed the crackers, cheeses, and champagne.

The waiter returned just as their glasses needed refilling, and asked if we were ready to order. Maria, always hungry, made her choice of a cup of vegetable soup, cherry apple salad, and the Balsamic steak tips with mushrooms and garlic mashed potatoes.

"I thought you might go for that, you like your potatoes."

Tom ordered a cup of French onion soup, the restaurant's Caesar salad, and the pan fried perch that included an herbed wild rice blend, and steamed broccoli. After he looked over the wine list, he selected what looked like a good Pinot Noir that would go well with both their choices.

"Excellent choice, sir. I'll have your soups out in just a moment and I'll bring our special fresh bread to go with it."

"Tom, you must have been paying attention to Doug. You ordered that wine like you've been doing it for years."

Tom smiled. "Doug has many talents, doesn't he? I wish I knew more about his background. He rarely shares much about his past. I think he's had quite a few adventures, but he keeps everything pretty close to the vest."

As they sipped their soups and nibbled on their salads, the talk moved to the speed of the last few days. So much had happened in such a short time. It was such a relief to be away from the pressure even if it was only for a little while. Maria asked, "Do you think you'll be able to get another teaching job?"

Tom said, "I'm sure I will. It is just a matter of time."

"Is there any way you can apply and as well find out if their theatre program has an opening for me?"

"I don't know but I'll try. Why don't we just forget about those things right now?"

"You're right. This is our wedding night."

"Right. And the honeymoon already started," Tom said with a twinkle in his eyes.

Maria smiled at him. "We've just got started," she whispered softly to him.

When their main courses arrived, the waiter opened the pinot noir, let Tom taste it and when he nodded, poured their wines for dinner. Maria's steak tips were great as were Tom's lake perch. They traded bites so each got an idea of the tastes.

Tom said, "These perch are supposed to be the best, but I don't think they are as good as Doo Drop's. What do you think?"

"I agree. Now what's for dessert?"

He laughed. "Now why did I know you would ask that? They have a very special sundae made of their very cherry ice cream covered with an elegant hot fudge topping. What do you think?"

"I'd love it with some coffee."

They finished their sundaes and even though it was early, they went back to their suite, arm in arm.

The next morning, they had breakfast brought to their room while they got ready to go out to explore Traverse City. They walked hand in hand out of the Park Place lobby to a sunny September morning. The temperature was 74°, warm but not too much. It was a perfect day for shopping. Maria moved to her right to look at some flowers and pulled Tom with her. They heard what sounded like a car backfiring, and the next thing Tom felt a sting in his left arm that had him spinning around. He went down taking Maria with him. A second shot zinged past them. Tom asked, "Are you hit?"

Maria said, "No."

"Don't move. He'll think he got both of us. I hear the sirens already. He'll have to leave."

"Are you hit?" Maria cried.

"Yes, my left arm. It's not too bad, but I'm bleeding. We can't move till we know he's gone."

They heard a car door slam out on State Street and a car start to move away. Other guests and staff crept to the door and looked out the windows of the hallway to see what happened. The first police car pulled up in the Park Place entryway. Two officers got out and took up their station on the side of the car away from State St. One called out to Maria and Tom, "Are either of you hurt?"

Maria answered, "Yes, my husband is bleeding badly."

Other police cars were now positioned on State Street. After they determined it was safe, one of the first officers on the scene came to Tom and Maria and told his partner to call an ambulance.

"Tell me your names. Ok, you hang in there, Mr. O'Banion. We'll keep pressure on the wound with this bandage. It looks like a flesh wound but it took a pretty big piece of flesh and that's what the bleeding is from. An ambulance is on the way. Are you hurt, Mrs. O'Banion?"

"Just some soreness from the fall."

"Don't move. Let the ambulance people take you to emergency."

Two ambulances drove up into the entryway and loaded Tom into one. They were going to put Maria in the other. She said no, she hadn't been hit. She was staying with Tom.

Tom said, "Ask your Chief to call Chief Jim Johnson of the Muskegon police. I think this might be tied to a case down in Muskegon. If it is, I can't figure out how he found us up here."

∾

TOM WAS BEING TAKEN care of in one room and Maria was in another. She soon convinced her ER doctor that she was ok except for some bruises. She was with Tom in his cubicle when the Traverse City police chief walked in. "Well, Mr. and Mrs. O'Banion, this is not a good first visit to our city. I called Jim Johnson as you asked, and we have a lot of officers looking for the gray car. We knew of the Mayor's murder, but he filled me in on what had happened on the case."

Tom said, "Well, Chief, if what I suspect is true, we brought the trouble with us. The thing is I can't figure out how. I was watching for the gray car all the way up."

"Jim asked me to get details, so why don't you tell me what you remember about the shooting."

Tom told him that they stopped momentarily at the door and looked outside for the gray car. Since they didn't see one, they walked out hand in hand toward the steps down to the street. Maria wanted to see some flowers to her right, so she tugged Tom over there with her. "That's when I was hit and we both went down. The second shot missed both of us. It probably hit the hotel somewhere."

The Chief said, "It's a good thing your wife pulled you to the right with her. It likely saved a more serious injury or maybe even your life."

"See, darling, as the saying goes, you saved my life and now you have me for life."

Maria just shook her head. "Tom O'Banion, we're already committed for that."

"I know. I know. And it's the best thing that ever happened to me."

The Chief said, "I'll go now and call Jim down in Muskegon to tell him what we know. Are you going back to the Park Place?"

"We are if they'll let us. But we'll probably cut our visit short. Maria will have to drive home. This arm really hurts."

The ER doctor finished up his work on Tom's left arm. "We have it patched up, the bleeding is stopped. We've got it cleaned up so there is no danger of infection. It took a chunk of muscle out of the upper arm and it will be sore for some time. I'll give you something for the pain. You may need it for a few days. Have your doctor look at it early next week."

Tom asked, "Will it impair movement? I'm a choral conductor and piano player."

"You may need some rehabilitation therapy to gain full movement and strength, but in the long term you will be just fine."

The chief took them back to the Park Place and saw them up to their room. He said, "I'll call you in the morning. Jim and I will likely work out some escort for the trip back. I doubt if there will be any trouble, but we don't want to take a chance."

The next morning after breakfast in their room, they checked out and waited in the lobby for a police escort. They were followed out of town by a Traverse City police cruiser down to somewhere near Manistee where they were met by a Muskegon police cruiser. There was no trouble on the way home, but Tom hadn't expected any since the shooter probably thought he got them.

They were settled in a newly rented apartment by 4:00 p.m. Both sets of parents showed up shortly after they were called with takeout for dinner. After much hugging and a little bit of crying, both sets of parents settled down. The conversation revolved around the incident.

Maria's mother said, "I'm so glad it wasn't worse. Thank heavens you wanted to look at those flowers, Maria. I shudder to think about what we would be doing right now if you hadn't. You're going to have quite a honeymoon story to tell those children of yours someday."

Her dad asked, "What are your immediate plans?"

"Maria will be back in school on Tuesday. I'm due to go in to see Jim and fill him in on the happening."

Five voices in unison asked, "You're not going back to work on the case, are you?"

"No, I'm not. Jim was here shortly after we got home. We talked about what happened. Jim agrees with you all. I need to lie low for a while and let this arm heal. I'm concerned about Maria driving back and forth to school, but Jim said we'll have protection until we know that the killer didn't come back to town. Maria is not comfortable riding in a cruiser, so we'll see what happens. He has asked Maria to see if she can get a couple of weeks late start approved. He will also call the principal and lean on him to get it negotiated. We'll just have the rest of our honeymoon right here in our apartment."

Tom's dad said, "I think that's a great idea. We'd better let these young ones get settled in. Call us if you need us and do keep us up on what you are doing."

# 58

Harry thought he hit Tom with that first shot but didn't know about the wife. Both went down and he didn't dare try to move closer to get another shot. He decided to go as quickly as possible east to US 131 and take the long way back to Muskegon. He made it out of the Traverse City area without incident. He had spent part of the money to move into one of the long-term motels on the south side of Muskegon. It had a little kitchenette and he had laid in a supply of groceries before he left.

He could slip out every day and get a paper to get the latest on Tom and his wife as well as any news on their investigation. Wednesday's paper had a one column story about this honeymoon couple from Muskegon involved in a shooting while in Traverse City. Apparently, he missed the wife and only got Tom in the arm. The couple was staying in an unknown location for the immediate future.

Harry was determined to get another shot at them. When the wife showed up, he would follow her home. Once he found their nest, he could lay out his plan to catch them and take them out. When he took care of them, he would split and never come back again.

Harry thought he would call Joe and throw a little scare into him. He knew the group met on Saturday mornings and roughly what time it was. He called Joe early at his home before he left to go downtown.

"Joe, this is Harry."

"Harry, where are you? We heard about what happened up in Traverse City. Why did you do that?"

"I told you, Joe. I want them gone before I leave town. They've gone underground for now, but I'll find them."

"You should just leave. Call it off. They'll never figure it out."

"Nope, Joe. I'll let you know when the time comes."

THE GROUP MET for their usual breakfast at the Century Club. The first order of business was the incident up in Traverse City.

George asked, "Joe, have you heard from Harry?"

"Yes, just this morning. He's back in town. He won't tell me where he is, but he is determined to take Tom out before he leaves."

Tim said, "It sounds to me as if he's become unstable. I don't trust him. If he gets caught, he'll probably cave in, talk, and we'll be in trouble. Maybe we should get someone else to take him out."

Joe jumped back in, "We shouldn't do that. We don't want to dig a deeper hole. Leave it to me. I brought him in. I'll take care of it. I'll let you know when it's done."

George added, "We don't want to know how you take care of it."

"You won't."

## 59

Chief Johnson called Bob and Sara's parents and told them he had subpoenas that required them both to tell what happened on the Clipper. He scheduled them to come to the police station the next day after they got out of school. Both kids showed up with their parents and were put into separate rooms. Their stories didn't vary enough to worry about. It was just as Tom proposed in his theory. They witnessed a big man, as they described him, with something that looked like a body wrapped in a tarp with ropes all around it. When they took off out of the car, the guy took pictures and chased them upstairs, where they saw Mr. O'Banion and Miss Vitale, but turned and went the other way up the stairs to the upper deck.

They hadn't seen him since either at school or anywhere close to their homes. The Chief repeated his warning to keep quiet about what happened on the Clipper. The Chief said to each of them, "We don't think he is back in town, but you don't want to call any attention to yourselves. He doesn't seem to have any interest in the two of you so just try to keep your lives as normal as you can. Let me know if anything suspicious happens, anything, mind you."

The task force met the next morning without Tom. They all

reported in, Mark said that Tom was right. Two cement block pieces were found at the stern of the car deck. They decided to publish the police sketch in the Chronicle to keep up the pressure and to see what it might stir up. They continued the "be on the lookout" for the gray car but had no leads. Maybe the sketch would generate some new leads. Because the Chief had the search warrants for the Lakeside neighborhood, he wanted to start a house to house canvas of the area to see what this would turn up. This was to start this afternoon.

The next day, they got their first break. Late in the afternoon after the Chronicle was delivered, they had a phone call from a lady in Lakeside. Mark went out to see her and was told that she had seen someone who looked like the man in the paper. He was in and out of the little house across and down the street from her. She pointed out the house. Mark called in for backup.

They approached the house with caution. Two officers went around the side by the garage, looked in, and saw the gray car. As the officers coordinated, they knocked on both doors and shouted "Police, open up." When there was no answer, they broke in both front and back doors simultaneously. After finding no one in the house, they did a thorough search. They checked the kitchen, the refrigerator, and the sink. It was full of dirty dishes. No one had been there for a while.

Mark called and got a forensic team on the way. He got on his car radio and told the chief what they found. "This has been his hidey-hole, but he he's gone now."

They figured that he must have a new car. The gray car would be processed for evidence that Fred's body had been there. The next day they would get a crew to talk with car dealers along with the sketch of the killer to see what they could find.

Jim called Tom and told him the news. "Tom, this is why you didn't think you were followed up to Traverse City. We don't know yet what kind of car he has now."

"Is there any evidence that he is back in town? We'll go stir crazy here if we can't get out of here soon."

"No, we don't know. Let's give it another week at home. Maybe next Monday, Maria can go back to school and you can get out."

"All right, Jim, next week. Say, how about Saturday or Sunday? Do you think we could do a beach trip?"

"I'd rather you wait on that. We'll talk again before then."

## 60

J oe drove around town to all the motels. He figured that Harry was ready to run as soon as he finished what he had started out to do, get Tom O'Banion. He thought that if he were Harry, he would hole up in one of the long-term hotels south of town. He had checked out about half of them when he spotted a dark blue Chevy Impala outside of a motel on Old Grand Haven Road. The license plate number was the right one.

*Gotcha.* He circled back a couple of times more just to double check. He loaded his deer rifle, the Springfield M1903 model. Last fall, he had a scope mounted, and sighted in, so he could get a deer at a fairly long range. The rifle would let him take care of Harry if he could get within 300 yards. Now he had to find out what Tom O'Banion was up to. If he followed O'Banion, he was sure he would also find Harry. He would take Harry out before the O'Banions got hurt any more.

He found a gas station with a phone booth and called police Chief Jim. "Jim, Joe Antonelli here."

"What can I do for you, Joe?"

"I want to know if Sara might still be in danger. Do you think Fred's killer is still around?"

"We don't think he's around anymore. He probably never came back from Traverse City. It hasn't changed since I told you this earlier. So just keep on doing what you are, it's highly unlikely that he is after Sara or her boyfriend Bob."

"How about the O'Banions?"

"Why would you be concerned about them? I heard about your reactions to the trial that Sara put Tom through."

"Oh, that's in the past. Are they ok?"

"Yes, but they are still lying low."

"Thanks, Jim."

Joe went home and at dinner that night steered the conversation to how Sara was doing at school. Eventually, he found out that Maria O'Banion would be back to teach next week.

## 61

Tom and Maria no longer had a police escort. When Chief Johnson came by Friday morning to give the go-ahead for Maria to start back at school, he also reminded them about Harry's apparent change in vehicles. He said, "I suspect he has left town, but there is no way to be sure. Let's keep a tight watch through tonight. I'm just not comfortable without an escort for you. I'd rather keep it on indefinitely, but I'll lean to your wishes. We'll stop the close watch and just do an occasional drive-by of the apartment."

Tom said, "That sounds good, Jim. Maria, do you feel alright about that?'

"I do. Will the squad car follow me to school and back?"

The Chief hesitated and said, "Not anymore unless you want it."

Maria said, "I don't see why I need an escort now. I'll be extra careful where I park and if I feel uncomfortable, I'll get someone to walk me to my car. We can't keep living in fear."

Jim said, "Call me if you change your mind."

Tom asked, "What about making the move to my place? It will give us more room."

"Give it another week or two just to be sure."

Tom replied, "All right, Jim. Thank you for all your help."

Tom drove Maria to school on her first day back. His arm was gaining strength. He dropped her off at their usual parking lot and looked nostalgically at the school. He really missed that place and the kids. Maria turned and waved to him as he drove out of the lot. Neither of them paid any attention to the white car that pulled out and followed him.

Tom decided that he could finally go visit his thinking spot, the Ovals. He pulled into a parking spot near the pier and the white car parked back by the Coast Guard station. He walked to the end of the pier and sat in the sand a bit. When he headed back to the apartment, he didn't notice he was again followed by the white car.

When he picked up Maria late in the afternoon, they planned to go to Doo Drop for dinner. A dark blue sedan followed them from the school lot to the restaurant. They saw it but didn't think anything of it.

After an uneventful week, Maria and Tom felt safe enough to go out to the Ovals for a Saturday outing at one of their favorite spots, a walk along the beach at the Ovals and a picnic lunch on the beach. They went early in the morning so they would have the beach to themselves. They parked across from the concession stand and walked south toward the swings. The only other car they saw was a dark blue one across the street near Coscarelli's concession stand. As they turned back toward their car, Maria asked if anything had happened on the job search.

Tom said, "It looks more promising. I have several job applications out for a choral conductor position. Most said they would decide in the spring, so I should stay in touch. It won't be Muskegon High but at least I'll be teaching again."

"I've been on the lookout, too, Tom. I just don't want to stay after the way the principal treated you. He should have given you your job back after you were cleared. Hopefully, we can each find a job either at the same school or close to each other. For now, you have the jazz club work, right?"

"You bet! What do you think? Do you want to walk out to the lighthouse?"

"Come on, Mister O. I'll race you to the jetty and we'll walk back and have our lunch." They stopped for a hug and turned to walk down the jetty toward the lighthouse. Neither noticed the big man who got out of the blue car and now approached them with gun drawn. The man started shooting, scattering bullets all over.

Maria dropped first. Tom went down, hit in the leg. He landed close to Maria's feet facing toward the shooter and couldn't see that she was bleeding profusely from a head wound. Tom whispered, "Don't make a move. We have to make him think we're dead. Someone in the houses across the Ovals will have heard the shots and they'll call the police. He'll have to leave."

Maria didn't move. Tom laid still and watched. The man stopped, looked to see if they moved, and started across the road toward them. Tom heard two more shots, one right after the other, but with a different sound than before. Blood spurted from the man's left side and his head exploded. Tom moaned and passed out.

The police and an ambulance screamed to a stop near the shooter. The EMTs saw the man in the road first and determined that he was dead. As they started toward Tom and Maria, they called for another ambulance. Tom and Maria both were unconscious, Tom from loss of blood and Maria from her head wound. One pair of EMTs worked feverishly over Maria, her injury was severe. They got her in the ambulance and took off, sirens blaring and lights flashing. The other pair of EMTs staunched the bleeding from Tom's leg as best they could, put in an IV, and loaded him into the ambulance. Tom stirred and mumbled, "How is Maria? I have to make sure my wife is ok."

"She's in the other ambulance and we hear them talking with Hackley emergency room as we are too. She's still unconscious, Mr. O'Banion. The head wound was a severe one and she also hit her head hard on the concrete pier when she went down."

"You know my name?"

"Yes, we always check ID. We need your blood type. Is Maria your wife? She doesn't have the same last name as you."

"Yes, she is. We just got married. Is she going to be ok? My blood type is A positive and Maria's is O positive."

"I'll pass that along to the other ambulance. We'll be at the hospital soon. You can find out more there."

At the hospital emergency room doctors quickly patched up Tom's wound. No arteries were hit so he was coming around quickly. They told him he had lost a lot of blood, so they had started a transfusion. Tom asked, "What about Maria? How is she? I want to see my wife."

The ER doctor said, "She is still unconscious. The gun wound was a serious trauma. I suspect that alone gave her the concussion. When she fell, she hit her head on the concrete and both events were enough shock to her brain to put her into a coma."

"Oh no! We should call our parents. Their numbers are in my wallet."

"We called them and they are on their way."

Tom asked, "What happened to the man who shot us? Was it the same man who killed the mayor? Who killed him? And who shot him? I saw his head explode."

"The only question I can answer is the first one. He was dead at the scene. He has been taken downstairs to the morgue. The staff is checking his wounds to find out what kind of weapon was used to kill him. The chief of police called to see how the two of you were. I understand he is a friend of yours. He said he'll be up sometime later in the day to talk to you about what happened. He also called your friend Doug. He'll be up shortly."

"When can I see my wife?"

"As soon as that transfusion is done. You lost a lot of blood and you'll be weak. You were lucky the bullet didn't hit an artery. We'll get you in to see her in the next hour or so."

As the doctor left, Tom's parents rushed in. Tom told them his injury was not serious. The bullet went through his upper leg without hitting a bone. "The doctor cleaned the wounds thoroughly and told me that wounds like this will heal in time."

Tom continued, "I'll probably walk with a little limp for a while, but it will eventually get better. I lost a lot of blood so I'm weak. They want to keep me in here overnight, but I probably will be around here for a while anyway. I'm much more worried about Maria. She's in a coma and they won't tell me much more than that. I have to see her."

His dad said, "Her parents are in with her now. They'll be down in a little bit."

Doug came rushing in. "Hey there champ, I heard you were shot. How are you doing?"

Tom said, "Thanks for coming, Doug. I'll be ok. It's Maria I'm concerned with. I haven't seen her yet. They tell me she's in a coma but they won't let me see her until this transfusion is done. Where is she? Where's my wife?"

Just then, Maria's parents walked in. Her dad walked to Tom and took Tom's free hand in both of his, saying, "She's just two doors down from you, Tom. We're so glad your injuries weren't too serious. The doctor told us you should be up and around in a couple of days."

"That's right. He said that I would be weak for a while and probably limp as well. But he told me it would heal in time. How is Maria?"

"She is in a coma. She has a severe concussion that caused a lot of pressure on the brain. They have taken X-rays and don't see any evidence of a blood clot. They'll watch her closely, but they don't think she will get worse. They just can't get her to wake up yet."

Tom asked, "Do they have any idea when that might happen?"

"We were told there is no way to tell. We're in a waiting game. It could be tomorrow. It could be six months or a year away."

Tom cried, "Oh, no, why couldn't it have been me? It should have been me. Not Maria."

Tom's mother said, "You are going to be strong for Maria. She's going to pull through this. You love her very much. We all do so we'll just keep praying that she heals quickly and comes back."

Tom drifted off to sleep and woke just as the chief walked in.

"Hello, Tom. I'm so sorry about this. The doctor told me about Maria's coma and filled me in on your injuries."

"It's not your fault, Jim. We saw the blue car but didn't think anything of it. It looked like the man on the boat, is it him?"

"It's him alright. His name is Harry Walker. We took fingerprints and found him in the state police files. He's had some minor scrapes with the law. There may be more. There's more data coming in from around the state including no FICA or income tax records for him. That may mean the name is one he uses for this kind of work or he has just ignored these filings. He is apparently a muscle man for hire. This makes it more likely that someone or some group in town hired him."

Jim continued, "Here's what I think may have happened. I think that when he killed Fred, he went further than he was supposed to. When he kept after you and Maria, someone decided they had to get rid of him. The fact that they knew what his new car looked like means they probably supplied him with it. They must have gotten lucky when he left his house, picked up his trail, and followed him to the beach. The coroner found the bullet that went into his head so we know he was killed by a rifle. Whoever pulled the trigger is a good marksman. We think he might be a hunter. That's all we know at this point. Tom, I only wish that he had gotten off his shots before Harry shot the two of you."

"Did someone from the houses across the Ovals see anything?"

"My officers are there going house to house. There aren't many people up that early on Saturday morning. But the shots woke some up. One woman saw a man with fishing gear walking toward the Coast Guard Station. He could have had a rifle hidden in the gear. She said he got into a white car, but she didn't recognize the make. It will not be easy to find him but find him, we will."

Doug had been listening to every word and nuance. He was seething with anger but didn't let it show. Now he said, "Tom, I'm going down to Maria's room. I'll check on her and come back so we can talk later. I'll call Nancy before I come back."

Tom said, "Ok, Doug. Hurry back." Then to the chief, "You won't stop, will you? There's something not right here. Maybe it was the group of nine that Fred spoke of who were behind it."

"No, Tom, we won't stop, ever. You just get recovered and soon Maria will wake up and you can rebuild your life. We'll keep you posted on our progress."

# 62

When Doug slipped into Maria's room, her nurse was in there adjusting one of the monitoring instruments. Doug said, "Tom and Maria are my best friends. We are fellow teachers at Muskegon High School. Tom's room is full of people so I told Tom I would check on Maria. Is it ok if I just sit here a while with her?"

The nurse said, "I don't see why not. We moved her in from emergency an hour or so ago. She was in the coma when we got her and that hasn't changed at all. She's stable but we can't get her to wake up. It wouldn't hurt if you talk to her."

"Thank you, I will. Her parents probably told her that Tom is ok. I guess it won't hurt to say it again."

"You're right. Her doctors think it seems to register with them somehow. I'll be back to check on her in about 20 minutes."

Doug waited until he was sure she was gone and with another patient. He then reached over and took Maria's right hand. The left had a fluids IV so he didn't want to touch that one. As he held her hand, he said, "Maria, sweetie, I'm making you a promise. I have some skills you don't know about. I promise you I will use them to find the people who hired this Harry fellow. I'll take them all out, I can do it."

He sat there, in tears, making a vow to himself like the promise he had made her, adding, *No one is going to hurt the people I care about and live to tell about it.*

Doug didn't realize that Maria's nurse had returned and was watching and listening. She saw it all, heard it all and left just as he he kissed her forehead and turned to go.

## 63

Breakfast Saturday at the Century Club was somewhat somber and quiet. The news about the shooting at the Ovals had hit the papers the previous Tuesday. When the breakfast was finished, George opened the meeting with, "The events of the last week seem to be on our minds this morning. Anyone have questions or would like to start off the discussion?"

Tim said, "I've done a lot of thinking about this development this week. As I'm sure we all have. I believe we need to be extremely cautious about making any moves for a while. With Harry's death, we lost our information source about what is happening in City Hall. And the police are not talking at all about what they've learned or what direction they're looking for new information. We better be careful or everything will unravel."

"Good thinking," said Wendell. "I second those thoughts about caution. The only moves we can make are things that are really below the surface. For example, there are some options to purchase that either must be renewed or get an actual purchase completed. I think those kinds of things can be done safely. Any objections?"

George said, "I agree that those items can move ahead. I also agree with Tim that everything else is on hold until we find a way to know what City Hall and the police know. Does anyone have any knowledge of what is new in the police department?"

Joe chimed in, "These are all good ideas. I have a possible in at the district attorney's office. He and I worked together closely during Tom O'Banion's trial."

"I'm not sure that's a good idea," said Tim. "If you start asking him questions about Harry, it could stir up suspicions. And Joe, I have a question for you. When we talked about Harry going rogue, you said you would take care of it. My question is who shot Harry? Was it you, Joe?"

"I beg your pardon. I don't shoot people. I shoot deer, other wild animals, and that's all. Don't be insulting."

Tim persisted, "You told us not to worry and that you would take care of Harry. Just what did that mean?"

"It means what I told you when I said that. As you all know, I was the one who arranged for, as we all agreed, a car and the bonus money. He told me he was headed somewhere warm as soon as he got some little details taken care of. And, no, he didn't tell me what those were, just that he would be gone within two weeks. Well, obviously he didn't. According to the paper, the police believe he was the man who shot O'Banion up in Traverse City. I assumed after that he was gone, but obviously not. He came back to town to finish the job. Now he's dead. End of story."

"Alright, alright, sorry I doubted you, Joe. We're all uptight about this."

George asked, "What do you think about finding someone else to rebuild contacts in City Hall? I don't believe we should try to get tight with someone in the police department. Does anyone know whether O'Banion is back to work with the police department?"

He got nothing from the group. No one had a suggestion about a way to get in again. George got the feeling they were not about to go along with anything that looked like the arrangement with Harry. He didn't really blame them. He felt the same way. But he was uneasy about Joe. *If Joe had shot Harry, it could come back to them. He wondered whether something should be done about Joe. Maybe Joe needs to have a fatal accident.*

He said, "Look, let's all just keep our ears and eyes open just as we did before Harry. The mayor is no longer a problem and it doesn't look as though the interim mayor will be pushing Fred's agenda. Why don't we just go back to business as usual? It served us well for a long time. It'll work again."

They all agreed and went on their separate ways. Joe walked from the Century Club back to his restaurant thinking, *I dodged a bullet in there. George was looking at me with a suspicious look when Tim was questioning me. I'll have to play it straight until this cools down.* He had no idea the police were close on his trail.

## 64

T hree months later, Maria's parents came to her room at the long term care facility and found Tom reading to her. He said, "The nurses tell me it is important for me to talk to her and read to her. She may be asleep but sometimes it gets through and will help her to find her way back."

Maria's dad said, "Tom, we have something to say to you. We just had a consultation with her doctors. They told us that after three months, the chances of someone waking up are less than one percent."

Tom sighed, "I know, they told me the same thing. I just don't want to believe it. Every day I come in here believing that she will be awake."

"We want that too, Tom. We love you for the way you are staying by Maria's side. But we think it is time to get on with your life. Take one of those school jobs you've applied for or go back to your club work...or both. Just do something. We'll let you know the minute there's a change. We know you want to sit by her, read to her, but we think you should move on. What do you think?"

"I don't know. I don't feel right not being here."

"It's what she would want you to do. We'll come to see her often, talk to her, and read to her as you are. Think about it. We wanted you to know it is alright for you to move on."

"You know, I'm reminded of a conversation Maria and I had a while back. We talked about our long term future together and we made a pact. If anything ever happened to either of us, the other would move on. We both believed that one has to find one's way to fulfilling his or her life purpose. It was hard for both of us to come to this because we are both romantic souls and believed we would have lots of time to be together. I never thought it would be so soon. I can't leave yet. I appreciate what you just said. I'll have a talk with Dad and Mom and let you know what I'll be doing. I love you both."

# 65

The chief's secretary buzzed him and said, "Tom O'Banion is on line one."

"Thanks, Gerri. Put him on please."

"Good morning, Tom. Is that leg getting better? And is there any change for Maria?"

"It is, Jim. I still limp a little, but it gets better every day. Maria is still in a coma, no change. Thanks for asking."

"What can I do for you, Tom?"

"I need to talk to you. I'd like to catch up on the investigation and I have some questions that I believe you can help with."

"This is a relatively light morning for me. Can you be here by 10:00 am?"

"Thanks, Jim. I'll be there."

When Tom arrived, he was shown directly into the chief's office. Jim got Tom some coffee and asked, "What's on your mind, Tom?"

"Jim, I have some decisions to make. To make the right one, I need to know about the investigation."

"All right, I can do that..."

"Before you start, let me tell you about something that just happened this past week. Maria's parents, the Vitales, said something to me at the hospital. To be brief they encouraged me to get on with my life. They will let me know when she wakes up. I'm not going to abandon Maria, but I'm going to share her care with her parents and other people who love her. I'll always be there for her. Her doctors have told me her chances are less than one percent after this much time. I will be talking with my parents about all this over the weekend. Part of the answer is what to do...how to be involved in the investigation or even if I should. That's why I need to know what has happened."

"Well, Tom, here it is. Within a week of the shootings and Harry's death, we formed a new investigative task force. It is headed up by Dave Smithson of the State Police in Lansing, two other investigators from the local state police, my lead detective Mark, and me. We are being supported by a team at the state police headquarters in Lansing. They take information we send them, analyze it and provide us with direction to go further. We have an office and conference room here at police headquarters for the task force. We could have set it up at City Hall, but we have suspicions that there are leaks there."

"You still don't have an idea who that might be?"

"No, we don't. We have some suspects but have no proof yet."

Tom mused, "I think it might be either Sam, the city manager or Jerry, his assistant, or maybe both."

Jim went on, "Yes, those are our suspects. We've made some progress. Not as much as we would like. Dave has moved here temporarily, and he is taking the lead. We impounded Harry's new car. Dave took the VIN number and traced it back to a used car dealer on Getty Street. The car was bought there by a man claiming to be Harry Walker. But when Dave showed him a picture of Harry that we took after he was shot, the car salesman said that it was not the same man who bought it. Our guess is that the man who bought it is local, maybe part of the group of nine who we think ordered the hit on Fred, but all we have is the car salesman's description. We have a sketch of the man who bought it, but it is not that good. The man will not be easy to find. And oh yes, we have a statement from a lady in one of the homes at the Ovals? Like so many people who live there, she has binoculars handy to watch birds, and people on the beach. She saw a man walking toward a white car carrying a long duffle that could have held fishing gear. But she said he wasn't dressed for fishing. It might have been a rifle in the duffle. We know from the bullets we recovered that Harry was killed with a rifle. His killer may be a hunter and that was a long shot, so he's good. We have another lead to track down."

"Do you know whether Joe Antonelli is a hunter, and does he have a rifle?

"Tom, what makes you suspect Antonelli?"

"You remember that I saw him come out of that room at the Occidental with that group of men. And when Maria and I had dinner with Fred and Eleanor, Fred mentioned that Jerry said something that made him think that Antonelli was a member of the group. Maybe you could check and see if Antonelli is a hunter. He might have a deer license. And maybe you could have Mark show the car salesman a picture of Antonelli. He could have bought the car."

"Two good ideas, Tom. We'll do both and let you know what we find. If we can tie down one man in the group, it could lead to the rest. The hunting license won't take long to track down and if Antonelli did buy the car, he may be our start to unravel that group. It might mean that Antonelli is the leader or at least the group member who had direct contact with Harry."

"How about the consultant that Fred hired? Did anyone talk to him yet?"

"Yes, both Dave and Mark interviewed him together. He told them that he heard the name 'group of nine' from several City Hall workers, including city manager Sam Milford. The group seems to be common knowledge in City Hall. He didn't recognize the sketch of the man who bought the car either. But then that's not surprising. He said he has never seen any of the group."

Tom said, "So lots of pieces but no way that they all fit together yet."

"Wait, there's more. Dave had the team in Lansing checking properties along the lake front, working on the premise that the group didn't want any new industries coming into Muskegon. There aren't many recent sales but there seems to be a lot of options to buy. The options are all in the name of a shell company. And, of course, they can't find any of the names of the company owners. There is a bank account at one of the local banks, but we can't get a warrant to look at their signature cards without some other evidence. So yes, lots of pieces but the picture is jumbled."

Tom asked, "How can I help? One of the things I thought about doing is taking advantage of Dave's offer and getting some training with the state police. I'm not an investigator by profession but I'm a quick learner. Actually, I'm thinking of getting a private detective's license. What do you think?"

"You have good instincts. You would make a great detective but that would be quite a shift for you. My understanding is that you are a good musician. Maybe you should go back to that."

"I have been. I play regularly at some of the jazz clubs in Grand Rapids. I don't play here. I'm still edgy about being out in the public here. And I'm still looking for another teaching job at a high school. I don't have much to do to finish my master's in choral conducting. If I were to finish that, I could also look at jobs at community or junior colleges."

Jim said, "I'll tell you what, Tom. If you want, I'll get you copies of all the reports. Use those skills you have and feed your ideas back to us. Maybe you could meet with the task force and help us think through all the pieces. You could be a big help to us. Those new ideas about Antonelli show it. What do you think?"

"I think I'd like that. It is important to me to find the people who backed Harry and did this to Fred. And to Maria."

"Let's keep it between us until, and if, you decide to become more active officially. If you decide to do that, we'll get you started on the State Police training and get your license. We'll get them, Tom. For now, you go ahead and start rebuilding your life. We have a meeting next Monday morning. You would be welcome."

## 66

The next morning Tom called his dad at his office. "Hello Dad. I wonder if I could come by some evening soon. I have a decision to make and I'd love to talk to you and Mom about it."

"Of course. What's going on?"

"I'll tell you all about it. What's a good time?"

"Come on over tonight about six or so. I'll call your mother right away and tell her you are coming for dinner. She'll want to make your favorite."

TOM WALKED UP on the porch, knocked, opened the front door, and said, "Anybody home?"

"Come on in, son."

The smells of his mom's cooking made his mouth start watering as soon as he walked through the door. His mom came out of the kitchen. He got a hug from her and a handshake from Dad.

"Do you want something to drink, Tom?"

"No, Dad, I'll settle for a little wine with dinner if that's ok."

"Dinner is about ready. Be on the table in about five minutes."

Mom's fried chicken, mashed potatoes, and green beans were great. After Tom caught them up on Maria's status, most of the conversation at dinner was mostly about what Tom was up to. He told them that it was still mostly playing piano at jazz clubs in Grand Rapids and looking for another teaching job.

After dinner and clean up, they all took a glass of wine into the living room. Tom's mom asked, "Tom tell us what decision you are facing."

"It started with a conversation at the hospital. I was there reading to Maria and her parents stopped in. It was the first time we've crossed paths there in a week or so."

He filled them in on the gist of the conversations that he had with Maria's doctors and with the Vitales.

"It was a shock to me that the doctors said that the odds of Maria waking up were less than one percent after three months. I'm having a problem dealing with this. I can't believe my beautiful Maria might never wake up."

His dad asked, "Are they talking about taking her off life-support?"

"No, they didn't bring that up yet but it's sure to come."

"Have you given any thought to what you will do? It's going to be your decision you know."

"I know. But it's not a decision I want to make in a hurry. And I'll want to talk with the two of you, the Vitales, and Father Flannery. I can't give up yet."

Tom continued, "I know what the Vitales proposed is rational, that I move on with my life, and not spend so much time at the hospital. They said they would continue to come to hospital to read to Maria, and I would still go, just maybe not as often."

"What was your reaction to all that?"

"I'm not sure yet. It makes sense but I feel I need to be there. But there is that pact that Maria and I made."

"What pact?"

"We said that if something should happen to one of us that the other should move on, make a new life. I'm just not sure I can do that yet. It's only been three months. We never thought we'd have to deal with this so soon. We've only been married three months!"

His mom said, "It sounds as though she would approve though."

"And to complicate things more, I had a talk with Chief Johnson. You may remember that he and the state police both offered me a job as an investigator. The state police have a six month training program to learn the skills to become a detective. The course would work as a basis for either position as well as a third alternative."

"What's that?" they said in unison.

"I've also thought I would like to get my license as a private investigator and consult with either or both of them. Jim has already said that would work for him."

"Why would you want to become a private detective?"

"Mom, Dad, I want to be a part of finding out who is behind this killer who killed Fred, shot me twice, and put Maria in a coma. I want to know if it's the group of nine that Fred was worried about. It sounds like they resorted to some pretty strong tactics to discourage any new businesses from coming into Muskegon. You know that Fred's vision was to bring Muskegon into the future so if we can't figure out what they're up to, there's a good chance that Muskegon will suffer long-term because of what they are doing. But even more important is that they will have gotten away with murder. They are as guilty as Fred's killer."

"Suppose they hire someone else like this Harry," his dad said.

"They could do that. But I don't believe they will. I suspect they will sit tight for quite a while now. In the meantime, I'm sure they will move ahead with their plans for the city. Since Fred is no longer here, there's no one around to fight them. The only thing to do is, through the investigation, find out who they are and prosecute them, put them in jail where they belong."

"What about your music?"

"That's the hardest part of my decision. I miss my students and the music. I'd like to have it all, but I suspect I'll have to give something up, at least temporarily. I'm still at the jazz clubs in Grand Rapids. I have several applications in schools over there. One of the State Police training schools is taught over there. I'll figure it out. Mom, Dad, thanks for your help. I love you both."

## 67

The next morning Tom went to the hospital. He wanted to be there to talk with her doctor. The doctor normally did his rounds sometime between nine and ten. When he walked in, Tom had just finished another story from her favorite collection. Tom said, "I love you. I'm waiting for you, Maria. Hello, doctor."

"Hello Tom. Still here, I see."

"Doctor Franks, I have something to ask you in confidence."

"And what is that?"

"If a decision is to be made about pulling the plug on Maria's life support, who is the decision maker? Me or her parents or you? I still have to talk to our priest and my attorney, but I would like your input first."

"Tom, in the first place, we are a long way from having to ask that question. The primary consideration at this point is Maria. She is not brain dead — all tests show she is still in there. We know that so we have to take care of her body until she wakes up. I know I've told you about the odds, but patients like her do wake up. What prompted this question?"

Tom told him about the conversation with the Vitales, and his talk with his parents last night.

"Tom, I agree with them. You should live your life as though one day she will wake up and can join you in it. I can assure you nothing will happen to Maria without your knowledge. We just need to have a way to contact you at all times. And by all means talk with your priest and your attorney as well if you wish. She is safe here with us."

"Thank you, doctor. If things change when I make my decision about what to do, I'll make sure your office and the hospital know and can find me."

Tom spent another two hours with Maria, read her another story, and talked to her about his options. He left just after noon to go home, have lunch, and do some thinking. When he got home, he called the Chief and asked to be included in Monday's meeting of the task force. Jim told him to come in at 8:45 a.m. to talk before the meeting at 9:00 a.m. next Monday.

## 68

Tom was outside the chief's office at 8:45 a.m. He was shown right in. Jim stood and shook his hand. "Tom, I hope this means what I think it means."

"It does, Jim. I decided to become involved again. Do you know when the next State Police investigator training starts? I hope I can find a session in the Grand Rapids area. I could just commute and stay at home."

"I can find out about the training session for you. Give me a day or so. I'll call you."

"I don't know yet how I'm going to use this. For now, it is just to learn. And, of course, to get back involved on the task force. Where it goes from there is, well, we'll see what happens."

"That's fair, and for now, a good approach. How would you feel about a temporary six month appointment as a detective-in-training on the force? It would be ok with the city, as I said, and you could choose whether or not to become permanent after the training was done. Or you might decide to work for us for a year or so. I might be able to arrange for the department to pay the fee for the course. What do you say?"

"That's very generous of you, Jim. What do you and the department get out of it?"

"We get the skills and inputs of an already good investigator for the force. And maybe a top notch investigator for the department if you decide to stay."

"Thank you, Jim. I'll take the temporary appointment. I still have applications out for school positions. And I don't yet know what I will do if I'm offered one of them."

Tom told Jim about the conversations he had with the Vitales, his parents, and Maria's doctor. He told him there was still so much uncertainty in his life. Tom ended his story with, "I appreciate the opportunity you're offering, and I will give you full measure in return."

He shook Tom's hand and said, "I know you will, Tom. Let's get to the meeting and let you catch up on what we've done so far."

They walked into the meeting room together. Dave and Mark jumped up and said together, "Tom, good to see you!"

Dave continued, "Tom, you know Mark, of course. He's the lead detective on the case, and our two state investigators, Tony and Ken. Gentlemen, Chief Jim tells me that Tom is now on contract to the city as a detective-in-training. And by the way he starts his state police detective training next Monday."

"It's good to be back. I'm happy to be part of the group. I have some catching up to do. Jim told me a bit when we talked earlier but I'm sure there is more by now."

Mark asked, "Is there any change for Maria yet?"

"No, but we still have hope. Her doctors say it's early. We just have to wait and pray."

Jim said, "Dave, why don't you summarize where we are? It will get us all back right on top of everything and catch Tom up as well. Everyone hold your questions until Dave is done."

Dave gave everyone a neatly typed copy of the following five points.

1. We checked into Tom's suspicions that Sam and Jerry,

the city manager and his assistant, might be the source of leaks out of City Hall. Mark interviewed Fred's secretary Alice. She told us that she had alerted Fred that she thought Sam and Jerry had something going on besides city business. We think Harry might have been the go-between City Hall and the group. She has agreed to keep an eye out for anything they might do or other strange things that happen. Nothing else so far.

2. I checked the VIN number of Harry's new car and traced it back to a used car dealer on Getty Street. It was bought by a man claiming to be Harry Walker. And he remembered the sale because it was almost $10,000 in cash, but when I showed him a picture of Harry, he said that it wasn't the man who bought it. We got pictures from the Chronicle of Sam, Jerry, and because of what you said about Joe Antonelli, showed him that one too. Guess who bought the car? Joe Antonelli. This is our best piece of evidence yet that Joe is a part of the group.

3. Mark and I interviewed the consultant that Fred hired. He told us that he heard the name "group of nine" from a number of City Hall workers including Sam Milford. He didn't recognize the sketch of the man who bought the car. He hasn't met any of the group as far as he knows.

4. I had some team members in Lansing check out properties along the lakefront to see if they had changed ownership. The sales and the options are all in the name of a shell company. We don't have any names of the principals of the company. We need to get warrants to examine their books and check their bank account at New City Bank.

5. We checked the state records. Joe Antonelli has had a hunting license for deer for several years now. He bought a new long-range gun, the Springfield M1903 model. We found that last fall, he had a telescope mounted and

sighted in. The rifle would let him take care of Harry if he could get within 300 yards.

Dave paused, looked around the room, and then continued, "We are convinced that Joe Antonelli is a member of the group, that Sam and Jerry are somehow involved, and finally that the group of nine has a major project brewing for city property along the lake. The money involved is enough to lead them to hire someone like Harry. Our thought is that he was just supposed to put a scare into the mayor. But he got out of control, killed Fred, and tried to kill Tom and Maria. We think Joe Antonelli was the go-between for the group and Harry. When Harry went on his killing spree, Joe decided it was time to take him out. But we don't have a case strong enough to arrest Joe. That's what we have. It's good evidence but not solid enough to take action. Certainly not enough to get warrants issued. Any questions?"

Tom asked, "What are the odds that Joe will get rid of the rifle?"

"He won't if he doesn't know we're onto him," Dave said. "And that is the reason we need to keep a tight lid on what we are doing. No leaks."

Jim emphasized the point, "I agree with Dave, no leaks. Other questions?"

Tony, one of the local state police investigators asked, "Any evidence that someone other than Harry had driven the blue car, as in maybe Joe?"

"There was a fingerprint on the back of the rearview mirror that doesn't match Harry's. We ran it through our card file and the state police file but no match," said Dave.

Mark said, "That's another dead end."

Tom said, "Maybe not. Joe Antonelli is a businessman. He might have to have licenses for some of his businesses. I don't know if he owns businesses other than his restaurant."

Dave jumped in, "Liquor licenses might require fingerprints on their application. I'll check it out."

Jim said, "If we catch a break with this fingerprint, we could have enough to get a warrant to bring Joe in for questioning. We could maybe get a search warrant to cover his home where we could get the rifle and get access to the bank account. We might get another break there. Usually there is more than one signatory on a corporate account. Anything else?"

Tom asked, "How long will it take to get this fingerprint tracked down?"

Dave said, "I'll get someone to run it down to Lansing today and we should have an answer back by Thursday or Friday."

Jim said, "Let's meet here again Friday morning, same time. Depending on what we learn, we can plan our next moves on Friday and move in quickly. See you all then. And Tom, where will you be this week?"

"I'm going to be at home or the hospital or maybe my parents. I'll give you all the phone numbers but most of the time I'll be home reading these reports and thinking."

## 69

T om stopped at Etterman's on the way home. He needed to get some groceries and he wanted to get in touch with Doug. It had been a while since they had talked. He picked up a paper so he could catch up with the news.

He had a quick lunch while he scanned the paper. There was no news about the investigation. That was a good thing, nothing was getting out. There was a notice about a meeting of the city commission. The interim mayor had all but abandoned Fred's agenda and was building his own. Tom wondered how this one was fitting in with the group of nine's plans.

*I'll go down to City Hall and talk to Alice if she's still there.*

When he got to City Hall, he went right to the mayor's office. Alice said, "Hello, Tom. What a nice surprise. How is Maria doing? Any change?"

"No, no change. We're hopeful but her doctors can't tell us when she will wake up. How are things working out for you?"

"It's not the same, but it's working out."

"Alice, are Sam and Jerry still acting strangely as you put it before?"

"No, they seem a little lost."

"How do you mean?"

"It's almost as though they have lost some of their purpose in life. They are going through the motions of doing their jobs but they're different."

"As though they have lost contact with the world outside this office?"

"That's a good way to put it."

Tom said, "Keep all this under your hat, Alice. I'll keep you posted on what's happening when I can. You have my number at home and I now have an answering machine. If you hear anything new, please call me. But be careful who is around or wait until you are home to call me."

"Ok, Tom. Thanks for stopping by."

WHEN DOUG GOT HOME from school, there was Tom waiting on his front stoop. After a quick hug, they settled in to talk with a beer in hand. "Hey, Tom, almost like old times."

"Almost. As soon as Maria wakes up, it will be all the way back. How about heading for Doo Drop? I'm ready for some perch."

"I know it's not the same, buddy. It isn't the same without the two of you at school either. What are you up to now? A new teaching position open up yet?"

"I have several applications in throughout the Western Michigan area. I'm picking up a course in the winter term at Grand Valley so I'm getting closer to my Master's in Conducting. That's not the big thing that I have in the works though."

"What's up?"

"I'll give you the short version now. There's a lot we can't talk about at dinner. It's too sensitive. Someone might overhear."

Tom told Doug about his discussion with Maria's parents, her doctors, and finally his decision to rejoin the task force and take detective school with the State Police.

Doug said, "I haven't seen anything in the papers about a task force."

"That's good. That means we have no leaks. We don't want anyone to know we still exist. We are getting close to cracking the case against one of the members of the group of nine."

Doug looked up with surprise. "Who is it? I'd like to start looking too."

"Anyway I had better not say, at least without the Chief's permission. We're going to try to use him to get to the others. But as soon as his arrest hits the papers, we'll get together and I'll fill you in. If we can nail this first one, we'll be on our way to getting the rest."

Doug frowned. "What are you going to do with detective training, Tom? That's a long way from choral music."

"I know it is, but it's something I've thought about for a long time. I don't know what I'll do with it long term. We'll see. Right now, I have a six months temporary appointment as a detective-in-training with the Muskegon Police Department. By the way, Jim, the chief, has your number if he doesn't get me at home."

"That's fine. We had better get to dinner. I'm getting a little hungry."

## 70

Tom called his parents after he let Doug off and got home. It was only 8:30 p.m. so he knew they would be up. "Hi Mom, how are you both?"

"We're just fine, Tom. When are you coming over for dinner? It seems like too long since you've been here."

"How about tomorrow night?"

"That's great. What would you like for dinner?"

"Whatever you want to cook, Mom. I know it will be great. What can I bring?"

The next night Tom showed up at his parents' house with two bottles each of, their favorite red, a Robert Mondavi cabernet sauvignon and his mom's preferred white, a Stony Hill chardonnay. No matter what she chose to cook, one of the wines would work.

When he walked into the house, he could smell one of his favorite meals — baked whitefish, a brown rice pilaf, and steamed broccoli. But what really made his mouth water, the smell of her famous dinner rolls. They were so light, fluffy, and buttery. Mom bustled out, gave him a big hug, and rushed back into the kitchen, telling them it would be about twenty minutes. Tom and his dad took their drinks into the living room. His mom breezed in every few minutes to join them as she went back and forth to the kitchen. Tom was caught up on what was going on in their lives. His dad watched him thoughtfully, just waiting for Tom to share what was on his mind.

Over his mom's great dinner, the conversation was lively. Maria's condition and prognosis were discussed extensively. Tom's mom wanted to know if he was still good with the decision to not spend as much time at the hospital.

Tom sighed. "I think it's the right thing to do. It's what Maria would want for me. Her doctor said it was far too early to know what's going to happen. He told me it's still Maria in there and she's just sleeping. They are taking care of her body while we wait. And I need to get to work so I can be ready when Maria comes home."

"Dad and I are glad to see you thinking about the future. But we're puzzled about some of the choices you're making."

His dad said, "Something's going on, Tom. Are you ready to tell us about it?"

"Yes, I am. Mom, your dinner was great as always. Let's take our wine out to the living room and I'll you all about it. I'm glad you liked the chardonnay."

After they settled in the living room, Tom reminded them that he wanted to be a part of the investigation into Fred's murder and who was behind hiring the killer. And he wanted to be a part of the team that nails the group of nine. Tom told them, "I saw the Chief this morning and signed on to a temporary position. I'm going to get some training, work with them on this case, and see where this goes. He was happy to hear of my decision."

Tom's dad asked, "Are you sure this is a path you want to travel?"

"Yes, I am. I know I share in the blame for Maria's injuries and the fact that she is in the coma. And I just can't let it go. I want to play a part in bringing that group to justice."

His mom fretted, "You can't just let the police do their job?"

"No. I have some skills that Jim feels will contribute to making the case. I don't know exactly where those skills came from, but they are real. I see patterns and clues that lead to directions that others don't always think of. I learned in my math major about deductive and inductive reasoning. A mathematician also develops the skill for pattern recognition and that's useful in detective work. And one of my teachers was a physics researcher. He was always talking to us about observation, making sure that what you saw had registered. And of course, all of my reading during my illness was relevant. You know I read a lot of Sherlock Holmes back then. What I think is that things just came together to add up to these skills. I'm going to use them."

"Does this mean you have given up your career in music?" his mom asked.

"No, Mom. I'm enrolled in another course at Grand Valley to complete my Masters in Choral Conducting. I'm keeping all my options open. And I have had several encouraging interviews with schools about positions next fall. But in the meantime, I need to do this. Jim has offered me a six-month detective-in-training position with the department. He thinks he will be able to pay me a small salary and expenses as well as pay for state police detective training."

"It seems that you have already made up your mind."

"I have, Dad. You both always taught me to look at all the facts and make my own choices and I have. I sat in on a meeting of the task force yesterday. There is progress, but I can't tell you about it yet."

"What about seeing Maria? You still want to see her some, right? Are you sure about all this?" Tom's dad quizzed him.

"I am, Dad. Jim has not asked me for any decision to stay on past the six months. I'm free to make my own choice about what's next at that time. I'll still be with Maria as much as I can, just not 24/7."

"Son, you know we'll support you whatever you decide. We just want you, and Maria, to be happy."

After saying good night, Tom drove home thinking how much he loved his parents and appreciated their support. The answering machine was blinking when he came in the door. It was Jim saying they had an answer already from Lansing. "The fingerprint on the back of the rear view mirror is Joe Antonelli's. We have a solid case to get search warrants and to bring him in for questioning. We'll wait for the evidence to get back from Lansing and we'll plan our course. We'll have a meeting Friday morning to lay out our plan. See you there."

---

## 71

The next morning, Tom walked into Maria's room, went to her bedside, and took her hand. "Hello, sweetheart, I love you. I know you hear me. Open those beautiful blue eyes and talk to me."

There was no response. Tom didn't expect one, but he always hoped that one day he will walk in and see her smile, or she will squeeze his hand. "I'll tell you soon about some changes I've made. But for now, how about I sing to you a little until you do wake up?"

A half hour later, Tom was well into one of Maria's favorite musicals, *South Pacific*, playing all the parts as usual. When he started singing softly in a falsetto voice, *I'm Gonna Wash That Man Right out of My Hair*, he heard a little giggle behind him. He turned to see Maria's nurse grinning at him.

"Tom, you know, she's not hearing you," she said seriously.

Tom said, "Want to bet?"

"I wouldn't take that bet with you," she smiled, "I hope you're right."

"Let's step out into the hallway for a few minutes." After she pulled the door closed softly, Tom went on, "I didn't want her to hear this as though she wasn't there. I'm not going to be coming as often as

I have been. I've taken a new job so I'll be coming in at odd times. Do I need to talk to someone else about this?"

"No, you don't need to. I'll make a note of it in her chart."

"Here's another phone number where I can be reached when she wakes up. It's the number for the Muskegon police department. If I'm not at home or there, they'll know where I am and get word to me."

"She will miss you, Tom."

"I know, but it's also what she would want for me, get out, and start earning a living so we can get on with our life when she wakes up. I think she'll be excited about what I'm doing."

Maria's parents walked up and heard the last part of the conversation. Her dad said, "What's this, Tom? You're not going to be here as often? And what's this new job you're talking about?"

"Hello to both of you. Why don't you say hello to Maria, and we'll go downstairs, have lunch, and I'll tell you all about it?"

Tom waited patiently in the hall while Maria's parents went in to hug Maria. She looked so beautiful since her wounds healed. It really did look like she was sleeping.

Maria's parents came out and they headed to the cafeteria. After lunch and over a new cup of coffee for each, Tom filled them in on what he had decided.

Maria's dad was a little taken aback that Tom had gone back to the task force. He said, "I thought you were all done with that."

"Jim, the police chief, thinks I can help a lot. He offered me a temporary job, six months actually. If one of my teaching job applications pans out, I can make that choice for next fall. We'll see what happens."

"Do you think this group might bring in some other muscle?"

"No, I don't and neither does the rest of the task force. The feeling is that the group will lay low for a while and not do anything that will draw attention to themselves."

Maria's mother said, "I would think you might have enough of that business after what happened to Maria."

"Mom," Tom said, "you both know the battle I had over the guilt. I spent a lot of time talking to a counselor and with Father Flannery.

Now I just want to help find the people responsible for it. The man who shot us is dead, but the people who made it happen are still in the clear. We think we can get them, and I want to help do that."

She said, "I think I understand that."

"Me too," her dad said. "Get the people who did this to our girl."

"We will, you'll see. I can't say anything about where we are, but I'll let you know when I can."

"Ok, Tom. We'll stay close to her. You go get the bad guys."

## 72

The whole group was at the Century Club meeting room on time. Breakfast was served and as usual the initial conversation was just idle chit-chat, catching up on what everyone had been doing with their families. When the serving staff was finally gone, George, irritated, looked around the room. "Alright everyone. Let's have it. I hear you talking about what's going on in your lives. But there's a tension that I hear in your voices. What's on your minds?"

Tim said, "I don't know about the rest of you, but let me tell you how I feel. I have a lot of money tied up in this venture as most of us do. I don't like operating in the dark. At our last meeting, we agreed to sit tight and do nothing. We need to know what is going on. I think we ought to try to find some way to learn what the police are up to."

Several spoke at once. George boomed, "One at a time please. Wendell, what do you think?"

"I agree with Tim. Operating in the dark as we are leaves us open to making some mistakes. And mistakes may lead them right to us."

Joe said, "I don't see how anyone at the police department could connect us to Harry. I was the only one who had contact with him. While he knew my full name and how to find me at the restaurant, that wasn't true of any of you. And there is no evidence that he ever told anyone else my name. He was a loner. I impressed on him how important it was that we are under the radar and he understood the importance. And the police never caught up with him until he was dead. My thinking is that there is no way anyone could tie anyone, even me, to Harry and Harry ain't talking."

George looked at Joe thoughtfully and asked, "Joe, how can you be so sure?"

"It has been weeks since Harry got shot and there isn't anyone sniffing around me or my business. I feel pretty safe." Joe frowned and then caught himself not realizing that George watched him. *I wonder if the car lot salesman would remember me. Better not say anything about that for now.*

George went on, "It seems to me that we have two alternatives. One is to find out who Harry was working with. We could hire someone to talk to whoever turns up, not muscle necessarily, but someone who is good at sniffing out info. Our attorney likely has a private detective on retainer. I'll see if we can hire him for some snooping around. I'm not hearing any scuttlebutt about the electronics company from our previous contacts, but it would be good to know. Second, we could try to get to someone in the police department. And maybe there is a third alternative. We could get some muscle again and go after Tom O'Banion. Any of you know another 'Harry?' But no, let's leave that one until we get some more data."

Joe said, "I've met the city manager, Sam. He is a regular at my restaurant. I could have lunch with him sometime, just a casual meeting, and just talk about things in general as far as the city goes."

"I'm not so sure that's a good idea, Joe. One little slip and it will be a problem," Tim said.

"Trust me, if he was a source for Harry and us, he'll be a little skittish. He just might let something slip. I'll be careful."

Larry said, "I know a policeman. We went to high school together — he's a good friend. I can ask him to let me know if any action starts up. Anything new being checked out. Something might turn up."

Again, George studied Joe and finally said, "The two of you do that. Just be very careful. And I'll have a chat with my friend in the D.A.'s office over coffee or lunch. The rest of you keep listening to local talk, be a little aggressive, but careful about it. Let's meet again in a couple of weeks unless something breaks. We'll see you all at 8:30 Saturday morning at the Occidental."

## 73

W hen Tom walked into the task force room, he could feel the energy and excitement. Something else must have broken. Tom knew the fingerprint was a big break, but this level of excitement must mean some other evidence had surfaced.

He poured himself a cup of coffee and met the two new State men and Ken. They were chattering excitedly about big breaks. Tom was anxious to know what was going on. Just then the Chief came in with Mark and Dave.

Dave took over the meeting. "We sure are glad you joined us, Tom. Those two ideas of yours paid off. We have Antonelli solid for buying the car – the salesman identified him, and we have the fingerprint match now. We have Joe Antonelli cold. His fingerprint taken from his liquor license application matches the one on back of the mirror of the blue Chevrolet. We need to build a strategy to bring Antonelli in and pry the rest of the names from him."

"Tony, why don't you tell us what else you found out about Antonelli?"

"We told you at the last meeting that Antonelli has had a deer hunting license for the last four years and that he has a long range rifle with a mounted scope that gave him a shooting range of 300 yards. We checked the range from where a man with a white Buick LaSabre had been seen with what could be a rifle. The range was just less than 300 yards. We also confirmed that Joe Antonelli owns a white Buick LaSabre. When we can compare the bullets from Harry's body with those from Antonelli's rifle, we may have him for murder."

Ken stepped in, "My specialty is financial forensics. I was able to figure out where they bank by finding out that Joe has two accounts at New Shores Bank, one for his restaurant and the other, a mystery. We're getting warrants to get a look at those accounts. When we get the warrants later today, we'll see if there's anyone else on the mystery account. Antonelli's name is on it because we tracked it through his social security number. Hopefully, there's another name that will help us figure out who the other eight are. And we will be able to see how much money is involved in their scheme and what they're paying out. I also have some team members in Lansing checking out properties along the lakefront to see if there has been any ownership change in the past year and what's pending. I know they set up a shell corporation, but I'll keep following the money and see who we can tie the purchases to."

Mark reported, "Dave and I interviewed the consultant that Fred hired. He told us he heard the name 'Group of Nine' at City Hall notably from Sam Milford, the city manager. This fits in with what Fred's secretary said about Sam's behavior. He would either rush to his phone or suddenly have an errand out of the building whenever he heard news about Fred's plans for the city. Alice also shared some other news — she said that about a year ago, Fred was trying to bring a second casting business to town. A man named Larry Olsen came to see Fred. There was shouting in Fred's office and Mr. Olsen stormed out of Fred's office slamming the door behind him. She said she had forgotten the incident until now. All of this is circumstantial and not enough to bring them in for questioning, but it is strange behavior and should be followed up."

The Chief said, "I don't need to tell you this, but I'm going to anyway. We have to be careful how we do this. If word gets out that we are looking at properties and bank accounts, the group may just go to ground. We might never find them."

"And when we bring Joe Antonelli in, it also has to be done right. My initial thought was that we arrest Antonelli and charge him for the murder of Harry and hiring Harry to murder Fred. With that he can be held without bail, I think. I need to get with our legal people to see how this works. If he isn't handled right, he could demand a lawyer early in the game and we lose some of our advantage with him. We need him to get at the others in the group.

"After I talked to Dave and Mark about this, here's what we think we should do. We'll bring in Antonelli without fanfare, get him into an interrogation room, and start the process by letting him know we have him on murder and that we know he is a part of the group of nine. We'll let him know he can help himself if he will help us to get the rest. We won't charge him immediately unless he asks for his lawyer. Comments?"

Tom asked, "Should we hold off on Antonelli until we get at least one other name? We might have more success if we can play one off against the other. Hey, I just remembered something. Maria and I were having dinner with Fred and Eleanor back around Christmas and Fred mentioned Larry Olsen, told me the same story as Alice, and asked if Olsen might be a member of the group. Dave, should we look into this Larry Olsen? Could he be a member of the group of nine?"

Dave said, "Good idea, Tom. Let's see what we can find out about him. Tony, why don't you look into Olsen, low key and behind the scene? See who he hangs out with and who he goes to dinner with. Do you think you can have something by next Monday?"

Tony replied, "I'll get right on it after the meeting. I should have a good start by Monday's meeting."

"Ken, keep digging on the bank account. It seems likely that there would be at least two names on the bank account. We could figure out two more of the group. Maybe we'll get lucky and identify another couple of the group?" Ken nodded.

"Who wants to check out the Occidental and see if anyone there can tell you about a group of men who regularly met there – that seems to be the place where this group would get together?"

Tom jumped in, "I'll take that. I know people there since we always held our Christmas concert there."

The Chief said, "Let's meet Monday morning 9:00 o'clock. We may need to move fast when those warrants come in. We'll be looking for any new ideas about how this should be done. If we do this right, we can get them all."

## 74

The Chief's secretary, Gerri, knocked on the door. "Chief, sorry to interrupt. The interim mayor, Mr. Svensen, just called and is holding to talk with you."

Jim told her, "Tell him I'm just finishing up a meeting, and I'll be there in a couple of minutes." When she left, he looked around the group, and said, "I wonder what he could want? He hasn't been too anxious to meet with me. He seems to be settling into the Mayor's job pretty well. Don't go away – I'll be right back."

He returned about five minutes later. "He wants to meet, says there are some problems he wants to talk about. He thinks I might be able to help him with them. He wouldn't tell me what's going on – says he can only talk about them in person."

Dave asked, "Jim, what do you know about him? Do you think he's in the Group's pockets?"

"I don't know. I've never actually met him. As the Vice Mayor, he has to stand in until we can hold another election. All I've heard is that he is a pretty straight shooter. I'm going to go see what I can find out. I'll be careful not to leak anything. Why don't you go ahead and have lunch? I'll come back to fill you in and get your reactions."

IT WAS a quick five minute walk to City Hall and the mayor's office. Alice said, "Good morning, Chief. He's ready for you. I'll show you right in."

"Thank you, Alice. I hope you are doing alright with all this change."

"Yes, Chief, I am. I was with Fred ever since he came. But it's working out." She opened the door and let him in to the mayor's office.

"Good morning, Mr. Mayor."

"Good morning to you, Chief. Please call me Al."

"I will if you call me Jim. What can I do for you?

"Well, Chief, er...Jim, it's like this. Until Fred's death, I was sort of a nonentity at City Hall. No real responsibilities, not many people came to me for opinions. Oh, Fred kept me up-to-date on what he was doing but I was just a figurehead. Since Fred's been gone, I've been thrust into the fire so to speak and I'm not really up to speed yet. I'm learning but it's slow. Alice agreed to stay on, and she has been a big help. In fact, she brought something to my attention that I want to talk about with you. I'm going to ask her to tell you about it."

He buzzed Alice and asked her to come in. When she did, he asked her to sit and tell the Chief, Jim, what she had told him before.

She started slowly, "Jim, I told you or maybe one of your detectives about Sam and his assistant Jerry. The minute that something new was discussed about Fred's plans for the city, the two of them would ask to be excused for meetings they had out of the building or a phone call they had to make. Sam would usually be on the phone and Jerry would leave the building. What I didn't say before is that I followed Jerry one day to the Hostess café and saw him meet with the big man you have now identified as Fred's killer. Jerry didn't see me, I know it. He had his back to me and was engrossed in his conversation with the man. When I saw the picture being circulated, it all came back. Fred's killer was the man Jerry was talking to. And now, since Fred's been gone, they hardly leave the building at lunch time."

Jim nodded. "We've had our suspicions for some time about Sam and Jerry. Fred told me that he couldn't figure out some of the things they said, things that didn't make sense. Al, can you get them in here on some pretense? Ask them to step in about ten minutes from now. During that time, I'll call the office and get two detectives here to tail them and see where they go."

"I can. Go ahead and make your call. Alice, would you do as the chief said? Don't tell them anything other than he has some questions."

When Sam and Jerry came to the Mayor's office, Alice announced them and showed them in.

Al said, "I think you both know the Chief, Jim. Jim...Sam and Jerry."

Sam asked, "Good to see you again, Chief. What's up? Alice said you have some questions for us. Is this about Fred's murder? I thought that with Fred's killer dead, the case would be closed."

"You're right – we do know who killed Fred. What we don't know is why. We're just trying to get some notion of why all this happened." They spent the next fifteen minutes answering his questions about Fred, what had been going on at City Hall during that time, and some questions about Harry. Both of them swore they had never seen the man before. Jim thanked them and let them go. When Sam and Jerry were out of the room, Jim said to Al, "Well, we'll see if they react."

Both Sam and Jerry left their offices within five minutes of being dismissed and headed for the door. The chief was talking with Alice with his back to them, but Alice had a clear view. Alice told him the two had left together. Jim radioed his men, "On the way out." He said to Alice, "They took the bait, now we'll see where they end up. Thanks, Alice. Let us know when they come back."

Sam entered Joe Antonelli's restaurant and was shown to a booth. He ordered a drink and asked if Mr. Antonelli was in. "Would you ask him to come and see me. Tell him that Sam Milford, the city manager is here, and would like to talk with him."

"Sure, Mr. Milford, I'll get him for you."

The front door opened, and a man came in. As he removed his

topcoat, he spotted Sam in the booth. He said to the hostess, "Could I have a table over in this section?"

She said, "Are you alone? And wouldn't you prefer a booth? We're not busy yet today."

"Thank you, but no. The table will be fine. Would you let my waitress know I'd like some coffee? I have to go back to the office, so no drink for me today." He smiled apologetically. As the hostess took him to his table, the waitress she had signaled was right there with the coffee and a menu. He took the chair that angled away from Sam so he could still see Sam without being obvious about it. As the waitress left with his order, he saw Joe Antonelli go to Sam's booth and sit down across from him. Antonelli was almost facing him, but he had never met Antonelli so he wasn't worried about being made. Joe and Sam were engaged in a heated conversation. They paused and Antonelli signaled the waitress to bring Sam another drink. They calmed down a little but kept talking.

Antonelli stood up, Sam took his drink, and they both walked toward the back of the restaurant. The detective told the hostess that he had to go to the car for a moment, but he would be right back. Since he had left his coat on a chair, she said, "Fine, we'll get you some fresh coffee and bring your sandwich when you come back in."

He went to his car, radioed the Chief, and started to tell him what had happened. The Chief said, "Hold on. Let's not take a chance that someone is listening to the police channel. There should be a pay phone near the restaurant so call me back on that."

The detective went back into the restaurant and asked for the pay phone's location. After he filled in the chief, he asked if he should follow Sam when he leaves. The Chief said, "No, finish your lunch and come on in. We don't want the waitress or the hostess to get suspicious. By the way, Jerry was followed to his home. His tail is sitting on him to see if he comes back out and goes somewhere else. You know what? I changed my mind. Finish your lunch in a hurry and follow Sam when he leaves. Keep me informed."

# 75

W hen the chief walked back into the task force room, he said, "We just set a trap for Sam and Jerry at City Hall and one of them, Sam, took the bait. He went right over to Joe Antonelli's restaurant, had a heated conversation, and then they both adjourned to the back room. They probably went to Joe's office or one of the private dining rooms in the back. Sam came out a few minutes later. I have a tail on him. The long and short of this is that we should move this afternoon to pick up Antonelli and maybe Sam too. What do you think? Should we move today? The warrants just came in and I don't want this to blow up in our face. Talk to me."

The room erupted with comments and questions. Dave slapped his notebook on the table. "Whoa, guys, one at a time. Chief, can we get a tail on Joe right now?"

"Mark, get Ed to tail Joe Antonelli. Tell him Antonelli drives a white Buick LeSabre. Antonelli should still be at the restaurant so Ed should get right there. Tell him to stay on him and keep us posted."

He continued, "Dave, I think you're headed in the right direction. We need both of them and we need to get them as fast as possible. We can't risk them talking to anyone else. I want to be on the team that goes after Antonelli. I want to see the look on Joe's face when we get him. And remember, don't go in shooting. Let's get them in here quietly."

Dave started issuing orders, "Team one will be the Chief, Mark, and Tom. They will connect with Antonelli's tail and bring Antonelli in. Team two will be Tony, Ken, and I. We will meet up with Sam's tail and bring him in. If we do this quickly enough, no one will know where the targets have gone. Let's go do it. Be careful out there. Antonelli may be armed, Sam not likely but you never know."

Team one caught up with Antonelli and his tail as Antonelli was turning into the Ovals area. Antonelli was circling around the Ovals toward the Coast Guard station so Mark turned left onto the service road and got in front of Antonelli. Antonelli parked close to the walk out to the lighthouse, took what looked like a bulky covered fishing pole out of his trunk. Mark pulled in behind Antonelli's car from the left and his tail behind from the right. Tom stayed in his car since he wasn't armed. Jim and Mark approached Antonelli with guns drawn. Jim said "Hello Joe, we'd like you to come with us."

Joe started backing toward the water. "Why, what's going on?"

Jim replied, "We have some questions about Harry Walker's murder. What's in the bag? Looks pretty heavy. Can we take a look?"

Joe blustered, "This is just my new fishing pole. I was going out on the lighthouse pier and try it out. I hear they're running today."

Mark reached for the fishing pole. Joe held it back, but when Mark insisted, he reluctantly handed it over. Mark opened it and there was a rifle with a mounted scope.

"Joe, were you about to throw this away? We need to check out this rifle. We think this is the gun that killed Harry. We also have your fingerprint in Harry's car. And we have a witness that saw a white Buick LeSabre parked close to where Harry was shot, and you own a white Buick LeSabre. Between this rifle and your fingerprint from Harry's car, we have all the evidence we need to charge you. We'll tell you all about it down at the station. Into the car, now!" Joe's shoulders dropped and he went docilely to the car. The Chief put him into the back seat of the car. Joe looked up as Tom came up to speak to the

Chief. "What are you doing here? Is this your doing? Wasn't it enough that you humiliated my daughter?"

"I didn't humiliate your daughter, Joe. She brought that on herself. And it appears that you did this to yourself – it's your gun and fingerprint."

Team two found Sam in a Peck St. bar where he was slouched over the bar with three empty shots lined up in front of him. Dave and John went into the bar. Ken and the tail waited around back in case Sam ran. Dave and Ken walked up to Sam and stood one on each side. Dave said "Sam Milford, would you come with us?"

"Who are you?"

"I know you don't want us to show our badges in here. Just come outside with us and we'll tell you all about it."

When they got outside, Dave said, "We're state police detectives. The chief told us about his conversation with you and we just have a few more questions."

"I should call my wife."

"That's all taken care of. There's a team at your house as we speak letting your wife know that you are at the police station answering our questions. How you answer will decide how you quickly you get home."

Once Joe and Sam were stashed in separate interrogation rooms, Mark gave Ken the warrant to serve on the bank and told him to get started analyzing the data. "As soon as you get any name or names on the account, give me a call."

## 76

The team was gathered in the task force room talking about the success of the arrests of the two men. The upbeat tone in the room was palpable. Jim said, "You all did great work this afternoon. Now, we need to work fast to get all we can from these two men before they lawyer up." Just then, Gerri knocked and said, "Chief, Ken is on the phone from the bank. Shall I put him through to here or do you want to take it in your office?"

"Put it through to here, Gerri. I want everyone to hear what he found." Jim grabbed the phone on the first ring and said, "Hello, Ken, what do you have for us? We're all here. Are you in a place where you can speak freely?"

Ken spoke up loudly, "Yes, I am. The bank has been most cooperative. I'm in a private office. The first name on the account is..."

Jim broke in with, "Don't say the name, Ken. Is it one of those we have here?"

"Yes, it is. And there's one other name on the account. Do you want to know that name?"

Jim paused. "No, hang on, Ken. John Strahan is still president of the bank, right? Do you know if he's in?

"He is. He personally set me up in here. He gave me all the files that we'll need. He also gave me his direct line so I could call him if I need him or other files."

"Good job, Ken. I'll need that phone number. We'll get Mr. Strahan to come in shortly and sign a release for all the files we'll need. He can lock up all the files and give you the key along with access to the building. In the meantime, keep working on the files to find out all you can. We'll be here late tonight. The interrogation teams will be working on each man within the next five minutes."

Jim called John Strahan and first thanked him for his cooperation. Everything he asked for was granted. Mr. Strahan said, "Jim, if there is any way I can do more, please let me know. Do you want to send an officer over here to guard the office where your investigator has the files? Or do you want me to box them up and send them along for you?"

"The warrant covers the contingency of removing the files to here. That would work best if you could get it done. We will be working late tonight on this so this would free you and your staff to get the files here and go home normally. And Mr. Strahan, it is important that no one else know what account we are investigating. Understand? No one. I could have Mr. Swensen, the district attorney; call you if you need his assurance that this is necessary."

"No need for that, Chief. We'll have the files in your hands and mum's the word. I'll give Ken my home number. Please call me there any time if you need me for anything."

"Thank you, Mr. Strahan." Turning to Gerri, he asked her to get the district attorney on the phone.

The phone rang, "Hello, Jim, this is Harvey. What's going on?"

Jim filled him in on the afternoon's work and said, "We're about to start questioning them. Do you want to be involved?"

"Not at this time, Jim. But as soon as you get all you can and you think I should be directly involved, call me back, even if it's tonight or this weekend. By the way, have they lawyered up yet?"

"No, not yet. Sam hasn't seen the need, but he is only a minor player. Joe is so tired and worn out over the whole thing that he is ready to spill it all out. I'll let you know what we get."

Jim joined Mark in the interrogation room where Joe was hand-cuffed to the table. He looked up when Jim entered the room and said, "Jim, is this necessary? Do you think I'm going to cause a problem? I just want to get this over with. By the way, could you have someone call my daughter, Sara? She shouldn't be alone. Tell her I want her just to go stay with her aunt and uncle until I can talk to her."

Jim signaled Mark to take the cuffs off. "No, Joe, I don't believe you will cause a problem. We have a strong case against you. There is certain to be a match of the bullet we took from Harry's body with the one from your rifle. We have your fingerprint from the new car you bought Harry and an I.D. by the man you bought it from. And we have your name on a bank account that has a lot of money in it."

Joe just sat shaking his head. "I'm so tired of it all. I got in over my head."

"So why don't you tell us the whole story? I'm going to record it since I may have to step out a couple of times. When I do, I'll call Sara personally. Just start wherever you want." Joe wiped his eyes, started to speak, but was so choked up, he couldn't get started. "Do you want some coffee or water?" Joe just nodded. "Go ahead, Joe. Tell us the names of all the other members of the group and as best you know it, how it started, and where it was heading."

Joe started talking. Once he started, he couldn't stop. As asked, he named the rest of the group. Jim stopped him periodically to clarify what role each of the men played and how long they had been together. He told Jim that the group had been operating for several years. Joe said he got involved when he had overheard a conversation at his restaurant and asked how he could help. Eventually, he was accepted and worked his way up to becoming the contact and financial person of the group. That's why he was the first listing on the bank account. He was their primary contact. They all knew him at the bank because of his restaurant. He told Jim that he thought they were just a bunch of powerful guys who wanted to develop Muskegon the way they wanted. He was proud at first that he had been accepted and made the money guy. He realized later that they were keeping their distance so Joe would be the fall guy if things went south. The only other guy that knew what was going on with the money was Larry Olsen. There needed to be two names on the account and he was sort of second in command so he's got access to the books, too.

Gerri knocked and opened the door quietly. "Jim, that call you have been expecting just came in."

Jim turned to Joe. "Joe, keep the details coming. Gerri will bring some more coffee for you. I'll be right back."

Jim went directly to his office and picked up the phone, "Hello, Judge McVie. Thanks for calling. I know it's late so I'll get right to the point. We executed the warrants you gave us for Antonelli and Milford today, but now I need eight more warrants – Joe Antonelli gave me eight more names. They're all going to be meeting Saturday morning. Joe is going to wear a wire to the meeting so we can get them on tape confirming what Joe told us."

Judge McVie said, "Ok, Jim. Do you have enough to arrest them?"

Jim answered, "Well, Judge, we have their names from Joe's confession. Joe stated on the record that they voted unanimously to bring Harry Walker in to put pressure on the mayor, and then when he wouldn't give up, they voted to 'use whatever force necessary to get rid of him'. We have them at least for conspiracy to commit murder. Our forensic detective has linked them to the shell company that has purchased property on the lakefront and put options on other land. But we need the tape that Joe's going to get at the meeting to make the case solid. We need the warrants now so we'll be ready to arrest them. This all needs to happen quickly before they hear of what's coming down. We don't want them to leave town."

The judge said, "Give me the names. I'll fill out the warrants and have them ready for you. But you need that tape, Jim, before I'll sign them. I have my secretary on the other line, and she will record them and prepare the warrants."

As Jim soon as gave the names, the secretary left to prepare the warrants. Judge McVie got back on the line and said, "Jim, are you sure about these men? They are quite prominent in the community."

Jim said, "I know, your honor. Because of their prominence, they will likely insist on bail right away. They won't want to spend the weekend in jail."

"Alright Jim. Call me when you have the tape and make sure the tape has the evidence we need. I'll be at home if you need me for anything else."

Jim thanked him and said, "I will, your Honor."

Jim called Sara next. When she answered, he said, "Sara, your Dad is here to answer some questions for us. He asked me to tell you to go to your aunt and uncle's and stay with them until he calls you."

She asked, "What's this all about? Is he ok?"

"Sara, it's just routine questioning. He just doesn't want you to be alone."

"All right. Please tell him I'll get right there and not to worry. Thank you for calling me."

Sara wondered, *What's going on. She had no aunt or uncle. That was their code for me to get to the place up on Scenic Drive. I'd better pick up some groceries and get up there.* Sara packed some clothes, took the suitcase out to her car. Dad had gotten the car for her as soon as she turned sixteen and passed her driver's test. She didn't drive it to school. It was just for times like this. She thought, *I'd better take Dad's gun with me.* But when she went to the gun cabinet, it wasn't there. She looked in a couple of other places it might have been to no avail. *What's up,* she wondered. She locked the house and headed out.

As he went back to the interrogation room, he was greeted by a tired Joe Antonelli, just now winding up his statement. Joe said, "Jim, I think I'm done. What happens now?"

"First off, I called Sara. She agreed to go to her uncle and aunt's house right away and not to worry about her."

"Thank you," he said, thinking, *Good, she got the signal. She'll be at the Scenic Drive cabin when I get out of here.*

With the recorder still on, Jim continued, "Gerri, my secretary, will type up your statement and bring it in for you to sign. It will be witnessed by two people and will go into the record as your official statement."

"What's to happen to me?"

"Joe, are you willing to wear a wire to the meeting? We need to get these guys to admit their role in hiring Harry and Fred's death. Otherwise, it's your word against theirs. You're going to have to get them to say on tape that they voted unanimously to take Fred out. And that they're behind all the purchases on the lakefront. Killing Harry was wrong. If you do this, it will go a lot easier on you."

"Yes, Jim. I can do that. This has gotten way out of hand. I just want this to be over and for my daughter to be safe."

"Ok, Joe. It's not going to be easy. To make sure we don't tip them off, I'm going to let you go tonight, but not to go home. We made a reservation for you and your daughter at a lodge in Whitehall. Tell your daughter that you just need to get away for a couple of days. You'll be guarded all night and we'll bring you back in tomorrow after the meeting. In the meantime, try to act as normal as possible. Don't tell your daughter what's going on. She'll be safer not knowing."

"Jim, should I get an attorney?"

"That would be a good thing for you to do, Joe. You'll need a good criminal attorney. If you don't have someone in mind, we can help you get an attorney."

"Well, I'll think on that over the weekend and call someone Monday."

"Fine, Joe. If you have nothing more, I'll turn off the recorder. These officers will take you back to your car and then follow you to Whitehall and get you checked in at the lodge. One will stay there as well. Just stay there and we'll get you to the meeting. We're going to have undercover officers at the meeting posing as waiters so we'll see you there. And they will be there to protect you if something goes wrong."

Jim left and went to the second interrogation room to see how that team was doing with Sam Milford. Dave stepped out of the room and said to Jim, "We have all we're going to get from him. He was just a supplier of information about what was happening at City Hall. I don't know what the district attorney could charge him on."

Jim frowned. "We can't take a chance he'll leak something. We have to charge him with something. Can we build a charge on his meeting with Joe Antonelli? Joe said he was passing on information and that he wanted more money when he started having direct contact with Joe."

"That should work. You may have to clear it with the district attorney."

"Alright, I will. We need to keep him over the weekend and by then, we will have picked up the rest of the group."

"Good, I'll let him know he's going to the holding cell. When he talks to his wife, have him tell her that he has been put in a safe place, but she should tell anyone who asks that he is out of town until Monday or Tuesday. And remind her she should say nothing to anyone that no one should know about this until later."

Jim added, "Good work, Dave. When he's been taken care of, please come to the task force room. We'll be working on our strategy for tomorrow morning."

Jim went to his office and called his wife. "I'm working late tonight sweetheart. If any of the gang calls and asks where we were, just say that I was working on something at the department and we couldn't make it. We'll see them next time. I won't likely be home until between nine and ten. Love you."

---

The phone rang, George's wife said, "I wonder who that could be this time of the evening. It's almost bedtime." She answered it and said to George, "He said he wanted to talk to you, it's not a voice I know," handing the phone to George.

George took the phone and walked into his office. The voice on the phone was his contact in the DA's office.

"George, I have some news for you. There is a State Police specialist looking into bank accounts around town. I don't know which bank has been targeted."

George asked, "Have you heard any names that they are trying to tie to the accounts?"

"No, no names yet. I'll nose around and let you know right away if I hear any names."

"Thanks, call me anytime. This is crucial. If you get anything new by tomorrow morning, I'll be in a meeting at the Occidental at 8:30 a.m. They'll get me out of the meeting to answer a call from you."

"Ok, I'll be in touch."

---

J im entered the task force room with more energy than he'd felt in a long time. "Ken will be here any minute with boxes of files from the bank. You all have been working so hard. I know we're not done yet, but I think we need to celebrate. Do you all like Doo Drop Inn perch?"

A loud chorus of "yes" erupted in the room. Dave patted his stomach. "Yes and some of their onion rings I've come to like too much."

"Ok. Perch dinners and onion rings it is. We have soft drinks, iced tea, and coffee here. I'll send someone to pick them up for us. While we're waiting, we can recap what we know and what's going to happen."

Jim continued, "Joe Antonelli confessed that he found Harry and brought him to the group. He knew him from his restaurant. The group wanted Harry to scare Fred so he would quit trying to bring in businesses to the lakefront that the group didn't want. When Fred didn't go along with the warnings, Harry upped the ante and took him out. Joe said the group voted unanimously to kill Fred. Joe also confessed that he shot Harry because he didn't want Harry to hurt anyone else like he did Tom and Maria. He's agreed to wear a wire to the meeting on Saturday and record the group confirming what he says in his statement. Did I miss anything, Dave?"

Dave added, "He gave us the names of the rest of the group. And he told us that Larry Olsen is sort of next in command and the second name on the checking account. Olsen knew about all the property deals."

Tom interjected, "He confessed to bringing in Harry? He's responsible for what happened to Fred and Maria and me? He's going to rot in jail or worse!"

"Calm down, Tom. We've got him and he's going to pay. Now we have to make sure the rest of the group pays, too. Let's talk about what we're going to do tomorrow."

"Here's the plan," Mark started. "Joe is going to be wired. We're going to use some of our officers undercover as waiters. When the meeting is over, Joe is going to pass the tape to one of our undercover people. Once we have what we need, we'll get the warrants and arrest them Sunday morning at the Century Club."

OFFICER PETE THOMPSON strolled by the conference room and asked the desk sergeant, "What's going on with all the perch dinners? Gotta be Doo Drop Inn perch. I'd recognize that good smell anywhere."

She laughed. "I don't know. They've been in the interrogation rooms all afternoon with a couple of guys. One is down in the holding tank, and I saw the other one escorted out by a couple of our officers. Now they're back in the big conference room, talking and eating perch dinners from Doo Drop. I have no idea what it's all about."

He looked again at the conference room door. He could only make out the Chief – everyone else had their backs to him. He was puzzled and wondering what was up. Larry had asked him to call him if there was anything unusual going on here. Could this be something Larry would want to know about? Interrogating a couple of guys all afternoon? He wondered who was in the holding cells and who got escorted out? He thought, *Why not go down there and see for myself?*

He clocked out and finished packing up his gear, then went down to the holding cells. There was a middle aged man in one, reasonably well-dressed. He didn't look like a criminal. He looked like a businessman. What could he be in here for? Pete went to the officer in charge of the cell block and asked, "Who's the guy in the holding cell?"

The guard frowned and said, "I'm not supposed to say anything about him to anyone."

"Aw, come on. I'm off duty. I'm just curious about what's going on. There's a bunch of guys holed up in the conference room now and the desk sergeant said they interrogated this guy all afternoon. Who is he? You can tell me and I won't say anything about it."

"They told me not to say anything. They didn't even tell me what his name is or what he was being charged with."

Pete went back upstairs to try again with the desk sergeant. "What's with all the cloak and dagger? Why all the secrecy? What are those guys doing in there?"

She shrugged. "It's above my pay grade, and yours, too."

On his way home, Pete wondered if he should call Larry Olsen. Larry had taken good care of him a couple of times when he needed a loan so he owed him, but he didn't really know anything other than a couple of guys got questioned. He had dinner with his family, wife and two children. After playing a game of Clue with his wife and the kids, at which he made several mistakes that he usually didn't, the kids went off to bed. His wife turned to him and asked, "What's got you so preoccupied tonight? Your mind wasn't on the game tonight."

He told her it was nothing. Just something strange going on at the station. *None of my business.* He thought that he had better call Larry on the way to work tomorrow.

# 79

---

Tom leaves the station and goes to talk to Doug. He swears him to secrecy and tells him that Joe has confessed to bringing in Harry and to killing Harry. Doug can barely control his anger.

Tom said, "Joe also named the other eight. I can't tell you those names yet."

Doug remembered that Tom had told him about Larry Olsen. That he was the one that Fred thought was squashing the deal with the electronics firm and, earlier, the other casting firm. He wondered, *Maybe he is one of the eight others.*

Doug asked, "What is going to happen to all of them."

Tom said, "Joe is going to wear a wire to the meeting on Saturday and gather the rest of the evidence they need to link them to Harry."

Doug asked, "Why can't you tell me who the others are? I'm not about to tell anyone else."

Tom jumped on him. "Doug, I shouldn't have told you about Larry Olsen. I will let you know it all when the meeting is over tomorrow."

Doug glared at him. "It seems you don't trust me, Tom. What's going on?"

"It isn't that I don't trust you. I'm just trying to do right by Jim. The chief has set me up to be a part of the investigation team."

"Ok, buddy. But I'll be looking for some answers soon. After all, this group hurt people I care about."

"I know, Doug. We'll talk tomorrow night."

After Tom left, Doug sat pondering, *It looks like Joe will get what's coming to him. I better fix on Olsen.* He checked his phone book and there was his address. *He just had to figure out how to take care of him.*

## 80

P ete stopped at a pay phone about ten minutes from the station the next morning. He called the number that Larry had given him, and when Mrs. Olsen answered, he said, "Mrs. Olsen, this is Pete, an old high school friend of Larry's. We bumped into each other a day or so ago and he suggested I call sometime for coffee or something. Is he home?"

She said, "Of course, I'll get him. Larry, Pete is on the phone, says he is an old high school friend."

Larry came on and said, "Hi Pete. What's up?"

"You wanted me to call you if anything unusual was going on at the station. Well yesterday afternoon, there was. A group of men led by Chief Jim were meeting in the conference room, even having dinner brought in. They had interrogated a couple of guys all afternoon, and they put one in a holding cell and the other was escorted out by a couple of officers. I talked to another guy in the locker room and he said the one escorted out was late 50s with a big handlebar mustache, slightly balding and a little on the heavy side. The guy in the holding cell was younger, dark haired, small goatee. I couldn't get their names from anyone without raising some eyebrows."

Larry thought the first guy sounded like it could be Joe Antonelli

– there aren't too many guys with a handlebar mustache. Before he could say anything, Pete started up again, "I remember thinking that I've seen the younger guy before, maybe in the paper, something to do with the city." Larry thought that could be the city manager, Sam.

Larry said, "Thanks for the call, Pete. I can't make it today but maybe next week. I'll give you a call."

He hung up and said to his wife, "I didn't want to get together with Pete today. I've been thinking about a surprise for you and the kids. We're taking a trip today."

She said, "Where to? We can't just drop everything."

He casually continued, "Aw c'mon. We haven't had a weekend vacation with the kids in a while. Pack up a few things for all of us. And don't forget the bathing suits. Don't take any phone calls. I don't want to be delayed. I'm going out to do a couple of errands and we'll leave around 10:00 o'clock."

She said, "Well, ok, Larry. But where are we going?"

"It's a surprise for all of you. I've got to gas up the station wagon and go to the credit union. I'll be back before you know it and Up, Up, and Away we'll go."

She said, smiling at last, "This is going to be fun. And you're right; we haven't done this in a while. The kids will love it. Love you."

Larry said, "I love you too."

As he drove to the gas station and filled up, he thought, *should I call George now or wait until we are gone? I think it should be later after we're on the road. I'll tell him that I had an emergency meeting at one of the other plants and would call him after I get back.* He didn't notice the truck that pulled to the other pump at the gas station nor that it followed him. It was an ordinary truck except for the big wooden bumper on its front end.

## 81

The Occidental was very cooperative in setting things up for the police. There were two groups of officers and detectives, one on each side of the meeting room, in case Joe got into trouble and they had to move in fast.

At 8:25, two plainclothes officers in Occidental staff clothes, wheeled brunch tables in and unloaded on tables in the back of the room. There were eight men already drinking coffee. Comments by the group included, "Ah, that smells good. Let's get started." Joe, looking a little uncomfortable, talked quietly with Tim.

The two other undercover policemen finished setting up the table and left. One asked, "Anything else, Mr. Anderson?"

"No, that's fine. Oh, wait; could you bring us back another pot of coffee? This one's nearly empty."

"I'll have it back in a few minutes, fresh and hot."

George asked, "Does anyone know where Larry is? It's not like him to be late." George looked around at the group. "Does anyone know if he had any weekend plans? I'll try his wife." George called Larry's home number. No answer. "Well, he'll be here soon I'm sure. His wife has probably taken the kids to the library or something."

The waiter returned with the hot coffee and offered to fill their cups. George was busy chatting with Wendell and didn't notice when the waiter paused by Joe's cup a moment longer. Joe looked up and nodded wanly.

George tapped his water glass to get their attention. "Wendell has some good news. We just exercised our option on the last piece of property on the lakefront. Now we won't have any businesses coming in that we don't want."

Wendell added, "We don't have to worry about that electronics business. Their board voted to drop their application for land here."

Tim piped up, "So does that mean we don't need to resort to any more rough stuff?"

"I don't know what you're talking about, Tim," George warned.

Tim went on, ignoring George's comment, "I know we all voted unanimously to bring in Harry and then to have Harry kill the mayor since he wouldn't play ball, but I don't want to be a part of any more violence. That got out of hand and I'm sorry it went that far."

"Shut up, Tim." George looked at Joe. "As long as we keep our mouths shut, we've got nothing to worry about.

"Sorry, Tim," George apologized. "We've all been under a lot of stress. Let's finish our breakfast and adjourn early. A change of scenery would probably do us good. Let's meet at the Century Club in their private dining room tomorrow after church. I'll find out where Larry is and make sure he's at the meeting. Wendell can fill us in on the details about our latest deal."

They all nod and begin to leave the room. George follows Joe with his eyes as he moves slowly out of the room and crosses into the men's room. A few minutes later, Joe emerged followed by one of the waiters. When Joe emerged from the side door of the Occidental, he walked up Third Street, turned left and was met by his escort. Joe gave the tape to him and was driven back to the lodge in Whitehall and left with his guard.

# 82

Larry went to the credit union to withdraw some cash for his "vacation." He couldn't tell his wife that they might be gone for a while. He had a bad feeling about whatever was happening at the police station yesterday. Things felt like they were spinning out of control.

He noticed the big black truck with the wooden bumper that waited behind him at the light. He thought he'd seen the same truck at the gas station, but he dismissed the worry. There were a lot of black trucks on the road – but not many with wooden bumpers. It seemed to be the most popular color for trucks. He could never understand it. He liked nice beige for his vehicles.

He turned left on Henry Street to head back home. There was a lot of traffic for a Saturday morning, but occasionally he caught a glimpse of the black truck. He kept making turns, but the truck stayed behind him. He turned onto an old gravel road.

He thought he could shake him on it. There was a bridge coming up. The driver kept pulling up close to Larry and bumping him. *What's the matter with him?* Irritated, Larry sped up. *There's no way you can pass me. There are too many blind curves.* The truck pulled up close to Larry's bumper and nudged him again. Larry wondered, *what the heck is going on?* He began to be a little afraid. He sped up again and just as he hit the 35 mph curve at 60, his car caught some gravel on the road, and started to fishtail. Larry yanked on the wheel too hard and sent the car into a spin. One more bump from the truck sent him into the guard rail. The last thing he thought when he broke through the guard rail was that he wouldn't see his family again. He quickly sank out of sight in the lake.

## 83

J im called the judge. "Judge McVie, I have Joe Antonellli's taped confession plus the group's confirmation that they all agreed to kill Fred on the wire that Joe Antonelli wore at the morning meeting. I'll have both transcripts sent to your office on Monday."

The judge signed the warrants for conspiracy to commit murder, one for each of the eight members of the group Joe had named. He told the Chief, "I will ask my secretary to pick them up and bring them to the station."

"Your honor, I would be happy to send an officer to pick them up."

"I would rather she bring them over and hand them to you directly. She will be there within the next half hour."

"Thank you, your honor."

The Chief hung up and called Gerri in. "Judge McVie's secretary is bringing over eight warrants. As soon as we check that they are all there, I would like you to call Dave Smithson and let him know we are on for tomorrow and we should meet here at 10:00 am. We'll be moving out at 11:30 to execute the plan. He should notify all the others. Then, Gerri, you can head home for the day. I appreciate you putting in the extra time today. Don't forget to submit your overtime pay. Thanks, Gerri."

The phone rang just then. Gerri answered it and told the Chief it was a Mrs. Olsen.

"Mrs. Olsen, this is the Chief. How can I help you?"

"I'm concerned about Larry. He left this morning to run some errands and he hasn't gotten back yet."

"Is this something he has done before?"

She answered, "No, he has not."

"Mrs. Olsen, I'm sure there is a good reason for his delay. We can't start an investigation for a missing person yet. Let's be in touch again if he is not back by tomorrow. I'll tell you what, tell me what kind of car he is driving and if you know it, the license plate number, I'll have my patrol cars be on the lookout for the car. If anything turns up, I'll let you know. How does that sound?"

"Thank you, Chief Johnson. You're right. He'll likely come in soon."

## 84

The Century Club had been cooperative in setting things up for the arrest team. There were seven officers and detectives in teams in rooms on each side of the meeting room. All were dressed as servers at the Century Club.

The group showed up at the Century Club at 1:00 as George decreed. At the stroke of 1:00, George asked, "Does anyone know where Joe or Larry is? There's no one home at Joe's place and he hasn't been in the restaurant yesterday or today. And Larry's wife is worried. He went out yesterday morning for gas and didn't come back."

Alarm registered on everyone's faces. "This is bad," Tim stammered. "What do you think is going on?"

"I don't know, but I don't like it. Larry's been missing since yesterday. I talked to his wife early this morning. And where is Joe? He was here yesterday. Did he seem like he was acting strangely?"

Wendell replied, "Now that you mention it. He did seem nervous. He didn't talk much which is pretty unusual for Joe."

The door burst open. A mass of policemen, detectives rushed in and stood around the front and sides of the meeting table with guns visible though not pointed at anyone. George said, "Jim, what's the meaning of this?"

"George, all of you are under arrest for accessory to murder before the fact. We have the warrants. Please be advised that other charges may be added. The district attorney is waiting at the station."

George blustered, "What murder?"

"The mayor of Muskegon, Fred Thomas."

George said, "You can't just march seven of this city's prominent citizens out of the Century Club on a charge like that."

The Chief said, "We can and will. There are separate cars with drivers and an officer waiting out back. Officers are stationed at the front door so you can't leave that way. No one will see you leave if you don't raise a fuss."

George said, "I'd like to call our attorney."

"You can do that when you get to the station."

George said to his group, "Gentlemen, as an attorney, I'm advising you to say not a word until we can get our attorneys to the station, not a single word. You may all want to call your attorney when we get there, but if not, our group's attorney can serve for all of us."

He continued to the Chief, "We're going to remember what you are doing to us."

The Chief said, "My officers and detectives will keep their guns out of sight, but they will use them if necessary. Please don't do anything to create a problem and we'll get to the station without fuss. You will all be in one room until you make your decisions about attorneys. If you choose to get your own attorney you will be taken to individual rooms with your attorneys. We'll get to you all as quickly as we can."

After everyone got down the back stairs and into the cars, there was a caravan of unmarked vehicles down Clay Street to the police station and the process started. As Jim had expected, they all opted to use the group's attorney.

An hour or so later, the entire group of the seven was in the task force room, drinking coffee but not saying a word. The district attorney, Harvey Swenson, was meeting with the group's attorney, Harold

Evans. They were going over the charges. The district attorney only wanted to talk about the charge on which they had all been brought in.

Evans said, "Harvey, we need to know all that they're facing."

Swenson replied, "You don't need to know all the charges at this time. Accessory to murder before the fact is enough for the judge to hold them."

"Does Judge McVie know about the other possible charges?"

"He does, but he doesn't want to muddy the waters with them now. He just wants to get this done and get back home. He says that we'll deal with the others later."

"Are you open to bail for these seven men?"

Harvey replied, "I am, in an appropriate amount. It's true that these are prominent people in the community, but the charge is a serious crime. We know they have the resources to be a flight risk. The judge will be the final decision-maker on the amount."

"Who is the accuser? What evidence do you have that they were involved with killing the Mayor?"

"We have the proof. I'm going to let the judge make the decision on whether to reveal that name. The judge has read his statement and will make his decisions based on that statement."

THERE WAS a knock on the door. The Chief's secretary, Gerri, told them that Judge McVie had arrived and was set up in a room large enough to accommodate the bail hearing. The group of seven would be brought in after the attorneys were in place. They went quickly to the room. The group was brought in and seated around the defense attorney's table.

Judge McVie came in and all stood as though they were in his courtroom. The judge was seated at a table that had been elevated with a platform. To his right was the court recorder ready to transcribe the hearing and a bailiff had been brought in as well.

Judge McVie said, "This hearing is now in session. This is a somewhat informal hearing, but don't doubt that it holds the same status as if it were in my courtroom. We are doing this here because of who you men are. Since it is informal, I will be reading the charge to all of you and ask if you understand the charge. If you do, you must answer verbally. A simple nod won't do. If you understand, please answer one at a time from your left to your right by saying, 'yes, I understand the charge.'"

He continued, "Each of you is charged accessory to murder before the fact. This charge does not mean that you committed the murder but that, in your case, each of you said yes to do it before the act was committed, the person murdered was Fred Thomas, at that time, the mayor of the city."

"I now ask you as a body and individually, do you understand the charges against you?"

Each of the seven members of the group in turn, said, "Yes, I understand the charge."

Their attorney Harold Evans stood and said, "Your Honor, I would like to speak for the group as a whole and have the same pleas for each individual."

Judge McVie said, "I understand that you represent the group as one and each individual in it. What do you want to speak to?"

"Your Honor, the defendants singly and as a member of the group want to know what the evidence of the charge is. That is to say, who is accusing them of this?"

The district attorney objected, saying, "Your Honor, the charge is being brought by an individual who was brought in last night on a murder charge that is related but who is also being charged with accessory as are these defendants. We see no need to reveal the identity of this person until this comes to trial to present the evidence."

"Objection," said the defense attorney, Harold Evans.

Judge McVie asked, "On what grounds?"

"Your Honor, these men may be in custody because of this testimony. They are entitled to know who the accuser is."

Just then, George Anderson said something to Evans, who said, "Your Honor, may I have a moment to confer with my clients?"

"Yes, make it brief."

Evans said, "My clients indicate that they know who their accuser is now because of what the district attorney said a moment ago. They would like the court to move on to the question of bail."

"I happen to agree with you. Mr. Swenson gave it away in his objection. Mr. Swenson, do you have something in mind on the bail question?"

"Yes, your Honor, I do. This is a serious charge for these men. I am asking for bail in the amount of $250,000, cash, no bond, for each individual."

There were gasps among the group. Mr. Evans rose to say, "That is an outrageous request. These men are long-standing citizens with deep roots in this community. Who among them has a quarter of a million dollars just lying around? They each have business commitment here and are not a risk for flight. I ask that they be released on their own recognizance."

Judge McVie turned to Mr. Swenson, "And what do you say to that?"

Swenson said, "But for two pertinent facts I would agree. The first is the fact that two members of the group are already missing, whereabouts unknown. Our thought is that somehow, they learned of the impending arrests and decided to leave. They have not been found yet. The second fact is because we have knowledge obtained by a warrant issued by this court that there is enough money in the group's bank account to cover the $250,000 per person."

Again, there were gasps from the seven men. Until that moment they had not known that their bank account was now an open book to the police.

Judge McVie said, "I am aware of those facts. If we assign bail in cash, can we get the money today?"

Swenson said, "Yes, your honor. I've already called Mr. Strahan, the bank president. The bank is ready to transfer the funds when I call him about it. I will do so when this hearing is done."

Judge McVie said, "I'm assessing bail in the amount of $250,000 per individual. As soon as the funds are transferred to the court, you gentlemen are free to go. On Monday when regular court convenes I will be setting a date for your arraignment. I expect it to be sometime next week. Your attorney will be informed, and he will notify you. Be there. This hearing is done."

---

## 85

Joe looked out the window of his lodge room over White Lake. He was glad he had a few minutes alone. He had finally told his daughter what was going on and Sara left to return to their cabin. Joe's stomach was upset because of the events of the last two days. The arrest, giving his statement, and now being held in a strange place. Even so, it was better than sitting in a jail cell. He knew the Chief had been lenient with him – giving him this last weekend with his daughter. He had asked the bellboy for a glass of milk.

The officer who was staying at the lodge with him was having his dinner.

The bellboy was late getting the milk delivered because of a strange encounter in the elevator. A distinguished looking man had come on the elevator at the last moment and overloaded the elevator. The elevator balked, darkened as though there was a short. The bellboy said, "I know how to fix this. Happens every now and then. Would someone hold this tray with my milk order?"

The distinguished looking gentleman took the tray and while everyone was distracted, emptied the contents of a little vial of a clear liquid into the milk. He shook the tray slightly, no one could see in the near darkness.

The bellboy fixed the problem, retrieved his tray with the glass of milk, and went on to make his delivery.

The light knock on the door startled Joe. But it was just the bellhop with the glass of milk he ordered

He was hoping the milk would settle his stomach. He tipped the guy and went back to the window, sipping the milk.

The lake was so beautiful and the light on the trees shimmered with gold and yellow. He finished the milk and thought the wind must have picked up because the trees were waving and swaying. *I hope the milk wasn't spoiled. It tasted a little funny. I think I better lie down a minute before I get dressed.*

He turned toward the bed, stumbled a bit, and fell face first on the bed.

When the officer returned, he knocked on the door. Strange, there was no answer. Mr. Antonelli must've fallen asleep. The officer used his passkey and opened the door. He saw Mr. Antonelli lying across the bed, legs hanging off slightly. He tried to rouse him and when he couldn't, he felt for a pulse, none there.

The officer called the chief and told him what happened. "Sir, there is no evidence of foul play but something just doesn't seem right to me."

The chief sent for the coroner and he took the body back to his laboratory. He called the chief, "Jim, it looks like he was poisoned. I haven't identified what the poison is yet, but there is no sign of trauma. It could be a heart attack but I won't know for sure until I finish the autopsy tomorrow."

---

## 86

The group's attorney, Harold Evans, had met with them for a few minutes after the hearing at police headquarters. He took the opportunity to emphasize that they should say nothing to anyone, even their families. He said he expected Judge McVie to call for the arraignments to happen toward the end of the week, most likely Thursday. He added, "I intend, with your permission, to appeal the amount of the cash bail required. I believe I can convince the Judge or an appeal judge that it is an excessive cash bail that has been imposed. It is, in my judgement, an effective shut down of your business operations. I am hopeful that I can prevail and get it reduced. That said, I would remind you again, don't say anything to anyone."

The room erupted with questions, such as, "What is the likelihood that all of this will leak out? Is the press onto this already and how should we react if we are sought out by the media?"

Evans answered, "The notion of 'don't talk to anyone' applies to the law and to the media in addition to your families and friends. I repeat, say nothing."

George asked, "I think we know that the police have Joe Antonelli in custody, and he is the one who turned on all of us."

"I'm sure that is true as well. The same thing applies here. Say nothing about Joe Antonelli or the fact that he is likely to be the one who is being held and has turned on all of you. It can only make things worse for you. I will be pushing the district attorney for a transcript of Joe's interrogation. We need to know what Joe has said. Let me check on whether the funds have been received."

Evans returned a few minutes later. He said, "Mr. Swenson has just let me know the money has been transferred to the court. You are all free to go. Remember, no talking about this with anyone. I'll be in touch about the arraignment day and time."

With that, Evans left them in the room. Several began to ask questions, but George signaled them to stop. He held a finger to his lips in a shushing manner. He held up a piece of paper with the words, "I will call each of you tonight at home. We need to meet tomorrow."

---

## 87

Everyone on the task force assembled in the room where they had worked. Jim came in. "Good morning. I think it is still morning. I want to congratulate you all on a job well done. But it's not quite over. We have all but two of the nine. Larry Olsen is somewhere into the wind. He hasn't been seen for three days now. I had a call from his wife two days ago. He left to gas up the car and never returned. There is a BOLO out for him in Michigan. Something may have happened to him. Dave and his crew will be following up with interviews of his friends and other family members that may live in this area."

Dave asked, "Why did you say all but two?"

"We were still holding Joe Antonelli for murder one in the shooting of Harry Walker. We were going to bring him back in this morning."

Dave asked, "What do you mean, 'were'?"

Jim answered, "I just had a call from the coroner. Joe was murdered last night at the lodge in Whitehall."

They all burst in with questions. Jim held up his hand. "He was found dead in his room by the officer who was there to watch him. He had just finished most of a glass of milk that the bellboy brought him.

The coroner found the poison in the milk. He will undoubtedly find it in Joe's body."

Dave inquired, "So where does this leave us?"

"Our primary job as a group is essentially done. As I said, we will continue to look for Larry Olsen. I'm thinking he may be dead as well. Judge McVie told me the arraignments will go ahead as planned Thursday morning. It's now in the hands of the local courts. Some or maybe all of us might be called to provide testimony at trials, especially Mark and Dave as heads of the local police sector and the state police."

Tom asked, "Where does this leave me now? This has been a rich learning experience watching you professionals work."

Jim answered, "Tom, you have made a number of contributions to this process. You are well into your State police training. We hope you stay with it, but you also have other irons in the fire. Both sectors, the locals and the state police, are interested in you."

"I thank you both for that interest. I also have the option of returning to the teaching career that I love so much. I have two offers from other school systems in West Michigan. We'll see. I will complete the training and stay on as long as you think I can help. And as soon as I decide what my direction should be, I'll let you know. Can I tell my parents and talk to Maria about it?"

Jim said, "You can, Tom. Just don't share the details. Just tell them that it is now in the hands of the court system. Let's all finish up those reports. Ken, you have a big job with your financial forensics report of the group. Would you like some help in getting that finished?"

"I think not. I'll be able to finish it by sometime Wednesday."

Jim added, "Once again, my congratulations. This has been an excellent effort by all of you and a great example to others of cooperating jurisdictions. My report to the mayor and to the State Police commission will reflect that. Let me know if you need anything in the way of support from me as you wind this up. After conferring with Dave and his bosses in Lansing, I should be able to tell you what we might have to do about Joe's death and maybe Larry's as well."

## 88

The seven met Sunday afternoon in the home of one of George's friends. The friend and his family were on an extended trip to France and had left the keys to the house. George was watching the house for them. The group had been brought to the house in an unmarked van from George's company. George had picked them up at a downtown parking lot.

They settled into the big living room with soft drinks and snacks. George said, "Please use coasters and let's not leave a mess. I don't want my friends to know that we were here. I'm sorry about the subterfuge but we need to be extra careful right now."

When the room erupted with questions, he continued, "One at a time please. We need to plot a new strategy on how to get out of this and get our bail money, our operating funds, back. I spent time last night thinking about our situation. We've got a lot at stake here."

"Why did we ever let Joe talk us into hiring Harry?' Wendell whined. "If Joe hadn't gotten Harry involved, the mayor would still be alive."

Tim said, "Is there a way we can blame this all on Joe? Isn't it his word against ours?"

"And where's Larry? I'm getting nervous that we haven't heard from him. You don't think he's gone against us?"

George sat back and listened. Finally he spoke. "Maybe there's a way to shift the blame to both Joe and Larry. What if we could get to the evidence?"

"How can we do that? Isn't it guarded at the police station?"

George continued, "Larry told me he had an in with the police station – a Pete someone. He also told me that Pete owed him money. Maybe we can get Pete to help us out."

"How are we going to do that? Bribe him? Blackmail him?"

"If we have to. Here's what we'll do…"

He continued, "Now, let's all get back home, and each get ready to do your job when I call with final instructions."

## 89

Two city workers were responding to a call from a citizen who had seen a big hole in a fence near a particularly deep area of Muskegon Lake. The citizen thought it was not safe to leave it the way it was.

The workers drove up and saw the size of the hole in the fence. "Something pretty big went through that fence... It could be a car or a truck. The water is deep here. It may be down there somewhere."

The other said, "We had better let the boss know. They may want to get a diver or two out here."

Within the hour, there were two divers in the lake and a tow truck waiting to pull out what they might find. As all were watching, there was a shout from the lake, "There's a car down here with a body in it."

When they pulled it out of the lake, the body was that of a white male, likely about 38 years old. Another job for the coroner. It didn't look as though there was any bruising or holes in the body.

One of the city workers said, "I'm going call the police. This is not a part of our job."

He called the police and spoke to a detective named Mark.

He drove out to see for himself. The driver must have been speeding to go through the chain link fence like that. He sent the license number into headquarters where they quickly found that it was Larry Olsen's car. The car was impounded and the body taken to the morgue. They had found Larry Olsen. There would have to be an identification of his body and a forensic analysis of the car. It looks like another one of the nine was now gone.

## 90

Tom and his Mom and Dad were at a Sunday brunch where they had a somewhat private booth. They were served breakfast and sat talking. They were relieved to hear about the arrests and coming arraignments. Mom said, "Do you know what you will do yet?"

Tom had told them earlier in the week about the new school job offers and now he reminded them of his status with the police department, his state training, and his status on the private detective license. Tom said, "So it seems that I have a number of options. I'm thinking I will accept one of the teaching options so I can see Maria more often. My training sessions and my obligation to the police department should both end before the semester starts next fall. We'll see where things go after that." They lingered over coffee until it was time for Tom to go see Maria.

Tom walked into Maria's room with a dozen red roses. Her parents had come by after church and had been talking to her about what was going on. They were just about to leave. Tom asked them to step outside for a few minutes so he could share some things with them.

Tom spoke to the nurse and she set them up in a doctor's conference room. When they were alone, Tom said, "Well, it is almost over, just a few pieces of the puzzle to fit in. By the end of the week, all the remaining seven will be arraigned. What will happen to them is now up to the court. We have no way of knowing how long it will take."

Maria's dad asked, "What's your take on it? Will they get what's coming to them?"

"I don't know. We have a strong case on them. But who knows?"

Maria's mom asked, "How about you, Tom? Do you know yet what you will be doing?"

He told them about the offers from two school districts and the fact that his state police department training was ahead of schedule. And that he still owed the police department some time since that was a part of the arrangement he had made.

Tom continued, "The thing is I don't know if I'll ever use the license. But I do have more options to consider now. What I really want is for Maria to wake up so we can go on with our lives. But that's out of my hands. While I wait for that to happen, I just want to be close enough to see her, talk to her, and while waiting, go on building the kind of life that we can have together when she's back."

Maria's parents hugged Tom and left. Tom went back into Maria's room and told her the news. The news that meant they could finally put all this behind them. He told her, "Maria, sweetheart, we can move on, you can wake up now, you're safe. I'll be here more often and will tell you what I'm doing. Whenever you're ready, I'll be here. I love you, Maria. Come back soon."

## 91

Doug was sitting on Tom's front porch when he got home. Tom filled him in on the wiretap and arrests. He also told him that both Joe Antonelli and Larry Olsen were dead.

"If Fred was still here, he would only need seven more expensive funerals to make the changes he wanted for Muskegon. As it is, those guys are going away for a long time."

Tom told Doug that he had a lot of options now – teaching, working with the local police, or even working with the state police. He just didn't know which way to go yet.

Doug could sense that there was more — Tom wasn't ready to let it all come out. He got Tom a beer and another one for him and sat waiting. He saw Tom was hurting and didn't want to intrude. He thought Tom might need him to just listen.

Tom turned with tears in his eyes and said, "She's just lying there. She may never wake up. What do I do now?"

"What was it she always said to you? You should follow your heart. You always told her she could have made it on Broadway but that wasn't what she wanted. She wanted you and a family, even if adopted. She made her choice, following her heart. Now you need to follow yours."

"But if I had stopped looking for Fred's killer, she would still be here."

Doug said, "Tom, it happened. You can't change a decision you made and because of it, you and Maria have been dealt a bad hand. But you know she would want you to move on. Do you remember that she told you that we always need to be re-creating ourselves? She had a favorite quote from a naturalist, don't remember who, 'When the path you are on closes off, a new one opens up. All you have to do is jump to it. The net will appear.' Your best tribute to her is to do that, make the jump. When she wakes up, you'll be on a good path. You two can put it all together again."

"But..."

"None of that now. You'll find the way and make the leap. You always have."

# ACKNOWLEDGMENTS

I have so many people to thank. Let me start and end with my children and grandchildren who are first, last, and always my encouragement and inspiration. Thank you all.

Thank you to all my teachers of writing craft beginning with my hometown writing group, Stirrings. Thanks to Angie Maloy who brought me in, who continued to teach and inspire, who set up the structure of the sessions so that we all got lots of feedback, both good ideas to correct problems and praise when we had done well. You all taught me so much about how to write and tell stories.

Thank you to my teachers and friends at the Bear River Writers' Conference who taught me with your praise and critiques. There's one person I especially have to thank. Laura Kasischke, you are a genius teacher. I was in your class for three straight years. You awakened the writing muse in me and look where it has taken me. To those conference teachers with whom I have not studied yet, patience, I'll soon get to your class. I have learned so much from all of you during your readings and our private conversations.

Thank you to my teachers and mentors for various aspects of the writing craft and the business of writing when I attended the University of Madison Writers Institute. Thank you, Christine DeSmet, for your Master Class in novel writing. I appreciate your time generosity after the session when you critiqued my early pages and led me in a new direction. You said, "Try again and do this." I did that and it worked as you said it would.

Thank you also Phil and Jean, Michael and Cheryl, my brothers and your wives, for your unwavering support and encouragement in my writing efforts. Your big brother is taking a new step. Who knows what's next!

Thank you to my beta readers, Nancy Wittkopp and Larry Zadonick. Your commentary both encouraged me, and led me to several new chapters to provide an ending where the bad guys got their due.

In a Bear River staff presentation, Keith Taylor, then director of the conference said this, "Get yourself a good editor and listen to her/him. He/she will help you make it a better book." I took your advice and she did just that. My daughter, Deborah Smith Cook, edited the book and as you said she would, made it a better story. She caught things I missed and helped me find a better way. Thank you, Deb.

Kitty Bucholtz was my self-publishing consultant and Deborah was my coach while I was learning the independent publishing side of the business. Kitty and Deb are such good teachers and brought my first book to where it needed to be. Thank you, Kitty and Deborah.

And finally, again, thank you to my children and grandchildren. Your constant encouragement and support helped me bring this book to reality. I love you all.

# A NOTE FROM HAYDEN

Thank you for reading my story. This novel had its beginnings some time ago back when I was still teaching physics and mathematics at our local community college. More than once while having lunch in the faculty dining room, we discussed what we were reading. I've read mysteries most of my life, a habit I inherited from my dad. Often I mentioned at those lunches that I would like to write a mystery novel, and that I already had an idea for a story.

I read many novels and sometimes actual news stories about towns that were run by a group of powerful men. Having lived in Muskegon, Michigan, since I was nine years old, I knew my hometown better than anywhere else I had lived. It made good sense to me to set the novel here in Muskegon. Singing, acting, and teaching are other passions of mine, so it was a natural thing that my protagonist, Tom, and his lady friend, Maria, were choral music and theatre arts teachers in the local high school, Muskegon High School, from which I graduated a whole lot of years ago.

The places and restaurants that my characters visit are real, or were real, as some have been torn down, burned out, or just closed up. Many of these have been, and continue to be, my favorite places to visit. The Occidental Hotel was, sadly, one of those torn down.

Some incidents are factual like the burning of Drelles Restaurant. The Milwaukee Clipper is real and is today being converted into a museum.

The story is entirely a work of fiction. Names, characters, and other incidents are products of my imagination. Any resemblance to an actual person, living or dead, or an actual event is purely coincidental.

If you have already read the story, I hope you enjoyed it. If you have not read it, please do so and enjoy! I enjoyed writing it.

The next book in the series, the first sequel, is in the works. It is a story of revenge on those who caused all the problems. Who carries out the revenge? Stay tuned for the continuation of the story, to be released late 2021 or early 2022. Check out the first chapter at the end of this book!

# ABOUT THE AUTHOR

Hayden Smith is a research physicist by education and experience. After a satisfying and productive research career of 14 plus years, he came home to Muskegon to be near his children. With an interim time in educational sales, he finally turned to a new career as a physics and mathematics instructor at the local community college. This was one of the most fulfilling times of his life. After a total of 22 years, he retired. During his teaching time, he would often say, at lunch with colleagues, that he would like to write a novel, that he had an idea for a story.

After he retired and his second wife died, two things happened. One of his daughters, who knew about his wish to write, told him about the Bear River Writers' Conference and sent him to it. At about the same time, a dear friend and former colleague remembered the lunch conversations and suggested he join the writing group that she led. He did both, attended the Bear River Writers' Conference and joined the writing group in his hometown. He is so grateful for both suggestions. His life was changed forever. He found a new passion that he didn't know he had. In addition to all the other writing he did along the way while learning his writing craft, his novel began to shape up.

Now he has five passions that feed and gratify him. The first and foremost passion is to stay close to his children, grandchildren, and great-grandchildren. They are his joy. What else? He is getting back to his roots in music and theatre, both performing and attending. Look for his third cabaret show in 2021. He is passionate about travel

– especially to France, Ireland, and Italy, and around the great United States. He particularly loves the wine regions in California, Oregon, and Virginia. Hayden continues doing research in physics and physics-related subjects. And of course, writing fiction and the stories of his life. He often says, "It is a great, full life!"

# VENGEANCE SERVED COLD
## A SNEAK PEEK

**Coming Soon**

Tom was enjoying the fireplace that was crackling away, taking away the chill from the late March winds. His stereo radio was playing a soft and easy jazz for the dinner hour. He laid his book down, thinking, *I'd better get something cooking.*

An insistent loud knock on the door made him jump. He thought, *that sounds like a Doug knock.* When he opened the door, sure enough, Doug stood there with a large Scrib's pizza and a cold six-pack of beer. "Let me in, this March wind has a nip to it."

"Welcome, pizza guy, get yourself in here. Let me take that pizza while you get your jacket off. I didn't know you were coming tonight."

Doug smiled. "A little surprise. I thought you might like an old friend for company. And I'll bet you haven't had dinner yet."

"Nope, just thinking about it. Do we need to heat that up a little?"

"It's piping hot now, so let's get to it."

After setting up TV tables, they sat by the fire and were quiet while they went after it.

Tom was reaching for his next piece of pizza when the phone rang.

He hurried to the phone table, picked up, and said, "Hello."

"Tom, this is Jim Johnson. Something has come up that I need to talk about with you. I don't want to do it over the phone. I know it's short notice but I wonder if I might drop in."

"Of course, Jim, come on over. By the way, Doug is here. Will that be alright?"

"I think so. I'll see you in about a half hour."

After he hung up, Tom sat back down on the sofa, looked at Doug, and said, "I wonder what is going on that couldn't wait until tomorrow."

Doug said, "I was puzzling over that too. Is it ok that I'm here?"

"If Jim said you could, I'm sure it is. I'm still on the temporary status as a detective in training. I've finished my State Police program and a little more than two months to go on the last courses for my Master's in choral conducting. And to answer your unasked question, what will I do then? Truth is, I don't know yet."

Their conversation continued as they cleaned up all but two pieces of pizza. Jim might want some.

Tom let the chief in a few minutes later. "Welcome, Jim. Can I warm up some pizza for you and get you a beer? You remember Doug, don't you?"

Jim shook hands with Doug, then chuckled. "I'd better not have pizza. Martha's holding dinner for me. I told her it would be between 7 and 7:30. We better get to business."

Doug asked, "Chief, would you like for me to leave?"

"No, Doug, but I will ask you to keep this to yourself until it hits the *Chronicle* tomorrow. And even then don't talk about some of what you will hear, except with Tom."

He continued. "Tim Samuels is dead. He was shot sometime late yesterday as he left his office. You will remember that he is one of the group of nine."

Both Tom and Doug started with questions when Jim paused.

Jim slowed them down saying, "We don't have a clue about who did this or if it is related to what went down last fall. It may be something else in Tim's past. The forensics and autopsy aren't done yet. We'll see what that tells us."

Tom asked, "What will you do next and how can I help?"

Jim replied, "I haven't figured that out yet. But then late this afternoon this showed up in the mail." Jim pulled a letter out of his pocket along with two pair of police evidence gloves. He continued, "It was addressed to you but we were concerned about what might be in it. We took the liberty of opening it and finding nothing bad in it, had it checked for fingerprints. Nothing there. There is more analysis we can do yet at the State Police lab. For now, I'd like you, Tom, to put on these gloves, take it out of the envelope, and read it aloud."

The message was made with cut out letters glued to an otherwise blank piece of generic white paper. The words read, "O'Banion, Samuels is number three. You are on the list as well and I want you to know I'll get to you before I'm done."

Tom gasped. Doug shook his head. Tom said, "Jim, do you think this means what seems obvious at first reading?"

"I'm afraid it does. It sounds as if someone is out to get the other six members of the group of nine plus you."

"Are you going to reassemble the task force?"

"I will soon. I haven't talked to the State Police people yet but on Monday I will."

Jim continued, "Doug, I don't want anything about this letter to get out. No one else should know yet. You and Tom can talk about it, but no one else. Understood?"

Doug nodded. "I've got it, chief." But he thought, *someone else is out there. That's ok. That's one more I don't have to get. And now Tom needs to be protected as well.*

Made in the USA
Monee, IL
27 October 2021